FOR THE FIRST TIME

Her body heated. Fire churned in her belly and her breath grew shallow and rushed. She had no illusions about her purpose here, but her body's reaction to him confused and surprised her all the same. Lucian Patras would use her for his own sexual satisfaction. She was perfectly aware of what that would entail. She'd been exposed to the act of sex at a very young age, seeing many adults perform such acts with no regard to privacy or onlooking eyes.

What she was unprepared for were the sensations flooding her blood. Scout never expected her skin to feel so hot, so hungry, her limbs to grow weightless and too heavy at the same time. She was incredibly aware of her hips and the space in between them.

Lucian pulled back from her mouth and she found herself extending, chasing his touch. He chuckled arrogantly and she hated her need. His mouth worked over her jaw and down the slender column of her throat. He sucked on the flesh over her racing pulse. His tongue skittered to her ear and his breath tickled the hollow, sending chills up and down her spine . . .

FALLING IN

lydia michaels

BERKLEY BOOKS, NEW YORK

THE BERKLEY PUBLISHING GROUP
Published by the Penguin Group
Penguin Group (USA) LLC
375 Hudson Street, New York, New York 10014

USA • Canada • UK • Ireland • Australia • New Zealand • India • South Africa • China

penguin.com

A Penguin Random House Company

This book is an original publication of The Berkley Publishing Group.

Library of Congress Cataloging-in-Publication Data

Michaels, Lydia.
Falling in / Lydia Michaels.
pages cm.—(The surrender trilogy ; 1)
ISBN 978-0-425-27507-8 (paperback)
1. Love stories. 2. Erotic fiction. I. Title.
PS3613.I34439F35 2014
813'.6—dc23
2014017374

PUBLISHING HISTORY
InterMix eBook edition / October 2013
Berkley trade paperback edition / June 2014

PRINTED IN THE UNITED STATES OF AMERICA

10 9 8 7 6 5 4 3 2 1

Cover design by Rita Frangie.
Interior text design by Kristin del Rosario.

This book is dedicated to my amazing husband, Michael.

Without you, nothing else matters. You are the other half of my soul, and I thank God every day that I found you. You are my most coveted treasure and my truest friend. You are as depended on and indescribable as the air I breathe. You are the meaning behind my favorite song, the magic of Christmas morning, the sparkle in our daughter's eyes, and the inspiration behind every unwritten romantic thought hidden between the lines. I can accomplish anything, so long as you never let go of my hand. Thank you, Mike, for always supporting my dreams and for sharing that secret part of your soul with me that no one else gets to see.

I love you.

scout

one
. . . . .

CAUGHT

THE early morning sky was the color of steel wool, sharp, ominous gray hanging low over the city without a hint of softness, but Scout Keats's trajectory was somewhere brighter. She hustled down Randolph, past the urban district, and into the commercial quarters of Folsom. Only after crossing that invisible divide from the hidden shadows of the impoverished sections of the city to the streets teeming with endless opportunities of prosperity did she take her first full breath of the day. A sense of possibility invigorated her every time. Scout's lungs filled with hope and her weariness ebbed with each step as the world she coveted awoke and slowly began to flow around her.

Today was a day to be proud. After two weeks of learning her way, mimicking those who had it already figured out, she had done it and would finally see some of the results of all her hard work. Her heart raced each time she imagined clocking out at the end of her shift and being handed her first big fat paycheck.

This was it. This time it would be different. Being a maid at Patras, although nerve-racking, was going to change Scout's life.

Like scenting the snow before it fell, she could sense change approaching, and every cell of her being told her that Patras Hotel was the key to her escape.

She couldn't say how she knew, but she knew. Parker had come to simply roll his eyes each time she fell into fanciful ramblings, warning him that her evenings at the shelter were numbered, that one night she simply wouldn't return and when that night came, he should celebrate, in memory of her, Scout Keats, the dragon baby who outran her destiny and made it in the real world.

She was aware of what Parker thought. She knew how they *all* saw her. While much of the transient population seemed to accept their hand in life with bitter surrender, Scout never would. Their cynicism ran deeper than any still waters could wash, but she refused to let herself drown in their doubts.

Born in a back alley, ripped from her mother's womb by claws sharp enough to make her scream to a point of delirium, she came into this world running. She was chasing the dragon before she could even crawl. Ironically, her mother had been running from it as far back as her memory held.

The dragon killed her daddy before she ever knew him. No pictures to tell her if her silver blue eyes were his or how he wore his hair. All Scout had was a collage of mumblings, broken bits of her mother's jigsaw mind to tell her the kind of man her daddy was. Didn't matter anyway. He was dead before she was born.

Death favored the poor. People of wealth had an astounding ability to not see them. As insignificant as litter, they were merely unfortunate crumbles of trash lining the curbs they hoped would soon blow away, and each night they did, retreating back to the warmest corners of Folsom to barter their scavenged finds of the day, sleep with one eye open, and strategize how to outmaneuver their pretend friends the next morning, because in reality, you had no friends when you were homeless. You only had yourself and your only objective was to stay alive.

Parker had been a concession she made at the age of fourteen. She supposed she could call him a friend. He did kick Slim's ass when Slim kept leering at her that one year, and she sort of liked him then. Not that she needed a hand defending herself. It was nice of Parker to do that, but that wasn't what made him her friend. Scout decided he could be her friend when she found out he could read and he offered to teach her.

But friends were liabilities. Survival was easiest when emotion stayed out of it. She was getting off the streets and she didn't need to be liable for anyone when she already had her mother to worry about.

Pearl had long ago surrendered to a doomed existence that worried Scout sick, but Pearl brought her into this world and no matter how much Scout hated the life her mother chose, she'd seen it enough to know she really didn't choose it at all. She merely flirted with a dragon that swallowed her whole at first chance and traded her soul for the poor excuse of the life it let her slip away with.

The woman who raised her was gone, replaced by a flesh-covered skeleton who whispered gibberish in her momma's voice, but she loved her all the same. Heroin was Pearl's weakness and she was Scout's, and damn Parker for intruding on her meager list of those she cared for, but Scout wouldn't let him hold her back no matter how many words he taught her to read or how many leering creeps he beat the piss out of. Parker was a lifer and she was not.

He often made fun of Scout and her obsession with words. He didn't understand why she had such a fixation on expanding her vocabulary. At this point in her life, it was humiliating not to know how to do such a common thing as read. It wasn't something she shared about herself easily. Words, however, she could memorize.

Anytime she heard a word she didn't know, she'd ask Parker

what it meant and he'd tell her. She made it a point to think and speak those words as often as possible. It made her feel educated in a way she knew she was not. Some day it would benefit her, once she moved out of the gutter class and into a more prestigious one.

The black ribbon of road slowly crowded with yellow cabs. That sleeping scent of the city, a little bit bitter with a trace of dewy air, was slowly replaced with the smell of exhaust and early morning eateries opening their doors.

Two sizes too large, her worn black sneakers clopped over the pavement and were slowly humbled by the gentle roar of pedestrians in their finery. The cadence of leather-soled loafers and stilettos built like a distant wave, washing out the unsophisticated rhythm of her steps.

The choking clouds were pushed back as the buildings grew in size, each one an enormous trophy of some self-important man's arrogance and a supplement for his inadequate anatomy.

The buildings pierced the canopy of haze, like beams beneath a heavy circus tent. The analogy made her smile. She was leaving what would be the gypsy caravans squatting in ramshackle functionality and heading for the better-dressed performers of the main event. Like a child smiling over a tuft of cotton candy, she grew excited at the nearing presence of the fancy-dressed ringleaders of the world with their bedazzled accessories and self-pronounced confidence. One day she'd be among the glamorous women who swung high above the rest and were respected for their courage and grace. Scout longed to be a part of the big show and leave her less-appealing brethren behind.

Pushing her fanciful musings aside, she hefted her cumbersome bag over her shoulder as she moved deeper into the congested commercial district. Men of industry, demigods, built these impressive structures, smudging out even the sun until nothing but a slice of sky showed a mile above. On lackluster mornings like this one when the clouds hung low and the rooftops raked through the dull cotton bluffs, she truly understood why they were named skyscrapers.

Her strides doubled when she turned onto Fenton and the great clock showed there were only ten minutes to six. Three blocks to go and she still needed time to clock in and check her cart. In another hour these hollow roads would be clogged with taxis, and the walkways would suffer as civilized a stampede as human nature could produce.

Scout rounded the corner of Gerard and there, like a dove among pigeons, sat Patras Hotel. Its white granite walls with opalescent luster gleamed even under the overcast wedge of sky. Thirty-foot pillars guarded the structure, sweeping the grand marble staircase in a soft glow of controlled lighting where shine boys already waited at their benches with boxes for their wealthy clientele. Velvet roping sectioned off the affluent guests from the covetous passersby. One didn't set foot on that red carpet leading through those eighteen-foot gilded doors unless they were entitled to.

Scout quickly walked past the fringed runner and around the corner of the building. Practically taking up a block on its own, Patras Hotel was the beauty among the motley buildings that neighbored it, and in such a swank section of Folsom that proclaimed it to be the best of the best.

At the back of the building was a subtle awning, pristine enough not to detract from the hotel's beauty, but lacking the pretentiousness of the front enough to be overlooked by those who weren't in the know. She slid her badge through the discrete keycard lock beside the door and waited. When the green light signaled and the lock disengaged with a snick, she pulled the heavy door open and let herself in. The scent of freshly arranged flowers greeted her and mingled with the familiar whispered clatter in the distance of the waitstaff preparing the restaurant for the breakfast crowd.

Traveling in the opposite direction of the lobby, Scout again reached for her badge and slid it through the service elevator's lock. The bell dinged softly and she stepped into the unembellished car. She keyed in for the basement and moments later entered a bustling underground world of service.

The air was heated with the clean scent of detergents and presses. She loved the fragrance of the laundering facilities. Such a luxury, to not only sleep on fresh sheets every day, but to have them pressed as well. Her feet hustled through the corridor and turned into the employee locker room.

Approaching the docking station, she breathed a sigh of relief as she slid her badge through the mechanism clocking her in for the day at 5:58. Perfect.

Turning to her locker, Scout quickly stowed her belongings without making eye contact with any of the other employees. Down here, in the bowels of the hotel, they were all janitorial staff. Good thing, too, because the lobby employees with their fancy blazers and ticked, tuxedo-style pants intimidated the crap out of her.

The maids all wore the same poly-blend shapeless dove gray dress with white Peter Pan collar and cuffed sleeves. They didn't intimidate her one bit. She simply didn't meet their gazes so as not to inadvertently suggest she was interested in making acquaintances. She wasn't. She was there to do a job.

Once her dainty, completely ornamental white apron was tied at her waist, she pinned the small accordion cap in front of her bun. Hoisting the last of her items into the tight metal locker, she tucked the bulge back and forced the door closed, moving her fingers just in time for the latch to catch before her cumbersome belongings could be regurgitated onto the floor. Looking left, then right, she spun the built-in combination lock several times until convinced her possessions were secure. Everything she owned was in that locker.

By the time Scout made it to Tamara's office, other maids were already on the move with their carts. Behind her, some employees were just arriving. Quickening her pace she turned into the office labeled *Housekeeping General Manager* and greeted her GM with a smile.

"Good morning, Tamara."

"Good morning, Scout." She smiled, her teeth clean and perfectly straight.

Scout had an odd obsession with hygiene and frequently noticed people's teeth and fingernails as some sort of personal grading system.

"Here's your list for the day. Bridget's out so I put you on the penthouse suites if that's okay," Tamara said.

Like she'd admit if it wasn't. "That's fine. I'm happy to help."

"Good, and while I have you here, your paperwork was sent back from Human Resources. You forgot to fill in your social when you did it. They're going to need that in order to process your paycheck this afternoon."

Crap. Parker had done her paperwork. Tamara's curvy frame twisted in her fancy leather chair as she reached into a paper tray. She slid the familiar paperwork across the desk and Scout forced her hand to remain steady as she picked it up.

There was nothing condescending about Tamara. She was in her midthirties and seemed to be one of those pleasantly chubby women who chronically dieted and would never truly recognize the beauty they held within. Scout appreciated her easy pleasantness and genuine candor.

Her eyes raked over the application. Parker's penmanship was neat and bold. Scout admired the confident way his letters stroked in tidy order across the small blank spaces.

"What did you say was missing?"

"Your social security number. See, there, on the top right. Just fill that in and you'll be good to go and I'll have it sent back before payroll cuts the checks this afternoon."

Tamara wore a floral-scented perfume and Scout couldn't help breathing in the bouquet without a touch of envy. It mixed nicely with the fragrance of her hair and skin.

She found the blank spot Tamara was referring to. Nine little blank lines needing to be filled.

"Why do they need this?"

"For tax purposes mostly." Her fingernails were painted red. Scout self-consciously tucked her clipped nails into the shelter of her palm.

She didn't have a social security number, or if she did she'd never been told what it was. She could've been honest, but honesty in this situation would only delay and complicate things. The key to fitting in was being as low-maintenance as possible.

"Do you have a pen I could use?"

Tamara handed her a pen and Scout squatted low at the corner of the desk. Her fingers deliberately formed the numbers. Scout was very aware of how unpracticed they appeared next to Parker's well-developed letters. Quickly, she made up three groups of numbers she could remember in case she had to recall them for something in the future. One-three-six, because it was the number of her locker. Twenty-two for her age. And nineteen hundred because it was the address printed on the awning out back of Patras. If they checked it and realized she made it up, she'd act like it was an honest mistake and figure out what to do when and if that time came.

"Here you go." She slid the paper back to Tamara.

"Great." She grinned, slipped the paper back in the tray she pulled it from, and handed Scout her assignments for the day.

"You'll need to use your badge to access the penthouse floors. Level thirty's all individual entry, so once you get off the elevator your normal house key will work, but from there you'll have to use the private bank of elevators located just outside of the private ballroom on thirty-one. There're four master penthouses on the thirty-second floor. Three of them are vacant this week so you'll only need to attend Suite C. Each has its own elevator that will deposit you directly in the room. I usually have the girls take only what they need with them. The master suites have a supply closet your general house key will open, where you'll find a sweeper and basic supplies to replenish the amenities. Here's the keycard for Suite C. Make sure you deactivate it at the end of the day."

It had taken the first week to lose the knot in her stomach over starting a new job. By the second week Scout found her rhythm and acquired a keen understanding for how long a room took to clean and freshen. She'd never done a penthouse before, let alone a master suite. Scout wasn't even sure what a master suite was. Forcing a calming breath into her tightening lungs, she maintained an expression of capable confidence and took the list and keys from Tamara.

The idea that she had no clue about the pace she'd need to keep that day terrified her. Scout needed this job and she'd have to hustle her ass off in order to get everything done before the end of her shift. She usually sat on a bench down the street for her lunch break, being that she never packed a lunch, but today she'd work straight through her entire shift in order to make sure she finished in time.

Not until ten o'clock did she breathe relatively normally again. She completed her first circuit of common-area maintenance. The upper floors were much like the lower ones. There were more seating areas and therefore more furniture to dust, but for the most part they took the same amount of time. Although the suites were larger than the typical rooms, they were pricier too. That meant fewer guests. Tamara must have realized that when she made the schedule for the day.

By Scout's third suite she had herself timed at twenty-two minutes per room, but there were only fifteen rooms she was responsible for on level thirty. That would leave her with two hours to complete the penthouse master suite C.

By one o'clock she was left waiting for one guest to get the hell out of his room so she could clean it and then she'd be finished with the thirtieth floor. Scout hovered for a few moments and decided it would be better to come back after she finished the master suites.

She rolled her cart to the service elevator and returned it to the lower level with the rest. Collecting a small basket from the shelf, she quickly packed it with shampoo, conditioner, soaps, and anything else she might need while up there.

Scout's anxiety returned as she found the private elevators on the thirty-first floor. Unlike the other guest elevators, these were quite lovely. There were four of them, simply numbered with the letter dedicated to each individual master suite. Each one was made of glass and lined with delicate brass bars. As she stepped into the one labeled *C*, she felt like that bird in a gilded cage from one of the stories Parker had read to her.

The ride was only a few seconds to the thirty-second floor. The gilded cage opened with practiced ease and Scout stepped across the threshold to a frosted glass–paned set of French doors.

She knocked lightly.

"Housekeeping."

When no one answered, Scout slid the private keycard through the lock and slowly turned the knob. The level of luxury the room announced at first sight was sweltering. She found it difficult to breathe among the thickly papered walls, richly upholstered furniture, and heavily padded carpet.

Silently, she walked down the long, private corridor.

"Hello? Housekeeping . . ."

No one was there, but she found comfort in her own familiar voice. Looking down at her shabby shoes, her self-esteem faltered for a moment. Such opulence. Such contrast.

Chandeliers dripped from beveled fixtures on the twelve-foot ceilings. Antique settees and decorative side tables created various sitting rooms. There was an enormous private bar, somehow dwarfed by the mammoth window facing the east.

Approaching the window slowly, the effect was dizzying. It felt as though she were an angel spying on mortals below. It was a powerful and jarring vantage point to hold. She was on top of the world. Well, on top of Folsom, but still . . . this was the highest she had ever been.

There was an identical window facing the north. A unique executive desk was the centerfold of that backdrop. She wasn't quite sure what to do with the personal items she noticed scattered on the floor around the grand desk so she let them be.

Moving to a pair of double doors, Scout discovered a bedroom. It wasn't as extraordinary as she'd expected. The bedding was of a finer quality than the typical guest rooms at the hotel, but a slight wave of disappointment washed over her because it was somewhat ordinary in comparison to the rest of the penthouse.

Then she discovered another set of doors.

Pressing them open, she gasped at the audacious splendor that was obviously the master bedroom. It was a palace. A king-size bed shaped like a sleigh was the central piece of the room. The decadent bed was draped in heavy silk blankets reminding her of something from a story called *Arabian Nights* that Parker had read to her.

Velvet pillows littered the floor and plush, heavy satin draped from a spherical sconce above the bed. The canopy gathered at the wall in several places, held by thick golden ropes with tassels the size of horsetails, and cascaded like a waterfall to the black marble floor.

Her hand coasted over the luxurious textures and her body hummed with excitement. Never before had she seen such a display of exquisiteness. Turning, she noticed a set of three French doors leading to an oval granite balcony complete with heavy metal furniture softened by more sensual fabrics.

Her feet glided over the plush carpet and her fingers closed around the heavy pewter knob. The color scheme was flawless. Warm earth tones blended with spicy cinnamons and sultry reds.

Scout's fingers moved over the plush cushions reverently, almost sensually, fondling the sumptuousness. What must it be like to sit on such bursting softness? She couldn't quite understand how such material survived the elements.

The air was much cooler at this altitude. Cautiously, she walked to the dense, stout columns making up the wide granite railing. The balcony was the size of a regular guest room.

As she stepped to the edge, her heart raced. Wisps of hair came loose from her bun and whipped across her face in the blustery, uncontained wind. From such heights there was neither rhyme nor reason to the breeze, nothing barricading or stifling its power.

Overwhelmed by the magnitude and quite aware of her insignificant part in this grandiose world, Scout quietly panted, her heart somewhere in her feet as she tried to fathom the height, scale, and intentional point of power she occupied in those brief seconds. It was a completely unfamiliar feeling, staring down at the tiny people bustling about their lives on the pavement below.

Scout tried to imagine the person entitled to stand in such a position of supremacy, but her mind came up short. She had no image of reference for such an omnipotent being. All guests of Patras were wealthy, but whoever stayed in this master suite was a king.

She saw the guest as a master of the world in her mind, yet he or she remained faceless, and without detail. Power was the only characteristic she was sure of.

A sudden stab of unease had her stepping back from the edge. Never had she felt so out of place. Wealth to this degree was beyond her comprehension and she was defenseless against it, outnumbered and small, meaningless. She suddenly wanted to be done with this place.

Scout quickly returned to the warmth of the room and pulled the heavy doors shut behind her. Like a trespasser on the run, she sought her supply basket and headed toward what she thought to be the supply closet.

Get done and get out.

There were three bathrooms in the master suite, each one more lavish than the last. She began with the largest one and quickly worked in a clockwise motion around the restrooms until the marble fixtures shone like jewels. Next she made the beds, fluffed the pillows, refreshed the soaps and towels, and dusted the furniture.

When Scout went in search of the vacuum, she accidentally found a clothing closet. The sheer volume of clothing baffled her. Suits. All men's suits. A large silk robe the color of onyx hung on the inside of the closet door and as she leaned close she could smell a delicious trace of some sort of masculine fragrance in the material.

There were so many clothes. Over twenty pairs of expensive shoes, shined to a point that she could see a distorted reflection of herself in each toe. She added large feet to the powerful, faceless guest occupying this space.

It occurred to her that this was more than just a hotel room, more than just a temporary penthouse. This was the apartment of some very wealthy long-term guest. She wasn't sure what gave away the resident's permanent status at Patras, but once it crossed her mind that this guest was more than some wealthy mogul passing by, she became certain of it.

The suite didn't smell like the other rooms in the hotel. It had a warm, unique scent of its own. There was an astounding amount of lived-in subtleties she'd first overlooked, the amount of papers tucked here and there, the clothing, the wooden hamper in the master bath. She wasn't sure what to do with that.

Curious about the mysterious resident, Scout wandered to the large desk in the sitting room. She debated organizing the papers that seemed to have floated thoughtlessly to the floor in no particular order, but her better judgment told her to let them be.

There was a calendar with notes jotted in every square. She tried to read the thickly scrolled handwriting, but it was in cursive and she was hopeless with those peculiar, curly letters.

Her fingers grazed the shiny pewter letter opener. It reminded her of a dagger. She lifted it, testing the heavy weight in her hand and smiled when she discovered a pearl set in the hilt and something engraved beneath the gem. She wasn't sure what the one loopy letter was, but she thought the other was a *P*.

She turned the substantial tool, handling it this way and that and admiring the effect the subdued sunlight had on the pearl. As she turned to better see the scrolled detail of the handle, her apron brushed across a sheaf of papers and to her horror, the pages went fluttering to the floor. They coasted and furled in their descent, losing any sense of order and mixing with the papers already matting the floor.

"Shit!"

She quickly tossed the heavy dagger to the desk, wincing when it landed with an obnoxious clank on the soft wood surface, and dropped to her knees. She wasn't sure what the papers were or if they went in any sort of order. Scout tried to pinpoint similarities in the typed words to tell the difference between the pages intended for the floor and the ones she'd accidentally knocked over, but they all looked the same to her.

She tried to sound out some of the words, hoping to see some clue that told her where they belonged, but the words were all very long and unfamiliar other than the occasional *the* or *and* she recognized. Her fingers trembled as she panicked, and then she heard the beep of the front door.

"I don't care what he thinks he's entitled to. His lease locks him in for one year and reoccurs indefinitely until either he or I give written notice of change. And even then he's responsible for a minimum of six months' notice," a deep, booming voice shouted.

Scout froze on the floor, shaking, pages clutched in her moist palms as she trembled with dread. Staying low, kneeling, slightly hidden by the clawed foot of the mahogany desk, she jumped as the voice bellowed, "I don't fucking care what his reasons are! He can pack up or ride it out, but he's responsible for the next six months and that's *after* he gives me written notice. Until I have that, he's pegged."

The voice got closer and she held her breath. The bang of a cabinet made her flinch. There was a clank of something glass followed by the soft chink of what sounded like ice filling a tumbler.

Scout froze. *Don't even breathe.*

"Well then he better have a good lawyer, Slade, because I'm not fucking around here. I gave up a two-point-six-million-dollar tenant to get him in there on time. He dicks me now and I promise he'll be the one getting fucked in the end."

The sound of liquid moving over ice and trickling over glass, then, "I don't fucking—"

The room was suddenly submerged in silence. Too quiet. Terror gripped Scout's heart and she slowly looked up into the most intense set of black eyes she had ever seen.

"I'll call you back," he said and slipped his phone into the pocket of his suit.

He was stunning. Dark hair clipped close at the sides and slightly longer at the top with the tiniest beginnings of silver peppered by his temples. Deep olive skin, a straight nose, and two menacing, black slashed brows scowled down at her. His jaw was strong and shadowed with coarse black hair.

He was tall, much taller than her and likely taller than most men. Her heart raced as she took in his cuffed shirt adorned with sharp snaps at the wrists; long, expensively dressed legs, and her hunched, terrified reflection shining back at her from the toes of his dress shoes.

"Mind telling me what you think you're doing?"

There was nothing friendly about the way he spoke to her. Scout frantically tried to say something, but her brain had short-circuited and all of her words seemed to have fallen from her head.

"Answer me."

She jumped at the sharp lash of his voice and lost her balance. She'd been crouching so long her foot had fallen asleep and her knees had gone stiff. As Scout caught her balance, she inadvertently landed on her knuckles. Her fist closed over his paperwork and crinkled it slightly. She might've whimpered, but she couldn't hear over the heartbeat suddenly roaring in her ears.

In two swift steps his legs ate up the distance between them and he was standing over her, still scowling.

"What's your name, girl?"

"S-Scout."

He frowned as if her name were unacceptable to him. "What kind of name is Scout?"

She opened her mouth to throw out some sharp retort, but luckily, her better judgment crept in and she merely gaped at him. He gave an exasperated sigh and set his glass on the corner of the desk. He moved so quickly she flinched as he grabbed her forearm and abruptly hoisted her to her feet.

Her legs wobbled beneath her, pins and needles attacking her foot. Gasping, she caught her weight on the desk. He was very close and the scent she had picked up on in his closet was now intensified and heated by the warmth coming off his body.

"What does that say?" he barked and jammed his finger to a note scribbled on a slip of paper sitting in the center of the desk.

Scout stared at it, hating the cryptic cursive letters. She thought the first letter was a *D* and then an *O*. After that she couldn't tell. She may have detected a *T*, but there were too many letters she still didn't recognize.

Finally he snapped, *"Do not touch the desk!"* He enunciated each word with a stab of his long, thick finger on the note. "If I took the time to leave you instructions not to touch my personal items on my desk, what makes you think I'd be okay with you rifling through my paperwork?"

Scout gasped as he ripped the pages out of her hand.

"Sir, I—"

"You're not Bridget. Where's Bridget?"

She needed to get this guy to not freak out. If he told Tamara, she might wind up getting suspended or worse, fired. This guy couldn't submit a complaint with her managers or she might lose her job.

"I'm sorry, Bridget called out today. I'm new. I didn't mean to touch your desk, but I accidentally knocked over a pile of papers."

A piece of ice settled in his glass and she jumped as she waited for him to speak. She wasn't usually this skittish around others. Long ago she had mastered keeping her emotions behind an iron expression of indifference, but she was completely out of her element in the presence of this man. She'd observed his wealth and power firsthand by simply admiring the world he existed in, and Scout had never been more aware of her insignificant position in this life.

His cold black eyes scrutinized her dress and gazed dispassionately at her too-large sneakers. He frowned.

Scout batted away a wisp of windblown hair that had fallen loose and accidentally knocked her paper bonnet askew. Righting it quickly she said, "If you'll just let me collect my belongings I'll be out of your way."

He stepped aside, not providing much space for her to pass,

and waved his hand for her to be gone. He was broad and daunt-
ing, hulking in his power suit over her slight form.

"By all means," he purred. "Please remove your things."

Scout scurried past him like a mouse running for its life. Her
hands shook as she gathered the vacuum cleaner and wound the
cord over its handle. Very aware of him watching her, when her
shoe caught on the thick tread of the carpet she whimpered, but
kept moving.

She couldn't remember where she left her basket of supplies.
Frantically she searched the surrounding area.

"Looking for something?" He glared at her, his arms crossed
over his wide chest, stretching the sleeves of his crisp silk shirt.
When her gaze reluctantly met his, she froze.

"M-my basket. I forget where I left it," she stuttered, hating
the way her voice wavered.

"Perhaps you left it with more of my personal items." His
clipped accusation had the effect he'd intended.

Shame and fear for her transgression choked her. Scout's eyes
suddenly spotted the basket of supplies beside his desk. *Shit.*

Knowing she couldn't leave the items, she pulled back her shoulders and met his gaze with as much bravado as she could fake.

"Sir, I'm sorry I disturbed your things. I didn't see your note,
but I assure you it won't happen again." Her eyes glanced at the
basket on the floor pointedly and he followed her gaze.

He looked back at her but said nothing, and Scout had the
sense he was daring her to retrieve her things. Her lips twitched
nervously at the challenge in his eyes.

She was outmatched. Quickly, she brushed past him and collected her items. He didn't make room for her to pass and she
again found herself cornered behind his desk. The gaping glass
view made her feel as though she were on a plank suspended high
above the city, being backed into her death by a formidable pirate.

"Whom do you report to?"

Scout's heart sunk to her knees and she quickly blinked back the sharp sting of tears. Her voice cracked. "Tamara Jones, sir."

His eyes moved over her face and she took his inspection as her penance, lowering her gaze to the floor. She needed this job. In that moment Scout let go of all her stubborn principles, realizing she would do anything to keep it.

The touch of his fingers below her chin caused her breath to quicken. His large hand tipped her face up so that her gaze met his. His glare narrowed as he inspected her.

She felt naked under his watchful eyes.

"What did you say your name was? Skip?"

"Scout, sir. Scout Keats."

"And how long have you worked at Patras Hotel, Scout Keats? I don't recall seeing you here before."

"Two weeks."

He nodded. "Are you new to the Folsom area?"

"No, sir. I've lived here my whole life."

His fingers tightened on her chin and turned her face to the left. "You have very unusual eyes, Ms. Keats. How old are you?"

His question caught her off guard. She had always known her eyes were unique. Against her dark brown lashes, the blue irises appeared almost white. Witch eyes, Parker called them. Once she tried disguising them with a makeup pencil she had found, but their glasslike color within the dark ring only became more startling.

"I'm twenty-seven," she lied. Adding five years to her actual age seemed necessary, like those five imaginary years could somehow protect her against this superior being.

Scout shifted her feet, the weight of her basket becoming awkward in her hands. The motion attracted his attention. He looked down at her burden and suddenly released her face and stepped

back as if the collection of cleaning products worked as a reminder of her situation. Peasant in the presence of royalty. Recalling his balcony, she decided it was more a throne than anything
else. She imagined him holding court there as all of Folsom gazed
up at him.

"You may go."

His sudden dismissal had her gaining control of her faculties,
and in a split second she rushed toward the penthouse door.
Quickly setting the basket there, she returned the sweeper to the
supply closet. He followed her at a distance, watching her as if to
make sure she didn't steal anything. Scout didn't make eye contact. She simply kept her gaze lowered to the ground and collected
her items and left.

On the ride down to the next floor she regretfully accepted
that this might be her last day at the hotel. Likely the man would
submit a complaint about her to Tamara and they would care
more about keeping the in-house billionaire pleased than keeping
their homeless new housekeeper employed. This paycheck would
have to last.

two
·····

THE TRACKS

STEPPING out of the pawnshop where she had her check cashed, Scout walked directly to the gas station across the street. Once inside the public restroom, door locked, she deposited her bag on the rusty sink. Her fingers rifled through the wad of soft money in her hands and her heart raced. Counting slowly, focusing on her numbers, Scout formed four piles of one hundred dollars and recounted each to be sure.

Once certain she was given the right amount she folded each stack tightly. Each faded green pile sat neatly on the tank of the toilet. Inside her bag she found her jeans, regular shoes that fit, a hooded sweatshirt, and her money belt. Stripping out of her uniform, she folded it as best she could so that it wouldn't be wrinkled in the morning.

After strapping the belt tightly around her ribs, she inserted three of the piles into the zipper compartment. Pulling on her jeans, Scout divided the remaining hundred dollars into four stacks, slipping a stack deep in each denim pocket. Once dressed, her hands compulsively checked that her money was secure.

Parker would be waiting for her. There were only two hours until curfew, but she needed to find Pearl before she returned to the shelter. If she didn't make it in time, she'd have to sleep at the tracks, which wasn't something she enjoyed doing, especially with four hundred dollars on her person, but she couldn't go back without taking care of Pearl.

The sun never made it through the haze that day. The blustery autumn wind chased litter along the back roads of Folsom beneath the webbing of vapor-bloated clouds. Past the point of beauty, brown leaves clogged the gutters and pathways. As she turned deeper into the forgotten crannies of the city, signs of life showed less and less.

Decrepit planks of pavement made up broken sidewalks. Faded abandoned buildings created the backdrop for graffiti. Barbed-wire fences formed treaty lines separating frightened drivers who accidentally lost their way from those hiding from the world.

Cutting directly to the hidden section of fence that'd been previously ripped from its poles, she lifted the heavy chain-link sheet, rolling under the sharp edge. Striding quickly and with purpose, Scout kept an eye on her surroundings and favored the fastest route to the tracks.

The scent of burning trash and sulfur from the nearby refineries irritated her sinuses. A cold trickle ran toward her lip from her nose. She brushed it away and hoisted herself onto the ledge of a loading dock outside of an abandoned warehouse. Lowering to her belly, she rolled under the metal garage door propped open by a cinderblock.

The vacant mill was silent, but Scout could detect the signs of life, never forgetting those who wished to remain unseen were watching her. Stowed belongings were stashed in secreted corners, secured by makeshift safeguards serving only to bring peace of mind, but lacking any real purpose.

A man wearing a belt of water bottles filled with various fluids rocked in a shadowed nook. He spoke to an emaciated cat as he tended to a small fire built between four bricks. Something cooked within the coffee can resting above the flame. He paid her no mind and she reciprocated in kind.

Sallow eyes followed her. Dirty faces turned as she made her way deeper into the belly of the abandoned mill. The scent of rotting life and urine forced her to breathe through her mouth. The farther Scout traveled, the darker her surroundings became. Boards covered windows, showing only the tiniest slice of light. Occasionally, a broken windowpane permitted a burst of light, a beam no wider than a finger width, but it was too dim to depend on. Her eyes adjusted to the darkness.

Needles and crack pipes marked the way to the more populated quarters. Recognizing the familiar ductwork at the entrance of a long passage, a sense of unpleasant nostalgia filled her. Home.

The stench of fecal matter made her eyes water. The glow of a flickering flame bounced like a strobe past the last door in the vacant hall. The quiet mumblings echoed like a child playing alone, whispering over dolls or imaginary friends. Scout entered the chamber.

Pearl sat huddled on a flattened cardboard box sorting through a torn plastic bag filled with crushed cans. Quiet, incoherent words whispered past her cracked lips as she took inventory of her treasures. A sharp sadness had Scout swallowing hard. Pearl's gaunt, jaundiced flesh hung off of her protruding cheekbones. It had become almost impossible to equate the pretty woman from Scout's childhood memories with the woman crouching before her now.

"Momma?" Pearl hugged her belongings defensively and scowled at her. It hurt, waiting for her mother to recognize her. "Momma, it's me."

"Scout?" Pearl grinned, cracked lips stretching over gray gums. "Oh, you should see all the goods I scouted out today. Traded a can of fruit for this here sock. What you got for me, Scout?"

Scout reached into her bag and pulled out a small jug of milk, a half pound of sliced turkey, a handful of bananas, and four cans of stew. Pearl cooed and greedily took the bounty.

"Good, good," she mumbled as she eyed the door and quickly stowed the food out of sight, keeping a banana and peeling it back.

Scout sat on the edge of her mother's pallet and rifled through her bag. "I also got you these, Momma." She dropped a collection of half-used shampoos and bars of soap from Patras.

She picked up a bottle and frowned. "What is it?"

"Soap."

Pearl tucked it away in the corner and continued to eat her banana, quietly singing over each bite.

"I'm going to bring you more stuff tomorrow. Do you need anything specific?"

"I need a hit."

Scout sighed. The life of a heroin addict was a never-ending cycle of scavenging for that next fix and strategizing ways to secure it. Finishing the banana, Pearl tossed the skin into a pile of odorous compost in the corner. Flies and maggots terrorized the new addition.

"How much do you have left?" Scout asked wearily.

"A bit. Hank'll be back tomorrow. I can get some from him."

"Don't do that, Momma. I'll give you the money."

There was no use not giving her the money for a fix. Pearl couldn't make it more than a few days without it and she'd do anything to get it. *Anything.* Scout's lectures about sharing needles and sexual favors had fallen on deaf ears, and Hep C was the only competition heroin had in the race to end her mother's life. Her gaze purposefully avoided the slavered candle in the corner next to the filthy spoon.

"I gotta go, Momma." Pearl never asked about her job or where she got her money. She was too far gone in a world of her own. "It's almost dark."

"How come you don't bring your friend?"

"Parker's at the shelter."

"He treatin' you good?"

"You know it isn't like that between Parker and me, Momma."

She gave her a look of skepticism. "He reminds me of your daddy. You bring him back here with you next time."

"I will."

Scout nodded and wearily stood. Some days it was so hard not to take her mother into her arms and hug her the way she used to. It'd been years since Pearl let Scout touch her like that, like a daughter. It was for the best, considering her health.

"I'll be back tomorrow night, Momma."

Leaving the mill, Scout's energy abandoned her. Streetlights flickered above as she slowly headed back to the shelter. Her cold fingers shook and pulled the hood of her sweatshirt over her hair as the bitter wind snuck down the collar of her shirt. Thoughts of the day played through her mind and she tried not to worry about what would come tomorrow. Scout still wasn't sure if she had a job to return to in the morning.

By the time the black silhouette of St. Christopher's showed in the distance, her hunger pangs had converged into a dull throb. She spotted Parker's tall form in the shadows before stepping onto the cracked pavement of the old church's courtyard. He pushed off the wall and met her by the broken steps of the shelter.

"You went to see Pearl." It wasn't a question. Parker wasn't her keeper, but he liked to pretend he was.

"I needed to drop her off some things. She wants you to come with me tomorrow."

"You're going back?"

"Yes."

There was no need to explain that she'd gotten paid and wanted to bring Pearl more supplies. It was none of his business. She'd be going back with or without him. Like Pearl and her reckless lifestyle, Scout could be unbending too.

"You almost didn't make curfew, Scout. You can't keep going there this late at night."

"If I miss curfew I'll just stay there."

He stilled and then quickly caught back up to her as she pulled the heavy door to the church open. Her muscles were tired and weak, begging for a break. "I think you should only go there on the days you don't work. It isn't safe to go there when it's dark."

"I grew up there, Parker."

No matter the years Parker had been on the streets, he'd never fully understand what it meant to be born there, to never have any other option or never know what it might be like to have a roof over your head no one could take from you. His background was very different than Scout's. The streets of Folsom were all she'd ever known.

He'd long ago given up asking why her mom couldn't stay in the shelter and she was grateful he had. Scout rarely took the time to explain herself, but Parker was her friend. He worried. It was easier when he accepted this was the way it would be, and his opinions wouldn't change what was.

They walked into the church and down into the basement. The scent of stew and boiled carrots had her cramps returning with a vengeance.

"I'll go with you," he said as he held the door for her.

The subdued chatter of the residence greeted them. Following

Parker to the line of people, she secured her bag over her shoulders and lowered her hood. They each grabbed a tray.

"You don't have to," she told him as they followed the sluggish line.

Parker's eyes focused on the new resident three spaces ahead of them. He was an older tan-skinned man whose left eye never moved. The man had stared at them the entire time they ate the night before, and Parker already decided to hate him.

"Ignore him, Parker."

"I don't like the way he leers at you."

"He's harmless."

Moving through the slop line, they filled their trays with potatoes, rolls, wilted salad, and what looked to be beef stew. Parker followed her to the end table where they sat and ate in silence. Scout tucked her roll in her bag at her feet for lunch tomorrow. The potatoes were flavorless and too mushy to cut. Gently scooping one into her mouth, she chewed as her cheek stretched over the boiled tuber.

"How was work?"

The watery potato disappeared down her throat with little flavor to herald its journey. "Good, but I might've gotten in trouble today." They ate in silence for several minutes, food taking precedence over all else.

Once their plates were mostly clean, Parker asked, "What happened?"

Scout's fork scraped the last of her stew into the crease of her bowl, hoping to get one last bite. Her stomach was already cramping with fullness, but she couldn't waste the warm sustenance.

"I had to do the penthouses today because the girl who usually does it was out. There're people who actually live in there. Can you believe that? The place I cleaned was so luxurious you would've pissed yourself, Park. It was insane."

"So how did you get in trouble?"

Parker never commented on her references to others' wealth anymore. He found it unimpressive, whereas Scout found it fascinating how rich people lived. He'd constantly told her that her standards were screwed up, and people like them shouldn't fixate over a life they'd probably never have. She didn't see it that way. There was no predicting what the future could bring.

"Well, I accidentally knocked over some papers and of course the guy who lived there walked in the moment I was picking them up. I don't know what he does for a living, but whatever it is I'm pretty sure he's good at it. He was terrifyingly powerful."

Parker scowled, his soft green eyes taking on a menacing glare. "How so?"

"Just in the way he carried himself. Even his shoes were intimidating. He was tall and handsome and rich. I think he thought I was snooping. He sort of cornered me and gave me an inquisition."

"Did you tell him to go fuck himself?"

Scout rolled her eyes. "Yeah, Parker, I told the billionaire to fuck himself. Are you nuts? I need this job."

"There're other jobs, Scout. You don't need to take any crap from some self-important asshole. You should've told your boss if you felt threatened."

"I didn't say he threatened me. He just intimidated me. It doesn't matter. I'll probably never see him again. I may not even have a job in the morning. Whatever was on those papers, he seemed pretty protective of."

Parker was no longer listening to her. She followed his gaze, and the older man who'd been watching them the night before was leering at her again. Scout sighed and stacked her dishes. "Let it go, Parker."

"I don't like him."

"He knows."

Following supper they walked over to the old school. Parker headed to the men's bathroom and Scout visited the ladies' room. Once she used the toilet, she went to the sink and unraveled a bar of Patras soap. After scrubbing her hands and face vigorously and picking any flecks of dirt from under her nails, she took a wet washcloth into the stall to clean her body. Changing her pants and underwear, Scout shifted all her money into her money belt and tightened it around her ribs. Her belongings were stuffed back in her bag and she headed to the girls' quarters.

Selectively, she pulled a mat from the pile, discarding the stained one at the top of the heap, and carried it to the far corner. The echo of a baby crying from the family quarters overwhelmed the silence.

Scout's blanket withdrew from her bag in as practiced a move as a magician pulls flowers from his sleeve. She shoved the bag to the head of her mat as a pillow.

Nimbly, her fingers removed the laces from her shoes and tied them into one long string, then threaded the frayed edge through the tiny zipper of her bag and tied the other end around her wrist. As the last of the overhead lights shut off, leaving only the dim glow of the emergency signs, she settled in for the night.

The baby eventually stopped crying and other than a spontaneous cough, the room was quiet. Scout's tired mind reflected her mother and what she'd bring her the next day. She thought about the man from dinner and decided to stay away from him in the future. But her last thoughts before she fell asleep were of startling black eyes and the warm scent of lived-in silk.

three

·····

WHAT'S IN A NAME?

TAMARA handed her the key and Scout frowned. "Isn't Bridget here today?"

"Yes, but Mr. Patras specifically requested you tend to the penthouses from now on."

"P-Patras?" The man from yesterday must've really been upset to complain to the owner of the hotel. "Tamara, I don't know what the man from the penthouse told you, but I want you to know I wasn't snooping. I accidentally knocked over his things and he happened to walk in just as I was trying to straighten up the mess."

The GM frowned at her. "He didn't say anything about you snooping. As a matter of fact, he called down after you left yesterday to tell me how pleased he was with your attention to detail."

Scout's restless fingers twitched and smoothed her apron. "What about my other rooms?"

"Don't worry about them. I put Miguel on your old section. We have a guest coming into master suite B tonight so you'll need to clean that room tomorrow. Today you just need to freshen it up. In the service kitchen you'll find fresh fruit and flower arrangements to take with you. Ask Raphael. He'll show you which ones."

Building trepidation made it difficult to focus on what her GM was saying. Scout wasn't sure who Raphael was and only had a general idea of how to get to the service kitchen. Rather than allow her dread to ruin her day, she found her cart and took the elevator to the penthouse floor to do the general guest suites first.

Scout finished the thirtieth-floor rooms by noon and used her lunch to locate the service kitchen. Aside from the common areas and guest rooms, there was an entire labyrinth of service passages the staff used.

Reluctantly, she finally asked another maid named Mona where the service kitchen was. In broken English the maid explained it was in the lower level. Scout needed to take the west wing all the way down until a sign appeared that read "Kitchen," then follow the arrows. This was going to be a problem.

Once in the west wing there were signs on every corner. Scout looked for words that started with *C*, hoping she'd find the word *kitchen*. No luck. Tears of frustration blurred her vision after more time than her lunch break allotted had passed. Taking a breath she slowly tried to sound out each word on the sign.

Her eyes focused on the first word.

Incinerator.

Scout had no idea what that said, but she knew it didn't say kitchen.

Accounting.

Shaking her head, she firmed her lips and wiped her eyes. It had been too long since Parker and she had sat down to practice reading.

There were three more big words that she skipped because they didn't look like they spelled kitchen either. Scout considered going to find Mona again, but the other maid seemed hassled to begin with.

Startled by the sound of someone coming, she discreetly wiped her eyes. A man in a white jacket came from a door down the hall. He had a smear of red on his cuff and carried a rag. He sort of looked like a chef.

Straightening her shoulders, Scout waited until he came closer and then asked, "Do you know Raphael?"

He stilled as if he hadn't seen her standing there. "I am Raphael," he said in a clipped accent that sounded French.

A huge sigh of relief puffed out her cheeks. "Oh, thank God. Can you show me where the service kitchen is? I'm supposed to pick up flowers and fresh fruit for the penthouse master suites."

"I was wondering when you were going to show up. No Bridget today?" He said the other girl's name like *Brisheet* and for some reason that pleased Scout.

She shook her head. "I'm assigned to that floor this week."

He looked at her then, his eyes assessing her critically. Only because Scout was dependent on him to show her where the supplies she needed were, did she not snap her fingers in his face and demand he stop looking at her that way.

"I think you will have the top floor longer than a week, child. You're prettier than Bridget."

"What's that got to do with anything?"

"Everything. Follow me." He turned briskly and Scout rushed after him. He led her into the doorway he'd come from and she was suddenly in a bustling underground kitchen.

Stacks of pots billowed with steam, and wonderful fragrances of food made her mouth water. A man shouted in French and Raphael quickly said something back she didn't understand.

Dishes clattered and phones rang. There was a computer screen overhead and a man assembling fruit cups at a counter read from the screen as he worked. Mesmerized, Scout watched him multitasking with nimble dexterity and bumped into Raphael. He turned and glowered at her, but then his features softened. Raphael had a nose too wide for his face.

"You like honeydew, *Cendrillon*? You taste this honeydew. It is so fresh it will bring tears to your eyes."

His clean fingers reached to the counter were the man worked, and plucked up a green ball wrapped in some sort of pink meat.

"What is it?"

"It is prosciutto. Delicious. You taste and then tell me what a culinary genius I am." He smiled and held the wrapped fruit out to her.

She carefully took the fruit from him and sniffed it. It was cool in her warm fingers. The sweet and refreshing scent of melon filled her nose. The meat had an earthy, smoked smell to it. Glancing to the chef one last time, he nodded.

"Just pop it in your mouth. Trust me. Delicious." Raphael had very nice teeth.

Hesitantly, she placed the morsel in her mouth. Its salty, sugary flavor burst over her tongue and she moaned. Her teeth cut through the delicate, thinly cut meat and melon juice exploded over her taste buds.

"Oh, my God."

"It is spectacular, *oui*?"

"Very good!" Her fingers covered her mouth as she chewed and swallowed.

"*Bon*. Now come with me, *Cendrillon*. I show you where your flowers and fruit are."

Once Scout had the flowers and fruit loaded on a cart, she returned to the private bank of elevators and slid her key through B. No one was in residence yet and it was quick work, unloading the items for that suite.

Master suite B was quite different looking than the other master suite. Less lived-in and more generic. It had an air of luxury to it for sure, but it lacked the level of wealth and power the other suite projected.

Her heart raced as she took the lift back down and moved to

the private elevator for master suite C. The ride to the top was way too short. Moisture built under the sleeves of her dove gray gown and her sweaty palms nervously smoothed her apron and adjusted her bonnet. He wouldn't be there.

Pushing her cart out of the gilded car, she sighed and approached the entrance. Her knuckles rapped lightly on the frosted window of the door.

"Housekeeping."

Reaching for her key, Scout's relief was short-lived as a shuffle sounded on the other side of the entry and she stilled. The handle moved and the door opened. Smooth black patent leather shoes stepped into her view.

"Ah, Ms. Keats, do come in."

Her jaw unhinged as her gaze traveled up expensively clothed, long tapered legs, a trim waist evident under a neatly tucked shirt, broad shoulders, and a tanned throat with a dark shadow of beard. The man from yesterday. He smiled at her. *Very* perfect, white teeth. His visage was nothing like the irritated expression he'd greeted her with the day before.

"I—I can come back at a better time," she stuttered stupidly.

"Nonsense. I was just sitting down to have lunch. Have you eaten?"

Scout's eyes blinked as her brain worked. His silk sleeves were rolled up to his elbows. The top button of his shirt was undone and his tie hung loosely at his neck. Parker was the only man she ever really looked at. Parker's skin was still youthful, while this man's skin was tanned and roughened slightly with the dark shadow of coarse hair under the surface.

Her dry throat swallowed back a lump that had formed some-where over her voice box. He heaved a sigh and suddenly reached for her cart and pulled it over the threshold.

"Oh, sir, no. I can do that."

Scout followed him and her cart into the apartment like a kitten chasing a string. He needed to stop touching her things. He parked the cart at the end of the hall and turned. She staggered to a stop.

"You didn't answer my question."

"Your question?" she repeated stupidly.

"Have you had lunch?"

"I just finished my break. If you don't want me to come back later, I can be finished here in a few minutes. I didn't mean to interrupt your lunch."

Scout reached to the bottom of the cart for her bag of supplies, but he grabbed her arm. His large, tanned hand circled her wrist like a manacle and he pulled her toward the seating area.

"Wh-what are you doing?" she stammered. Her feet quickly hurried after his much-longer strides.

He released her arm and turned. "Sit."

Instinctively she dropped her weight to the edge of the settee. He lifted two pewter covers and the scent of warm, rotisserie-style meat filled the room. Her stomach cramped at the reminder of her hunger and her mouth watered.

Some sort of small chicken sat on each plate. There were long green beans with slivered almonds in a buttery sauce, and a fancy-shaped pile of mashed potatoes that looked more like toasted ice cream the way it swirled into a peak. It suddenly occurred to her that there were two of everything.

"You were expecting someone."

"Yes."

He sat beside her and she was intensely aware of the way his warm thigh touched the naked flesh on her knee peeking from below her uniform.

"These are Cornish game hens. Have you ever had them before? They're a bit tougher than chicken, but equally as savory when prepared properly."

Her eyes went wide as he spread a linen napkin over her lap. She shot to her feet, catching the napkin before it fell to the ground.

"Sir, I can't eat your food."

"Of course you can. I ordered it for you."

"You—you ordered this for me?" *Why would he do that?*

"Well, not all of it. Half is for me." He smirked, only the corner of his mouth participating in the expression.

She shook her head. "I'll lose my job. I'm sorry. I'll come back later." She quickly turned and walked toward the hall.

"Evelyn."

At the sound of her legal name she froze. Slowly, she faced him. "How did you know my name?" she whispered.

"It was on your paperwork."

"What paperwork?"

"Your application."

"You read my application?"

He raised one dark brow. "You rummaged through my desk."

"I—" This was insane. "Sir, I've already apologized about that. I promise you, it wasn't what it looked like."

"And what did it look like, Evelyn?"

No one used her real name aside from her mother, and even she rarely called her that. She hated that name. It didn't fit her.

"Like I was snooping," she admitted shamefully.

"Were you?"

"No!"

"Good. Now that that's all cleared up we can eat."

He replaced his napkin on his lap and sliced into the small bird on his plate. Succulent juices spurted from the crispy skin as his polished silver knife created neat little slices like fallen dominos. Her stomach made an obnoxious whining sound and she blushed.

"Come sit, Evelyn."

Her feet carried her across the carpet and her eyes glazed with hunger as his nimble fingers worked. His silverware was thick and shiny, nothing like the dull stuff workers gave them at the shelter. He speared a small bit of the tender white meat and popped it in his mouth.

"Mmm. You should really try some while it's still warm."

"Sir—"

"Lucian."

"What?"

"My name is Lucian."

Scout shook her head. He took another bite and groaned.

"Lucian, I thank you for the offer, but I'm an employee and I have a job to do."

"I'm quite aware of your purpose, being that I pay your salary. I find your work ethic quite admirable, Evelyn, but you're spoiling my thoughtful gesture."

As his words set in she stared at him. She couldn't move. Did he just say he paid her salary?

"What did you say your name was?" she asked in a hoarse whisper.

He sighed and placed his fork on the edge of his plate. His fingers swiped quickly over the linen napkin and he leaned back. His eyes studied her for a long moment and she fought the urge to cover herself from his penetrating gaze.

"I'm Lucian Patras, hotel tycoon and seasoned entrepreneur. It's a pleasure to make your acquaintance, Ms. Keats. Now that everyone's been introduced, I'd like to eat."

No. It couldn't be. No.

He sighed and crossed his arms over his broad chest. His strong build was evident even covered by the silk of his dress shirt.

"What's the problem, Evelyn?"

"I—I don't . . . understand. You own the hotel?"

"Correct."

"Are you firing me?"

He laughed. "Why would I fire you?"

"Because of yesterday."

All humor fled his expression. "You told me it was an accident, that you weren't rummaging through my personal papers. Did you lie to me, Evelyn?"

"No." Her jaw trembled. What was happening here?

"Then you have nothing to worry about so long as you never lie to me." He paused and looked over her clothing. "Your shoes are too big."

Scout awkwardly tried to hide her feet from his view. "I don't understand what's happening here, Mr. Patras."

"Lucian."

"I can't call you that."

"Why not? I have no problem calling you Evelyn."

"No one calls me that."

"Scout's no name for a beautiful woman."

His words made her incredibly uncomfortable. Her brain ran out of things to say. Lucian Patras was a man of great determination and she found his presence exhaustingly challenging. He was breaking her down, but she wasn't sure why. Her hunger had become more than the unending nagging ache it always was, and she was suddenly very weary.

He narrowed his eyes at her then reached for the phone. She stood silently as he dialed.

"Ms. Jones, Lucian Patras. Evelyn Keats is finished for the day. She'll be back in the morning. Please make sure she's paid for the rest of the afternoon." He waited a moment. "Very good." The phone returned to the cradle with a light click.

four
.....

IN GOOD COMPANY

"SIT down, Evelyn. We're going to eat and then we're going to talk."

Her body slowly lowered to the settee. Lucian pulled her plate closer to him and made quick work of slicing her meat. Once the white meat was stacked in neat little bite-size pieces, he slid it closer to her and handed her a fork.

"Eat."

The silverware was cool and heavy. She slowly stabbed a piece of food and placed it in her mouth. She wanted to say she was too shocked to process the flavor, but that would be a lie. It was perhaps the most divine thing she'd ever tasted.

They ate in silence. The beans were so fresh and flavorful Scout could've cried. The potatoes were unlike anything she'd ever tasted before, crisp yet fluffy, nothing like the bulbous, mushy spuds they served at the shelter. She wanted to bring some back for Parker to taste, but that would be impossible.

As her mouth closed over the last bit of food, embarrassment had her blood rising. Lucian still had quite a bit of food on his plate. With a trembling hand she placed her fork on the edge of her plate like he had done. The touch of heavy silver to the delicate china seemed all too loud and uncultured to her ears.

"Thank you. That was amazing."

"I'm glad you enjoyed it. Do you like working at Patras Hotel, Evelyn?"

Her limbs trembled, knowing what was coming. He'd lied. He did plan on firing her.

"Yes, sir."

"Where did you work before you took this job?"

Her fingers nervously wrung her napkin in her hands and she looked at her lap. "I was a waitress for a while."

"And before that?"

"I worked at a car wash and answered phones for a mechanic."

He nodded and eased his body back against the back of the settee. "A jack of all trades."

"And a master of none," she said dryly.

He chuckled. It was deep and rumbled from within his chest. "Not everyone is intended to be a master, Ms. Keats. Why did you leave your previous jobs?"

"I lost my waitressing job when my register came up short."

He raised an eyebrow. "How short?"

"Three hundred seventy-six dollars."

"Did you take the money?"

"No. I don't steal."

"Good. And the job at the mechanic's?"

"I was young. It was me working with three men. I didn't like going there after a while."

"Why?"

She glared up at him. He only met her challenge with endless patience in his stare. Her shoulders lowered.

"The youngest mechanic was the owner's nephew. He used to wait for me outside of the bathroom and try to make me . . . pay a toll before he'd let me go back to the front office."

His jaw ticked and she sympathized with anyone who came face-to-face with Mr. Patras in business. He had a menacing presence when he wanted to show one.

"Did you pay the toll?"

"No," she said clearly. "I broke his nose."

He laughed long and hard and she found herself laughing too, perhaps a bit out of nervousness.

"I like you, Evelyn. You're a lot feistier than you first come off."

His compliment made her oddly proud. Their laughter faded and her lips twitched, wanting to keep the moment going, but she had no more to add.

"I have a proposition for you, Ms. Keats."

Scout stilled, all merriment gone. While Lucian Patras was acting the perfect gentleman, she was not fool enough to underestimate him. He was a man with determination in spades, who did not easily accept being told no. While she wasn't necessarily what people would consider book smart, she was street smart and worldly enough when it came to men. They all thought along the same lines no matter what social position they held.

She swallowed apprehensively. "A proposition?"

"Yes, a business deal, if you will."

Scout wasn't equipped to make business deals with a man like Mr. Patras. She remained silent and he continued.

"I find you . . . appealing. I want to know you better. I'm a very busy man, Ms. Keats, and while my social schedule is not lacking, I find myself . . . bored with the selection. How would you feel about attending some parties with me?"

"Parties?"

"Fund-raisers, soirées, the typical high-society bullshit."

"I don't have the means for such things," she admitted, figuring he couldn't argue with the truth.

"I'd make arrangements for everything you would need. You wouldn't be required to spend a penny of your own money. I'd arrange for you to have a line of credit at the best boutiques, which my driver would take you to. You'd have the use of the hotel's salon whenever you needed and I'd arrange for you to have your own penthouse."

Her unblinking eyes stared at him dumbly. Was this a joke? Slowly, she pinched her arm and his fingers smoothly settled over hers.

"Don't do that, Evelyn," he gently reprimanded, and she stopped.

She thought of Pearl, memories of men coming and going throughout her childhood while she was told to wait outside the door. He couldn't mean that.

"What would you get in return?" she asked.

"Your company."

"Define 'company.'" Her heart was beating uncomfortably fast and her delicious lunch had become a heavy weight in her stomach.

"I find such things can't be determined until the time comes. I could tell you my expectations, but who's to say what they'll be tomorrow? I'd much rather our association develop over a natural course of time before we try to pigeonhole it with labels."

"I'm not stupid," she whispered defensively, unable to meet his gaze.

"Of course not. I have no interest in surrounding myself with stupid people."

"I know what you're asking."

"Good. I'd hate to think I wasn't clear."

The calm manner in which he danced around her questions was infuriating. "I'm not a prostitute."

The word didn't slow him. "Also good. I hate involving myself with legal situations. I much prefer to keep things on the up-and-up. We'd merely be two consenting adults sharing each other's company."

Her fists tightened on the linen napkin.

"Mr. Patras, no matter how you pretty it up, my sexual favors are *not* for sale."

"Everything's for sale, Ms. Keats," he replied silkily. "The currency simply varies in order to meet social standards."

"I'm not."

"While your paychecks may read Patras, Evelyn, they are only in exchange for housekeeping. I assure you, what I intend to offer will pay for itself. You'll take as much pleasure from our association as I plan to."

His black eyes gazed into hers. She looked at this man, finding herself marginally more settled in his presence than the day before, but still ill at ease. His fingernails were clean. His thickly muscled arms were dusted with dark hair. He was so different than the malnourished men at the shelter or even Parker, who was surprisingly fit. Mr. Patras was undeniably an attractive man.

Her gaze scanned the penthouse, still clean from her visit the day before. Mr. Patras was a fairly tidy person. His desk was messy, but she'd never concern herself with that again.

As tempting as the offer of fine clothing and salon beauty treatments were, she was more concerned with proper-fitting shoes she could take with her when Mr. Patras no longer required her "company." Her situation in life had never, not once, allowed for any sort of indulgence. Scout's brain simply wasn't wired in a way that permitted such fantasies.

Her dreams consisted of warm clothing, shelter, and food to stave of her hunger. Mr. Patras could certainly provide that, but at what price? Indignity had her pride bristling. She'd witnessed

sex and found it undesirable, to say the least. She was very territorial of her own space and didn't favor anyone coming too close.
Yet, the thought of a man like Lucian Patras finding her attractive
did things to her. Her body warmed in places she wasn't normally
aware of. There was certainly a level of temptation hidden within
her to experience these unknowns with him.

If sacrificing her body and attending parties could bridge the
gap between her and the ordinary women of society, she probably
shouldn't dismiss the opportunity. Would she be able to abide a
man like Mr. Patras touching her, kissing her? The idea of such
acts appealed, but actually having the guts to follow through was
something else entirely. She had a stubborn side she couldn't always control. As her mind imagined what it would be like to have
sex with him, her stomach tightened in an unfamiliar way she
found disarming. She quickly generated a mental list of pros and
cons.

She wouldn't have to sleep at the shelter, at least for a short
length of time. There would be no more guarding her belongings
and cold, restless nights of sleeping with one eye open. This could
be that chance to finally rest peacefully.

She'd have an actual bed, complete with clean linens and plush
pillows. Her skin prickled with longing for such luxuries. She'd be
warm. Winter was coming and she didn't savor the idea of cough-
ing through another bitter season, chilled to the bone and unable
to thaw until the arrival of spring.

Would their arrangement last that long? Even if it got her out
of the unforgiving elements for a week it seemed worth it. Her
narrowed perspective of life was so limited, she could barely
fathom what such a life would entail, what such comfort would
feel like. Something deep down in her heart, something that was
frightened and indignant, told her chances like this didn't come
around more than once in a lifetime.

And then there was Pearl. Her mother would tell her to do it. She'd done the same for much less.

Scout could say no and continue on her slow trek out of poverty, but Mr. Patras was offering her a speed pass to the top. Her mind segmented as she rationalized the situation. Flashes of bodies rapidly flickered through her mind, colliding flesh and ticking clocks. Sex took only a few minutes. The more she considered his offer, the more curious she grew.

He was a stunning man. Her options for experimentation had never been so promising. There was a good chance she might enjoy him touching her. If not, she would simply send her mind somewhere else and all those luxuries could be hers.

It was a business deal. Her mind and emotions didn't have to come into play, only her body. The survivor in her eagerly awaited her acceptance. Mr. Patras was a handsome man. He smelled nice and had clean hands and nice teeth.

Her practical side told her sex was a small price to pay for the easy lifestyle he could provide, but her prideful side, that part of her that demanded she was better than that, indignantly objected. Shutting her eyes, she muzzled her pride in order to think.

Obviously, he found her attractive if he was bartering to have her body. Something inside of her preened that an upper-class man like Mr. Patras would see her as desirable. She wasn't fancy. She didn't pretty herself up in any way. Yet, he wanted her. However, he didn't have a clue about her real-life circumstances outside of the hotel. Scout was intelligent enough to know, if he assumed she was homeless he'd be more likely to chase her away with the dirty end of a broom than sweep her off her feet.

At first it seemed like she'd be sacrificing a great deal to oblige him, but now she wasn't sure who would actually be taking advantage. When she walked away, she'd be leaving him with nothing more than a memory, but she might earn uncountable assets in the process. She could use, pawn, or recycle a good amount of what he'd provide. That was headway.

Money was power. She wasn't materialistic. There was an infinite divide between her desire to have enough financial stability to not freeze, starve, or die another Jane Doe, and the desire to be dressed up and paraded about like some fancy aristocrat. She didn't care for superfluous wealth. She only desired stability, something she never had. Yet, no amount of rationalization let her dismiss the fact that, at the end of the day, she'd still be his loosely defined hooker.

No.

The rejection to his offer rang in her head, but temptation to take it fought hard against her will. Scout needed to get off the streets. Perhaps this was the fastest way to accomplish that. Attending parties with other rich people could lead to meeting someone who could offer her more than a minimum wage job.

Her gaze returned to the long, tapered legs beside her. He'd been waiting quietly as she considered his offer. One ankle crossed casually over his knee. His lean torso was barely camouflaged by his clothing. Her gaze caught on the shining, narrow silver buckle of his black leather belt.

"Look your fill, Evelyn. I plan to do the same."

Her stare jerked to his and his eyes creased with laughter. "I was looking at your belt," she informed him, offended he'd think she was looking anywhere else. As curious as she was, his quick accusation reminded her that the scales of life experience were extremely tipped in his favor. She'd have to be cautious about how much of her true self she allowed him to see.

"Of course." He peeked at his watch and sighed. "I'd hate to eat and run, but I have a meeting I need to get to downtown. Can my driver give you a ride home?"

"No." She couldn't let him see the shelter and she needed to visit Pearl again. "Thank you, but I prefer to walk."

"Then I believe I've given you enough to think about until tomorrow. Monday evening I have a benefit at the Westchester Museum of Natural Art. I'd like you to be my guest. Think about my offer and have an answer for me by tomorrow."

His dismissal was jarring. Was she still expected to finish her shift or did he want her to clean his suite the next day?

"Would you like me to freshen your bed before I go?"

She regretted her words the moment they fully left her mouth.

"That does sound delightful," he purred. "But unfortunately I must be going. I think I can manage until tomorrow, but I'll expect you to tend to my *needs* first thing. I don't like coming second unless the foreplay's truly worth it."

She stood and picked up her supply bag. He stood as well, engulfing her and the surrounding space with his size. At her cart she stowed the bag on the bottom shelf.

"Your flowers," she said, picking up the large arrangement and turning. Scout stopped abruptly, nearly smashing the flowers into his chest. He was right behind her.

His hand reached out and Scout's breathing stilled as he ran his thumb over her lower lip. "I can't seem to decide," he said softly, "if your eyes are blue or silver. They remind me of the sky, blue at first glance, but really some unnamable color made purely of reflections. They remind me of diamonds."

Mumbling a thank-you for the compliment, which he, in turn, thanked *her* for, her lashes lowered, breaking the spell, and he stepped away. She placed the arrangement on the sideboard and removed the wilting centerpiece from the week before. Scout was very aware of him watching her as she moved the bowl of fresh citrus to the bar.

He held the door as she backed the cart to the elevator, and he obligingly pressed the button. She couldn't bring herself to look at him again until the split second before the gilded glass doors closed between them. His expression was blank, but his eyes held a glint of promise. She knew in that moment she'd never leave this man's presence unscathed.

five

SECOND THOUGHTS

B Y the time Scout's feet dragged through the door of St. Christopher's that night, her head was still out of sorts. Pearl had been
stoned out of her mind and was barely able to speak when she
arrived. Her mother rested naked on her makeshift pallet, not thinking clearly. After Scout had settled her a bit, she bathed her as best
she could with the bottle of rainwater she'd collected, and cried.

Tracks from shooting up had disfigured her mother's flesh permanently. Her eyes were unfocused and as Scout tended to her
needs, her mother told her about her beautiful daughter, Evelyn,
who hadn't come to visit in a while. Some days Scout wondered
why she didn't just let her go and save herself the torture of watching her mother slowly kill herself.

By curfew Scout was nothing more than a rundown body needing a long night's rest. Parker wasn't waiting for her tonight. No,
he'd already be inside eating. She'd missed supper. Luckily her belly
was still full from the lunch Mr. Patras provided. Lucian Patras was
an entire other issue her mind was too exhausted to think about.

Wearily, her feet trudged up the church steps. When she reached the basement, the dining hall was empty. Sighing, she turned and headed back outside to the school.

"Hey."

Scout started as Parker suddenly jumped in step beside her. "Hey," she replied wearily.

"I thought you were coming here after work so we could visit Pearl together."

Shit. She'd totally forgotten he'd said he'd go with her. Made no difference anyway. If Pearl couldn't recognize Scout, her own daughter, she certainly wouldn't have recognized Parker.

"I'm sorry, Parker. I totally forgot."

"Hey." He frowned and pulled her to the side of the hall. "What's up? You look upset."

Scout hadn't realized how close to tears she was. "It's nothing. She was just really bad today. She didn't recognize me, and she was covered in her own filth. Probably some of someone else's too. I couldn't leave her that way."

A jerky gasp filled her lungs and she pressed her lips tight, refusing to cry in front of him.

Parker looked at her, not with pity, but the true understanding of a friend. Without promising something he couldn't guarantee, he did the only thing he could do to help. He pulled her into his arms and hugged her tight.

Scout leaned into his strong form and shut her eyes. Besides Pearl, Parker was the only person she ever let touch her, and even that was a rare occurrence. His arms wrapped around her and he whispered, "I'm sorry, Scout."

Swiping at her insistent tears, glad no one else was around at the moment, she said, "It's okay. It is what it is."

His large, firm palm rubbed over her back. He smelled nice. Her nose breathed in the traces of soap clinging to his sweater. He must've washed it recently.

"She's getting so thin. As I bathed her I could count her ribs. She doesn't even have breasts anymore. I'm so afraid of the day I'll go there and she . . ." A shaky breath cut off her fears.

"Shh, don't talk like that. You're a good daughter and your mother loves you. You're doing everything you can to help her."

Although Pearl was adamant about staying out of the shelters, with a little bit of money, Scout could maybe find a small place for her and Pearl alone. Her mother had been raped when she was in her thirties at a shelter, and since then had never entered another. If she could just get her away from the mill, away from the tracks and those assholes down there, maybe she could get a little better. Some days Scout saw signs of the old Pearl, but most days she was a realist enough to know her brain was too far damaged from drugs and hard living to ever return her mother to her.

Her mind switched to Lucian Patras and his offer. If she helped him, maybe he'd help her get help for Pearl. Maybe if she could afford a good doctor and could put her mother on some sort of medicine, she could get better. Pearl had to be less than ninety pounds at this point.

At the rate her mother was withering away, she didn't have much time left. Pearl was going to do what she was going to do. Every decision she made had a direct correlation to how she'd obtain her next fix. She'd sell herself to anyone to score a hit, and every time she did it brought her a little closer to death. Scout could sell herself just the same, but without the risks Pearl tempted with such dealings. Mr. Patras was worlds away from the men her mother dealt with.

Breathing in the last bit of Parker's strength and familiar scent, Scout straightened her shoulders and pulled away. Enough self-pity.

"Thanks, buddy. I needed that. Don't tell the others or I'll have to retaliate just to prove I'm still a hard-ass."

He smiled sadly and wiped away a tear her cold fingers had missed. "No one doubts your toughness, Scout. You're one of the toughest girls I know." He reached into his pocket. "Here, I saved you my roll from supper."

Her heart swelled. Parker was an awesome friend. "Thank you, but you keep it. I already ate my fill today."

There was no need to tell him. As much as she wanted to tell him about the amazing feast earlier, in the light of their existence it now only seemed cruel.

"You sure?"

His hunger was evident in the way he held the stale bread. She smiled. "Yeah, I'm sure."

By the time they made it into the gymnasium, it was already lights out. Scout said good night to Parker and went to the ladies' room. Sometimes it was nice to be the last one standing. She needed a good wash and having the restroom to herself made that a little more possible.

THE following morning Scout arrived extra early at Patras. She hadn't slept much the night before. The moment sleep found her, her dreams were restless. Horrible visions of her mother's skeletal form filled her nightmares. By the end of her last dream she realized it was not Pearl she was seeing, but her own reflection. As her body jerked awake her mind gave up on sleep, and Scout decided to dress for work.

The shelter didn't offer breakfast, and residents had to be out by eight. She often wondered where Parker spent his days. He never went far and most of the time he could be found at the Folsom library. Some days he'd take her there, and they'd find a quiet corner and he'd read to her. Other days he'd pick a children's book and guide her as she struggled through. She loved those days.

She decided not to mention Lucian Patras to Parker. He wouldn't understand, and she didn't feel like being judged. It wasn't that Parker was overly judgmental. He was just protective of her and worried like a mother hen at times. He also thought she had an unhealthy obsession with money, but from her impoverished perspective, money ruled the world.

After stuffing her belongings in her locker and taking inventory of her cart, she waited for Tamara outside of her office. Pulling an emery board out of her pushcart, Scout tidied up her fingernails as she waited.

Her mind of course wandered to Lucian Patras. If his offer still stood, she was pretty certain she was going to take it, with some conditions of her own. He was right, everything did have a price, and her morals seemed for sale at the moment. While the idea of visiting a salon and actually having her hair cut professionally for the first time in her life was appealing, it was also worthless. Clothing, however, could be sold and jewelry could be pawned.

It was wisest to think in matters of moving on. Mr. Patras was, in some odd way, attracted to her, but once he figured out how inexperienced she was with men he'd likely send her packing. She needed to go into this with a plan. Even if it only lasted a day, there was no way she was leaving empty-handed.

For a moment Scout allowed herself to fantasize about the bathtubs in the hotel. He'd said he'd arrange for her to have a room. One time she sat'd on the edge of a hotel bed after suffering a dizzy spell from not eating enough, and she was amazed at how soft and plush the mattress was.

If Mr. Patras actually did as he'd said and put her up in a room for a night, chances were she'd never want to leave. Scout wanted to know what it felt like to bathe in one of those grand tubs with the jets and use those fancy bath salts housekeeping left on the vanities for guests.

"You're here early."

She jumped as Tamara headed in her direction. Stowing her file in the pocket of her apron, she stood. "I couldn't sleep so I came in early."

Her eyes crinkled warmly. "Give me a minute to put down my stuff and start the coffee and I'll give you your schedule."

Scout waited by her office door as Tamara stowed her bag under her desk and hung her coat on a hook behind the door. It was a nice coat. Warm-looking and thick wool in a lovely royal blue. Tamara always had nice clothing. She wore something different every time Scout saw her.

"Okay," she said as she rolled her chair closer to her desk and pulled out a stack of papers. "It looks like today you have fifteen penthouses."

She handed Scout the slip of paper.

Scout frowned. "What about the master suites?"

"Mr. Patras didn't put in for housekeeping today. He usually only requests the maid services once a week. It was odd he asked for his suites to be cleaned two days in a row, but if there's one thing I know about him it's that he's eccentric. No use trying to figure him out. Hey, are you feeling better?"

Scout's head tilted in confusion. "Excuse me?"

"You left early yesterday. I assumed you weren't feeling well."

Her face flushed with embarrassment. *Damn meddling hotel owner.*

"Oh, yeah. I'm fine. I had an unsettling lunch." Not a lie.

"Oh, good, I'm glad it wasn't anything serious. With flu season coming up you can never be too sure. That reminds me. Here's my cell number. If you're ever sick, call there or text so I know before I get here. That way I won't be scrambling to find someone to cover your rooms."

Tamara slid her a glossy white business card, and Scout slipped it into her pocket. She didn't know how to text and didn't have a cell phone to text on, but there was a pay phone at St. Christopher's if she ever needed to reach her boss.

Leaving the GM's office, she passed the other maids coming in. Ignoring her disappointment that Mr. Patras had had a change of heart, she focused on her work. She'd just have to stick to her original plan. Work hard, make money, eventually have the means to afford her own apartment and get Pearl off the streets.

The pinch of regret hurt more than she'd expected. She should've agreed yesterday, while the offer was still on the table. All her anxiety about being intimate with him and her stupid, stubborn pride had wound up screwing her out of opportunities she'd likely never come across again in her lifetime.

Her original plan seemed to have lost a bit of its luster since she'd been offered a much faster solution. But that was no longer an option. She should be feeling like she'd made a lucky escape. She should have known better. Nothing was ever easy. She was a fool to assume a man like that could actually want her.

Scout pulled her cart off the elevator and onto the thirtieth floor, ignoring the unsettling feeling filling her belly as she passed the private bank of elevators to the master suites above. Focusing on her tasks for the day, she threw herself into dusting the banisters of the common areas and polishing the furniture at each sitting area until her reflection showed in the cherry finish.

By eight, guests had begun heading out for the day or simply traveling down to the restaurant for breakfast, and she started on cleaning the suites.

Just before noon someone called her name. "Scout? Are you in there?"

She turned and found a flushed Tamara looking for her. She was out of breath.

"Tamara? Is everything okay?"

"Yes," she panted and wedged her fist into the side of her nipped blazer. "Sorry. Cramp. Mr. Patras called. He expected you to tend to his suites first thing this morning. He must've forgotten to call it in. I need you to go up there right away."

Scout stood unmoving for a moment, spray bottle of disinfectant hanging in her left hand and a rag in her right. Tamara shoved a keycard in her direction. She quickly peeled off her gloves and took the card.

"What about this room? I'm not finished."

"I'll find someone else to finish it. Just go. Mr. Patras doesn't like to be kept waiting and he didn't sound happy when he called."

Well, that wasn't her fault. She quickly returned to her cart and replaced her items.

"Here, take what you need and I'll take this down for you," Tamara said quickly.

Scout had never seen her GM so flustered. Her stout form got behind the cart and quickly pushed it in the direction of the service elevators. Scout hastily grabbed a few necessities and cradled them in her apron. She pulled the door to the half-cleaned room closed and went to the private elevators.

Her heart skipped nervously in her chest as she rode to the top. It was impossible to determine if she was nervous or excited. The elevator quietly chimed, announcing her arrival. Her knuckles knocked softly on the private entrance.

"Housekeeping."

"Come in."

At Mr. Patras's sharp command, she slid her key through the lock and entered. He sat at his messy desk with a phone to his ear. His eyes drilled into hers and her steps faltered. He jabbed his finger through the air and pointed to the sitting area and mouthed *sit*. She didn't appreciate the way he scowled at her.

His outburst jolted her into motion and she quickly sat.

"Sell ten percent of my shares and then do your goddamn job and use your brain next time! What the hell am I paying you for if you can't even keep an eye on the market? I don't want to hear from you again today unless you're calling to tell me good news about my net worth."

He slammed the phone into its cradle and stood. "You're late."

She flinched as he shouted.

Scout's mouth opened and her head shook at his accusation. Refusing to be bullied, she snapped, "You didn't send in a request for housekeeping."

He stood and paced with the grace of a black panther. "I thought I made myself quite clear yesterday that you were to come here first thing."

The arrogance of him! "How am I supposed to do that without a key?"

He scowled. "What happened to your key from yesterday?"

"We have to deactivate them at the end of each day and put them back in the bin."

He sighed and walked to his desk, pulled open a drawer, moved some things around, and then returned to her, holding out a new keycard.

"Here, don't deactivate this one. It's mine. Next time I tell you to be somewhere I expect you there on time."

She bristled. "Mr. Patras—"

"Lucian."

"Fine, Lucian, I'm sorry you see this as my fault, but I couldn't walk up to my GM and just say, 'Oh, by the way, the owner of the hotel propositioned me yesterday and I'm to report directly to him with my answer. Please get me a key.' I would've lost my job."

"I'm your job."

"Well, I don't report to you," she snapped.

He smiled slowly and there was a dark glimmer in his black

eyes. "Everyone in this hotel reports to me, Ms. Keats. Now, you said you had an answer for me."

Scout shifted uncomfortably. Her brain tried to keep up. She'd thought he rescinded, but now the offer was back on the table again. Objections from yesterday tangled with residual disappointment from the morning. Everything was happening so fast. A bottle of Patras conditioner fell out of her apron and she bent to pick it up. He beat her to it.

"Are you stealing from me, Ms. Keats?" he asked jokingly, tipping back her apron with one long finger to see her plundered items.

She scowled at him. "I told you I don't steal. I didn't have time to get my supply basket. My GM was quite adamant I stop everything and go to you right away."

"Wise woman," he said, removing the rest of the items from her lap. He invaded her personal space more and more every minute. Once each little bottle sat side by side on the table across from them, he sat back and looked at her.

"Now, your answer . . ."

Her certainty wavered. Yesterday she was reluctant, but this morning she'd been so certain her answer would've been yes when she thought the offer was no longer a possibility. Buying some time, she took a deep breath. "I need to know how you see this working out."

He grinned, apparently already tasting victory.

"If you agree to my terms, I'll arrange for you to stay here at the hotel until our arrangement is over. You'll have a house credit, which I'll pick up the tab on. That'll allow you to use Patras's restaurant, bar, spa, salon, gym, pool, room service, and the boutiques downstairs. My driver will also be available to you if you wish to go into town for shopping or lunch. I expect you to be available to me for social functions and whenever I desire your company."

"Right, company," she said dryly, never forgetting his broad understanding of the word.

The corner of his mouth kicked up. "That's right, Evelyn, company. I am a very private man and I find crowds . . . tedious. Do you play chess?"

"Chess? No."

"I'll teach you. I'll also expect you to be pleasant and agreeable." His assumed power over others' moods baffled her. "I don't tolerate lateness, so I expect you to be on time. If it takes you three hours to do your hair, arrange for it. When I ask you to be somewhere I expect you there on time."

He was barking out his demands so quickly she had trouble keeping up. "What about my job?"

"Your job's secure. I don't see you needing it when I'll be providing everything you'll need, but it's there if you choose to return to it."

Scout could never put that much trust in another person. She feared becoming indebted to a man like Mr. Patras more than anything. This was not a man you fucked with. "I want to keep working."

"No." He didn't go into detail or offer any reason why she shouldn't work, he simply forbade it.

"Then I'm sorry, but this isn't going to work. I need this job." She prayed he wouldn't call her bluff. While his offer would provide more necessities at a faster rate, there was no stability to their agreement.

"There's no reason for you to work while our arrangement stands. If you're worried about not having a job when we end the agreement, don't; I have no intention of forcing you out of your position."

"It's not that. I need to work. I have responsibilities. I understand if you don't want to attend social functions with a recognizable employee from your hotel, and if it embarrasses you I can find work somewhere else—"

"I'm not embarrassed by your job, Evelyn. You come to work every day on time and put in an honest day's effort. I simply don't see the need for you to work when I'll provide everything you need. If it's a matter of paying your rent, I'll supplement it while you're staying at the hotel. I want you close for my convenience."

Her stomach cartwheeled nervously at his unspoken insinuation. "I'm sorry, I can't live with that. If it's the amount of time my job takes up, I'd be willing to ask my GM to cut back my hours temporarily, but I can't give it up altogether. What if I somehow managed to only work twenty hours a week instead of forty?"

"Ten."

"Fifteen."

"Nine," he countered.

"Nine? You went the wrong way!"

His eyes narrowed challengingly. "Eight."

She huffed. "Who works eight hours a week?"

"Seven." He crossed his arms over his chest.

Scout threw her hands in the air, completely exasperated. "Fine, ten hours, but I need to see if that's even possible."

"Consider it handled. Now, do you have any other conditions?"

She thought about Pearl. "I need two afternoons a week to myself."

"Fine. Why?"

"None of your business."

"I thought I explained that everything in my hotel is my business."

Scout folded her arms over her chest, mimicking his stubborn posture. "Well, that time won't be spent in your precious hotel so it doesn't count."

"Careful, Evelyn."

"Two afternoons or the deal's off."

His eyes narrowed, but she held his gaze. If this was going to happen, she couldn't continue to let him intimidate her.

"I don't believe you," he whispered, eyeing her critically.

"Try me," she said slowly, assuming her best poker face.

"Fine. Take your two afternoons for now, so long as they don't impose on my scheduled time with you. Now, let's talk about sex."

Her breath siphoned down the wrong pipe, and she choked. He patted her back as she sucked in tight gulps of air and coughed. Hand pressed to her chest, she leaned forward.

Lucian stood for a moment and returned, offering her a glass of water. She gulped half of it down and placed it back on the table, wiped her eyes, then turned on him.

"*What?*"

"Come on, Evelyn, you're a big girl. You knew what this was about the moment I suggested it. Eventually you *will* be in my bed, so let's just cut to the chase and put everything on the table. You seem like a straight shooter so I'm just going to lay it out there. I like control. Lots of it. I'm a healthy, virile male. I enjoy sex and like my female to be available to me whenever the mood suits me. She must know how to prepare herself for me and I expect her to see to my needs and grant me control. Now, I know that sounds like a lot, but I promise I've never had any complaints from my partners. Does this sound like something you could agree to?"

She gaped at him. How did one even reply to such a statement? She knew sex would be part of the deal, but he was so blasé about it. She'd thought they would agree to do the deed once every few nights. What he suggested left no room to hide. "You expect me to have sex with you whenever you want?"

"Exactly."

Scout reached for the glass of water and chugged the rest, then placed the empty container on the table and stared straight ahead, unable to face him at the moment. He stood, retrieved a silver pitcher, and refilled the glass.

It wasn't necessarily the control thing that bothered her. He'd have to be in control. She was clueless and inexperienced. Dear God, the thought of him touching her . . . A warm, buttery sensation tightened her stomach.

Her face was burning up. Taking the freshly filled glass, she held it to her forehead, resting her elbows on her knees.

"Is the idea of sleeping with me that upsetting to you, Evelyn? I like to think I'm a fairly good-looking man for my age."

"It's not your looks," she mumbled, still unable to face him.

"Then what's causing your hesitation here? Tell me and I'll fix it. I have no intention of sleeping with anyone else while our arrangement stands and the same will go for you."

She snorted. She couldn't help it. "Oh, that won't be a problem."

He didn't seem to see the humor. "Good. I also plan on having my medical records shared with you after you visit my physician and have your own physical done."

"Physical?"

Scout hadn't seen a doctor since she was eleven and visited the hospital with pneumonia. It was a horribly frightening experience being that Pearl had left her there and taken herself on a five-day bender. They had to escape once she sobered up enough to realize her abandonment of a hospitalized daughter had attracted the notice of Children & Youth. She had no desire to voluntarily step into another medical facility ever again.

"If you can't commit to having a screening, Ms. Keats, I'm afraid the entire arrangement is off."

Back to Ms. Keats again. She sighed inwardly. What if they discovered something terrible? Her mom was sick and she never allowed herself to forget that, but what if she'd somehow contracted hepatitis or some other illness? Knowing what diseases did to people, she wasn't sure if she could handle that kind of stress, but on the other hand she was rarely sick. Her body had a high threshold for pain and a fairly tough immune system based on her track record. If she were sick, there would probably be symptoms. Maybe it was best to know.

"Okay, I'll see your physician."

"Good. I'll make the appointment for this afternoon. Are you on the pill?"

Everything was moving so fast. "The pill?"

"Birth control."

"Um, no." She couldn't look at him, but sensed her answer disappointed him. He'd likely be disappointed about a lot of things once he discovered how ignorant she was about this sort of stuff.

Again, he jumped topics without warning. "Now that we have the majority of our agreement taken care of, how about if I order up lunch and make some calls? The concierge can get your room situated and I can inform Ms. Jones about your schedule change. After that I'll have Dugan bring the car around and we can do some shopping for any personal items you might need."

Before she could answer, he was already moving to his desk and ordering lunch. She thought about Parker. He'd be worried sick if she didn't return to St. Christopher's this evening. Why hadn't she told him this was a possibility the night before? Oh, right, because he'd never understand.

Lucian put a call in to his physician and had lunch ordered

and on its way within minutes. She excused herself to use the bathroom and when she returned, he was on the phone with someone else and room service was delivering lunch. This time they carried in a sharply dressed table and two chairs.

"Right there's fine, gentlemen," Lucian said, and the men quickly placed the trays on the table and backed out of the room.

One man made eye contact with her before the door cut off his view. It was incredible, the amount of shame and judgment that swamped her in the span of that brief glance. Did they know?

"Wonderful, Ms. Jones, I'll let her know."

Scout turned at the mention of her general manager's name.

Lucian hung up the phone. "Your new schedule's been arranged and you'll be occupying suite 3000, just below. A key's being sent up."

She simply stared at him. She always knew money made anything possible, but actually witnessing its influence was something else entirely. And now Tamara will know what she'd done.

Lucian stood and went to the table. He acted so nonchalant about all of this. Was this something he did all the time? How many women came before her? How many would come after? She figured ignorance was best in situations like this. Too much self-examination and she'd worry herself into a moral meltdown.

six
·····

CHECK UP

AFTER lunch there was another visitor, Dr. Vivian Sheffield. Once Scout was over her initial shock that Lucian could arrange for house calls at the drop of a hat, she realized Dr. Sheffield was intimidatingly striking. The doctor also seemed to have a standing rapport with Lucian on more than a professional level.

They moved to the sitting area and she waited silently, not quite sure what would happen here.

"Did you bring it?" Lucian asked.

"I did." Dr. Sheffield gracefully sat on the edge of the club chair, one long leg crossing delicately over the other. She lifted her briefcase and removed a folder.

"Here are all your most recent test results." She passed the file to Lucian who in turn passed it to Scout. "You're in perfect health, Lucian, but you already knew that."

She smiled charmingly at him, her deep red lips curling softly over her pearly teeth.

Lucian looked at Scout. "Go ahead and see for yourself."

Opening the blue folder, Scout found a typed list of sorts and pretended to read it. Turning page after page at what she hoped was an appropriate reading pace. Somewhere around the fifth page, Dr. Sheffield gazed over at her, her long neck extended gracefully, and her sophisticated diamond stud earrings winked in the light.

"Oh, you don't need to read that, Ms. Keats. That's just the HIPAA contract."

Scout blushed and shut the folder, handing it back to Lucian. He grinned and tucked the folder away on the seat next to him. "Ready?" he asked, looking at her.

Scout felt incredibly stupid. "For?"

"Dr. Sheffield came to take your blood work and give you an exam," he said as if it were obvious.

"Here?" No hospital?

The doctor smiled empathetically. "I assure you it'll be quick. And don't worry. I'm excellent at drawing blood if needles bother you. It'll be quick and painless."

Growing up the way she had, needles were the least of her worries. She had gotten over any squeamishness years ago.

Scout turned to Lucian. "Where will you go?"

He frowned. "I'm not going anywhere."

The doctor hesitated a moment then gently said, "Lucian, perhaps Ms. Keats would be more comfortable if she had a little privacy."

"That's ridiculous. I'll be reading all her results anyway—"

"But I'm sure you can understand this must be a bit awkward for her. I'll take her to your spare room and we'll return in a few moments."

The way Dr. Sheffield handled him amazed Scout. The next thing she knew they were sitting alone in the spare bedroom of the suite and Lucian was waiting, alone, in the common area of the suite, sulking.

They sat on the edge of the bed and Dr. Sheffield softly said, "Do you mind if I call you Evelyn?"

Scout shook her head and the doctor's kind eyes softened.

"Okay, Evelyn, let's start with a few questions. Be as honest as you can and I want you to know that if at any time you change your mind about sharing this information with Lucian I'll respect that. You're my patient and as such, how much information I share is completely up to you. However, I won't lie. Do you understand?"

"Yes."

"Good." The doctor opened up a new folder and picked up a pen, quickly jotting down some words.

"How long since your last physical?" She waited with her pen poised just above the paper, eyes on the folder.

"I've never had a physical."

Dr. Sheffield moved to write then stilled. "Excuse me?"

"I've never had a physical. When I was eleven I was admitted to the hospital with pneumonia, but that was it."

"Surely, you had physicals when you were younger in order to get your vaccines."

"If I did I don't remember."

Dr. Sheffield blew a deep breath past her red lips. "Okay, let's start with some general background information."

Dr. Sheffield asked her about her family's medical history. Scout didn't want to tell her about Pearl and other than that she didn't have many answers. For almost everything the doctor asked, Scout said she didn't know, and she could see her frustration mounting, but the doctor never became short with her.

After she'd asked Scout a long line of questions, she listened to her heart, looked in her nose, mouth, and ears, examined portions of her skin and pressed her fingers along her spine. It was odd being touched in so many places by a stranger.

Dr. Sheffield wrapped a cuff around Scout's arm and pumped it full of air until it hurt. After making some notes she asked, "How much do you weigh, Evelyn?"

"I don't know."

Her brow puckered. "Okay, let's have a look at your legs and stomach. Do you mind lying down for a moment?"

Scout scooted onto the soft bed and eased onto her back. It was the most comfortable place she'd ever rested her head. Shutting her eyes and going to sleep was tempting.

The doctor gently lifted her legs and bent her knees, checking her range of motion. "I'm just going to feel around your organs for a moment. My hands may be a little cold."

Scout's back pressed into the mattress as if she could somehow save herself from being touched in such intimate places. Dr. Sheffield's contact was clinical and quick. She pressed into her stomach at various places, asked if anything hurt.

"When was your last menstrual cycle?"

"It ended three days ago."

"Have you ever been pregnant?"

"No."

"Are you on any form of birth control?"

"No."

"Are you currently sexually active?"

"No."

Her pen quickly moved across her notes as she recorded each of Scout's answers.

"I know they don't have a scale here, but I'm a bit concerned about your weight, Evelyn. You're quite thin. Do you diet?"

"Not by choice."

Dr. Sheffield stilled. Her gaze slowly met Scout's and understanding dawned. "When's the last time you've eaten, sweetheart?"

"We just had lunch."

"And before that?"

She swallowed. "The day before, when Mr. Patras offered me lunch."

"Do you usually only eat once a day?"

Tears of humiliation blurred her vision. Refusing to be ashamed of who she was, Scout looked the beautiful doctor in the eye and admitted, "When I'm lucky."

She closed her folder. "I see. Does Lucian know this?"

"I don't believe so. Are you going to tell him?"

She sighed. "No, I don't believe I am. Lucian's been my friend for many years. I think you'll find he can be difficult and demanding most of the time, but he's a good person. I promise to keep this between us if you promise to see me in another two weeks and have a little more meat on your bones by then. Fine dining's a vice of Lucian's so it shouldn't be a difficult task."

"Okay."

"Now, I was going to ask about your last gynecological exam, but I'm assuming you never had one of those either."

Scout shook her head.

"Would you mind if I examined you quickly? I can't perform a pap, but I can at least see if everything looks healthy."

"Do I need to undress?"

"Only partially."

"Okay," Scout said and Dr. Sheffield stood to lock the door. Scout unbuttoned her dress and the doctor directed her to lift her arms. Dr. Sheffield examined her breasts and Scout's cheeks flushed with heat. She explained how she should perform her own breast exams monthly and then instructed her to button back up.

Once her gown was back in place, true mortification set in. Lying back, she lifted her skirt and Dr. Sheffield looked at parts of her no one had ever seen. She wanted to crawl into a hole and die.

The doctor touched her there and Scout thought she'd pass out from embarrassment. It lasted too long, but at the same time didn't take more than a few minutes.

Dr. Sheffield removed her gloves and tossed them into the wastebasket as Scout adjusted her clothes back in place. Looking at her, worry marred the doctor's otherwise perfect face. Her lips pressed together as she seemed to consider her next words.

"Evelyn, are you being coerced into this?"

"Excuse me?"

"Are you here of your own free will?" she asked, as if the words pained her to say.

Scout recalled her mentioning that she and Lucian had been friends for a long time and understood her discomfort at asking such a thing.

"I'm here because I agreed to be. Mr. Patras didn't blackmail me or anything like that if that's what you're worried about. Why, is something wrong?"

"I hope you don't mind my saying this, but you do understand that he expects to be intimately involved with you, to my understanding."

Scout nodded. "That's why he wants me to have a physical. Am I sick?"

"No, sweetheart, you're not sick. You're a virgin."

Well, duh. "I know that."

Dr. Sheffield's little red mouth hung open for a moment, and Scout imagined this was likely the weirdest checkup she had ever performed.

"Does Lucian?"

"Well, no, but I don't see why that's any of his business." And it wasn't.

Dr. Sheffield rested her head in her hand and massaged her forehead. "Oh, Lucian," she mumbled to herself. Taking a deep breath she sat up, professional mask back in place and said, "Okay, all we have left is the blood work. How are you with needles?"

"Fine."

After her blood was drawn and capped off in neat, tiny vials, and the doctor had given her some reading material on birth control, which Scout would never read, they returned to the common area of the suite. Lucian was pacing by his desk and pivoted the moment they stepped out of the room.

"What the hell took so long?" he demanded.

"I do a thorough job. Don't fret, Lucian, I'll bill you for every minute of it."

The doctor's charming demeanor was back intact and her finesse with Lucian soon had him calming down. Scout admired the way she could maneuver him with such unfaltering poise. The doctor collected her belongings.

"So far, everything looks good. I'll have the blood work back by the morning. You can call my office for the results. I'll be sure to leave instructions with my front desk."

"Thank you, Viv. I appreciate your promptness."

Dr. Sheffield paused for a moment. She turned to Lucian and cryptically said, "You know, Lucian, a little patience never hurt anybody. Sometimes things are worth not rushing into."

As soon as the doctor left, exhaustion set in. Scout's shift would've ended hours ago. She had been running nonstop for days and wanted to lie down.

Turning, Lucian said, "Let's go shopping."

Scout tried not to wince. Did this man ever stop?

seven

· · · · ·

JUST A KISS

SCOUT'S shoulders drooped as she wearily accepted her status for the next several days. Everything would be according to the wants and needs of Lucian Patras.

"Evelyn? Is something wrong?"

She sighed. "No. I just . . . I'm still in my uniform. My bag's still in my locker downstairs. I can't go shopping until I change."

He stepped closer and a wicked gleam set into his dark eyes. "I find myself quite fond of your little maid's uniform."

His finger reached out slowly and he gently caressed her cheek. Her breath filled her chest and held as his hand moved to her hair and removed a pin from her bun. It landed silently on the plush carpet. He removed another and then another, until her dark auburn hair was tumbling down her back.

Lucian sucked in a breath. "Evelyn, your hair . . . I had no idea it was so long." His hands lifted the wavy curtain and spread it over her shoulders. "It's beautiful."

His feet shifted and he stepped closer. He'd never been this close to her before. Her heart raced. She could see the shadow of hair beneath the tanned skin of his jaw, the fine fleshy line that outlined his full lips, the dark onyx flecks in his chestnut eyes. They were more deep ebony than black or brown.

His eyes appeared softer in that moment. Stunning. He had lashes so thick they were almost feminine. The dark crests gave his visage a pirate's sharpness as if his piercing eyes were lined with soot, making his penetrating gaze all the more menacing. His tanned skin was smooth. He really was quite striking.

His scent cocooned her, made her slightly light-headed. Scout's lips parted as his thumb gently traced the plump curve of her lower lip.

"I'm going to kiss you, Evelyn."

Her pulse jumped as his head lowered. His palm sifted through her hair until he cupped the back of her skull. Chills skittered down her collar and underneath her clothing. A warm pinching sensation tickled her belly. It was like falling; frightening, but slightly more pleasant.

He pulled her into him. His breath coasted over her lips, warm. Barely making contact, his lips brushed over hers and her belly pulled tight. Scout's thighs suddenly felt oddly disconnected from her numb knees, and then his mouth was on hers.

Her eyes opened wide as his closed. She squeaked, as the kiss grew firm. His other hand trailed below her arm and around her back. He pulled her closer until her front was pressed into his, her breasts crushed against the hard muscle of his chest. Then his mouth opened.

Lucian's head tilted and the kiss became moist. She tensed as his tongue traced the seam of her slightly parted lips. He nuzzled her cheek and sealed his mouth over hers, his slowly opening and closing coaxingly.

His touch was gentle. Her arms hung lifelessly at her sides as his palm slid possessively low on her back. His teeth closed over her lower lip and her neck extended. Scout gasped and he took full advantage, plunging his warm tongue deep into her mouth.

Stepping forward, as if he intended to walk through her, his grip tightened. He tipped her head back and kissed the corner of her lips. The hand at her back massaged gently. His head tilted and his tongue was back at it again, licking deep into her mouth.

Suddenly, he tickled the roof of her mouth and her own tongue instinctively lifted, dueling with his. He groaned and chuckled.

"That's it, Evelyn, kiss me back," his mouth whispered against hers.

The touch of their tongues was warm and soft. They caressed one another, his battling for control. The kiss was more enjoyable if she let him lead. She also figured out that when her eyes were closed it was easier to concentrate. She lowered her lashes and let him take command of the kiss.

Her body heated. Fire churned in her belly and her breath grew shallow and rushed. She had no illusions about her purpose here, but her body's reaction to him confused and surprised her all the same. Lucian Patras would use her for his own sexual satisfaction. She was perfectly aware of what that would entail. She'd been exposed to the act of sex at a very young age, seeing many adults perform such acts with no regard to privacy or onlooking eyes.

What she was unprepared for were the sensations flooding her blood. Scout never expected her skin to feel so hot, so hungry, her limbs to grow weightless and too heavy at the same time. She was incredibly aware of her hips and the space in between.

Lucian pulled back from her mouth and she found herself extending, chasing his touch. He chuckled arrogantly and she hated her need. His mouth worked over her jaw and down the slender column of her throat. He sucked on the flesh over her racing pulse. His tongue skittered to her ear and his breath tickled the hollow, sending chills up and down her spine.

"I cannot wait to get inside of you," he whispered over her warming flesh.

His palm slid down to her butt and she froze. It wasn't the fact that he was touching her rear that had her tensing. It was the possessive way in which he held her. His hand had moved directly to the crease of her ass and his fingers clamped down on her private parts where no man had ever touched her intimately before.

It was too much. He was overwhelming her and she was thinking outside of her head, constantly forgetting what she had been considering from one second to the next, as her body struggled to feel. Scout lifted her palms to his chest and pushed, but he only pulled her closer.

His tongue plundered her mouth again as he took from her with such entitlement. Her hands curled into fists. No matter how much she was aware of what she was permitting herself to become, actually giving herself over to what it meant hurt her pride.

The unsettling thought lanced through the warmth churning in her body and chilled her warming blood. Scout turned her face away and broke the kiss.

Lucian waited, his breath beating over the low curve of her shoulder peeking past the collar of her uniform. She hated herself in that moment. Hated what she was surrendering herself to.

A few days, she told herself, a couple of weeks at best. She'd do this thing, and then the position could be passed along to the next pathetic charity case that stumbled into Lucian Patras's life.

He was a beautiful man. It wouldn't be difficult to give herself to him if she could just get off this moral cross. She was simply trading one title for another, and then she'd set aside all labels and live a normal life.

This had to be better than homeless vagrant. At least one led to some sign of improvement in the end. All of this was the cost of her financial independence.

Scout turned in his hold and his grip on her loosened.

"I need a moment. I . . . I'm sorry." *Get a grip, Scout!* She turned away from him.

Stepping away, needing some space, she caught her breath. He was silent, but she could feel him watching her. Her mind painted him as a giant, crouching behind her in a shrinking room. When his hands pressed into her shoulders, she flinched.

"You need to get used to my touch, Evelyn. I can't have you flinching every time I touch you when we're out in public."

Scout's arms wrapped around her waist protectively only to have his follow, the heat of his front scalding her spine. He held her wrists and slowly pulled her banded arms back. Entitlement. He was entitled to touch her. She was expected to surrender. His palm flattened on her torso and pressed until her back was flush against his front. Hands moved over her, caressing, feeling, mapping her every curve.

As his fingers tripped over the money belt fastened tightly under her gown and around her ribs he momentarily paused. She could sense him frowning curiously, but he moved on. His thumb grazed the underside of her breast and he continued on his exploration of her. Her breath hitched as he drew sensation after sensation from her untried body. His hands slid up her front until he was cupping her, holding her to him in a way no man had ever held her.

His thumbs traced over the protruding tips.

"Why, Evelyn . . ." he whispered, amusement laced in his voice. "You're not wearing a bra. Is this something I can expect on a regular basis?"

Her belly quivered and there seemed to be some fine thread connecting where he touched her and her lower body. He was like a puppeteer pulling her strings and commanding her body to do as he wished. He pinched her there, but it didn't hurt.

"Please . . ." Scout was confused and overwhelmed.

He squeezed. "Please, what?"

Her small hands covered his, still shaping her breast. "Please stop."

He froze. A chill filled the air and a moment later he released her and stepped away.

She couldn't face him. "I—I'm sorry," she stammered. "Next time will be better. You just took me off guard."

"It's fine." His words were terse and forced. They bit through her faltering courage and she shivered. "When you're ready, we'll go."

Go? Did he still expect to go shopping? She sighed. "I need to get my bag."

"I'll have it brought up."

"It's in my locker."

Scout had no doubt he could somehow manage to retrieve her things regardless of some measly locked metal box that held them, but she didn't want someone else handling her stuff. Everything she owned was in that locker.

She explained, "I'd rather get it myself."

"Fine." His fast concession surprised her.

Scout frowned. Maybe he wanted her to leave. She was about to ask if that was the case when he said, "I'll have Dugan bring the car around. Meet me out front in ten minutes. Do not be late."

Ten minutes wasn't a whole lot of time to make it all the way to the basement, get to her locker, change, and make it back to the front of the hotel. She needed more time, but before she could ask for it, Lucian turned and held his phone to his ear, already summoning Dugan.

eight
·····

REFLECTION

WITHOUT attracting much attention, Scout kept her head low and speed walked through the lobby of Patras. A man dressed in pristine Patras livery held the heavy glass door as she stepped out of the softly lit hotel and squinted at the sunny street. Cabs lined the curb as finely dressed guests alighted to the gold-fringed red runner at the bottom of the grand marble stairs. Brass luggage carts were stacked with designer cases and garment bags, and she had never felt more like a sore thumb in her life.

Scout shifted her raggedy backpack over her shoulders and looked for Lucian. He wasn't out there. Stepping as far into the shadows and out of the way as possible, she searched.

A man with a neat brimmed hat and Patras blazer spoke in rapid French to a guest. Footmen traded keys with valets, and the line of vehicles moved on. A shiny black limousine took up a large portion of the shoulder as a chauffeur aptly stood and awaited his passengers.

The sun was drifting behind the high skyscrapers. A blustery wind slithered over the pathways, mingling in and out of people passing by, and she shivered, fisting her hands deep within the front pocket of her hooded sweatshirt. The denim of her jeans had long ago worn thin and didn't do much to shield against the gusty November chill.

The chauffeur twisted as the sleek black window of the limousine lowered half an inch. He listened then turned. His gaze landed on her and his bushy eyebrows jumped. His mouth remained tight beneath the handlebars of his mustache. Straightening his shoulders, he walked in her direction.

Her back stiffened. Lucian would be furious if she wasn't waiting for him when he got here. If this man was approaching to chase her away, he had an argument coming. She had every right to be here. She'd be interested to see what he had to say when he learned she was waiting for the owner of Patras, Lucian Patras himself.

Squaring her shoulders, Scout opened her mouth, prepared to tell him she wasn't moving, when he surprised her by saying, "Ms. Keats?"

She fumbled. "Y-yes?"

"Mr. Patras is right this way. If you'll follow me?"

Her lip trembled as she got hold of her bearings and followed the chauffeur. He was quite an enormous man up close. Returning to his position beside the shiny black door of the limo, he opened it with a gentle click as she stepped nearer. The interior was low and dark. Scout bent to peek inside.

Lucian sat, a look of exasperation on his face, amber drink in his hand. He glanced at his watch dramatically and back at her and sighed. She quickly scurried into the car.

The soft leather seats cushioned her inelegant landing and she scooted in as the door closed with a quiet snick behind her. Blue lights accented small wooden compartments and a crystal decanter held securely on a small counter.

"Drink?"

The car pulled away from the curb and she lurched back in her seat, not used to being in cars. She looked at Lucian. "No, thank you. I don't drink."

He raised an eyebrow, but said nothing more on the subject. They drove a few blocks in silence. Lucian's gaze raked over her, scrutinizing her attire. She tried not to fidget, but failed.

The clink of ice in his now empty glass drew her attention. "I can see we'll have our work cut out for us."

Scout's spine stiffened. She didn't appreciate his comment. If he didn't want such an undertaking he should've asked someone else for their "company." She sighed. This wasn't how she imagined this going. He'd done nothing he hadn't said he planned to do. It was her own wavering thoughts that were making her irritable and jumpy. She needed to jump into this thing with both feet or back out now.

"Lucian, I'm sorry about earlier. I've been up since three a.m. and I'm not at my best."

He frowned. "If you were tired you should've told me. This could've waited."

She had been tired, exhausted really, but since stepping into the limo her adrenaline kicked in. "I'm okay now. I must've gotten a second wind."

He studied her face a moment then said, "I expect you to be at your best, Evelyn. If you require eight hours' sleep, take it. If you need ten, then make sure you get them."

His words were bossy and rude, but there was also a bit of concern beneath his censure. Underneath all of the gruff and growl, she suspected there was a soft little puppy. No, not a puppy, more like a bear cub or baby lion. She hid her smile.

They arrived in a section of the city she had never visited before. "Is this still Folsom?"

"Yes, the Upper West Side."

Scout looked out the tinted window as the lavish stores and boutiques rolled by. Shoppers patronized the ritzy strip in high heels and designer suits. Glancing down at her tattered clothing and worn-through sneakers, she frowned.

The limousine pulled to a stop outside of a pristine store she couldn't read the name of. She swallowed as a lump formed in her stomach. Lucian placed his glass aside and flattened the front of his suit jacket. He'd forgone the casual air she'd grown used to seeing him in while in the comfort of his penthouse. Scout liked that Lucian better.

Dugan came around and opened the passenger door. She couldn't move. Well-dressed patrons bustled past her vantage with dogs dressed finer than her. Her breath was coming too fast and she was going to be sick.

"Evelyn? We're here."

She looked at Lucian and he frowned. He leaned over her lap and said to Dugan, "Give us a minute." He then pulled the door closed, submerging the heated car in silence.

"What's the matter, Evelyn?"

"When you said shopping for personal items I thought you meant we'd hit a drugstore or something."

He pressed his lips together and, again, took visual inventory of her clothing. His fingers pinched a loose flap of her bag distastefully, rubbing together as if he touched something unsavory.

"You can't expect what you're wearing to be appropriate for the places we'll visit. You need clothes."

"But you said the dinner wasn't until tomorrow."

"That's right, we have a function tomorrow, but we still need to eat tonight. I have no problem with lunch or breakfast in the penthouse, but dining out is something I enjoy. What difference is there if we purchase some items tonight or tomorrow? Either way, you need an entirely new wardrobe."

He was right, of course. Dressed the way she was, Scout was an embarrassment to a man like him. She looked out the window. But did they have to shop here? She'd be uncomfortable at a department store. This was beyond swank.

"Come on," he said, nudging her leg and smiling. "Let me treat you. Clothing is armor. I prefer you feisty and I'm prepared to spend a great deal of money on you in order to have you that way. Let's go buy some courage."

"People will stare at me."

"You're beautiful, Evelyn. People will stare at you no matter what you wear."

His words were sweet and warmed her heart, chasing away some of her trepidation, but not all of it. She sighed, resigned, and he tapped on the ceiling. The door opened and Dugan took her arm as she climbed onto the sidewalk.

Scout shivered and Lucian stepped out beside her. "Where's your coat?" he asked, again frowning.

"I don't have one."

Her words seemed to render him momentarily speechless. He didn't comment, merely nodded and headed toward their first courage outlet.

A woman with hair the color of silken wheat greeted them. Her nails were long and painted white at the tips. She carefully ignored Scout's presence and purred up at Lucian. Scout's brow pinched and she decided not to like her right off the bat.

"Mr. Patras!" she cooed. "What a pleasure to have your company today. Is there something particular I can show you?"

Scout curled her lip at the woman's ridiculous advance. Lucian typed something into his phone. Without even looking at the woman he said, "Evelyn here requires an entirely new wardrobe. Do you think you can help her with that, Simone?"

The woman pouted. "Sonia."

Lucian tucked his phone back in his pocket and looked at her in confusion. "Excuse me?"

"My name's Sonia, sir."

"Of course." He nodded a halfhearted apology and came to Scout's side. Slipping his hand around hers, lending some of his power and strength to her, he squeezed her fingers and smiled, sending her a sidelong glance.

Did he know the attendant's name? Was he fucking with her? Scout's lips twitched as she hid her smile. She squeezed his hand back. It was the first time he made her feel *with him* rather than against him or below him.

They were taken to the back of the store. Dugan arrived with Lucian's laptop and the ladies of the boutique brought him coffee and a table. He soon had himself his own little squatter office. He worked as one woman after another presented her with beautiful garments and accessories.

Lucian might have been otherwise occupied, but he always had a bead on what was happening around him. All Scout had to do was look in his direction and she'd find his gaze on her. He'd offer a slight nod or a shake of his head, and the women of the boutique would either discard or hang the garment he was rating. She found it amusing that a piece of clothing the women would rave about one moment could become a travesty of fashion in the next if it was something Lucian didn't favor.

Scout was soon bustled into a large room with mirrored walls and a button-upholstered round ottoman that reminded her of the inside of a genie bottle. Sonia began to tug at her clothes and she backed away. The attendant smiled, but some of the sincerity she recalled from when they were on the floor had left her eyes.

"You have to undress if you plan to try on clothes, honey."

Scout scowled at her patronizing tone. "I've been undressing myself since I was a child. I'd like some privacy."

The snobby attendant pursed her lips and shrugged. She backed out of the dressing room and left Scout there with a variety of outfits.

Quickly kicking off her shoes, she stuffed her oversized wool socks into them. Sliding out of her jeans, she folded them. Recalling the selection of undergarments Lucian had approved, Scout grimaced at her black cotton panties.

Her fingers reached under her sweatshirt and unlatched the clasp of her money belt and carefully stuffed it in the leg of her jeans. Taking a deep breath, she pulled her sweatshirt over her head and added it to the pile. As she turned to select her first outfit she gasped and jerked to a stop.

There, staring right back at her was her reflection. She hadn't seen herself so completely naked since . . . well, the last time she saw herself like this her body was very, very different.

Her lips parted and she blinked. Her hair was still down, forming a dark curtain of waves to her narrow hips. They barely swelled beneath her nipped-in waist. Her breasts were full, the tips darker than the rest of her skin, and pointed.

A half smile tickled her lips. She was quite pretty like this. She scrutinized her legs. They lacked any of the grace she noticed in the women's legs in the boutique. Scout recalled the beautiful Dr. Sheffield. Trying to mimic her grace, she awkwardly crossed one foot over the other. Her nose wrinkled. Her knees were knobby and juvenile. She stood on her toes. That helped.

When her gaze traveled back up to her face, she deflated. Her flesh-colored lips were lost on her plain skin. Her nose was small and unremarkable. Her eyes had always been her most unique quality. They were more silver than blue and had a way of getting lost against the whites of her eyes. Dark sapphire rims centered them and kept her appearance on the right side of that fine line between captivating and bizarre. Her lashes were long, but not as thick as Lucian's.

Her fingers gently nudged the loose skin beneath her eyes. It was deep purple and slightly bruised. She looked exhausted. Her cheeks were a little gaunt and she suddenly could see the slight resemblance between herself and Pearl. Scout averted her gaze, not wanting to look anymore. How had she gone from seeing someone beautiful moments ago, to hating the ugly person before her now?

There was a loud knock.

"Evelyn? What's taking so long?" Lucian's deep voice startled her.

She jumped. "J-Just a minute."

Her hands quickly grabbed the first item she found and yanked it off the hanger. It was a dress, or something . . . She slipped it over her head and tugged the material around her behind. Perhaps it was a handkerchief. Yanking up the top, it covered her breasts, but she frowned when half of her curves were still hanging out.

Lucian knocked again. "Evelyn."

She snapped her lips and scowled at the door. "I said I need a minute. It's too small."

The door suddenly opened and she backed up. Her arms covered the ridiculously small scrap of fabric attempting to be clothing as Lucian stepped in. The mirrored walls created a hundred Lucians. Too many Lucians.

"What're you doing? You can't come in here!"

He tilted his head and rolled his eyes, telling her exactly how ludicrous he found her statement. "Let me see."

She shook her head. "It doesn't fit. I look ridiculous." Her protests only made him step into her personal space and force her arms to her side. He stilled.

"See . . ." she mumbled.

He stepped back, his eyes growing even darker. His gaze wandered over her like fingers. His Adam's apple bobbed under the stubble covering his throat as he swallowed. "You look . . ." His voice was a hoarse whisper. "I like it."

"Lucian . . . It doesn't fit."

"We'll take it. I want one in every color."

Her palms slapped into her thighs. "It doesn't even make sense. There're no pockets to hold my stuff. It's November. I'll freeze."

"Then you'll wear it in spring."

"I won't be here in spring."

His head jerked and his eyes narrowed. They stared at each other for a long moment, each seemingly challenging the other, but about what she wasn't sure.

"Every color, Evelyn. Try on the next outfit." He turned and left the genie bottle, taking all ninety-nine other Lucians with him.

Scout groaned. Would she ever get her way again?

nine

GLASS SLIPPERS AND QUEENS

SCOUT'S weight shifted from foot to foot as she waited for Lucian beside the counter of the boutique. A man in a Patras blazer arrived and quickly carried boxes out to a delivery truck intended for the hotel. It was all too much.

Lucian had spent enough money in the past few hours that could probably feed the shelter's homeless for a year. Scout understood he was filthy rich, but seeing him in action was something altogether different. This was beyond rich. This was pure wealth.

Lucian had requested she wear one of the more casual outfits home. It was a pair of skintight midnight blue jeans and a loose gossamer blouse that hung open at the collar and gathered around her waist with a delicate little beaded belt. On her feet she wore very pointy high-heeled shoes that were impossible to walk in. They reminded her more of weapons than footwear.

Scout had to turn away when Lucian signed the receipt. She didn't want to see such excess wasted on her. She'd sell it all, she vowed. Sell it and buy enough food to feed everyone at the tracks for months.

Thinking of the tracks made her think of Pearl. She hoped her mother was better today than she'd been the day before. Had she found the food Scout left her?

A warm, wool camel-colored trench coat was draped over her shoulders. Lucian took her arm and led her back to the limo. With tiny ticking feet like a bird, she tiptoed beside him in the silly shoes. Stepping close to the limo, she stilled with the oddest sense she was forgetting something.

"My bag!"

"It's in the limo," Lucian said, directing her there as well.

Scout dug her sharp heels into the pavement. "My clothes!"

"You just got an entirely new wardrobe, Evelyn. Let the other pieces go to Goodwill."

She was Goodwill!

Yanking her elbow out of his grip, he scowled at her. "That's my stuff, Lucian. I'm not leaving it."

Scout turned and trotted stupidly back into the boutique. *Fucking asinine shoes. How was anyone supposed to get anywhere quick in these?* She was just in time. Sonia, the bitch, had her Botox lip curled as she dangled Scout's belongings, pinched between two fake nails, over the wastebasket.

"Hey!" Scout snapped and click-clacked over to her with as much dignity as she could manage. Yanking her stuff out of the woman's manicured hand, she quickly felt for her money belt and let out a deep breath when she found it still wedged in the leg of her pants.

"This is my stuff!"

Sonia gasped, and she had to give her credit. She at least had the good sense to look frightened. Scout turned in a huff and stilled when she spotted Lucian standing by the door. Great. His arms crossed over his chest as he leaned carelessly against the wall, taking in the scene. He was laughing at her, the bastard.

Scout rolled her eyes and trot-marched back to the limo. When he climbed inside the vehicle she scowled at him. He'd schooled his expression, but not very well.

His eyes still creased with laughter. "Remind me not to piss you off or take your stuff, Ms. Keats. I think Sonia just wet herself."

Scout threw her shoe at him. He was lucky it was her old one and not the dagger on her foot. He caught it with a speed and precision that seemed impossible.

Glancing at the offensive shoe, he raised a brow and turned his gaze on her, dark promise of retaliation showing in his onyx stare. He chuckled and put the shoe aside. "Oh, Ms. Keats, I do believe you're going to be a handful I will enjoy handling."

A hint of the sexual predator he was hiding beneath that power suit announced itself and her body responded with a jolt of nerves. The car was too small for all the tension suddenly filling it, the tension she could barely breathe through, yet he seemed to be getting a thrill from. She looked out the window and hid her reaction with her best impression of indifference when she was anything but.

WHEN they returned to the hotel it was after nine o'clock. They rode the elevator to the top floor and Lucian used his key to let them in.

"I thought we'd go out for dinner, but I know you're tired. How do you feel about ordering in?"

She thought about her promise to Dr. Sheffield and smiled. Perhaps this man had the ability to end her days of roping off waistbands and bulky, ill-fitting clothing. For the first time in her life, she might actually get to a place where she was comfortable with her weight, gain some curves, and not feel her bones protruding beneath her flesh. "Okay."

"I'm going to change out of this suit. I'll call down and have them bring up something, and then I'm going to give you your first lesson in chess. Any special requests?"

He slid off his shoes.

"Um, explain it slow and don't get upset when I ask you to repeat yourself?"

He paused. "What?"

Her head shook. "What are you asking me, Lucian?"

He laughed and came over to her. He placed his hands on her shoulders and smiled. "Have I told you how much I enjoy hearing you use my name?" He pinched her chin. "Dinner. I was asking if you had any *special requests* for dinner."

"Oh." Her cheeks heated. "Whatever you choose is fine."

He tilted his head, his eyes moving over her curiously. "What's your favorite food, Evelyn?"

She shrugged. She didn't have a favorite food. Food to her wasn't what it was to Lucian. To rich people it was a ritual, an experience, a display of beauty. To her it was what filled her belly at night and fought off her hunger pangs for a time.

"I don't have one."

"Well, what do you like?"

He seemed to really want to know what kind of food she enjoyed. She thought about Raphael. "Um, there're these little melon things. They make them downstairs. They're wrapped in this fancy kind of meat."

He grinned. "Prosciutto." The ethnic word rolled off his tongue almost sensually.

Her fingers snapped. "That's it!"

"Why don't you pour us some drinks and meet me in the sitting area. The chessboard's in the case along the wall."

Scout did as he asked. She wasn't sure what Lucian usually drank, but there was some stuff in a crystal decanter so she poured him a tall glass of that with some ice. Taking a bottle of water from the fridge, she poured it into a glass for herself.

The chessboard was housed in a glass hutch. It was heavy and very old and looked to be made of marble. She told herself it was marble because she didn't want to consider that the antique game might actually be made of ivory and some poor elephant might've died so that rich people could play chess. *Babar* was one of her favorite stories that Parker had used to teach her small words.

Carefully placing the heavy game on the table, Scout sat and sipped her water. Lucian spoke on the phone with the front desk and she waited patiently.

She liked the colors Lucian used in his decorating. They were warm and cozy. He looked good against them.

When Lucian emerged from the master bedroom all thoughts scattered from her head. He wore loose-fitting silk pants and no shirt. Muscles existed on him where she didn't even know there were muscles. She had never seen a real person with a body like his. The image appealed to her in a fundamental way. He looked like the models she saw in magazines and on billboards. Her mouth was suddenly very, very dry. She gulped her water.

"Dinner should be here shortly."

Lucian sat next to her on the sofa and pulled the heavy marble chess board onto the cushion between them. The action caused his arms to bunch and flex. His tanned torso twisted. His nipples were very dark and flat.

Scout needed a distraction. Plucking her shoe off her foot, she asked, "Do you mind if I take off my shoes?"

"Not at all, make yourself comfortable, but you may want to hear my rules first."

She stilled, shoe hovering in her hand just above the floor. "Rules?"

He expertly placed the various-shaped pieces on different

squares. "I find people learn fastest when under a bit of pressure. I expect you to give me a decent challenge. Playing chess is one of my favorite pastimes and I'm in need of a good opponent. We'll be playing strip chess."

"*What?*"

"You heard me. For every piece I take of yours, you remove an item of clothing. The same goes for me when you get my pieces."

"But you're only wearing pants!"

"Very good, Evelyn. It takes a keen sense of observation to excel at chess." His sarcasm was playful, but she was too afraid of what he was suggesting to laugh.

There was a knock at the door. Lucian stood to answer it. She kept her gaze averted as the men delivered the food.

"The coffee table's fine, gentlemen."

Dishes were spread across the low table beside them and they were soon alone again. Lucian removed the covers and her stomach pinched with excitement. She never wanted to forget how wonderfully he fed her during their time together. There was that melon wrapped in prosciutto; a tray of various cheeses and grapes; bread topped with salmon, some sort of cream, and dill; salad; and mini crab cakes.

"That's a lot of food," she said, as he passed her a linen napkin.

"Not really. It's all appetizers. I figured we'd pick."

"Pick?"

"Yeah, graze while we play."

Scout took a grape off the cheese tray and popped it in her mouth. The splendid juice burst over her tongue, tart and sweet. Lucian bit into a crab cake, then placed it aside.

"Okay, Ms. Keats, the objective is to get a checkmate. In other words, threaten my king with an inescapable capture. Each piece moves in a unique way. This is the king. He can move any way he wants, but only one block at a time."

"Figures," she mumbled and he arched a brow.

He purposefully cleared his throat. "This is the queen. She's the most powerful piece. She can move any direction and as many blocks as she chooses. Her duty's to protect the king. She must never stray too far and she'll sacrifice herself if it saves her king."

Scout cocked her head and shifted her legs beneath her, careful not to jostle the board. "I was impressed until the end of that spiel. Some protector he is. Okay, can we start the game?"

He tsked. "Evelyn, first, chess is not a game, it's a sport. Second, it requires a great deal of patience. When done right, it can be a beautiful thing, lyrical even. It can be a great show of aggression and surrender that's charged with deep emotion. You must pay attention. It's quite rare for a male to be topped by a female. No, don't look at me like that. I'm only telling you the truth. Some say it has to do with the basic human nature of each sex. Females are naturally martyrs in many aggressive situations, while men are natural aggressors. And as far as the purposes of the king and queen, make no mistake, the queen's the fiercest aggressor on the board. She holds more power than any other piece and is, without a doubt, the king's greatest asset. Because she's so valued, she's also coveted. She can lure any piece into the king's territory."

His fingers swirled over the round tip of the queen as he talked, and she had a feeling he was explaining more than the rules of chess. She gazed at the board, seeing the resemblance between royal order and the pieces.

"Are these the guards?" she asked, motioning toward a horse-shaped piece.

"They're the knights. Their duty's to the queen, but also the king. You must always be aware of your king. As the players move, so does he until one opponent finally outmaneuvers the other. Then . . . checkmate."

"It's a big game of chase."

"Yes, but it isn't fun to simply chase one player across the board. Chess is about taunting your opponent, seducing them out of their comfort zone."

She swallowed. The way he explained the rules in that deep gravelly whisper, it somehow made her very aware of her being female and him being male.

"You'll notice, Evelyn, that I prefer to keep my queen close to the king. I like her innocently uninvolved with the politics and safely tucked away in my back row, always there for me when I need her."

Pressure built in weird places she wasn't used to noticing—until meeting Lucian, that is—and she squirmed. "You explain it like a war game, but describe it like a relationship."

"How much difference is there really, in love and war? Both require a great deal of passion and plotting. Chess is a display of training that ends in social intercourse. Chess is a competition that's never lost, but the triumph of one competitor's ego, the declaration of who is truly the master."

"What's this one?"

"These are your bishops. Quite powerful. They can move diagonally any distance. The X the bishops draw are said to represent Saint Andrew's cross. Are you familiar with that? No? We'll save that for another time, perhaps."

He replaced the bishop and picked up the piece that resembled a castle. "This is the rook. He's the voyeur. His tower's tall so that he can watch over the game. He sees all, but rarely interferes. His movement is limited to the linear advances that are only ever in *cooperation* with the more powerful players of the game."

He replaced the rook and waved his hand over the lined up small pieces in the front. "These are your pawns. They're your front line, your servants, and essentially, the foundation of your power. They're here to serve and sacrifice for their king and queen, but we must never undervalue their importance. Shall we play?"

Crap. She was so going to end up naked. "I suppose."

"Good. You may make the first move."

Her lips twisted and she frowned over the boards. Everything was packed in tight like little sardine soldiers. Shrugging, she slid a pawn two spaces forward.

Lucian quickly made a move, and she had the feeling his was a lot more thought-out than hers. Scout moved another pawn. Lucian did the same. This continued for some time until the other pieces seemed a bit less confined.

She found herself relaxing into the flow of the game and growing less intimidated. Chess wasn't that hard.

Suddenly, Lucian jumped a number of pieces with his knight and took her pawn. "Hey!"

"It was bound to happen, Evelyn. You can't expect to challenge me without retaliation. You owe me an item of clothing."

She huffed and removed her shoe. "They were hurting me anyway," she said snidely and moved her knight, mimicking his strategy.

His bishop slid out of nowhere and captured her knight.

"Son of a bitch!"

She bolstered her confidence with a lot of mental smack talk, but knew she was losing her shirt. Literally. It took courage she wasn't sure she possessed to actually go through with this and not forfeit. Her pride told her not to be a chicken, but her conscience told her she was about to be humiliated in more ways than one.

Would he draw back when he saw her skinny shoulders or unspectacular breasts? She wasn't used to having such personal parts of herself scrutinized. She wasn't used to having herself scrutinized period. But since meeting Lucian Patras that seemed to be what her every word and action brought about: scrutiny. How would Lucian perceive her? She didn't know why she cared, but she did. For the first time in a long time, she pretended a level of confidence she didn't possess.

He laughed and her other shoe came off. The game continued and Scout regretted her earlier cockiness. She was soon sitting across from Lucian in her panties and shirt. Each item of clothing peeled away with a bit of her dignity.

"Don't forget the power of your queen, Evelyn."

She scowled at him. "Maybe I don't want you to take off your pants."

"That's fine. I can quite enjoy your naked body while I'm clothed."

He was so arrogant. She hadn't taken a single piece of his and she wanted to more than anything. Every opportunity she found to advance on his pieces put her queen at risk.

"You know," he said contemplatively. "When the game gets too complicated, sometimes you have no choice but to sacrifice your queen."

"Never," she hissed vehemently.

Eventually, it didn't matter what she did. Lucian captured her queen. "Checkmate."

She stared at him, brow puckered and pathetic. Her eyes glazed and her lip quivered. Shamelessly, she evoked his pity and hated herself for it. All she had left was her newly discovered article of clothing called a camisole, and panties, and at the moment that meant more than her pride.

He laughed. "Oh, Ms. Keats, really? Here I thought you to be a fair opponent."

She blinked at him and he sighed.

"Very well. It's late anyway and I have a meeting downtown first thing in the morning. You played a good first game."

She was shocked he was letting her go, but also incredibly grateful. She smiled and then his words sunk in. "What should I do tomorrow?"

"I've made you an appointment at the spa for ten."

"What about work?"

He frowned. "Ms. Jones is expecting you Wednesday morning. You'll work five hours then and five hours on Thursday."

The concession he was forced to make regarding her job still apparently bothered him.

"Thank you."

He nodded, brushing off her gratitude. "Get dressed. I'll walk you to your room."

Standing, he stretched as she quickly replaced her clothing. Glaring down at the spiked heels, she opted to walk to her room barefoot. It was after midnight and she was exhausted.

Lucian escorted her to the thirtieth floor and handed her a keycard when they reached her room. She couldn't believe she was actually going to sleep in one of the Patras suites. As the door opened, she gasped. She'd cleaned these suites several times, each one was the same, but this one was somehow different.

Beyond the numerous boxes from the boutique, stacked along the wall were beautiful arrangements of flowers. The room was filled with the soft fragrance of lilies. Scout laughed and went to admire the flowers, caressing the delicate petals and sniffing their gentle scent. Turning, she found Lucian watching her, a slight grin on his face.

"You did this?" she asked, an unfamiliar buttery sensation curling inside of her.

"I didn't know what flowers you liked. I see lilies were a good choice."

"They're beautiful. It'll be like sleeping in a fairy-tale garden."

The bed was turned down and a soft silk nightgown was laid

out at the foot of it. This would be her reward, her one indulgence for trading a bit of her dignity to be here. At the moment, seeing such opulence offered to her, she suffered no form of regret.

Her fingers ran over the material, softer than a whisper. She had never slept in something like that. What if there was a fire and she had to get out of the building quickly?

Lucian cleared his throat. "I'll be in and out all morning and probably won't see you until just before our dinner tomorrow night. Everything you need you should have. It's a formal affair, so one of the gowns we bought today should do. The girls at the salon have their instructions and if you need anything else I've left you the number to my assistant, Seth. He can answer any questions you have."

After the intimate way they had spent their evening, his instructions struck her as awfully businesslike, jolting her conscience back to awareness of their arrangement. She nodded and stepped back, taking on what she hoped signified a more professional and refined position. Her expression sobered.

"Thank you for everything." She wondered if she should address him as Mr. Patras now that they were being formal again.

"I'll see you tomorrow. I expect you at my suite, ready to go, by six. Latch the door behind me."

Remaining a safe distance behind, she followed him to the door. He stepped into the hall and hesitated as if he wished to say something. "Good night, Evelyn."

"Good night."

He turned away and Scout shut the door. Gently closing the latch, she exhaled for probably the first time since that morning. Had it really only been one day since she agreed to this? It had been the longest day of her life. And the strangest. And, if she was honest, the headiest.

She went to the bathroom and washed up. There was a basket

of toiletries. She brushed her teeth and even flossed with the fancy little flossers provided. Her heavy eyes stared at the Jacuzzi tub longingly. She was so tired she'd likely drown if she took a bath. Sighing, she turned and went to the bedroom.

The empty drawer slid quietly open. *Drawers! Never had any of them before.* How bizarre her situation was.

A pang of guilt skewered her when she thought about Parker. He was likely worried sick about her. Lucian said her appointment was at ten. Scout was usually up way earlier than that. Her guilt eased as she decided she'd go see Parker in the morning and explain everything then.

She gently took off her delicately sewn, expensive clothing and laid it out in an empty drawer. Her toes tapped as she eyeballed the little nightgown on the bed. In her old bag she found her worn-in jeans, slid them over her legs, and attached her money belt to her waist, then slid the nightgown over top. It was so soft it was like being nude.

Her tired body climbed into the bed and crawled under the heavy covers.

"Holy fucking shit!" she moaned. She was sleeping on a cloud.

ten

.....

TEMPER

SCOUT woke at five, her body used to getting up for work. The first thing she did was sigh blissfully when she realized she wasn't dead and the reason her body didn't ache was simply that she'd slept on the most decadent bed in the world. Scrambling up, she rushed into the bathroom and filled the tub.

In the basket of toiletries she found bubble bath, bath salts, shower gels, soaps, some gritty stuff she couldn't read the name of, and various other potions and lotions. She hadn't a clue how to use such things or in what order they should be used, so she simply waited for the tub to fill and dumped them inside.

When she pressed the button for the jets they roared to life and everything began to churn and bubble. She hastily removed her clothes and climbed in the warm soothing bath.

Sweet mother of all that is holy!

With her body in the water, she giggled. The soaps and salts gave the water a satin feel. She simply luxuriated in it for a long while. As the water grew cold, her pruned fingers unplugged the drain and filled the tub with fresh water. The dirt washed away from her skin and it was like nothing she ever imagined. She was finally, for the first time she could ever recall, fully clean.

Her gaze found the basket on the counter, then moved down to her legs. She lifted her arms and frowned. After only a few minutes of consideration, she climbed out of the tub and dribbled over to the basket. It was cold outside of the water. She quickly found the razor and shaving cream and jumped back in the tub.

Scout examined both objects. Luckily, there was a little folded paper stuck to the shaving cream with pictures on it. Shaving couldn't be that complicated.

Popping the cap off, she squirted some of the cream in her palm. It smelled like peaches and was actually more like jelly than cream. Her finger spread it around and it turned white and fluffy.

Getting the razor out of the packaging was no easy task. It required another trip out of the tub and the use of a small set of scissors she found in a little kit with a nail file and clippers. By the time she had everything she needed her water had run cold again so she did a refill, this time forgoing all the soaps, salts, and jets.

"Okay, Scout, you can do this. Time to get girlie."

She squeezed a big pile of peach-scented gel into her palm and spread it thickly over her leg. Swishing her hands in the water, she picked up the razor. It glided up her calf slowly like a snowplow clearing away a blizzard. The blade immediately needed to be rinsed, and she repeated the process.

Five minutes later she was sitting in hairy, peach-scented sludge and completely grossed out. No longer clean. Worse, although everything looked good at first, her skin had begun to bleed where she'd accidentally made little nicks.

"Shit."

Growing frustrated, she abandoned her plan to also shave under her arms, and stood. Reaching blindly beneath the sludge, she felt around and released the plug. The water drained, leaving a slimy film at the bottom of the once-shiny tub. Embarrassment flooded her and she suddenly wanted to cry.

Scout ignored the mess, needing a shower more than the tub needed one. Moving to the enclosed glass stall, she turned on the water and rinsed away the proof of her disastrous first attempt at being girlie. She felt marginally better after she shampooed her hair with a lovely, foamy wash. Her hair had never been so soft.

Once she dried herself off and attached little scraps of tissue to the nicks that refused to stop bleeding, she cleaned the tub. By the time all was said and done it was seven o'clock. If she planned on catching Parker she needed to get a move on.

Forgoing the numerous boutique packages and bags, Scout slid on her jeans, hoodie, and old sneakers, ensuring that her money belt was wrapped tightly around her waist. There was no way she was walking all the way to St. Christopher's in death shoes. She quickly made the bed, and because of her own stupid embarrassment, she placed the Do Not Disturb sign on the door and left.

It was cold and she regretted not waiting for her hair to dry or taking her new coat. She walked fast, taking advantage of all shortcuts, and cursing herself for not bringing Parker one of the apples from her room. Dodging into an alley, quickly pulling five dollars from her money belt, she made a detour to a bakery and bought him a huge muffin. The cost was exorbitant for what was basically bread, but she had been eating so well, Parker deserved a treat too.

Scout made it to the shelter just in time. She spotted Parker's brooding face as he came out of the school doors. He hunched into his sweater, shielding away the cold, and she ran over to him.

"Parker," she called and he turned, relief clear on his face.

"Jesus! Scout, where the hell've you been? I've been worried sick."

"I'm really sorry. I couldn't make it back in time. I knew you'd be worried and I felt terrible. Here." She handed him the muffin.

"Where'd you get this?"

"It's a present. Don't worry about it."

He frowned then leaned close and sniffed her. "Where were you? You smell different." He bit into the muffin.

"It's a long story. Where're you going right now?" He shrugged and they made their way to a low brick wall where the old school courts used to be. "How's the muffin?"

"Incredible. Scout, what's going on? Why aren't you at work? And you better not tell me you slept at the tracks last night."

"I didn't sleep at the tracks. I slept in a bed."

He froze. Putting the muffin aside, he faced her, something akin to fury darkening his otherwise calm expression. "Whose bed?"

"Well, Mr. Patras's. I stayed in the hotel."

"Is that allowed?"

This was going to be hard. She figured keeping things as honest and simple as possible would be best for now.

"Yeah, the owner of the hotel actually suggested it. They sort of changed my hours and adjusted my job description. I'm going to need to be at the hotel a lot more."

"Well, that's great. Maybe one of these days I can come visit you at work. Do you think anyone would give me shit if I tried to get in there?"

"No. That'd be awesome if you came to visit. I want you to, but I need to sort out some things first."

He seemed genuinely happy for her. "That's really great, Scout. You may actually make it in the real world after all. I'm glad you're getting out of this shit hole. St. Christopher's isn't any place for a girl like you. You know that new guy, the one with the eye? Well, I knew I didn't like him for a reason. He snuck into the girls' room last night and attacked Deborah."

"Oh my God, is she okay?" Her hand went to her throat. Deborah was a little older than her and very tiny.

"Yeah. George heard her scream and got there before any real damage was done. The cops came and took him away, but you know how that goes." He swallowed the last bite of muffin. "The sad part is Deb took off. The temperatures are going down and I hope she comes back."

So many people over the years had died from hypothermia. December through March were the scariest months of the year for their people. She looked down at Parker's thin sweater. Holes had worn into the elbows. He still looked handsome with his scarf wrapped tightly around his neck and his fingerless gloves, but being homeless wasn't about making a fashion statement. It was about survival.

"Parker, do you need anything? I can get you stuff. I have people who . . . if there's something you need, would you tell me?"

He smiled sweetly. "I don't need anything, Scout. Got everything I need right here." He patted his bag. She understood his pride wouldn't let him take much more than a muffin from her.

"Can I ask you a favor?"

"Anything."

She smiled. That was Parker, always willing to give her anything he could. He was the best friend she'd ever had. Her only friend.

"I'm gonna be busy in the next few weeks," she said. "If you can manage it, do you think you can get down to the tracks to check on Pearl for me?"

He sighed. He hated the tracks. It was where his mother had died not long after losing his father. Parker's family's descent into the bowels of Folsom had been a swift and sad one. She hated asking him to go there.

"Yeah, I'll keep an eye on her so long as you promise not to go there in the dark by yourself. I know you. You won't be able to stay away. I get that you're busy with your job and all, but you can't keep going down there when it's dark, Scout. It's dangerous. You shouldn't be down there at all. Wait for me and I'll go with you, but only when it's light, okay?"

She nodded. Unable to voice a promise she wasn't sure she'd keep.

Something seemed so final in the way Parker hugged her good-bye. Her hand ran over his wool cap and she stared into his soft green eyes, so different from Lucian's. She wished she had some meaningful thing to say in that moment, but all she could think of was, "Stay warm."

As she walked back to Patras she didn't have her earlier pep. Taking the longer way back, she kept her head down. Unused to walking through Folsom during this time of day, the crowds were stifling. Everyone seemed to be rushing off to one place or another. What must it be like to live such an urgent life? Scout never had anywhere to be except for where she chose to go.

Crossing into the more prominent section of the city, she tried to blend in as best she could with the finely dressed population. She appreciated seeing others in sneakers and jeans, but no one else's clothes seemed quite as tattered as hers.

On Gerard, she debated taking the service entrance into the hotel. Looking up at the repeat of yesterday's rich-and-famous parade of limos, luxury cars, and guests, she decided that was exactly what she'd do.

Scout walked quickly through the crowd, careful to avoid the fancy red runner and its gold tassels. There was a lot going on, various languages being spoken, carts of luggage being wheeled, cars idling, guests checking in with the attendants.

Someone shouted. Head down, she kept walking. As she was turning the corner some brute grabbed her arm and she was nearly yanked off her feet.

Her arm jerked, wrenching her hand from the pocket of her sweatshirt and she turned ready to attack. *"What the fuck?"*

Lucian, dressed in his long wool coat and a tailored black pin-stripe suit, stared down at her. His jaw ticked and he wasn't blinking. "Evelyn."

She relaxed. "Jesus, Lucian, you scared the shit out of me."

He quickly looked around and then took her hand and pulled her toward the front of the hotel.

"What are you doing?" she hissed and dug her feet in, but he was much stronger than her. "I can't go in that way. I look like crap. People will stare."

"And whose fault is that?" he snapped. "I spent thousands of dollars on a new wardrobe for you not twenty-four hours ago, yet here you are walking around looking like you're homeless. Where the hell's the coat I bought you?"

And that, apparently, was her limit. Scout yanked her arm free and stomped her foot. "Stop! I'm not some little kid you can just boss around. I've been taking care of myself longer than you've probably been on your own. I never had a dad and I don't need one now."

"Are you finished?" he asked through gritted teeth.

Searching her mind for a moment in case there was anything else, she paused. Yes, she was finished. And now she was shaking. Fury blazed in his eyes, but he had no right to manhandle or boss her like that.

Adrenaline rushed her system, making her feel cornered and off balance. Lucian didn't look like the easygoing man who took her shopping yesterday or the man who taught her to play chess last night. He looked every bit the menacing industrialist prepared and qualified to take over the world.

Shit.

"Lucian, I—"

"Not. Another. Word. It's ten minutes to ten and I'm now running late. You have an appointment. I'll see you tonight at six at which point you *will* be dressed appropriately for the evening. We will have dinner, make our rounds at the benefit, and return home, at which point I expect to hear all about where you spent your morning. Any questions?"

He didn't leave much unexplained.

She gritted her teeth and narrowed her eyes, hopefully making it clear that he wasn't the only person pissed off at the moment. "No." She just wanted to get away from him.

He turned and whistled. About fifty people, the majority of them wearing Patras uniforms, turned and stared at them. Scout wanted to crawl under a manhole cover and die.

"Philippe," Lucian called. The man jogged over. "This is Ms. Keats. See that she gets back to her room safely. She's in suite 3000."

Philippe looked at her and his judgment caused her to shrink. He had to be French. She was proven correct in the next moment when he began speaking to Lucian in what she now recognized as French. Naturally, Lucian spoke back to him in Philippe's native tongue, probably flawlessly.

Once he'd given the attendant his instructions, he turned and left, without even a good-bye. Scout was pissed, but more frustrated with herself than anything. It hurt, for some reason, watching Lucian walk away from her without even a glance back.

Ridiculous.

There shouldn't be such confusing emotions warring inside of her. This was a simple arrangement, one where she needed to keep her head and not underestimate him or lose sight of who he really was.

She should probably feel guilty for snapping at him, but her stubborn pride wouldn't allow it. She may be younger and smaller than him, but she wasn't anyone's kicking post.

The limo pulled away. Let him be angry. She was angry too.

"Mademoiselle? I shall take you to your room now as Monsieur Patras instructed."

Her shoulders drooped. Even in his absence he seemed to maintain control. "Yes, all right. Let's go."

eleven

FEMALE TORTURE RITUALS

AFTER changing into a more "appropriate" outfit for the day, Scout quickly rushed down to the spa. She wasn't sure if she needed anything. A sweet girl about her age with beautiful teeth and a cheery smile greeted her.

"Evelyn?"

"Yes. I'm sorry I'm late."

The girl came around the counter. "That's no problem at all." She held out her hand. "I'm Beth."

"Evelyn," she said stupidly and blushed. "But you already knew that. I might as well just tell you I have no idea what I'm doing here. I've never been to a spa before and I'm not really sure what I'm supposed to do."

Beth grinned and somehow her trepidation vanished. "You'll love it. Just be yourself. Mr. Patras arranged for you to have quite a full day. We're going to start you off in the salon. Mr. Patras made it perfectly clear that your hair was to remain long, but we should clean up the ends for you. They have some great hot oil treatments as well. Once you get back to Isabella you guys can discuss color if that's something you're interested in. From there you'll meet with Ivone for your massage, then Katelyn, who'll help you select the right kind of makeup for your coloring. You have beautiful skin, by the way. After that, Richard will style your updo and then it's back to Katelyn for your makeover."

As Beth spoke she led Scout back to the salon. Various scents fought over the airy space. Everyone wore black and had perfect hair. Even the one stylist with spiky pink hair had managed to accomplish the perfect spiky pink.

Scout was ushered to a cushiony seat and introduced to Isabella, who also appeared to be quite nice. Her hair was taken out of her ponytail and fondled by several stylists. She tried not to flinch at being touched. They each commented on its thickness and how lucky she was to have such nice natural waves. An unfamiliar pride filled her with each kind word.

They each put in a suggestion of the type of cut and style she'd look best with. Scout had no opinion on the subject, so she remained silent. She was brought to a small sink where magical fingers massaged her scalp and delicious-smelling products were rubbed into her hair.

When the first snip came, a mixture of excitement and sorrow swirled in her belly. She'd never cut her hair. They said it would remain long, but as each coil of brown fell to the polished floor she fought the urge to tell them to stop. It was just hair, but oddly, watching it fall to the floor made her sad, like she was saying good-bye to part of herself.

Everyone was so nice. The massage was a chore of sorts. At first she couldn't relax. She wasn't used to being touched, and her personal space was something she took very seriously, but eventually Ivone had her practically weeping as her hands worked over her flesh.

When the masseuse lifted her arms, she quietly asked about

Scout's shaving situation. She blushed and explained that she was too afraid she'd cut into an important artery if she shaved anymore. Ivone smiled and suggested she see a girl named Patrice to get waxed.

Waxing sounded worse than shaving, but Ivone swore it was the way to go. She also hinted that Mr. Patras would probably like it. Her comment turned Scout's cheeks scorching hot with embarrassment, but also convinced her she was right.

It was very hard not to punch Patrice in the face after she pulled the first sticky strip away during what she called a Brazilian.

Brazil must be filled with a bunch of sick, sadistic bastards.

Her underarms weren't that bad, but it took serious courage to allow her to put wax on her eyebrows. Patrice applied a topical cooling cream to her face, which helped. She also gave Scout something for the damage she'd done on her legs.

After the waxing fiasco was over, Katelyn yelled at poor Patrice because apparently it wasn't the best thing to have a wax the day of a makeup consultation. Poor Patrice. She had been nothing but badgered all morning. Scout decided next time Patrice helped her get pretty—*if* there was a next time—she'd ignore the temptation of attacking her when she caused her pain. She truly understood now what the girls at the salon meant when they joked that "beauty is pain."

Richard styled her hair in a crown of cascading curls that exposed her neck and swept off to the side of her face and over her shoulder. She looked like a woman from the 1920s. Once her makeup was done, Scout could hardly recognize herself. She smiled the entire way back to her room as people stared at her admiringly.

It was only four o'clock and all she had to do was dress. She decided she'd wear an ice blue gown that gathered at the lower back. The bottom reminded her of a mermaid tail. Out of navy blue heels and strappy silver ones, she wasn't sure which matched. She went with the strappy silver ones in the end.

Being that she had some time to kill, she walked around in her underwear and shoes for a while. She had terrible balance. How did women manage to get around in these things? What if she needed to run for some reason? She didn't want to stumble and embarrass herself or worse, break her neck, so Scout spent the better part of the hour simply walking back and forth, back and forth until she worried her toes might bleed.

A light was blinking on the phone beside the bed and she stilled. There were all kinds of instructions written on it, but they were useless to her. The first group of words was next to the number nine. She pressed it but nothing happened. Next was the number zero followed by more words. She pressed zero.

"Patras front desk, this is Kevin. How may I assist you this evening?"

"Um, hi, my name's Evelyn Keats and I'm in room 3000."

"Good evening, Ms. Keats. Are you enjoying your stay?"

"Uh, yes, thank you. There's a light blinking on my phone. Do you know what that means?"

"That would mean that you have voice mail. Just dial 'star' and your room number and it will connect you."

"Oh." She had no idea who'd leave her a voice mail. Perhaps it was Tamara calling about her schedule change or Lucian calling to cancel and tell her he no longer wanted to see her again after the way she spoke to him. A sick ball of dread rolled in the pit of her stomach. She thanked the man at the desk and did as he instructed.

"Hello, Evelyn. This is Dr. Vivian Sheffield. I'm calling to let you know that all of your tests came back perfectly fine. I'd still like to see you again in a few weeks if that would be all right with you. We also need to discuss contraception when you're ready. If there's anything you need me for or any questions you have please don't hesitate to call." She left her number and Scout quickly formed the numbers on a notepad labeled with the recognizable Patras logo.

Scout looked down at her sloppy handwriting and thought about what this meant. Did Lucian know her blood work came back clean? Yes, he probably knew before she did. She was substantially relieved she wasn't sick. So many people had so many different sicknesses, and although she was always careful with her mother, there was always a risk.

Her gaze landed on her underwear. Perhaps she should change into something a little fancier. Her stomach did a cartwheel at the thought. She tucked the number into her bag and walked some more. On her fifth trip past the bag with all the fancy panties, she stopped and pulled out a lacy blue pair.

At ten minutes to, she brushed her teeth, freshened her lip gloss, and slipped into her gown. She couldn't get the zipper all the way up on her own. She didn't want to walk through the hotel half dressed, but she tried to reach every which way for the zipper and couldn't. Slipping on her shoes, Scout grabbed her key and, again, placed the Do Not Disturb placard on the door before she left.

When the gilded elevator arrived at Lucian's suite, she was ridiculously nervous, her anxiety causing her stomach to cramp painfully. She wasn't late, but feared he'd be upset with her anyway. Maybe he was still mad about this morning. She'd had time to cool off and wanted to forget about the whole thing. She took a steadying breath and knocked, realizing she forgot the room key he'd given her.

twelve

.....

SCATTERED PICTURES

THE door opened and Scout's mouth gaped. Lucian was dressed in a sleek black tuxedo and looked incredible.

"Evelyn, my God, you look . . . words fail me."

She smiled nervously. "Fail you in a good way or a bad way?"

"Good," he rasped. "Definitely good."

"Glad to hear it, because I got the shit kicked out of me at that torture chamber you're passing off as a spa down there. Can you help me zip my dress?" She stepped in and hid a smirk. Seems she had rendered Mr. Patras, hotel tycoon, bazillionaire, entrepreneur extraordinaire, speechless.

He stepped back and shut the door. Presenting him her back, she shivered at the soft touch of his fingers as they slowly pulled the zipper up. Her back was still very exposed, but at least now the dress fit properly. She turned.

"Thank you. You look very handsome, Mr. Patras."

"You're stunning, Ms. Keats. I'm wondering if I should keep you here instead."

Scout tilted her head. "Why?"

"Protect my queen." His reflective compliment was incredibly flattering. Warmth spread through her chest and she smiled at him for a moment, not quite sure what to say next. He turned briskly.

"I have something for you."

"You do?" She followed him to the common area and he handed her a large, heavy gift box with a navy blue bow. "What is it?"

"Open it. I saw it this afternoon and thought of you."

Grinning foolishly, she pulled the satin ribbon back. It gathered in a large loop and fell to the ground. She placed the box on the seat of the settee and shimmied the fitted lid off. When she saw something furry, she jumped. "What—what is it?"

Lucian reached into the box and pulled out a stunning white, silk-lined fur coat. "I realized we forgot to get you a dress coat for formal functions. Here, try it on."

"Is it real?"

"Quite." He held the coat open for her to step into.

"Don't people hate people who wear fur?"

"They're all hypocrites. The Americans slaughter billions of animals a year for clothing, cars, furniture, shoes, and exotic food, but protesters only seem to care about the cute fuzzy ones."

He had a point.

She slipped into the coat, its silk lining cool against her skin. It engulfed her. The fur was heavy, but it was likely the warmest, softest thing she'd ever put on her body.

"My God, Lucian, it's beautiful."

"I'm glad you like it. Shall we go?"

She simply stared at him. The coat must have cost a fortune. She reached for his hand and slowed his escape.

"You're very generous," she whispered. "No one's ever done so much for me in my entire life. I'm not even sure how to accept such openhandedness."

He frowned. "It means nothing to me. It's just a coat."

As he presented her his back, she was shocked by how hurtful his words were. Means nothing? Perhaps purchasing a coat like this was the equivalent to purchasing a roll of toilet paper to an ordinary person. Scout found herself blinking back tears no matter how she spun his comment.

Her emotions baffled her. This was not supposed to be an emotional exchange. She was being overly sensitive and needed to knock it off.

Lucian returned wearing his own coat. "Ready?"

She merely nodded, her voice lodged somewhere in the pit of her stomach beneath her bruised heart.

They took the limo and rode in silence. Lucian seemed preoccupied. Scout stared out the window the entire time, but also studied him in the reflection. Sometimes she saw him looking at her and wondered what he was thinking.

He was so difficult to read. At times he was charming and sweet and in the next moment he was cold and distant. She wondered if this entire arrangement had anything to do with her specifically or if she was just filling a slot. She hoped the latter wasn't the case, which contradicted every barrier her common sense insisted she maintain.

He was beginning to affect her on a personal level, and that was dangerous. His praise or disregard shouldn't affect her. She needed to stop being so damn vulnerable. She mentally chastised herself to disassociate any personal feelings. It was a job. So why did his opinion of her suddenly seem to matter?

At this point, after all the money he had spent and everything he provided for her, she was already indebted. She'd follow through with her part of the deal regardless, but it would be a much easier job if she believed Lucian Patras actually liked her.

The Museum of Natural Art was interesting. It was a cross between artifacts, plants, antiques, and quirky art, all sort of blending in with what the aristocrats called the contemporary craft movement.

Scout remembered being at some sort of office building with her mom when she was little and watching a show called *Gilligan's Island*. Her mom had meetings there at the same time every week and she loved it because she got to watch TV. A character on the show was a millionaire. He used to talk with his front teeth clenched together. She realized that was how she expected Lucian's friends to talk. They didn't. They were all normal people.

The women, married, single, young, or old, all loved Lucian, she quickly learned. Men vied for his attention as well. She smiled politely when someone spoke in her direction, but no one really talked to her. She didn't have much to contribute to the conversations anyway. Stocks, bonds, the economy, politics, it was all above her head.

Lucian kept a hand on her the entire night even if he didn't speak to her much. As they moved to find their table, she panicked when she saw there was dancing. There was no way she was dancing in these shoes. She could barely dance in bare feet.

The tables were draped in glossy linens, and ridiculously large topiaries acted as centerpieces. The chair backs were made of bronze-painted branches and the silverware was heavy to hold.

Lucian entered a heated debate over the new permits needed for redevelopment in lower Folsom with the gentleman to his right.

"These things really are silly, aren't they?"

Scout turned at the soft comment coming from the older woman sitting next to her. "Pardon?"

"These events. I mean really. Five thousand dollars a plate to support art. What ever happened to supporting a real cause?"

Scout choked. "Fi-five *thousand* dollars, did you say?"

"Ridiculous. I know," the woman went on. "I mean, I don't

even know how half of the knickknacks out there are considered art. My grandmother used to make crocheted plunger covers. Perhaps I can find a spot to display her work here," the little woman said sarcastically.

Scout stifled a laugh. She had to be almost eighty. Scout introduced herself and the woman replied, "Lovely to meet you, dear. Yvette Constance Whitfield hyphen Baldwin. My husband's running this event."

Scout snorted. The woman was a riot. Her laughter attracted Lucian's attention. He greeted Mrs. Whitfield-Baldwin. "Thank you for inviting us, Yvette."

"I was just chatting with your lovely date, Lucian. About time you found yourself a respectable woman. She's quite exquisite."

Scout didn't appreciate being appraised as if she were made of stone and incapable of hearing. Lucian nodded his concurrence. "I quite agree, Yvette."

Scout gritted her teeth but held her smile.

The dinner was nice, but the extravagance of it all was baffling. From the clothes to the cost of the tickets, to the amount of news coverage, it was all obscene. Mrs. Whitfield-Baldwin was right. How about supporting a real cause, like stamping out hunger or solving the job crisis or finding a cure for AIDS?

As they drove home, they again were quiet. Lucian's introspective mood seemed to turn brooding. Scout was already nervous about the remainder of the night, so she figured she'd better try to lighten the mood.

"Lucian?"

He turned to her.

"I shouldn't have spoken to you the way I did this morning." She wouldn't apologize, but she would let him know her behavior hadn't ranked as one of her proudest moments. She was usually much more in control of her emotions than that.

He scowled then sighed. "It's over. Let it go."

"But you're still mad."

"Who says I'm mad?"

"Well, you haven't really spoken to me tonight. I figured . . ."

"Where did you go, Evelyn? It occurred to me this afternoon that I really don't know much about you other than what I read in your paperwork."

She fidgeted with her dress. "I had to go see someone."

"Who?"

"A friend."

"A male friend?"

She frowned. "What difference does that make?"

"I find it makes quite a bit of difference. Until our time together expires I expect you to treat our situation monogamously."

"I will."

He was quiet for a moment and they both looked out opposite windows. "Who is he?"

"Who?"

"The gentleman you were with this morning?"

"How do you know I was with a gentleman?" He gave her a dubious look and understanding dawned. "Oh my God, you had me followed!"

"Don't act so surprised. Do you mind telling me what you were doing all the way in lower Folsom? My man tells me you were in one of the poorest sections of the city."

"Your man?"

She was still reeling at the idea of being followed. She thought about last night and Lucian's descriptions of the pawns in the game of chess. He was the king and she was his asset and his pawns would do everything in their power to protect the queen.

"I cannot believe you had me followed! Where I went and who I was with is none of your business."

She turned away and he gripped her arm tightly, almost painfully.

"Be very careful, Evelyn. We have an agreement. Until you or I end our arrangement, you are, for all intents and purposes, in my care. I wouldn't drive my favorite car in that section of Folsom. Don't expect me to let something much more valuable go there."

"Some*thing*? Do you hear yourself? I—am—a—person! Not a thing!"

He narrowed his eyes. "I'm aware that you're a living, breathing, flesh and blood woman, Evelyn. It hasn't slipped my attention since the moment I found you rummaging through my desk."

She scoffed. "I was *not* rummaging."

"Regardless, I don't want you visiting that part of town again."

Scout turned and scowled out the window, seething. That part of Folsom was her home. *Big, stupid, rich moron!*

After several minutes Lucian said, "I spoke to Vivian."

It took her a moment to realize he was referring to Dr. Sheffield. When she did, she stilled. He could not expect sex after they just had an argument.

"She seemed very adamant that we proceed slowly. Care to tell me why?"

"I don't know what you're talking about," Scout said with feigned indifference.

"Don't play games with me, Evelyn. I want to know why Vivian's so concerned with my intentions toward you."

"Maybe she's just being nice. People *do* like me, Lucian. Maybe she liked me and is just trying to be a friend."

"She is a friend. *My* friend. Now tell me what she meant."

Her shoulders sagged and she faced him. "She meant nothing. I'm clean as a whistle so we can go on with our arrangement as planned. Whatever the reason behind her warning, I assure you, it isn't necessary. I'm a big girl and I know perfectly well what I'm getting myself into."

He contemplated her for a moment. When they arrived at the hotel he said, "No, I believe I'll wait. Dugan, please see that Ms. Keats makes it to her room safely. I'll stay here until you return."

Scout turned, shocked. "You aren't coming up with me?"

"Not tonight, Evelyn. I think I'll go out for a bit."

She wanted to throw something at him. Her nerves had been a wreck all night, and where the hell did he think he was going? Her eyes suddenly glazed with tears of frustration. She lifted her chin and turned on her heel, marching right up and over the damn red runner with gold tassels.

Once she made it back to her room, she shut the door on Dugan and threw her shoe at the wall. What was happening to her? Her trembling fingers wiped her eyes and she was appalled to find she was crying.

How silly. Almost as silly as a five-thousand-dollar dinner at an overvalued flea market showing off a hodgepodge of crap!

Scout stripped out of her dress and went to the bathroom to wash off her makeup, hating Evelyn, wanting Scout back. Sniffling, she plucked the pins from her hair and tossed them all over the vanity, some pinging to the tile floor.

She looked like the bride of Frankenstein with her hair still sprayed into place and mascara marks beneath her eyes.

"You are a jerk, Lucian Patras," she said, narrowing her eyes at the mirror. Something about being in that man's presence unhinged her, leaving her raw and vulnerable. Such self-doubt was unfamiliar and unwelcome.

Her gaze moved to her underwear and the fancy lace bra she wore. None of this was her. He may have thought she was being stubborn, but she was actually trying very hard to be what he expected. Scout stripped out of her underwear and dug through the bags of clothing. Nothing was right.

From the closet she pulled on the big terrycloth robe, then grabbed her old bag and curled up on the bed, tucking her feet beneath her. Digging deep in the inside pocket, she found the picture she was looking for. She stared at it and wiped her eyes as the tears continued to fall. She was overwhelmed by so many unfamiliar things, angry at her inability to keep up with this sort of life, and, most of all, frustrated that he'd somehow managed to affect her in such a way.

The sketch was of her and Pearl, twelve years ago. They were sitting on a bench together, a bag of all their possessions to their left. It had been raining and her mom insisted she wear that ridiculous rubber hat. Scout hated that hat.

A watery chuckle rose in her chest. She could hear her mother's voice telling her it was the hat of a famous sea captain and he'd be sad if she didn't wear it with pride. She was so full of crap. That was when her mom still acted like a mom, before Scout started calling her Pearl.

Even when she went to the tracks and talked with Pearl, she still left missing her mom. Scout hated what drugs had done to her. Her mom had never come back to her and every day Scout loved her it hurt a little more.

Scout hugged the drawing to her chest and carefully folded it back up. It was tearing where the creases were. She should find tape and fix it before it fell apart. After tucking the picture back in her bag, she lay down. The heavy covers warmed her body, but she shivered anyway.

Faces swirled behind her closed eyes. Parker and Pearl and Deborah and the scary man from the shelter. She thought about the crying baby she'd heard the other night.

Her mind randomly recalled a conversation she'd had with a

nursing mother several years ago. The mother had told Scout that her body had become so malnourished that she could no longer produce milk. Scout hated when that woman was at the shelter. Her infant would scream all night long. Every cry cut through her like a hot blade, and she'd never been so furious or felt so helpless. Scout wanted to help that starving baby and she couldn't. She hated when that woman was at the shelter, but Scout hated when she left more because she never knew what happened to her or that baby.

That was her life, people coming and going and no one sticking around long enough to ever depend on. She had been the one afraid to depend on Parker, afraid to call him friend. But now she was the one abandoning him. Would he hate her for leaving him? If he left her she'd never forgive him. It was a complicated thing, her way of thinking. She hated letting people in, but once she did and she began to care for them she never wanted to let them go.

thirteen

ROOKS AND VOYEURS

A sharp, shrill alarm sounded and Scout jerked upright. Instinctively, she reached for her bag as the alarm sounded again.

Fire?

Her eyes landed on her unfamiliar surroundings and she remembered she was in the hotel, and the annoying sound that had woken her was coming from the phone. She leaned over and answered it.

"Hello?"

"Get dressed. Something casual, but nice. Meet me out front in thirty minutes."

Scout wiped her eyes and scowled. She was still angry from last night. "Where are we going?"

"It's a surprise. Thirty minutes," Lucian said and hung up in her ear.

She replaced the phone and glared at it. After a few minutes of refusing to move, eventually she gave in and went to take a shower.

She dressed in a pair of fitted jeans and knee-high boots. The boots, although heeled, offered more support than the pumps. Finding a soft corded sweater the color of rust, she slipped that over a lacy brown camisole.

Katelyn had given her a dainty bag full of makeup the day before, and Scout sorted through the little tubes and compacts for some magic quick fix that wasn't there. Locating the mascara, she pulled out the black wand. Her eyes flickered rapidly as she tried to swab her lashes with the goopy stuff. When she finished, she wasn't pleased. Her eyes looked startling. *Witch eyes.* She tossed it back in the bag and found some powder.

There were ten different brushes. Selecting a fluffy large one to use with the powder, she dabbed the compact. Blending was a talent that took skill she lacked. Growing frustrated, she grabbed the clear gloss, slathered it over her lips, and left.

Her hair was still damp, so she twisted it into a bun as she waited for the elevator. Scout wasn't sure how she'd treat Lucian today. Part of her wanted to hurt him the way he had hurt her, but another part of her missed the way they'd been that first night. And then there was the part of her that constantly reminded her she shouldn't care that much.

There was no paying him back for the things he had given her, and her stubbornness refused to allow her to bow out at this point. If she let people like Lucian intimidate her, she'd never make it in the real world.

Squaring her shoulders, she stepped off the elevator. The lobby was politely hushed as people checked in and out. She could smell the restaurant and wondered if they'd ever dine there.

As soon as she stepped outside she recognized Dugan. She pulled the lapels of her camel coat tight against the wind and took the red runner toward the limo.

"Ms. Keats," he greeted and opened the door for her.

"Good morning, Dugan." She slid into the warmth of the car.

Lucian was waiting for her. Folding the newspaper he was read-ing, he inspected her from head to toe.

"Your hair's wet."

"And my eyes are blue. Where are we going?"

He didn't appreciate her comment. "It's November, Evelyn. Do you enjoy pneumonia?"

"Not particularly, but you didn't leave me much choice with your demands for promptness."

He looked back at his paper. "I can see this morning will be full of your charming wit."

The limo pulled away from the curb, and they rode in silence. The sound of newspaper pages turning interrupted the stillness of the ride every few minutes. The city rolled by quietly, buffeted by the sleek glass of the car, and appearing somewhat artificial.

"Care to read a section of the paper?" Lucian asked.

"No, thank you."

"We need to stop by my office before we get to where we're going."

Scout nodded her understanding.

"I plan on introducing you to some colleagues this morning, Evelyn."

"You're working?"

"I'm always working."

They arrived at a tall building in a section of the city she wasn't familiar with. The door of the limo opened and Lucian climbed out. She scooted over toward the door to follow when he turned and said, "I shouldn't be more than ten minutes." The door shut in her face.

Scout spent the time snooping around the limo and testing each button. She found an apple in a small refrigerated compart-ment and ate it. She wasn't sure what to do with the core, so she wrapped it in a napkin and held it in her lap.

When she found the radio, her fingers rolled the dial until locating a station that wasn't fuzzy. Accidentally pressing the wrong button, the music cut off and a grinding sound came on.

"Crap." She panicked, but a second later music came on again. There must be a CD in the player somewhere.

Soft, jazzy-sounding vocals filled the limo. Sitting back, she listened, realizing the words were being sung in a different language, but it was still nice. Her booted feet tapped as she waited for Lucian.

Finally the door opened and she spotted Lucian exiting the building with a stack of papers in his hands. His strides were confident and people seemed to defer to him. He climbed into the limo and smiled.

"Now we can go."

As Dugan drove she noticed the buildings growing farther and farther apart and the sidewalks becoming less populated with people. The denseness of Folsom eased and suddenly there were houses and grass and then they were speeding along a raised section of highway.

"Are we still in Folsom?"

"No."

Panic filled her as they left the city she had never been outside of. She felt powerless as if she were being whisked away without choice. A sense of getting lost choked her as her world slipped farther and farther out of view, until the tall skyscrapers she'd grown up under were nothing more than specks along the horizon.

"Evelyn?"

She didn't want to turn away from the remaining view of the city, fearing if she lost sight of it she'd never find her way back home.

"Evelyn, what's the matter?"

"You didn't tell me we were leaving the city."

"Does it matter? We'll be back by tonight." His words only slightly reassured her. "Come here."

She jerked her gaze from the window and faced him. His papers were all neatly tucked away in a briefcase and he patted the space beside him on the bench seat. Hesitantly, she looked back out the window one last time and moved to his side.

His fingers undid the buttons of her coat and slid it off her shoulders. "You're tense." His thumbs pressed into the back of her neck and rubbed in firm, but gentle circles. Her shoulders slowly relaxed as he soothed the tension out of her muscles.

His touch moved up to her bun and tentatively turned the knot of hair.

"Take this out."

Her fingers unraveled the rubber band and her hair uncoiled down her back.

"I prefer your hair down."

Fingers sifted through the brunette strands, parting and separating the long locks over her shoulders. Her hair was different since she'd had it cut, softer, smoother at the ends. Lucian continued to play with her hair until he'd coaxed her into leaning into his shoulder. His fingertips delicately traced whorls over her collarbone. It was nice.

The music played and they fell into a much more welcome silence than how the ride had started out.

"I want you to spend the night with me tonight, Evelyn."

She prided herself on hiding any physical reaction to his words. "Okay."

"I've thought about Vivian's cryptic warning and decided there's no use postponing the inevitable." She silently agreed with him.

"I assume by your presence that you still consent to our agreement."

"I won't back out," she assured him.

"Good."

They arrived at a tall iron gate that opened to a sprawling lawn. As the limousine eased slowly uphill, an enormous home came into view. It was pale yellow with rounded soffits and a terracotta roof. She moved to sit up a little straighter, and Lucian released the hold he'd kept on her for the majority of the drive.

"Is this somebody's house?"

"Yes. Mine."

She looked back at him and found honesty in his gaze.

"Do you like it?" There was a hint of vulnerability in the question, nearly hidden, but making him seem more human, less godlike.

"It's the size of a hotel."

"This one's all mine."

They parked at the curve of a cul-de-sac outside a six-bay garage. It occurred to her that she never considered much of Lucian's life outside of the city, outside of Patras Hotel for that matter. She suddenly had a terrible thought.

"Lucian?" When he didn't hear her rasp she forced herself to speak a little louder. "Lucian?"

He faced her.

"Do you have a family?"

His expression shuttered. "I have sisters and a father."

Scout relaxed, but needed to make completely sure. "Have you ever been married?"

She could not do this if there was another woman. If she was the *other* woman.

"There's no one else, Evelyn. I've been single for quite some time."

It was obvious by his tone and the set of his features no other questions were welcome. He climbed out of the car the moment Dugan opened the door. She breathed a sigh of relief. After a few deep breaths, she followed.

They walked up to a set of Gothic French doors that opened before they crossed the top step. A young woman, wearing the same dove gray gown that housekeeping wore at the hotel, held the heavy wooden door as they stepped through.

"Good morning, Mr. Patras."

Lucian removed Scout's coat and heaped the heavy wool into the maid's arms. "Good morning, Lucy. Have my guests arrived?"

"They're in the library, sir. Breakfast will be served in the dining room. Would you like me to escort your guests there?"

He undid the large buttons of his coat. "That won't be necessary. Please send coffee to the library. We'll eat in a bit. Come on, Evelyn."

Scout still held her apple wrapped in a napkin. She looked down and at the maid. She couldn't ask her to take her half-eaten apple core. Holding it low by her hip, she hoped no one would notice and followed Lucian, keeping her eyes peeled for a trash can.

The house was like a museum. Every step echoed and she was very aware of her prattling steps in the wake of his much surer paces. There was a long winding staircase made of white marble, and shutters on the inside of the windows that lined the upper floor. It was like a courtyard, but inside. Vines and bright botanical plants filled corners, and mosaic vases topped random side tables.

They approached a set of pocket doors, and masculine voices boomed as Lucian slid them apart.

"Gentlemen."

"Ah, here he is. Lucian, I was just telling Slade how I took you to the bank on the course the other day," a man with startling green eyes, golden curls, and rosy skin announced.

His gaze fell on Scout and she looked down.

"My, my, who's this?" He stepped in front of her and offered his hand. "Shamus Callahan. My friends call me James or Jamie."

That was a mouthful. She took his proffered hand. "Nice to meet you. I'm Scout."

James smiled. "Scout? What a unique name." He laughed pleasantly. "It takes a lot for a man named Shamus to say that."

Lucian stepped to her side and placed his palm at her back. "This is Evelyn Keats. She's a friend of mine from Patras Hotel."

The dark-haired man standing behind Jamie made no attempt to introduce himself. He had blue eyes and striking skin. Darker than Lucian's, his complexion was the color of warm caramel. His observant blue eyes studied her with such intensity that she fought the urge to cover herself.

"Slade, I see you made it out of the city in one piece," Lucian said as Lucy returned with a tray of coffee.

"It isn't good for my constitution to be this far out in the country."

"This is hardly the country," Lucian mumbled as he doctored up two mugs and handed her one. "And it never bothered you before. Time to get on with life, my friend."

Cradling it close to her chest, Scout stepped back from the men. She wanted to slip away, but thought it would be rude to take a seat before everyone else.

The coffee was sweeter than she usually had it. She didn't take her coffee a certain way though. When it was offered, she simply took.

"If I can't spot a cab on every corner, I've left my comfort zone. Are you planning on feeding us?"

Lucian laughed. She hadn't heard him laugh often and when he did, she savored it. She felt herself smiling beside him.

"Come on, James, I guess we better take this to the dining room before our fragile friend here faints from hunger."

Everyone replaced their barely touched coffees on the silver tray and exited the room. It struck Scout as blatantly wasteful, but also gave her a chance to ditch her apple core.

The men walked ahead of her and talked quickly of people and things she had no clue about. When they reached the dining room a man, also in familiar Patras livery but without the name-tag, pulled out a chair for her.

Plates of steaming eggs, bacon, and toast were brought out. A brightly colored bowl of fruit was placed at the corner of her placemat. There were bright green cuts of fruit, slices of some-thing peach tinged with red, and bright pink berries. It was very exotic.

The men discussed business as she focused on her meal. She realized she had a problem with eating past the feeling of fullness, but it would be a shame to waste such fine food.

"Well, you can sure put away a meal," Jamie commented with a grin and Scout blushed, aborting the last of her toast. "I can't imagine where you're hiding it. Such a little thing, you are."

"Don't be rude, James," Slade grumbled. She turned and found his sharp blue eyes analyzing her again.

Scout frowned uncomfortably. He looked at her like he knew her, but that was impossible. She would have remembered.

"Do you want some more, Evelyn?" Lucian embarrassed her by asking.

"No, thank you, I've had more than I should've."

"I like a woman who isn't afraid to enjoy a good meal," Jamie commented.

Breakfast was cleared and briefcases were popped open.

Papers slid across the table as their conversation flowed. It soon seemed all very chaotic to her. Papers traded hands and more coffee was served. A phone was brought in so that Slade could make a call, while Lucian spoke on his cell and Jamie sent a text to his secretary.

"I know I had it," Jamie said. "Nancy handed it to me just as I was packing my briefcase."

"Maybe it got mixed up with the leases," Slade said as they all rummaged through pages.

"Here, Scout, do me a favor and look through this stack for a page that says Cambridge Development on the top." Jamie slid her a stack of papers and continued to sort through the stack in front of him.

Her hands trembled as she gently slid the papers closer. With extreme care she flipped one page then another.

Sweat moistened the skin beneath her arms and she forced herself to breathe steadily.

"Here it is." The page she was holding was torn from her hands. "She was staring right at it," Slade said in a huff as he slid the paper to James.

"Thank you, Scout." James smiled apologetically at her then turned to glare at Slade.

"What kind of name is Scout, anyway?" Slade asked as he continued to loom over her.

Lucian came back into the room. She didn't recall him leaving. "Did you find it?"

With undue credit, Slade announced, "*Scout* found it."

Lucian frowned at his friend then glanced at her. "Evelyn, you okay?"

She nodded and distracted herself with stacking the papers still in front of her in a neat pile. Jamie picked up the discussion they'd been having before, and everyone's attention was eventually directed back to the business at hand. Everyone's except Lucian's.

He stood behind her chair, gently resting a large hand on her shoulder as they continued their business. She was very aware of him and he seemed to intentionally stick by her side. She wasn't sure if the action was to comfort her or to make a statement to the other men.

An hour later their business had concluded, and Slade was the first to go. He took a great deal of her tension with him. Lucian and Jamie settled into their chairs and let go of a bit of their professionalism.

"Wow, it's noon already," Jamie said. "How about a drink?"

Lucian nodded at Lucy, who was idling at the edge of the room. She nodded back with understanding and left only to return moments later with a tray.

"That will be all, Lucy."

The maid left and quietly slid the pocket doors closed. Jamie poured himself a drink and raised an eyebrow in Scout's direction.

"No, thank you," Scout said, appreciating the offer anyway.

Once they each had their drinks they eased back in their chairs and sighed. "Slade was in a mood today," Jamie commented. "Do you think it's Monique?"

"He's always in a mood." Lucian rolled back his sleeves and tossed his jacket onto an empty chair. She liked seeing him like this, rumpled and relaxed.

"So, Scout, how is it you managed to charm Lucian?"

Her mouth opened, but no words came out. She looked to Lucian and he grinned. He took a long sip of his drink then placed it on the table. Propping his arms behind his head he said, "Don't worry, Evelyn. Jamie and I have been friends since we were in diapers. We have no secrets from each other." He faced Jamie. "She works for me."

Jamie nodded. "What do you do?"

Before she could answer, Lucian said, "She pleases me."

James laughed. "I see. Do you find Mr. Patras difficult to please, Scout? I'm much easier to content than my friend here, you should know."

Heat rose under her cheeks. Lucian chuckled and grinned at her. "Come here, Evelyn."

She hesitated. The look in Lucian's eye was patient, yet indomitable. Slowly she rose on shaky legs and walked around the table until she was standing beside Lucian. She was very aware of Jamie's smiling gaze on her.

"Don't be shy," Lucian said as he took her hand and pulled her to sit on his knee.

His fingers pulled at the collar of her sweater, exposing a slight bit of skin. Her spine stiffened as his lips pressed there.

"Relax," he whispered against her neck. His mouth kissed up to her shoulder and to the curve of her neck.

She looked into Jamie's green eyes. They were no longer creased with laughter. He watched her carefully under lowered lashes, his hands folded over his chest. He was completely undisturbed by Lucian's show of affection.

Lucian's arm banded around her hips and she was pulled farther onto his lap. "I like being watched, Evelyn. Does that bother you?"

His fingers lazily traveled up and down the sweater covering her tummy. Her heart began to race. *Watched doing what exactly?*

"Jamie is a voyeur. Do you know what that means?"

When she didn't reply he said, "It means he does well with an exhibitionist as his friend."

Her lips parted as Lucian's fingers gently lifted her sweater. Jamie's gaze smoldered as he watched his friend's hand slip under her top. Lucian didn't expose her skin, but his touch was obvious.

Her sweater pulled tight over his hand as it continued to draw circles on her belly. His touch was hot over her skin.

Easing her back to his chest, his knees pressed between hers. He separated his legs, drawing her denim-clad thighs apart. His left hand moved over her hip and stopped at the apex of her thighs as his right hand landed softly over her lace-covered breast. She gasped.

"Shh, he won't see anything beneath your clothes. I'm just going to make you come."

Her body tensed as his palm pressed down over her jeans and he rocked his fingers back and forth, applying pressure, kneading the area between her legs.

Scout tried to draw her legs together, but he used his own legs to stay her. His touch grew firm, surer. Jamie quietly groaned, but her eyes remained averted from his intense stare.

Lucian's mouth continued to kiss her throat. "It feels good, doesn't it, Evelyn. You like having my hands on you, don't you?"

Her heart raced as a mixture of arousal and humiliation clogged her veins. Overwhelmed, she struggled to break his grasp, but his hold only tightened.

"Stay still."

Why was he doing this in front of someone she just met? Was he purposely trying to embarrass her? Punish her for something?

Tears prickled her eyes and she blinked. His fingers molded over her sex, spiking the pleasure that warred with her modesty. It was easier to give in than to fight him. Something told her if she said stop he would, but for some reason he wanted this and some twisted part of her wanted to prove she could give it to him, no matter the mixed emotions rioting in her head.

Forcing herself to surrender, she quietly breathed. Her body tightened and twitched in places she wasn't used to twitching. Her bottom clenched against his muscled thigh and his fingers moved faster.

"You're close. I can sense it." His voice and touch gentled her struggles.

Lucian Patras had some sort of horse-whisperer hold over her she couldn't figure out. He changed her in ways no one else seemed capable of. It made her hate him and like him a little bit more. There was no black and white here, only shadows of innuendos and seedy intentions she was too inexperienced to navigate through.

The lace was pulled away from her breast as his warm palm cupped her in its place. His thumb touched the tip of her nipple and her spine trembled. A frightened rush filled her blood as she stared at Jamie staring back at her. Lucian was breathing hard and his body was rigid beneath her.

She cried out as he suddenly pinched her. His moist lips pressed into the flesh just below her ear. "Shh, feel the pain transcend into a slow burn. Are you ready to come now?" His hand slipped out from under her sweater and he sucked two fingers into his mouth. The hand at the crotch of her jeans lifted and quickly undid the snap at her waist.

Lucian's wet fingers slipped beneath the waistband of her pants and pressed into an extremely sensitive place. A startled gasp escaped her as he rubbed over her bare flesh fast and hard. She reflexively jerked.

He held her down, pressed tightly to him, as she struggled with the intense sensations taking over her body. The hand under her shirt pinched her other nipple. His breath echoed over the shell of her ear and just before he bit down on her tender lobe, he whispered, "Come."

Her cry filled the room as her muscles locked. Moisture flooded her panties and her knees forcefully pulled together, locking Lucian's fingers between her legs. Her body throbbed and pulsed as her heartbeat filled her ears and Lucian's mouth sucked hard on her neck.

Scout didn't remember shutting her eyes, but when she opened them, Jamie's gaze locked with hers. His chest rose and fell beneath his dress shirt and he looked nothing like the good-humored man she'd met that morning. His eyes set in a narrow stare that made Scout all too aware of how vulnerable she was at the moment. Jamie suddenly seemed very much like Lucian. She recognized the predator hiding behind a friendly smile, a smile that had been replaced with parted lips. His expression was covetous.

Lucian's hand slowly pulled from between her legs. His fingers were glazed with moisture from her body. He brought them to his mouth and moaned. "Delicious, Evelyn, very sweet." He righted her clothes and briefly hugged her.

Embarrassed, she turned in his lap and pressed her face into his shoulder. He held her and kissed her temple. She was grateful her hair was down, for it created a much-needed barricade around her.

She heard Jamie stand. "Lucian, as always, it's been a pleasure. Scout, I look forward to *seeing you* again." The door slowly slid open and shut.

They were alone again.

fourteen
. . . . .

SAFE WORD

LUCIAN'S hands eased Scout back from his chest and sifted through her hair until he found her face. Tipping up her chin, he asked, "You okay?"

She couldn't look at him. "Why did you do that?"

"Did you not enjoy it?" His gaze moved over her face, taking in her upset. Softly, as if realizing how unprepared she had been for anything like that, he whispered, "I don't know. I'm sorry, Evelyn. We haven't reached that stage yet. I shouldn't have put you in that position."

Lucian Patras was not the kind of man who apologized easily. Somehow she knew that. She looked into his eyes and found nothing but sincerity. He was sorry. However, the part of his apology about not reaching that stage *yet* disturbed her. She had grown up in places where people fulfilled their bodily urges with no regard to their audience. She expected more from the upper class.

Nevertheless, there was something erotic in the act, something that created that reaction in her body. This worried her, worried her about the effect he was already having on her. She had the urge to sever any emotional link that may have stimulated such an emotionally charged result, but she couldn't pinpoint what it was. Did there have to be an essential connection for her body to react that way?

Lucian kissed her cheek and eased her off his lap. "I have to make some calls in the library. Why don't you go freshen up and then join me there." His words were confident, but she detected concern in his gaze. She nodded and went to use the bathroom.

Two hours later she was sitting on a cushioned chair, watching Lucian as he made phone call after phone call. He was like a fascinating storm she knew she should avoid, but couldn't. He moved quickly and made fast finite decisions that changed the world around him.

She analyzed his appearance. His power made him seem older than he was. He seemed much older than her, but in reality, she'd be surprised if he was over thirty-five. She thought of Jamie. He looked like he was in his thirties. If they'd been friends since they were babies, then that made Lucian about the same. How did someone that age get so much power?

Just from hearing these men work today, she'd learned that Patras was more than a local commodity. There were also Patras hotels in Europe. And she now knew Lucian did more than own a chain of hotels. He developed properties and did things with the stock market and worked on a slew of committees.

He hung up the phone and the room was suddenly quiet. "I'm sorry this has taken so much of my time today. I didn't expect to be held up here so long."

Scout closed the garden magazine she had been looking at. "That's okay. I didn't have plans," she teased.

He eased his leather chair away from his desk and lounged back, watching her. "What is it about you, Evelyn, that makes me want to go out of my way to make you smile? See, like that. When you smile you light up a room."

Warmth spread in her chest. "I like when you smile too. You don't do it enough."

He breathed in a deep breath and let it out slowly. "Well . . . you're certainly helping with that. Come on, let's get out of here."

When they returned to the limo, she grinned with delight. Lucian had one of the servants set up a chessboard for the ride home. Once they were on their way he said, "Okay, Ms. Keats, let's see how fast I can get you naked."

Scout returned his challenging glare with a smile. "You're on, Mr. Patras."

By the time they reached the city limits, she had lost her shirt, literally. She was still smiling, however, because she had managed to collect Lucian's shoes and tie.

"Check," he called as he cornered her king. Her only choice was to intervene and sacrifice her knight. She moved her piece, recognizing that the game would be over very soon.

"I'll take that lovely bra, Ms. Keats." A chill spread over her shoulders as she met his gaze. "Don't even try it. Last time I let you get away with those puppy dog eyes, but not this time. You should've protected your king better."

Moving her pawn she huffed. "Fine."

Reaching around her back, she undid the clasp and slowly slid the straps down her arms. Her breasts pulled tight as the cooler air touched her flesh. Taking a deep breath, she sat up straight and faced Lucian.

He stared at her with unblinking eyes as his hand moved one of his pieces. She frowned at the board. His move was foolish, but she wasn't going to give him the chance to take it back. Her bishop slid over and knocked out his rook.

He nodded in approval and without a word began unbuttoning his shirt. His eyes bored into her, and she suddenly realized what he was doing. Once his chest and arms were bare he moved his queen. "Check."

He hadn't even glanced at the board, but he was right. He had her in check again. She examined the board, curling her shoulders in and trying to hide under her hair. She was very self-conscious of him watching her. Her lips pursed. "If I move my queen you'll only take it. I refuse to give you my panties."

"There's always a consequence," he rasped, shifting as if he were uncomfortable in the tight space.

His abs formed a neat little stack of ridges, and his belly button was perhaps the most perfect belly button to ever exist. Wiry, dark hair traveled from his navel and disappeared somewhere beneath his pants. Oddly, she found his body exquisite and mesmerizing, where she found her own reflection lacking and flawed. She liked seeing him partially dressed, something she hadn't expected to enjoy.

"This isn't fair. You've had way more practice," she whined, crossing her arms over her breasts.

"You were quite aware of the rules when we started."

His fingers closed over her wrist and pulled her arms away, exposing her breasts once again. She watched as his drowsy eyes stared at her chest. Why did men have such obsessions with boobs? His fingers twitched and she scooted back an inch.

He looked at her then, stared into her eyes, warning her not to move again. Her chest filled with quick breaths as his hand slowly rose and cupped her breast. Warm heat engulfed her, and her lashes lowered. Her eyes opened as his fingers closed over the nipple of her other breast. She gazed down at his hands touching her body and found the image very erotic.

His palms slid to her sides, thumbs teasing the turgid tips, and suddenly she was being lifted over his lap. Her knees pressed into the soft leather seating on either side of his hips as he settled her thighs over his.

Hands squeezed over her hips and slowly traveled up her bare back. Lucian pulled her to him as his mouth crashed over hers. His tongue seared into her mouth, hot and wet. His hands gripped her to him, and she found her own hands holding the thick flesh of his shoulders tight. She didn't want him to let go.

Their heads tilted as they took from each other. Lucian growled as she tried getting a little creative and lost their rhythm a bit. Taking hold of her neck, he took back his control and showed her what it was to be kissed soundly.

Her thighs squeezed down on him. It was difficult to stay still. Scout pressed up on her knees, wanting to get closer. He directed her hips back down only to help them rise again. Guiding her motions, he remained in complete control. When she drew up on her knees another time, he ripped his mouth from hers and latched onto her breast.

Her head tipped back and she moaned. "Oh my God, Lucian!" Sensation burst inside of her.

He wasn't delicate with her. He sucked her flesh hard, bruising the tender tips, but it felt too good to ask him to be gentle. His mouth moved from one breast to the other and then back to her lips. It was a cycle she never wanted to end.

Scout thought about that morning and what he had done to her. She wanted to feel like that again. Boldly, she reached around to where he gripped her hips and nudged his hand. She closed her palm over his hand and directed it between her thighs. He pulled his mouth from hers and pressed his forehead to her shoulder. As he panted he looked down at where she had moved his hand.

Suddenly she was being flipped over, and the cool leather upholstery pressed into her back. Lucian dropped to his knees on the floor of the car and peeled her panties down her legs. Her heart raced as she watched him look at her there, completely bare, nothing to cover herself with.

"God you're beautiful." He kissed her hip and licked up to her breasts. His strong fingers massaged her ass, and then his mouth was between her legs.

"Lucian, no!"

She reached for his head as his tongue licked her slit. All of her pleasure vanished, suddenly replaced with extreme mortification.

Scout squeezed his head with her thighs and he yanked back.

"Stop." The command fell from his lips like a whip cracks through the air, sharp and precise.

He wrenched her knees apart and glared at her. His gaze was hard and had her shrinking away as if he'd slapped her.

"Why are you here?" he asked with intent. When she said nothing he barked, "Answer the question!"

"Because you asked me to be," she whispered, a little frightened.

"And how did I ask you to come to me? What were my conditions?"

Why was he acting like this? "Prepared. You get control."

"This is not a game, Evelyn. I either have the control when it comes to sex or it doesn't happen. If you can't agree to that I'll have Dugan gather your things and deliver them to your home and our agreement will be over. I will not *ever* tolerate being told no by my lover."

"But I'm not your lover," she whispered, and he looked at her menacingly, one last time, then sat up.

He retrieved his shirt and began to get dressed. She wasn't sure what was happening. He kept changing the rules. The weight of her sweater suddenly on her thighs made her cringe. What was she doing?

Dressing was a shameful experience. Each item of clothing acted as a reminder of how far she had fallen. By the time she zipped her boots, she was blinking back tears. Being whatever she was supposed to be to him was simply too hard.

She had never been so happy to see Patras Hotel before. She'd go change her clothes, grab her bag, and go. Tomorrow she'd beg Tamara to give her her old hours back. When the doors opened to the penthouse floor, Lucian went to the private elevators and she walked briskly toward her room. He cursed and called her name. She walked faster.

As she dug her key out of her pocket she saw him gaining on her. Thankfully she unlocked the door on the first try and had the satisfaction of slamming it in his face.

"Evelyn, open the door."

"Go away."

Disappointingly, that's all it took. He sighed and she heard his muffled steps walk away. He didn't persevere, didn't try to convince her further.

Once Scout got over the sting of being so quickly discarded, she began to pack. She rummaged through the drawers, putting any practical items aside, items she could carry with her, wear, or sell. She wasn't taking the majority of the clothes with her, because she simply couldn't lug it all, but she could at least put them back in the bags and boxes, so returning them wouldn't be a hardship for whomever got that job.

Pursing her lips, she contemplated her belongings. Were they truly hers? She hadn't met her side of the bargain. She didn't steal. Convincing herself that the items were likely inconsequential to Lucian, she stifled any protests from her conscience and stuffed them into a bag.

Her bed was made and her bags were packed. She tied her old sneakers and sighed as she placed her warm coat on the comforter. She'd need that once winter hit. There was a quiet beep, and then she heard the knob turning. Her jaw unhinged when Lucian stepped inside the room and slammed the door.

"What are you doing here? You can't just barge into someone's room!"

He looked around dramatically, taking in the walls, ceiling,
and floor. "I'm sorry. I thought this was my hotel."

Exasperated, she grabbed her bags and snapped, "Fine, stay.
I'm leaving." He gripped her arm and pressed her into the wall
before she could get to the door. "Get off of me, Lucian."

"You don't want to leave," he whispered, boxing her in with
his body.

"Yes. I do."

"Liar."

He was unbearable. Challenging him was like swimming up-
stream in a lead vest. She simply didn't have the energy. Her body
slackened. "I don't understand you."

"I'm very complicated," he whispered almost humorously.

"You're beyond complicated. I've never met anyone as frustrating as you. You can't expect me to be what you want if you
constantly change your expectations."

"I told you what I want."

She scoffed. "You told me to be on time, dress appropriately,
provide company, and stay away from lower Folsom. Other than
that I'm flying blind."

The corner of his mouth quirked up. "Don't go."

"Why should I stay?"

"Because you like me."

She did like him, the big jerk. The jury was still out on whether
or not that was a good thing, but that didn't make it any less true.
She liked the way he made her laugh and distracted her from all the
terrible things she was used to coping with, but at the same time he
somehow had the ability to make her feel terrible about herself. She
never second-guessed herself until she was around Lucian.

"This isn't going to work."

"Why not?"

"Because I don't know what it is you want!"

He suddenly pulled away and dragged her toward the bed. He sat down and tugged her until she sat beside him. He wouldn't let go of her hand.

"I'm fucked up, Evelyn. I need to have things a certain way and if I'm ever going to care about someone again I need to know I have complete control."

"Again?"

"Yes. Again. I don't usually share my past with others and I don't intend on changing. Suffice it to say I lost someone very important to me once and she'd still be here if she had listened to me and done as I said."

"Lucian, you can't control everything. What good would it be to have a relationship with someone who's had every bit of individuality stripped from them?"

"I *want* you to be an individual. That's not what I'm saying."

"Then explain to me what it is you want," she said, truly wanting to understand.

"I want your submission."

"My submission?"

"Yes. I want to possess you in a way no one else can or will. I want to own your body and I want you to surrender it to me willingly. I want to be able to spoil you and treat you, all in return for the comfort of knowing you'll be there waiting at the end of my day. I want to take care of you, but I also want you to take care of my needs in a way no one else can. I want you to trust me, Evelyn, to make the right choices for you."

She swallowed and tried to find her voice. That was a whole lot of expectations.

"Why me?"

"Because I like you. You're feisty, but also a natural submissive—"

She knew what *submissive* meant. And she wasn't that. She'd been running her own life since she could walk. "Lucian, I am *not* submissive. You have no idea what I'm like outside of your world."

"But you are, Evelyn. I recognized it the first time I saw you at my desk. You don't even have to try, and when you do surrender to my will, you do so with absolute grace."

She shook her head, her gaze climbing over the enormous stack of boxes at the wall. "I don't know you well enough to trust you that way. I don't trust anyone."

"Give it time. I promise I'll never do anything that puts you in danger. I'm a good protector, Evelyn, of that I'm certain."

If only he realized how much she wanted a protector, how badly she wanted to agree to everything he proposed. In time, if she could give Lucian what he needed, he could help her save Pearl and maybe even help Parker get back on his feet.

But the emotional surrender he was looking for wasn't something she could command. It was a useless negotiation chip because she had no control over her trust for others. It either existed or didn't. And all of her life, with every person she ever allowed herself to get mildly close to, it never had existed. Maybe she wasn't capable of such complete trust. Maybe she could fake it, use willpower to agree to the things he wanted no matter how it tore her up inside. If it wasn't real, then she wouldn't lose her head like some romantic fool. She'd know exactly what she was agreeing to at all times.

"Lucian, what you said in the limo about telling you no—"

"In bed. I do not accept being told no in bed," he clarified.

"But what if you do something I don't like."

"I'd never hurt you, Evelyn."

She rubbed her head wearily. "Physically maybe, but you can't take away my right to say no. I could never submit to that level. I just don't have it in me."

"Then we'll have a safe word."

"A what?"

His gaze grew hopeful, his eyes softening further, a hint of color returning to his face. "A safe word. A word you wouldn't normally say in intimate situations. You say that and everything stops. It'll be your ticket to end our contract. Game over. All you have to do is breathe it and I'll let you go."

Everything was always so final with him. He didn't have gears. There was no slowdown or reverse. It was full steam ahead or nothing.

Scout thought about what he said. She wasn't sure what had happened in his past to make control such an unbending need of his. For some reason it made sense that Lucian would perform best in that sort of dynamic. The question was, could she?

Resigned, she knew she couldn't just walk away at this point. She'd never forgive herself for turning down the opportunities he offered just because she was too afraid to try. It was sex. Sex was physical. She could do that, surrender her body, but hold tight to her emotions.

She also couldn't deny that he piqued certain unknown appetites. When Lucian kissed her, things happened. She was curious what else there was, what else he could make her feel. So long as she kept her mind grounded in the physical and avoided the emotional, she should be able to do this.

Sighing, she asked, "What would the word be?"

His smile was a true expression of deep satisfaction. It spread over his face slow and beautiful like a sunrise, chasing away the darkness. "That, my dear, is your choice."

The perfect word skated off her tongue before she even realized she had chosen it. "Checkmate."

fifteen
·····

TRUST

LUCIAN carried a bag of Scout's personal items onto the elevator as she held her housekeeping uniform. "I need to use your iron when we get upstairs. This is horribly wrinkled."

"I'll have someone come pick it up for dry cleaning."

She grimaced. "You're not sending out my housekeeping uniform for someone from housekeeping to clean. That's ridiculous. It can't be that difficult to iron."

He shrugged as they stepped off. "Never tried."

Weren't they a pair? He placed her bag on a chair in the seating area and flipped through a pile of mail on his desk. Scout scrutinized her uniform and brushed over some of the creases.

"You know I could have another one delivered for you, but I'm not going to do that because you know how I feel about you working in the first place."

Great. This again.

"If you don't want me working at Patras, I'll go get a job somewhere else."

Tossing the mail back on the messy desk, he took the uniform out of her hands and hung it from a sconce on the wall. He turned her until she was facing him. "I don't want you to work at all. I can provide everything you need."

"Lucian, that isn't practical. I need spending money."

"Why do you need money?"

She rolled her eyes and countered, "Why do you?"

"So that I can take care of you."

"Smart-ass." She carried her bag into the guest room and set her black shoes out for the morning after she unloaded her toiletries.

"Seriously, Evelyn, if you need money I'll give it to you. Just tell me how much you need." He gathered up her cosmetic bag and carried it into the master bath. He returned and picked up her sneakers and carried them into the master bedroom.

"What are you doing?" she finally asked when he picked up her bag.

"What are *you* doing? I told you where you were sleeping. My bed's that way."

Okay, then.

After she unpacked her minimal amount of belongings and discovered ironing was not difficult, but a pain in the ass, they sat at the small dining area in the corner and had dinner. Lucian ordered almond-crusted fish with rice and green vegetables. It was delicious.

The closer their meal drew to an end, the more reality seeped in. She was going to have sex with Lucian Patras. Tonight.

The thought was too surreal for Scout to actually form any kind of anxiety over. Curiosity kept her moving forward. The minutes ticked by and she figured she'd better just go with it. She did need to shower though.

When she came out of the bathroom, the master bedroom was empty. She smiled when she noticed a long black nightgown lying on the turned-down bed. Lucian must've run down to her room and brought the silk gown back.

Scout untied the towel around her head, glad she decided not to get her hair wet again. Sleeping on wet pillows sucked. She'd done that too many times in her life after using the facilities at the shelter just before curfew. After quietly shutting the door, she removed her robe and picked up the gown. It whispered over her skin like a delicious secret.

She hung the robe and waited. What now? Looking at the bed, she debated climbing in there and waiting for Lucian. The penthouse was set in dim lighting and bathed in silence.

Creeping past the door to the master bedroom on bare feet, she saw Lucian sitting at his desk. He was again wearing black silk pants. The sight of him in those pants with reading glasses low on his nose as he made notes inside a book made her smirk. They matched.

She cleared her throat and he looked up, definitely taking his attention away from whatever he was doing. He leaned back in his chair and she sauntered over to him. Taking her hand, he silently directed her to turn for him. His hands caught her hips and stilled her once she completed a full revolution.

Hands so large they spanned her waist, his thumbs dragged over the soft black silk covering her belly, causing sleek ripples. She removed his glasses and peeked through them before gently placing them on the cluttered desk.

They simply stared at each other for a moment, and then she leaned in and pressed her lips to his. He drew a deep breath through his nose and pulled her closer as his lips slanted over hers. She gasped into his mouth as he stood and lifted her with him.

The black gown gathered around her thighs. She wrapped her legs around his hips as he carried her to the master bedroom. He possessed such capable strength both physically and emotionally. The cool wall pressed into her back and she arched, pressing her front into his. His skin was so warm it practically burned her exposed flesh.

While one hand glided up her back, his other palm cupped her bottom. His mouth twisted and worked over hers and she found herself drowning in everything Lucian. He smelled delicious. Her cheeks burned from where his five o'clock shadow rasped against her softer skin.

They twirled, and he was moving again. Scout's arms wrapped tightly around his neck and broad shoulders, pulling her higher and tighter against his front. His tongue stole into her mouth and owned her. He took and she gave. In those minutes, the way he made her feel, he was like a drug. She wanted to give him everything. She would sell her soul if it meant the difference between his continuing and stopping. She wanted him in her, on her, running through her veins, heating her blood.

The sensation of falling took over, and she was suddenly cocooned in softness. Cool satin sheets slid across her back. She slid every which way he pulled her. His hot mouth sucked at the tender flesh of her neck below her ear as he settled on top of her. Nerves along her spine came alive and sang as his breath washed over her sensitized skin.

The straps of her gown were yanked over her shoulders, the slick material twisting at her belly. When the cool air caressed her breasts, her nipples puckered. Lucian's wet mouth drew upon the tips masterfully. Her body lifted into him wanting more, more, more.

"My god, I need to be inside of you," he whispered over her skin.

The bulk of his body filled the space between her legs. The warm muscles of his thighs pressed into hers and she realized he was no longer wearing pants. His fingers wrestled with the long nightgown wrapped around her knees and thighs, pushing it out of the way.

Need doubled inside of her. His hips came down into the cradle of her sex, and she felt him. Her body adjusted to accommodate the breadth of his hips. He was hard and smooth, hot. It would be soon. Her body wept for him. His hands were everywhere. He owned her then, took and gave pleasure unendingly.

Scout arched and moaned as he plumped her breasts and sucked hard. His hand worked lower over her body, a steady touch, caressing, kneading, never letting go. An ache formed in the pit of her belly. She could only describe it as need. A different kind of hunger than what she was used to.

His long fingers coasted over her dewy folds, and then he was probing. The intrusion was unexpected and awkward, but she didn't want him to stop. She waited for her body to adjust to the unfamiliar touch. His touch penetrated and sunk into her. She stifled a grunt of shock. It wasn't what she expected, but he was moving again before she had time to process.

His finger slipped in and out of her. Everything was slick and damp. She was being stretched and her body constricted over him. He was thicker now. She thought it was only his hand but worried she had somehow missed something. His touch became hurried. She couldn't stop the small noises that escaped her throat.

"I have to have you, Evelyn. I'm sorry, I can't wait any longer."

Cool air blanketed her and the absence of his weight struck her like a layer of flesh being ripped away. A drawer opened and slammed and he was back. The soft sound of foil tearing met her ears, and then he was nudging her knees wide, wider than before. Her hips stretched and he fit himself against her sex.

The sensation of flesh on flesh was interrupted by glossy latex. He separated her folds, and her mind retracted as he breached her opening. It was definitely his fingers before, because this was much larger.

"You're so tight," he whispered as he slowly rocked his hips.

Her mind had become too alert. Her arousal waned and she wanted him to bring it back. He softly grunted as he made shallow dips, poking her tender insides. Burning. A different kind. Nothing like the inner heat he stirred inside of her. This was a fire that blazed from the outside in. Nothing pleasant about it.

Friction built, detracting from the memory of the smooth glide they'd enjoyed only moments ago. Her temples grew damp with perspiration as he pressed in, burning her opening and stretching her painfully.

Scout bit her lip and when he thrust hard she whimpered. Her body stiffened like a corpse as he breathed into her shoulder.

"Jesus, Evelyn, just give me a minute . . ."

Tears leaked from the corners of her eyes and her mouth opened, but her sob was silent, trapped in her throat. She pressed her eyes shut and tried to pretend she was somewhere else.

Checkmate. Checkmate.

Lucian began to rock again and the pain subsided slightly. She let out a hard breath and his mouth kissed the corner of her lips. The more he pumped his hips forward the easier it became. Soon he was sliding in and out of her with ease. Pain fading, she slowly unclenched.

She realized she was holding his shoulders in a death grip and let her hands go lax. His hands found hers, but he didn't hold them. Rather, he wrapped his long fingers around her wrists and pressed them at her sides into the thick, cushiony bed. A touch of fear and helplessness surged through her, blurred by the unfamiliar presence of another person inside of her. Nothing was as she expected.

She forced her eyes open. His body arched over hers like a

wave, building and receding. His eyes had gone completely dark and his thick lashes hung low. His muscles bunched as his body plowed into hers and his chest wore a glistening sheen of perspiration.

His hands released hers and he reached down to where their bodies connected. He touched her there and she cried out at the long-awaited pleasure.

"Yes, Evelyn, let me hear you."

His fingers nudged her flesh in fast concise movements. The effect was quick and intense, washing away a great deal of her confusion and fear. Her body tightened around him and he grunted, his hips pumping faster.

"Come for me," he whispered, and there was a sudden release.

Her sex stuttered and spasmed around the part of him buried deep inside of her. She cried out as a wave broke over her, bathing her folds and easing his way. He probed faster. His fists gripped her thighs, pulling her into him as if he was not coming at her fast enough. The more he pushed into her, the longer the sensation lasted.

Slick and wet, together they fit, until finally he thrust hard and held himself buried deep inside of her. A guttural moan left his chest and his shoulders quivered. For the briefest second, she felt as though she was holding him and saw him as completely vulnerable. It was peculiar to see that flash of him so emotionally bared, unnatural and somehow secret. She blinked and breathed. That seemed the only function she had in the moment.

Lucian's shoulders rose and fell as he caught his breath. They were hot and sticky and covered in sweat. The silk gown had become like a tourniquet around her stomach that she needed to remove. Slowly, her body reconnected with her mind. Lucian's cock was softening, and little by little the pressure inside of her eased.

Her muscles were sore, and the tender skin between her thighs felt abused and messy. She wanted to clean herself up. Briefly, her mind touched on the fact that she'd just given herself to this man because he bought her pretty things and held the promise of better things for her and Pearl. She refused to examine that thought while he was still inside of her.

It was pleasant for a time, Lucian and her. When he kissed her, she liked it. Scout liked the way he touched her breasts and when he made her body tighten and release . . . it was insane. Sex, however, the actual act of intercourse . . . that she could do without.

Her damp skin was cooling, and she shivered. Lucian sighed, and then he withdrew from her. Her insides felt plumbed. He kissed her lips quickly and then stood. The chill of his absence weighed over her skin, seeming to take on a life of its own.

The light from the master bath flipped on. A toilet flushed and the rush of running water sounded. So clinical, lacking any sense of intimacy she may have expected. Gingerly, she rolled to the side of the bed and sat up. Her limbs ached and her muscles weren't working right. Her arms awkwardly slid back through the straps of the gown, and she stood. Walking as if her pelvis had been stretched, she eventually made it to the hall. Scout inched her way to the powder room, ran cool water over a washcloth, and cautiously cleaned her body.

When she returned to the master bedroom, Lucian was standing in front of the bed with his back toward her. She wasn't sure what people said after sex, so she quietly walked over to the bed and began climbing onto the mattress. She froze when she saw the expression on his face.

His eyes blazed intensely and stared unblinking. His shoulders rippled with tension and his fist clenched until his knuckles were white. He was furious.

"Lucian?"

His gaze jerked to hers and he practically growled. "Are you hurt?"

Scout took quick inventory of her body. She was sore, but not hurt. She just needed to sleep and she'd probably feel better in the morning. "No, I'm fine—"

"Then what the hell is that?" His finger shot out like a blade and pointed to a dark skid on the light satin sheets.

Oh my God!

Her mouth opened almost as wide as her eyes. Mortification choked her as she looked down at the evidence of her virginity smeared across his expensive sheets.

"I'll—I'll wash them." She quickly began ripping the sheets from the bed. Tears blurred her eyes and she was suddenly being jerked by her wrists in front of him.

"You were a fucking virgin?" The look of complete revulsion on his face when he said the word as if it were a curse crushed her.

She quickly rallied her dignity and got right in his face. "I *was*."

He released her arms so fast she practically stumbled backward. Through gritted teeth he growled, "How old are you?"

"What?"

"How old are you?" he roared. "You told me you were twenty-seven. I know that's bullshit. Your paperwork said you were twenty-two. Is that a lie too?"

She stared at him, just stared.

"Answer me!"

She jumped then quietly answered, "I'm twenty-two years old."

He shut his eyes and gave a humorless laugh. "A twenty-two-year-old virgin?"

"It's true. So what? I'm an adult. You didn't rape me. What's the problem?" She was growing more self-protective by the minute.

"The problem is I don't believe you," he seethed. He was no longer shouting, but she preferred him yelling at her to the icy calm he spoke to her with now. Those whispered words seemed underscored with the creak of heavy walls slamming up between them. The space flanked by them grew, though neither of them moved.

"Well, that's your problem then, because I'm telling you the truth."

"When's your birthday?" he snapped. When she didn't answer, he glared at her. "Well?"

"I don't know," she admitted pathetically. "I was born in the winter twenty-two years ago. I don't know what month." He suddenly ripped the top blanket off the bed and marched out of the room. "Where are you going?"

"I'm sleeping on the couch. You can have the guest room."

Scout didn't know how to cope with the unexpected pain accompanying this disappointment. He simply abandoned her there as though she was not worth the trouble. Her lip quivered and she blinked rapidly. She felt ashamed and used, but the worst feeling came from his admitted lack of trust.

This was never going to work. She was leaving tomorrow.

She didn't cry. There was no point. Her hands worked at removing the soiled linens as her mind replayed his words like some sort of loop of torture. She washed the sheets in the tub, never once letting a single tear fall.

sixteen
·····

GONE

S COUT left her makeup on the counter of the vanity, zipped her
bag, and crept out of the bedroom. Stopping at Lucian's desk,
the first place she had met him, she wished she could leave him a
note but figured it was for the best that she couldn't. Approaching
the door, she turned and looked back at his sleeping face one last
time. His black eyes were watching her.

"Sneaking out?"

Keep it simple. Keep it honest. "I have to go to work."

"I'll arrange for lunch to be sent up after your shift," he said,
not bothering to sit up.

Scout nodded. "Thank you, Lucian." She turned and left.

Work dragged. Her schedule was incredibly light and she suspected Lucian had done something to make it that way. By noon
she was dusting the same furniture in the common areas that she
dusted that morning. When her shift was over she went to the
basement to get her bag and slipped out the back entrance of the
hotel.

Paranoia that she was being followed hit her the minute she

stepped into the sunlight. Her legs quickly propelled her forward for a few blocks. Blood pumped through her veins, which helped to warm her body, but after she'd traveled about a mile her face was flushed from the cold and her fingers were chilled and starting to chap. She shifted her bag and pulled out her hoodie. After the sweatshirt was over her uniform she continued on her way.

St. Christopher's wouldn't be opening its doors for at least five hours. She had a good idea of a few places Parker might be, but she didn't want to waste any time. She hadn't seen Pearl in days and her worry had become almost too much to bear.

"Hey!"

Her skin stiffened. Scout turned and saw Dugan coming after her. She pivoted and ran.

Her legs pumped hard over the pavement. Ripping around a corner, she ducked into an alley. Her heart raced and she waited, too afraid to peek behind her. Heavy footsteps fell and a flash of black leather ran by. Waiting a few seconds, looking to see Dugan running in the direction she had led him, Scout pulled up her hood and went the other way.

Her cheeks were frozen when she got to the tracks. Slipping under the open garage door, she moved quickly to the hall where she'd find Pearl. The mill smelled of burning leaves, and there were many more residents now that winter had fully arrived. Scout passed a man tying off his arm as his companion pulled the end of a dirty needle over a battered spoon. She cringed and kept walking.

As she turned the corner into Pearl's hall, there was a soft flickering glow seeping from her door, and she was glad her mother had the sense to make herself a fire. She slowed her steps so as not to startle her. She turned the corner and found her hunched over a mirror sifting through a fresh batch of H with a razor.

When Pearl heard her she turned, her weathered, emaciated face vicious. Pearl shot her arm holding the razor out, as if to ward off a thief, and cradled her supply with her other arm. Scout stilled by the door and gave her a moment to recognize her.

"Go way," she mumbled.

"Momma, it's me, Scout."

Pearl narrowed her eyes and glared at her. "You're too fat to be Scout. She just a lil' thing."

"Pearl, it's me." Scout stepped forward slowly and lowered herself to her knees. "See?" She pulled her drawing of them out of her bag. Pearl stilled and stared at it.

"Where you get tha'?" she slurred. It was obvious she was already high.

"It's us. I got it from the man who drew it. Do you remember?"

Her mother's brittle laugh was slow and then too enthusiastic. "Scout hated that hat."

She smiled. "Yes, I did."

Pearl's dirty fingers went back to separating her stash. Her movements were painfully slow and unsteady. Dried blood crusted with the filth already clogging the little canyons of wrinkles on her brown fingers. Scout looked to the corner and saw the soaps she'd brought her a few days ago.

Once her mother had her supply in order and tucked away on her person, she found a bowl in the pushcart. It was dirty, but would have to do. She reached into her bag for a washcloth and poured some rainwater Pearl had collected into the bowl.

She scooted as close as Pearl would let her and drew her attention. "You makin' som'in?"

"I'm going to help you wash your hands."

"My baby does that when she visits."

"Does she?" Scout's throat tightened.

She carefully bathed her mother's fingers, hands, and arms.

Pearl chatted about a man she met by the water that Scout assumed was a figment of her imagination, and she also told Scout about how she was mad her daughter didn't visit anymore. She assured her mother that her daughter loved her and fought back her emotions. Life was quite unfair at times.

By the time she finished with Pearl's arms she was on her fourth bowl of water, and the little bar of soap was merely a sliver of black. Scout didn't want to use all Pearl's water, so she rinsed the cloth and washed her mother's face. Enough.

When she left, Pearl waved her away as if she were a stranger or a pesky stray dog. She didn't thank Scout and Scout didn't expect her to. Her mother had begun to nod out toward the end of her visit, and she promised herself she'd stay away, for her own good, for at least four days this time.

Looking into her mother's lifeless eyes and seeing not a speck of recognition was agony. She didn't know how many more visits like that she could take.

It was still light out when Scout arrived at St. Christopher's. There were cars in the parking lot of the old school, which was unusual, but not unheard of. The shelter had a board of trustees that kept it operating and dissuaded the township when they tried to close the shelter's doors permanently.

It was an ongoing battle for those who ran St. Christopher's to keep its doors open. Last winter had been a nightmare, never knowing if one day they'd return only to find the doors locked and the fancy billboard of a strip mall coming soon.

Seeing the cars there made her anxious. Winter was here. If they were going to shut the shelter down, they could at least wait until spring. She waited on the abandoned brick flowerbed beside the steps of the school. The cars parked along the dilapidated chain-link fence were all new and shiny. She was certain there was a meeting going on with the board.

Shivers transcended to a full-body seizure by the time the doors finally opened and the meeting let out. Scout cursed herself for not changing into her jeans before leaving the hotel, but her humiliation urged her to escape quickly and she hadn't been thinking. Already, the effects of living in the lap of luxury were affecting her common sense and making her forget the need for practicality. Curled into her sweatshirt, she tried to find a hidden pocket of body warmth. It crossed her mind that Lucian would be aware by now she wasn't coming back.

A few women bustled out of the building, followed by a man in an expensive trench coat with shiny leather shoes. He looked vaguely familiar. As he slowed, he removed his phone from his pocket and stood for a moment to press a few buttons. That's when she recognized those piercing eyes. Slade.

Shit. She ducked her head so he wouldn't recognize her. Out of her peripheral she saw him walk away.

"Holy shit! Scout! You're back."

Goddamn it Parker!

Scout looked up and behind a smiling Parker stood Slade, staring at her through narrow blue eyes.

"Hey, Parker," she mumbled, standing up and walking quickly through the doors of the school.

"Where you going? Aren't we gonna eat? Scout, wait up . . ." He followed her into the shadowed hall of the school. "What's going on . . . ?" His question faded as he followed her gaze. "You know that guy?"

"Not really."

Slade stared into the shadows after them and then turned and climbed into his car. When he pulled away she breathed a huge sigh of relief. Turning to Parker, she smiled.

"So . . . looks like I'll be staying here again," she said with false cheer. "Let's eat."

seventeen

INTRUDER

SCOUT awoke with a start and her back protested against the hard tile floor. Something was going on. It took a moment for her sight to adjust to the dark shadowy room. Eyes wide, she studied the door of the gymnasium. Bodies lay out like guests of a morgue after a natural disaster, creating an obstacle course around her.

Unseen voices carried over the sound of bodies breathing. She listened. She couldn't make out the words being said, but she sensed the hostility of the situation.

"Shit."

Scout quickly untied the shoelace around her wrist. Her fingers fumbled over the knot. The voices grew louder, coming closer.

"Fuck, fuck, fuck!" she hissed.

The knot came loose and she turned onto her knees. Rushing with fumbling fingers, she untied the laces attached to her bag's zipper. Footsteps echoed in the hall.

She recognized George's voice. "Sir, you can't go in there. If you don't leave, I'll call the police."

More voices added to the commotion, but others had begun to rouse. Moving blankets and whispered questions made it impossible to hear one thing clearly over another.

When the knot around her zipper came loose, she hurried to slip on her unlaced shoes. Preparing to sling her bag over her arm and haul ass out of there, grabbing Parker on her way, she turned.

"Evelyn!"

"Sir, you can't—"

"Scout!" Parker yelled as Lucian turned and grabbed George by the collar. She worried for George's heart condition, but Lucian released him the moment Parker tore into the gym. "Scout, run!"

What happened next had everybody screaming. Lucian grabbed Parker and Parker turned and punched Lucian right in the nose. Women screamed, men shouted, babies cried, and suddenly Dugan and Slade were there as well.

Scout lowered her shoulders and pulled up her hood, trying to remain unseen. Parker was pushed aside roughly and Lucian marched over mats as women from the shelter scurried out of his way. The gym was dark aside from the light spilling from the hall.

Lucian approached a woman with long dark hair. She gasped as he drew her close and he discarded her quickly.

Parker pushed away from Slade and shouted, "Scout, get out of here!"

She made to stand. Lucian towered over the fright-filled room and looked around. "Evelyn, don't move."

She froze. The sound of heavy dress shoes clicking over the linoleum came close until she found herself, once again, staring into their shiny surface.

"We're leaving."

Scout looked up at Lucian. He looked terrible. His hair was a mess and tension gave his dark eyes a haggard look. Parker skidded up behind him and jumped between them.

"Get away from her," Parker growled and Lucian cocked his head.

"Aren't you cute? Move."

Parker's eyes narrowed into a menacingly evil expression she had never seen before. "Fuck you."

"Evelyn, you have one minute to get your ass out of this building and into my limo. One second longer and I'll haul you out myself."

She didn't understand why he'd come looking for her. She gave him an excuse to let her go. He clearly didn't want an inexperienced virgin, or recently devirginized woman, in his bed. And now he knew exactly where she had come from. Her many kept secrets were getting exposed faster than she was comfortable with. Scout didn't like being so transparent.

Rather than cause any more of a scene, she figured it best to go with him. She'd let him say his piece. This was more about her leaving without permission than the fact she'd gone. He could have the last word and then she'd return to St. Christopher's tomorrow, all back to the way things had always been. But she couldn't afford to piss him off. She didn't need to look for a new job on top of all this.

Scout gently laid her hand on Parker's sleeve.

His pleading green eyes met hers. "Don't go anywhere with this asshole, Scout. You don't have to do a damn thing. He's not taking you anywhere."

"Parker," she said softly. "It's okay. He's my boss."

"That doesn't make him the boss of you."

"Wanna bet? Thirty seconds," Lucian said.

"Parker, listen to me." She forced him to turn and face her. Her friend was tense and ready to spring. "This is Lucian Patras. He owns the hotel. He's . . ." she sighed. "My friend."

"Ten seconds."

Parker looked at her with such desperation in his eyes. He whispered, "Don't go with him, Scout."

What a disaster. "I can't stay here, Park."

"Time's up, Evelyn."

She reached for her bag and Parker stayed her hand. Lucian caught his arm and growled, "You don't touch her."

"*Lucian!* Knock it off," she hissed and brushed his hand off of Parker's arm. "Listen to me, Park. Everything's fine. I'll be fine. I shouldn't have come back here. I need to go. I'll come find you in a few days." It should take that long to say her good-bye to Lucian Patras. "Do me a favor and if you get a chance—"

"I know, check on Pearl. I will."

He looked back at Lucian then turned to her and whispered, "Be careful, Scout. They aren't like us. Don't let them make you believe they are and get yourself hurt."

She smiled sadly at her friend. He would never leave this place because he'd been on the other side before and, in his mind, had failed. He'd never escape this world until he started believing he was good enough.

"I'll be all right."

She walked past him, lugging her bag, and Lucian grabbed for her arm. She yanked herself away from him and stomped out to the limo. Just because she was agreeing to go with him did not mean she was excusing him from embarrassing her in front of everyone at the shelter and getting Parker upset.

eighteen
·····

FRIENDS

LUCIAN scowled at Scout the entire way back to the hotel. He blanketed her with his body as he ushered her through the lobby. They rode the elevators in silence. When they reached his suite he went right to the master bath and began to fill the tub.

"Strip."

"Lucian—"

"I said strip." His words were bit out, but she could sense his fear through his resounding fury. Living on the streets, she'd learned to see through people's acts. Hostility often veiled insecurity or fear. Lucian was being hostile because he was afraid. She just wasn't sure if his panic stemmed from possibly losing her or losing what she represented to him or just losing in general. Either way, she was there now.

She could tell he didn't want to say more, but his words came rushing out anyway. "What the hell were you doing there, Evelyn? Do you have any idea how dangerous places like that are? People die in that section of the city all the time. I told you that you were not to go back there—"

"I *live* there, Lucian." The rush of water spilling from the faucet was the only sound. "I'm sorry, Lucian. I didn't want you to know. I'll leave."

"Will you stop running away from me!" His fingers forked through his messy hair. "Just give me a minute to think." He sat on the edge of the large Jacuzzi tub. "You live there?"

Pursing her lips, she nodded slowly.

"Your paperwork said you lived in the apartments on Locus Street."

"I needed a mailing address."

Scout shifted her feet. She didn't want to sit since it would only make it harder to leave. "Look, none of this is your fault. As a matter of fact, you've been nothing but kind to me . . . sort of. I know you didn't know what you were getting into when you made your offer. I should've told you about my situation. I'm sorry. I'm sorry about all of it, the shelter, causing you to worry, my virginity . . ."

His dark eyes drilled into her as the last word left her mouth. He shook his head slowly and whispered, "You're so innocent, Evelyn."

Scout laughed. "Innocent is the last thing I am, Lucian. I've seen things that would make your skin crawl. Just because I've kept my nose clean doesn't mean—"

"You *are* innocent. I cannot allow you to go back to that place."

She leaned past him and shut off the water. "It isn't your decision."

"Why do you fight me at every turn?" He took her hands and held them tight. "I've never met someone more determined to do things the hard way."

"I could say the same about you. Look, I'm not trying to be difficult. That isn't my intention. It just keeps happening that way. We're just *too* different, Lucian. You're beyond wealthy and I'm homeless. You're an extremely sexual person and I was a virgin twenty-four hours ago. You own a hotel. I clean in one. You're gorgeous and I'm—"

"Don't," he interrupted, his gaze suddenly hard. "Just . . . don't. What if I told you, knowing all that, I still wanted you?"

Scout put down her bag. This was not going to be a quick thing. "Why, though? You could have anyone you want. I see the way women look at you. It could be so easy. You're deliberately picking the most complicated person you can find."

"I enjoy the challenge," he said, a trace of hollow humor softening his solemn expression.

"Lucian—"

"Stay. Not because I'll make it worth your while, but because you want to. Stay with me, Evelyn, because you enjoy my company. Stay until you don't enjoy it anymore."

"And what about when *you* stop enjoying my company? People get on each other's nerves after a while. What we have . . . it isn't permanent and we both know it."

"Why can't we enjoy it while it lasts? I like you, Evelyn. I'm not ready to see you go."

He didn't deny that he'd eventually lose interest in her, and that was probably for the best. It was dangerous to start reading more into what wasn't actually real. She was a phase for him and if she stayed, she needed to be okay with that.

Weary didn't begin to describe how she felt. She was just so tired, tired of fighting, tired of the endless struggle to survive, tired of denying her feelings for this man. She wasn't sure what she felt, but it was more than a contractual association. Things were getting personal.

Scout sighed. Here was a man who could afford to hang with friends in the richest social circles of the world and it appeared he was the loneliest person she had ever met. "Okay. I'll stay."

He pulled her to him and hugged her. His arms held her tight and she breathed in his scent, which she now associated with everything Lucian—stability, determination, success, and a touch of sadness. Part of her wanted to give him this thing he asked for, because for a man who had everything, she was beginning to believe no one had given him anything in a very long time.

Scout's clothes were stripped away and she found herself being lowered into the tub. Lucian stripped and climbed in behind her. He held her in the cradle of his thighs and slowly washed away the day's dust with a soft sponge.

It felt right, sitting there in his arms, letting him touch her. He touched her as if he had a right to. Entitled. That was exactly what it was and she liked it. When Lucian touched her that way it made all her worries take a backseat for a while. She knew she could come to him with any problem and in no time he'd have a solution for her. Trust was extremely difficult for her, but Lucian seemed so dependable, Scout didn't think it would be hard to trust someone like him. She just needed the courage to surrender. And what's more, she wanted to know him.

He ran the sponge over her shoulders and water sluiced between her breasts. "Lucian?"

"Hmm?"

"Why am I different for you?"

He paused in washing her. Softly he said, "You see the world differently. You were more impressed by lilies than ten thousand dollars' worth of designer clothes. I know you respect money and the power it holds, but you see it only as a means to an end. Other people see *me* as that means."

There was such a fine line between being bought and what they were doing. "But you said everything has a price."

"Evelyn, if you could truly be bought I would've had you a hundred times by now. You would've been at my beck and call.

You would've dropped your job at the first chance. You certainly wouldn't let your hurt pride run you out of my penthouse and back to a shelter. You would've grinned and bore it because you had been bought off, but you didn't. There're certain things about you that simply aren't for sale."

Scout picked up the sponge and washed his arms and hands. Beautiful strong hands, so different than the hands she had washed that afternoon. "I don't have many friends," she said, not sure where the words came from.

He kissed the moist skin below her ear. "Me neither."

"What an odd pair we are . . ."

"Not odd," he said introspectively. "Just finding our way. It'll be easier now that we have each other's company."

nineteen

.....

HUNGER

THE satin sheets made a hushing whisper as Lucian rolled onto his back. "Where're you going?"

Scout stood from wedging her foot into her shoe. "Work."

He grimaced and leaned up on his elbow. The deep amber sheet slid from his chest. Rather than tell her all his reasons why she shouldn't work as a housekeeper at Patras, he said, "Don't go."

Her heart expanded and she walked over to the bed and kissed his cheek. "I have to. People are depending on me."

"Do you like cleaning?"

"Not particularly, but it's a good job."

He watched her for a moment, his fingers running over her apron. "I'll be waiting for you here as soon as your shift's over."

"I'll be here," she said confidently.

His lips kissed the corner of her mouth. "I have to run into town for a business brunch. Other than that I'll be here if you need anything."

When he kissed her like that, courteously, with a trace of intimate affection, emotions stirred that were better left dormant.

Scout wasn't used to such gestures, and the tiny thrill of joy little kisses from Lucian provoked in her. Each one was like a sifted grain of sand that could eventually lead to an avalanche. She didn't want to be swept away and eventually fall in.

Work was a repeat of the day before. Scout's schedule was impossibly light and this time she noticed everyone else seemed a bit burdened with larger than usual assignments. Rather than dusting the common areas over and over again, she finished her rooms and went down to Tamara's office.

Her knuckles knocked on the door lightly.

"Come in."

"Hi, Tamara. Are you busy?"

Her GM pushed aside a salad she was mixing at her desk. "Of course not. What's up?"

Scout stepped into the plain office and fidgeted with the slip of paper her schedule had been printed on. "I wanted to talk to you about my workload."

Her eyebrows shot up. "Is ten hours too much?"

"Oh, no. I . . . the hours are fine. If you needed me more I could do more. I was actually wondering why my roster's been so light."

She had the grace to blush. "Um, Mr. Patras said that you . . . I mean . . ." She sighed. "I'm kind of in a weird position here, Scout. Mr. Patras is my boss's boss's boss. What he says goes."

"And he told you I wasn't supposed to have more than a certain amount of assignments in a day?"

Her expression validated Scout's assumption. "I'm sorry."

Scout pinched the bridge of her nose. "It's not your fault. I'll talk to him."

When she returned to the penthouse, she was exhausted. Her stomach felt like it was slowly imploding it was so empty. Starvation was something she'd always tolerated, but since she'd been eating better, when it did hit, it hit with a vengeance. She was so hungry the thought of food made her frustrated and ill. She just wanted to sleep.

Lucian was at his desk when she came in. He tucked away what he was working on and stood.

"Hey, I need to talk to you," he said with a smile.

Scout put her bag on the floor and met him at the seating area. He kissed her cheek with restrained affection and she sat. "I need to talk to you too."

Her body sunk into the plush sofa, and her spine seemed to melt. She eased her head back and shut her eyes. Wearily she said, "Lucian, you can't tell my boss I can only clean so many rooms. Do you realize that maids make tips? The less rooms I clean the less tip money I earn."

"I hadn't thought about that. It doesn't matter anyway." She peeked through one eye at him. He wore a satisfied grin.

Dryly, she asked, "Why doesn't it matter, Lucian?"

"Because you've been promoted." He seemed quite pleased with himself.

She sat up. It took a lot of effort.

She wasn't sure she wanted to know the answer, but she had to ask anyway. "What do you mean 'promoted'?"

"Next Wednesday you start your new job at the front desk. You won't have to clean, the pay is better, and I'll know where you are in case I need to find you for some reason."

"Oh, Lucian, no . . ." All she saw in her mind were the computers that lined the counter and the pages printing from the machines and the receipts sliding back and forth. All things she didn't know how to use, all things that required a person to be literate. "I can't do that job."

"Why not? It's easy."

"For you maybe. Lucian, I don't know how to use computers.

I'd have to answer phones and . . . I'm sorry. I know you meant well, but I can't accept the offer."

"Evelyn, they'll train you. You'll learn—"

"Lucian, no. I'm not taking it."

"You're being stubborn. You're exhausted from cleaning all day—"

"I'm exhausted from thinking up things to do all day. I only had four rooms to do. Do you know how slow my day moves when I have nothing on my schedule? You need to tell Tamara to give me my old assignments back."

Rather than argue, he softly ran the pad of his thumb under her eye. "You look wiped. Did you sleep well last night?"

Scout wasn't used to him being so attentive to her comforts. "I'm just hungry."

"What did you eat for breakfast?"

"Nothing."

He scowled. "Did you have lunch?"

"I haven't eaten since I was at the shelter."

"That was twenty hours ago, Evelyn! You need to eat."

"That'd be great, Lucian, but there isn't always food."

He stood and picked up the phone. His finger punched down on a number. "That's bullshit and you know it. I told you I've arranged for you to have a credit here at the hotel. If you're hungry there's no excuse for you to starve. Yes, this is Lucian Patras. Send up some toast, eggs, and fresh honeydew wrapped in prosciutto. I'd also like a basket of nonperishables brought to my room every few days as well. Thank you."

He hung up the phone. "Why didn't you say something?"

Her shoulders shrugged. Scout was used to taking care of herself. She was responsible for herself. It didn't feel right going to someone else about her needs despite all her soul-searching thoughts and acceptances of her relationship with Lucian.

Scout changed the subject. "How was your business brunch?"

"Good." His gaze was unfocused for a moment. He seemed distracted as he smiled. "It was really good."

Lucian had all of her belongings brought up to his suite and moved to the guest room closet while they had both been gone. When she went to change and didn't come right back, he found her frowning at the closet.

"What's wrong?"

"All I have to wear are gowns and fancy clothes. It's weird dressing up just to sit around."

He left and returned a minute later with a button-down shirt. "Here, wear this."

She changed into his shirt and dug out a pair of thick wool socks from her bag. The shirt swallowed her, coming to her knees. Rolling the sleeves back several times, she sighed. When she came back into the common area the food had arrived.

"Aren't you eating?"

"I'm still full from brunch."

Scout picked at the toast and the fluffy eggs. Her stomach was hollow so everything she put in it landed in a way that made her painfully aware of its emptiness. When she couldn't stomach any more, she put her fork down. Lucian was sitting on the edge of the sofa, reading over some papers.

He looked at her plate. "You didn't eat enough."

"I can't stomach any more right now."

He frowned and pulled her to his side. His hand glided over her back and slowly undid her bun. As he read his paperwork, his fingers unconsciously stroked her hair. She sunk into his side, her head slowly lowering and her lashes growing very heavy. Drifting off, he continued to hold her, as if her presence brought him as much comfort as his brought her.

twenty
. . . . .

COLD

THE shrill ring of the phone awoke Scout from her nap. Lucian's hand rested over her hip and her head was using his thigh as a pillow.

"Patras," he said quietly, answering the phone.

Scout remained quiet and listened as the room came into focus.

He sighed. "Who is it? And what did he say?" He was quiet a moment. "She's resting." The sound of papers being rustled and placed aside was followed by a sigh. "Put him at my table at the restaurant. On my tab. We'll be down shortly."

The call ended and he brushed her hair away from her face. "Evelyn, we have to go somewhere."

Scout slowly sat up and swept her hair out of her eyes. "Okay. What should I wear?"

"Just something casual. Can you be ready soon?"

In the guest room she selected a pair of slim boot-cut corduroys, a brown camisole, and a tweed burgundy jacket. After slipping on a pair of beige death heels, she shrugged on her coat.

Lucian came into the room, dressed in a power suit and looking fiercely intimidating. She took in his outfit.

"You said casual."

"This is as casual as I get for things like this. You won't need your coat. We aren't leaving the hotel."

They took the elevator down to the lobby and Lucian kept his hand at her back as they walked toward Vogue, the hotel bar and restaurant. A hostess greeted them and announced that Lucian's party was waiting.

They followed the hostess's serpentine route and arrived at a secluded back corner of the restaurant reserved for private affairs.

Scout gasped, "Parker!"

Parker stood against the wall in his scarf and tattered sweater, looking like a rakish model. His soft jade eyes appeared worried and relief was clear on his face the moment he spotted them. He narrowed his eyes at Lucian, and Lucian's protective hand at her back slid to her hip possessively.

"Mr. Hughes," Lucian greeted, and she wondered how he knew Parker's last name.

Parker ignored the greeting and took her hands. "Scout, are you okay?" He shot Lucian an accusing glare.

"Let's sit. I'm afraid Evelyn slept through lunch so we'll call this an early dinner. Evelyn." Lucian held out a chair, nodding for her to sit.

They sat and Parker reluctantly followed suit.

"To what do we owe this pleasure, Mr. Hughes?"

A waitress silently handed each of them menus. Parker pushed his aside and eyed Lucian skeptically. "I wanted to make sure she's okay."

"Evelyn is quite well as you can see for yourself." She frowned as they talked over her as if she were incapable of answering for herself.

"What do you want with her?"

"That's none of your business," Lucian said as he put aside his menu.

"Uh, hello? I'm right here." Being the subject up for discussion, it would be nice if someone acknowledged her presence.

"You can't buy her or whatever you think you're doing," Parker hissed.

Lucian chuckled. "True, but only because I can't afford her. She's priceless and in case she hasn't told you, she's not for sale."

"Is this a joke?" Parker asked. "I'm serious. She won't let you take advantage of her."

"How charming, Evelyn, you have yourself quite a little champion here."

Parker's eyes narrowed. Muscles in his strong jaw twitched. "You think you're untouchable. You think you intimidate me with your nice clothes and fancy hotel? You don't. That crap won't impress Scout either. She's too smart to fall for all your glitz and arrogance."

The waitress returned. Parker sat back, apparently intending to order nothing, and Lucian said, "The three of us will have the sirloin, prepared medium rare, the arugula salad with pecans, and the sautéed asparagus."

The waitress took the menus. "Very good, Mr. Patras."

"I'm not eating," Parker announced with stubborn pride.

"Don't be a fool, Mr. Hughes. You're starving. I suspect you haven't had a meal like this in years. Don't cut off your nose to spite your face."

"You're an arrogant bastard, Patras."

Scout had heard enough. "Will you two stop it? Parker's my friend, Lucian. If you can't be polite, I'm going back to the room. Parker, I'm perfectly fine and here of my own free will."

The hurt that filled Parker's eyes made her look away.

"I see." He stood, and the way his body turned, she noticed how slender his hips were. She imagined Lucian's body and noted several differences. "I'll let you two enjoy your dinner."

"Parker, wait." She stood, and Lucian placed a staying hand on her knee.

"Good-bye, Scout. I'll keep an eye on Pearl for you."

He turned and left, quickly moving through the maze of tables and disappearing through the door. The tears that blurred her vision startled her.

Turning her scowl on Lucian, she hissed, "I'm sure you're pleased with yourself." With a flick of her wrist, her napkin was tossed onto the table and she stood, heading toward the lobby. Following the same maze Parker had taken, she left.

Her feet walked as quickly as she could manage without causing a scene or breaking her neck. Her tiny shoes ticked across the polished lobby floor like a tattoo needle. As a doorman held the door for her, she saw Parker cutting through a cluster of cabs and crossing the street.

The wind sliced through her clothing and sent her hair swirling and knotting around her face. "Parker, wait!"

He stopped and turned. The cold blustery weather flapped her light tweed jacket that was more of an accessory than anything else. His hands were rooted deep in his pockets and his shoulders were hunched. She twisted and noticed Lucian standing by the glass doors, watching them. Why did there have to be sides? With a frustrated huff, she crossed the street to Parker.

"Don't leave angry," she said as she stepped onto the sidewalk slightly out of breath.

"What're you doing, Scout?"

"I'm stopping you."

"Not now, with him? What the hell's going on? What does he have on you?"

Scout shook her head. "N-nothing. We're just friends."

He shot her a disbelieving look. Tentatively he reached up and tucked a long strand of hair behind her ear that kept catching in the wind.

"It doesn't have to be like this, Scout."

"Like what, Parker?"

"I see the way he looks at you. He watches you like he wants to devour you and treats you like a possession."

She flinched. True, their original agreement lacked any form of intimate knowledge, but sometime over the past few days that changed. She had to believe Lucian saw her as more than a possession. She certainly saw more to him than she originally assumed. If it were materialistic, things never would have gotten this complicated. Hurt pride and trust never would have come into play.

"Is that what you think? That he bought me?"

He fingered the lapel of her new jacket. "Didn't he?"

Her shoulders trembled, but not from the cold. She pressed her lips together and took a deep breath as hurt and rage chilled her bones.

"You're a jerk, Parker Hughes. He didn't buy me. He earned me. Unlike you, he knows I'm not for sale." She wished she had something better to say, but her shock made her dense.

"He doesn't love you."

"I don't want him to!"

Eyes searching, he looked at her. "Money isn't everything, Scout. You think it's power and what runs the world, but you're wrong. It owns a person. Don't let it own you."

Her jaw locked. Impatiently she stomped her foot. "Money is freedom, Parker. I've been homeless for twenty-two years. I won't make it twenty more. I refuse to be another Jane Doe."

"And does he see you as something more? Does he get the real you that I know or just some dressed-up imitation of what he wants you to be? How could you . . . how could you give yourself to someone who knows nothing about you? Don't do it, Scout."

Too late. Her fingers twitched with the urge to slap him. She was not a violent person, but fuck him. The quietly fierce whisper that slipped out was inconsistent with the rage building inside of her.

"Screw you, Parker Hughes. You don't know me any better than he does." Her throat constricted and her shoulders jerked with chills. There was such extreme judgment in his stare, she felt naked and resented him for pressing such shame upon her. He could accuse Lucian of buying her favors all he wanted, but Parker was the one claiming she came with a price tag, and by the way he was looking at her, it was a cheap one at that.

"Evelyn." Lucian, no longer across the street, now stood a few feet away. His expression was unreadable. "Dugan's going to take your friend home. His meal's waiting for him in the limo."

Scout glanced back at Parker, who scornfully watched Lucian. She couldn't do this. She turned and Lucian wrapped his suit jacket over her shoulders and escorted her back into Patras.

twenty-one
.....

COWARD

WHEN they returned to the penthouse, their meal had been delivered there. They ate in silence. Well, Lucian ate. She picked.

"You need to eat, Evelyn."

"How could he say those things about me? I am not a whore!" she whispered to herself.

Lucian's knife clanked to the table. "Friend or not, if I ever hear Mr. Hughes speak such words to you, he'll find himself without a tongue."

Scout looked up at Lucian, who was gazing back at her, his eyes intense pools of unfathomable black. She realized this was not a topic to discuss with him. They stared at each other for a long moment, neither of them saying a word, but understanding that certain truths of their association were too painful to hear.

Finally, needing to break the solemn spell blanketing the suite, she said, "Let's play chess."

Once deep in the match, Lucian was distracted. Either that or her skill was improving. She highly doubted the latter.

The match was quiet and lacking the usual cheer that accompanied their games. They had each removed their shoes, jackets, accessories, and Lucian had sacrificed his tie. She frowned over the board, recognizing several moves he could make that would rapidly end the game. If she was noticing these opportunities that meant Lucian had definitely spotted them and purposefully avoided them.

Scout didn't like playing with mock ambition. His moves felt charitable and she bristled at the sense of being pitied or coddled. Deliberately, she moved her queen before his rook, sacrificing her most powerful player. He looked at her.

"Evelyn . . ."

"What? I thought we were trying to see who could make the stupidest move. Go ahead. Take her."

"What're you doing?" he grumbled as she began to unbutton her pants. "Evelyn, stop. We don't have to play by those rules anymore."

She slid her pants over her legs. "Why not? Good company and competition, right?" She tossed her pants on the floor and knocked her queen off the board since he refused to take it. "Your turn."

He made an imbecilic move that left his king incredibly vulnerable. It was too rare an opportunity to ignore. She took his knight. He moved his bishop and exposed his queen. She took her. The game moved like this for several plays, leaving Lucian in only his pants, but looking no less in control. Then she finally saw what he was doing.

Checkmate.

One move left and she'd put his king in check. The only option he'd have to escape would lead her to capture his other bishop, her move inevitably ending the game, her calling checkmate.

He was sabotaging them. Why? She looked at him, hurt clogging her throat. How could he do that?

He stared back at her with not challenge but quiet defeat.

"Make the move, Evelyn."

With shaky hands she took his bishop and put him in check.

"Say it," he gritted, gaze focused on the board.

Her chin quivered as she stared back into his hard face. He was doing it again, pushing her into corners and pulling away. It always hurt. She didn't want to let him go. She didn't want to say those words. He was offering her mercy in his mind, but to her it only felt like rejection. She swept her hand across the board angrily, the heavy pieces clattering to the floor, and stood.

"If you want to hear those words so bad, say them yourself!"

She stormed into the bedroom and slammed the door.

How could he try to force her into a corner like that? He was the one who begged for her to come back, and in doing so, something frightening had been unleashed inside of her, something that said this was less about taking shoes with her when she left and more about experiencing *him* while she was here.

She wasn't ready to go. All his talk about trust and surrender, he'd tapped into a part of her she hadn't realized existed, a curious and eager part that wanted him, not because he'd coerced her or named her price, but because she really believed he wanted her too.

She'd been naïve to assume the physical act of sex could exist apart from emotional entanglement. For days she'd battled her emotions, unsure where this deluge of feelings had come from. Her life experience was limited. It didn't compute with Lucian's depth and understanding.

They'd just started to find their rhythm and now he seemed to be pushing her away. Why? Had he changed his mind?

After having Parker lay her bare and accuse her of being the one thing she wanted to avoid being, she was beginning to worry that was exactly what she had become.

No. Part of her couldn't accept that. There was something deeper here between Lucian and her. Something emotional others couldn't see and she didn't fully understand. Maybe Lucian didn't understand it either.

He tried to manipulate her, which he had done before, but this time was different. He was aiming at something final, something she wasn't ready to give now that he'd convinced her to stay.

His emotions ran about as calm as rapids breaking over the shore. She never knew if an encounter would run smooth or turn into a choppy mess. He hurt her. What he'd just tried to do was unexpected and surprisingly upsetting. It was the action of a coward.

twenty-two

HANDLE WITH CARE

LUCIAN came into the bedroom only minutes after Scout had changed and climbed under the covers. Her pillow was damp with tears. The whisper of his clothing was the only sound as he quietly undressed in the dark, and then the mattress dipped as he climbed in beside her.

He slid over and pressed his body into hers. His mouth kissed her shoulder. "I'm sorry, Evelyn."

She sniffled. "Why? Do you want me to go?"

He sighed. "No, but I need to know you're here because you choose to be, not because of anything I'm providing for you or because you feel coerced. I know, in the beginning, that was all this was supposed to be, but my needs are changing. I need to know you're here because you want to be."

She turned and faced him, squinting to see his face under the shadows.

"Lucian, when people find out my background they're automatically going to think I'm a gold-digging charity case. As someone who's never had money, I can assure you I want it, but only if I earn it. That's why I work. Being with you isn't the same. I'm here now because I like being around you.

"The clothes, the fancy dinners, the perfumes and expensive salon treatments, they're all very new and exciting, but none of it's necessary. You like eating at fancy places that require appropriate clothing. I'd go with you in my jeans and sweatshirt if I knew it wouldn't embarrass you."

"Evelyn—"

"Let me finish. I don't mean to say you're shallow, I'm just saying you live in a different world than I'm used to, one I can't afford.

"I could fill days with free things for us to do and still be very happy having your 'company.' When I came to you the other night it was by choice, not obligation. You've never made me feel like a paid-for whore. Please don't think of all those gestures as deposits for my time. If you start thinking of our association that way it'll only make it true. As much as I respect money and the power it wields, it's not why I'm here. Something's happened in the past few days—I'm not sure what—but I *want* to stay."

He touched her cheek. "If I ever make you feel indebted, tell me. I do those things for you because I want to, because I don't know any other way to show I care."

"I know." She smiled in the darkness and leaned in to softly press her lips to his. He stilled for a moment as if she surprised him, then slowly leaned into the kiss.

He pressed her back into the mattress as his mouth moved over hers with deliberate slowness. Her thighs pulled together as a small fire began to burn in her belly. His hand gently coasted over her hair and down to her shoulder. Something about his touch was different, softer.

Lucian tenderly stroked her arm and she waited for him to move further over her. When he didn't, she gently took his hand

and placed it on her breast again, taking him by surprise. He paused for a moment, then kissed tenderly down her throat. Scout arched into him as he palmed her breast over her nightgown, massaging pleasantly, but not taking it any further.

She sensed his need, yet when she tried to touch him, he diverted her motions and subdued her with a slow kiss. This went on and on, her trying in her own inexperienced way to timidly push things further, and him, the aggressor, gently rebuffing her efforts.

Their kisses fell into such soft caresses she grew sleepy. Lucian caressed her skin with long, soothing strokes. She felt as if she were being hypnotized. Eventually Lucian softly eased away and whispered good night. She was confused, but exhaustion made it difficult to figure out exactly why. Frowning into the darkness, her thoughts slowly faded into dreams.

twenty-three
.....

ASSHOLE

LUCIAN left early the following morning. Scout woke to find the bed cold and him dressing quietly in the dark. He said he had meetings downtown for most of the morning and suggested she spend the day enjoying herself. He told her how to order breakfast and recommended if she got bored she visit the boutique downstairs for a bathing suit and go for a swim in the hotel pool. She didn't do any of that.

Scout had a long bath and figured out how to use a blow-dryer. Her hair doubled in size and curled. She liked it because it was different, but she wasn't confident enough to actually leave the room that way.

She spent an hour practicing putting on makeup. She got a little carried away with her eyes and ended up washing it all off and starting over again.

For breakfast Scout ordered a bagel and an ice cream sundae. She was amused with her disregard for social order and three square meals until the attendant who delivered the sundae looked at her judgmentally. Then she felt juvenile and stupid. Luckily, the ice cream was exceptional and it soothed her embarrassment.

She dressed in jeans and a sheer blouse, then changed into a tight skirt with a loose green sweater and wide brown belt. Scout stood in front of the long mirror in the guest room and tried on one pair of shoes after another.

As she zipped up a sleek pair of leather boots, there was a knock at the door. Not wasting time removing the boots, she scampered to the front door and opened it. Her pleasant, easygoing mood evaporated.

"Ah, Scout," Slade greeted dryly.

"Lucian's not here." She stepped behind the door, wishing she'd left her jeans on and not changed into the short skirt.

"I'm aware. He should be here soon. He asked me to wait for him."

It didn't feel right having someone else in the penthouse. She'd come to think of it as her and Lucian's space, their hideout, like a little tree fort above the city.

"Oh, come in."

Slade stepped into the suite, and she shut the door. He walked to Lucian's desk and deposited some papers there.

Lucian didn't like people around his desk.

When he turned on her, Scout froze. They stood, facing off for a moment, then he moved to the bar and helped himself to a drink.

Gently, she sat on the edge of the settee, very aware of her posture and forcing her knees together, trying her best to mimic Dr. Sheffield's confidence. He turned and openly scrutinized her as he sipped his drink.

"How long did Lucian say he would be?" she asked nervously.

"He didn't. He said he was on his way."

She mouthed a silent *oh*.

"This must be quite different from Saint Christopher's."

Nothing like making an uncomfortable situation worse.

Scout decided then and there that Slade was a dick, and he wasn't going to intimidate her. "How is it you know Lucian?"

"We're partners," he said and offered no other explanation. Did Slade own part of Patras? Lucian had said he had sisters, but mentioned nothing of a brother. Was Slade a distant cousin or somehow a member of the Patras family? Perhaps by marriage. She looked at his hand. No ring.

"How long do you plan on being Lucian's . . . guest?"

She was distracted from her thoughts by his question. He said "guest" as if he were substituting it for a much more derogatory word.

"Um, we didn't really discuss a time period. I suppose as long as we enjoy each other or until we no longer do."

"No doubt you'll be enjoying the lap of luxury for a long time. Money does have a way of broadening one's tolerance."

Scout glowered at him. "What's that supposed to mean?"

"I'm just pointing out that the appeal's tipped in your favor. Where will you go once Lucian's done with you? It's a long way back to the dirty floor of a shelter from the top."

She was speechless. Eventually, she said the only thing she was sure of. "You don't like me."

"No. I don't." There was no hesitating about his confession.

The door opened and Lucian walked in. He was speaking on his cell phone and nodded in acknowledgement at Slade, then leaned down to kiss her temple. Slade relented with the stink eye and she took the opportunity to slip into the back room. She couldn't expect everyone to approve of her, especially when, like Slade, they discovered where she had come from.

Scout found the remote control on the table and turned on the television. TV was something she had rarely enjoyed. She couldn't find the show about Gilligan, so she put on cartoons. The cat chased the mouse and the mouse always got away. She settled onto the bed and watched, thoroughly entertained.

Laughter bubbled past her lips when the mouse caught the cat on fire. She wanted to catch Slade on fire. Smirking, she imagined him, in his tailored suit and fancy shoes, hopping around like the cat on the television as his devil tail smoked. She grinned evilly.

After the cartoon with the cat and mouse, a new skit with a road-runner came on. This one was more frustrating than entertaining. Lucian knocked on the door and she quickly shut off the television.

He smiled and looked at the blank screen. "What were you watching? I heard you laughing."

"Oh. Nothing." Scout moved to the edge of the bed and adjusted her skirt, the move distracting Lucian's gaze.

"Slade's invited us to dinner."

After her initial shock, she deflated. She'd missed Lucian all day and now that he was home she wouldn't be able to enjoy him. He was different around other people. Even when they'd visited his house and Slade left, he wasn't the same as he was when they were alone. Jamie was his oldest friend and she could even see a difference in Lucian in his presence.

"Do you not want to go?"

She could tell he wanted her to go. "No, of course I'll go. I just want to change."

He stepped close to her, his front pressing into hers as he ran a finger under the low-hung neck of her sweater.

"I like what you're wearing," he whispered.

Scout thought he would kiss her, wanted him to. With the high heels of her boots, she could almost reach his mouth. Pushing onto the toes of her feet, she leaned further into him. Her palms glided up his chest and over his shoulders and he gently circled her wrists with his fingers and stepped away.

"Slade's waiting."

When he left, she sulked, not understanding why he no longer seemed attracted to her. It wasn't fair, because she was growing more attracted to him by the hour.

Thinking about the night he took her virginity, she decided part of her adverse reaction was due to fear and ignorance. She didn't think it would hurt as much the second time, now that she'd already had him inside of her. But she was beginning to think she might never find out. Lucian seemed determined not to touch her.

They took the limo to a tiny, dimly lit French restaurant called The Speakeasy. Scout was silent on the drive over and sensed Slade judging her a little more with every mile. Lucian seemed oblivious to his friend's distaste with his choice in "company."

Since the menus were in French, Lucian declared that he would order for her. She didn't tell him that the language was irrelevant.

"Perhaps Evelyn would care to try some escargot," Slade said.

Lucian narrowed his eyes and ignored his friend's comment. When Slade called her by her real name he did so with theatric snootiness. She didn't know what was worse, the way he said Evelyn or the disapproving way he spoke when he called her Scout.

Being a glutton for punishment, she asked, "What's escargot?"

"It's a delicacy," Slade said with a reptilian smile. "You should try it."

She looked at Lucian, who was reading the menu. "Snails," he said without looking up, sensing her question.

Her lip curled and she glared at Slade. He chuckled and perused his menu. "It does require a more *sophisticated* taste," he grumbled under his breath snidely.

Did he think she was unaware of the difference in their backgrounds? She figured it was time to put an end to the cryptic jousting.

"You know, where I come from, if you eat bugs you're considered crazy, but you rich folk pretty it up with some fancy French name and feel superior. Seems, since I'm the one who's never been dumb enough to eat a snail, the sophistication rests on my side of the table."

Lucian chuckled and she smiled at him. With mirth in his eyes he turned to his friend. "Don't be a prig, Slade. She'll make you regret it."

Slade's color rose from warm caramel to the color of fresh maple syrup. He gave up his campaign to make her feel like a fool for the time being and she tried to enjoy as much of the meal as possible.

Lucian ordered lamb with a delicious mint jelly. There were baby carrots in some sort of glaze and tiny roasted potatoes. A person at a nearby table ordered snails and Slade looked at the dish longingly. She enjoyed thinking that it might've been her snappy comeback that made him too apprehensive to order the dish.

Scout one. Slade zero. Suck it, asshole.

Rather than take the limo back to Patras with them, Slade hailed a cab and headed home. Lucian pulled her to his side as they rode back. "Your friend doesn't like me."

"That's not true," Lucian said, holding her fingers in his where his arm draped over her shoulder.

"Yes it is. He told me."

Her fingers dropped.

"Slade told you he didn't like you?"

"Yup."

His eyes moved as if he were thinking. "Well, he's full of shit."

"Lucian, it's okay. I don't expect all of your friends to like me. Parker doesn't like you."

"That's different. I understand why Parker doesn't like me. Slade has no reason—"

She faced him. "Why does Parker not like you?"

Taking a moment to process her interruption, he frowned. "Because he's in love with you."

Her smile faltered. "Wha—Parker's not in love with me."

He stared at her for a long time. No words. It seemed everything he needed to say was in that meaningful look.

Scout was still reeling from Lucian's comment when they returned to the penthouse. She went to the bedroom and pulled out a nightgown and began removing her clothes.

Lucian came in quietly behind her and undid the clasp at the back of her bra. Moonlight formed puddles of blue on the floor around them. She turned slowly in his arms and faced him. His knuckles caressed the side of her breast and he watched as her skin drew taut. He gently stroked the side of her other breast.

Scout's chest rose and fell slowly with each breath. He reached down and took the gown out of her hands and slipped it over her shoulders. Not knowing what else to do, she docilely let him pull her arms through the straps and waited. He kissed the corner of her mouth and stepped back.

"I have some work to finish up."

She tried to hide her hurt, but she was really beginning to develop a complex. Nodding slowly, she climbed into bed. She didn't hear Lucian come to bed that night.

When she awoke next it was morning. Masculine voices from the other room mixed with the scent of coffee. After using the bathroom and brushing her teeth, she slipped a bulky Patras robe around her and knotted the front. The thick fabric engulfed her. The robe formed a train as she crept into the hall hoping to sneak discreetly into the guest room where her clothes were.

"Evelyn." She stilled. Lucian came around the corner and kissed her hair. "Did you sleep well? Come and have breakfast."

He took her hand, the billowy sleeve falling over their clasped embrace, and led her to the common area of the suite. Great. Slade was there.

Lucian gestured for her to sit at the couch and placed a dish in front of her. He lifted the top and there were two sunny-side eggs and a fat slice of French toast topped with strawberries.

Lucian's eyes creased with mirth. "Since the French toast is already rich, I figured you might want to skip the chocolate sauce this morning."

Confused, she glanced up at him. He smiled and placed an ice cream sundae next to her plate, sans the hot fudge. She blushed and he chuckled.

He left her side to return to his business with Slade. They made a conference call while she ate and listened, not really paying attention to what was being said. Once finished eating, she was stuffed. Slade nonchalantly tossed a newspaper on the table and her gaze immediately focused on the large picture on the page folded to the front.

It was Lucian, smiling, holding a gorgeous woman in his arms. The woman was smiling up at him, her dark hair a billowy cloud behind her curvaceous body, her dark eyes staring into Lucian's smiling face adoringly. Scout's delicious breakfast settled into the pit of her stomach like acid.

She couldn't tear her eyes from the picture. He wore the pinstripe suit she recalled from the other day when he had "brunch." This was a recent photo. Memories of asking him how his meeting had gone and the starry gleam that filled his eyes took on a whole new meaning. He said it went good . . . really good.

Scout's teeth clamped together and she breathed hard through her nose as she glared at the paper. Not wanting to draw attention to the issue she was having, she laced her fingers together and held still so she didn't *accidentally* shred the image and throw it across the room.

The conference call ended and Lucian excused himself to use the restroom. Slade settled in the chair across from her triumphantly.

"She's quite breathtaking, isn't she?"

Scout glared at him, refusing to be baited.

"Lucian cares very much for Isadora. Have you met her yet?"

Have I met her? No, she hadn't met her! Her limbs began to tremble. Lucian was right. Slade didn't dislike her. It was way more than that. He hated her.

Lucian came back into the room and stopped, noticing her upset.

"Evelyn?" He looked accusingly at Slade. "What's the matter?"

Scout stood up, kicked her robe around her ankles, and marched into the bedroom, slamming the door behind her. She barely had time to cool her temper when the door opened. Without a word, Lucian stormed up to her and swept her up and over his shoulder.

"Put me down!"

"Hush."

His hand swatted her ass, leaving her momentarily speechless. He marched her back into the common area and plopped her unceremoniously on the couch. She gave him her fiercest glare and refused to look at Slade the snake.

"Tell her," Lucian growled the command at his friend.

Not seeing the point in all this, she turned to Slade. He sighed and said, "Isadora is Lucian's sister."

The relief that swept through Scout was immeasurable. She may have actually moaned.

"It seems my friend here," Lucian began dryly, "needs to work on being a bit more unambiguous with his words. People seem to keep misinterpreting his meanings."

Slade's jaw ticked. "My apologies, Ms. Keats. I've forgotten my manners. It won't happen again." He was doing the *Gilligan's Island* rich person teeth-talking thing.

The apology was forced and she didn't believe one word of it was genuine. Scout wasn't sure how to react to such insincerity. There was a long, awkward moment of silence. Finally, Slade said something about making the next call but Lucian interrupted. "We're done here."

Stymied, Slade said, "Lucian, we have to—"

"I said we're done."

Realizing Lucian wasn't going to budge, Slade stood irritably and gathered his things. Once he had everything back in his briefcase, he turned to his partner. "You need to remember who you are and stop trying to be someone else."

"And you need to remember it's *my* name on the door," Lucian retorted, eyeing the other man intensely.

Slade turned. "Ms. Keats." He nodded and left in a huff that ended with a sharp click of the door.

She faced Lucian. He wouldn't look at her. "I'm sorry about that. Slade is . . . he doesn't deal with change well."

Scout stood, wanting to hit the reset button on the entire morning. "I'm going to take a shower." Nothing else was said.

twenty-four

TOO MANY SUNRISES . . .

S COUT took an extralong time in the shower. Her second
attempt at shaving her legs went a lot better than her first.
Rather than turn into the bride of Frankenstein with the help of
the blow-dryer, she simply braided her hair into one thick rope.
T-shirts had mysteriously appeared in her closet, and she chose a
soft cornflower blue one and a pair of plain boot-cut jeans. Then
she waited.

She sat on the bed and braided her hair again. After pacing a
rut in the freshly vacuumed carpet, she turned on the television,
but there weren't any cartoons on at the moment. She couldn't relate to daytime television and found it annoying. Unable to take
her silent restlessness anymore, she went out to bug Lucian.

Scout expected she'd be interrupting him, but his chair was
turned away from his desk as he stared out the window. He
appeared deep in thought. She approached quietly. He didn't seem
to notice her watching him.

She wasn't sure what made her do it, but she stepped close to
his chair and sat on the floor beside him. He looked down and she

pressed her cheek into his thigh, wanting to breathe in his closeness. His fingers picked up her braid and turned the long rope of hair.

"Your hair's so beautiful."

Her lips pressed tight as his praise fluttered through her chest. He draped the braid over her shoulder.

"Lucian?"

"Yes."

"Why are you avoiding me?"

He didn't deny it. He took a deep breath and returned his gaze to the world outside. "Would you like to do something today?"

More avoidance. She pivoted on her knees and faced him. Her fingers plucked at the button on his shirt. "If you're not busy we could go back to bed and spend the day there. It looks like it's going to rain. We could light candles and—"

"That's not what I meant, Evelyn."

His instant refusal threw her off. She had no experience with seduction, but she was a girl he had once found attractive. How hard could it be?

"I know that wasn't what you meant. I was making a suggestion."

The patronizing way he looked at her made her bristle. "I'm sure you'd rather do something else."

Her back teeth clamped down. *Don't get frustrated.*

"I'm pretty sure I just told you what I wanted to do. Why are you . . ." It hurt to actually ask such a question. "Lucian, did I do it wrong?"

His dark brows lowered over his dark eyes. "Do what wrong?"

Exasperated, she held out her palms and dropped to her bottom. *"It."* She knew he had done most of the work, but she wanted to have a second try. She felt a little braver now that she knew what to expect. "Are you no longer attracted to me?"

"God, Evelyn, no. I just . . . You're innocent."

"So? Is that so bad?"

He looked away.

"Lucian, I know you didn't expect me to be a virgin, but so what? I'm not anymore. You act like it's a bad thing. Look at it this way. You're all I've ever known as far as anything sexual. Rather than run from me, *teach me*."

Scout waited for him to reply, but he wouldn't even look at her. Brazenly she reached for his belt and began to undo it. He jumped up as if she had spilled scalding coffee in his lap.

"What are you doing?"

His look of contempt was so fierce she flinched. Her mouth opened and closed but no words came out. He glared at her and incredible shame snaked through her belly. He scowled at her as if she had tried to rape him. Tears stung her eyes.

"N-nothing. I won't touch you again," she whispered, and he walked away.

Scout sat on the floor, staring out the window for several minutes. When the front door of the penthouse slammed, she jumped. Maybe she should leave. Unsure if she'd be welcomed back at St. Christopher's, she chucked that idea. She didn't want to leave anyway. Lucian had become someone she was growing used to sharing her days with and she stubbornly wanted to see this thing through.

Her brain kept replaying Lucian's words about Parker in her head. The more she thought about Parker the more she feared Lucian was right. She decided she'd visit Pearl.

Her plans were dashed when a bolt of lightning webbed the solid sheet of sky like cracks in an old teacup, and there was a sharp crash of thunder. The skies suddenly opened and it began to pour. She had nowhere to go. Trapped.

Unable to sit in the suite any longer, she grabbed her room key

and left. Scout walked down to the lobby and looked at the paint-
ings of local architecture on the walls. She sat on a cushioned
bench and watched families and lovers dining in the restaurant.

The doormen all wore Patras ponchos and plastic caps over
their brimmed Patras hats. It made her think of the picture of her
and Pearl and that silly rubber hat.

After a while she walked through some of the boutiques. Her
eyes snagged on a black leather belt with a gunmetal gray, sleek
buckle. It reminded her of Lucian, hard, yet soft, attractive, yet
completely masculine. She asked if she could purchase it, and the
clerk asked for her room key to put it on her tab.

Scout knew it was silly, buying him a present with his own
money, but she'd never bought anything like that before. When
the clerk rung her up the bill was ninety-seven dollars. As she
reached for her room card Scout pulled it back.

"Wait," she said, hesitating as her mind worked.

The clerk's assistant who'd been gift-wrapping the leather belt
paused as well. "Is something wrong, Miss?"

"I'm not going to charge it to my room. Can you hold onto it
for a minute while I run upstairs? I'll be right back."

When the elevators deposited her on the top floor, she raced
into the bedroom. Lucian still wasn't back. Her hands dug
through her bag and pulled out a tight folded pile of twenties. Her
fingers shook as she counted out five of them. Once she had
enough money for the belt, she stuffed her money back in her bag
and wedged it under the bed.

Scout raced back to the elevators and impatiently bounced as
she waited for the car to arrive. She'd never spent this much money
on anything. She wanted to hand it over before she changed her
mind. The door opened and she jumped into the elevator.

Scout sped through the lobby to the boutique. The bills were
sweaty in her palm by the time she handed them over to the clerk.

They did a beautiful job wrapping the gift in black sleek paper and a diagonally tied silver bow.

"Did you want this delivered to your room, Ms. Keats?"

Scout agreed, feeling dizzy from doing something so spontaneous. An attendant in sharp black pants and a Patras blazer came and collected her package and carried it to the elevator. As the elevator doors closed, her eyes focused on the dial rising as ninety-seven dollars traveled farther and farther away from her. Then she felt like she was going to puke.

How could she have been so wasteful? Pearl could've used that money. Or Parker. It could've bought food for the shelter or a coat and a new sweater for Park. Oh, God, she was a terrible person.

"Evelyn?"

Distracted from her self-loathing, she turned and found Patrice, the waxing torture artist from the salon, beside her. "Patrice. Hi."

"You okay? You look a little pale."

Scout swallowed. "I just did something very, very stupid, but I'll live. Definitely a lesson I won't be forgetting anytime soon."

Patrice's lips curved with the practiced grace of someone who's always been beautiful, and she glanced toward the front of the hotel. "Look, I'm done for the day. I was gonna just go home and veg out, but I'll never get a cab in this weather. Wanna come with me to Vogue and get a drink?"

"Oh, thanks, but I don't really drink."

"Well, then how about coming with me to keep me company until the rain lets up? You can tell me all about the stupid thing you did and I'll make you feel better."

Scout was about to politely decline, but then figured what the hell. She was tired of being by herself and could use a break from her reality. "Okay."

They sat at the bar. It was high and long and supershiny. She'd never sat at a bar before. The lighting was dim and gave this part of the restaurant a reddish glow. A handsome man with tanned arms and big muscles came over to them. He wore a Patras golf shirt.

"What can I get you ladies?"

Patrice smiled. Every expression she made had a sultry appearance. This didn't slip the bartender's notice. There was nothing sultry about Scout.

Patrice moved like one of those fancy fish they sold in the Chinese section of Folsom, the kind with the long, fringed fins that flowed and swirled. Her arms crossed delicately as she leaned forward. Her long lashes moved over her pale blue eyes like wispy fronds fanning in a breeze. Her voice, when she addressed the bartender, was more of a purr.

Her lips curved slowly over every word. "I'll take a tequila sunrise and my friend here will have . . ."

Patrice looked at her and Scout panicked. It suddenly felt silly to be sitting at a fancy bar and ordering a water. "Make that two."

"Two sunrises, coming up."

He turned and began pulling bottles down from glass shelves and filling a silver cup with ice. He put on quite a show, raising his arm high as amber liquid poured down in a ribbon of gold. He shook the silver cup and the chilled liquor slid into a glass, causing the red juice he first added to rise like the sun.

Scout smiled. "It's so pretty."

"Like a sunrise," Patrice added, turning her slight smirk and long lashes in her direction.

The bartender slid the glasses in front of them. "Two beautiful sunrises for two beautiful ladies."

Liquor was a funny thing. It burned fast going down, then burned slow once it hit the belly. Scout had never had alcohol before and didn't really feel the effects. By the time she finished her drink she'd practically forgotten about the money she spent and was really enjoying herself.

"Can I get you ladies a refill?"

Patrice smiled and slid a twenty across the bar. Scout's brow puckered. She hadn't thought about paying.

"Wait," Scout said, stilling Patrice's hand. Her nails were very nice. Little, neat, and red. "You bought the first two."

"It's my treat, Evelyn." She smiled softly and Scout breathed in a whiff of her light flowery perfume. Her breath smelled like cherry grenadine.

"No, let me. I have a credit." Her fingers slid the room card to the bartender and he slid it through the machine.

He frowned and brought it back, looking uncertain. "Uh, this card isn't registered to your name."

"Oh." Scout didn't expect to be questioned for using Lucian's card, but she guessed that made sense.

Before she came up with an excuse, Patrice said, "Evelyn's Mr. Patras's guest."

The bartender looked at Scout in question, and she shrugged. "He said I should charge everything to the room."

With no easy way out of this predicament, the bartender jaggedly turned, skepticism slowing his progress, and made their drinks. As Patrice and she chatted, other patrons began to fill the establishment. Voices carried and they slowly began to talk louder, leaning in closer to hear each other.

After they ordered their third drink the bartender was flagged over by a man at the register. They spoke briefly and then the man looked at Scout. She wondered if they would be asked to leave. He made a phone call and left. She forgot about him by her fourth drink.

By the time the bar was full so was her bladder. Whispering to Patrice that she needed to visit the ladies' room, her friend decided to go with her. While she felt fine sitting at the bar, the moment she stood, she realized she was anything but. She lost her balance and Patrice caught her elbow. They giggled the entire way to the ladies' room. Walking in heels while intoxicated was like traveling on a tightrope.

When they returned to the bar, Scout had declared Patrice an excellent friend. She was in such good spirits she ordered drinks for the two men sitting next to them. The men were very appreciative. The one named Stephen stood beside them and told them about the convention he was attending while in town. Feeling loose and cheery, Scout leaned back in her chair and smiled. He didn't have such nice teeth, but he was still a very nice gentleman.

A while later she thought she saw Dugan in the crowd, but at that point everything had begun to swirl and blur. Patrice and she sat facing each other. Patrice laughed and placed her hand on Scout's thigh, little red nails rubbing gently. Stephen stood to her side, arm draped over the back of her chair. She was warm. It was a wonderful feeling, toasty and cozy in her skin.

The soft music that had been playing was turned up and people began to dance. She watched them longingly. Dancing looked fun.

Stephen followed her gaze and shouted over the crowd, "Wanna dance?"

Knowing she'd make a fool of herself if she tried, Scout said, "I—"

"She can't."

With a start, she turned and found Lucian and Dugan standing beside them. Patrice looked terrified.

"Hey! Dugan! What is up, my brotha?" The words just came spewing out of her mouth and then she burst out laughing.

Patrice giggled behind her hand, little red nails curling

delicately. Lucian frowned and Dugan's lips twitched, but his expression remained in its perpetual grimace.

"I thought you didn't drink?" Lucian leaned in and shouted over the noise.

Scout held up her glass in a salute. "I didn't, but I'm doing lots of things I never did before."

Stephen smiled boldly and gestured toward Lucian. "Who's this, Scout?"

Patrice shook her head nervously and Dugan's deep voice carried over the drunken roar of patrons without having to shout. "This is Mr. Patras, the owner of the hotel. Ms. Keats is his guest."

Stephen paled and slunk back into the crowd. Patrice laughed. "That wasn't very nice, Mr. Dugan."

The chauffer frowned at her. She ignored him and held out a hand to Lucian. "It's a pleasure to meet you, Mr. Patras. Patrice Devon. I work at your salon. Had the pleasure of waxing Evelyn the other day."

Scout snorted and felt herself blush. "She did!" She laughed, finding the comment hilarious. "She beat the shit out of my hoo-hoo!"

Pink spread around Dugan's bushy mustache and that only made her laugh harder.

Patrice pouted. "Hey, I did a good job. You know it's nicer now. I bet Mr. Patras likes it, don't you, sir?"

Lucian's lips twitched. Scout realized she should have probably stopped drinking some time ago.

When no one said anything, Patrice leaned forward and stage-whispered, "It's a very nice vagina."

Scout knew Lucian was pissed, but she lost it. Pressing her lips together, fighting a losing battle as laughter bubbled out of her nose and she put her head down on her arms. She leaned into the bar hiccupping with hysterics. Her finger shot up behind her head, telling anyone who was interested that she needed a moment to compose herself.

Patrice fell into peals of laughter right beside her. Scout turned and hugged her. Their arms slid over each other as they continued to cackle. Lucian tapped on the bar and signed something.

He turned and said, "Thank you for keeping Evelyn company, Ms. Devon, but I'm afraid it's time to call it a night. If you would allow, Dugan here will be more than happy to give you a ride home."

Lips pouting dramatically, Scout promised Patrice that they'd do it all again soon. Lucian escorted her to the elevators and her feet stumbled quite a bit. She was intensely aware that for as drunk as she was, he was sober. Her lips firmed to school her expression, but everything was making her giggle.

When they stepped into the elevator, she tripped and Lucian caught her arm.

"I know you think it's the alcohol," she heard herself slur, "but I swear it's these shoes. I can't walk in them." Her weight deposited itself awkwardly on one foot and she laughed.

"I'm sure it has nothing to do with the alcohol," Lucian mumbled dryly.

The door opened and she was suddenly lifted off of her feet as her world turned upside down. She squealed with laughter. Lucian's sweet ass was right in front of her face and her braid hung nearly to the floor. He walked them to the private elevators and she decided she should just *hang* in there. She laughed.

The door to the penthouse opened, and Lucian carried her to the bedroom and flipped her onto the bed. The world spun. She moaned as it righted itself.

"Shhh, stay still," she mumbled to the wavy room.

He plucked off her shoes and they hit the floor with a plunk. Her shirt twisted beneath her breasts and the cool air chilled the skin at her belly.

Scout arched and cooed, "Are you planning on undressing me, Mr. Patras?"

Lucian gave her a sardonic glance and unbuttoned her jeans and slid them over her hips. She lifted and helped him pull them away. Glancing down, she admired the midnight blue lace boy shorts. They looked sexy against her flesh. Tossing her arms over her head, she fell into the pillows so Lucian could have a better view.

"Shirt next," she purred with a giggle. How did Patrice *do* that?

The shirt was pulled over her head without finesse. Her torso lifted and she plopped back onto the soft mattress. More giggles.

Lucian went to the dresser and pulled out a nightgown. She saved him a step and undid her bra. Sliding it off she held it over the edge of the bed and said, "Don't forget this . . ."

He stilled midstride. "Evelyn . . ."

"Lucian," she said, lowering her chin and mimicking his disapproving tone.

He pursed his lips. "You're drunk."

She gasped and covered her mouth. "And naked!"

Rolling to her side, she crawled up onto her knees. When she lost her balance he quickly stepped forward and caught her by her upper arms. "Evelyn, you can barely hold yourself up."

"Then you better not let go," she whispered softly and pressed her lips to his.

To his credit, he didn't kiss her back . . . at first. She pressed her tongue into his mouth and his arms surrounded her, pulling her tight to his front. This was what she had been trying to accomplish for days. Once she had him she wasn't letting go.

Her fingers drove through his dark hair and she knotted her fists at the back of his head. He groaned and tightened his grip around her. The kiss deepened and he climbed onto the bed, kneeling with her. His hands slid down to her lace-bottom and squeezed. She moaned into his mouth.

Releasing her hold on his hair and shoulders, her hands slid down his chest. She yanked his suit jacket back over his shoulders and he quickly stripped it off. Her fingers went to his tie and yanked the knot loose. Once that was tossed away she hastily undid buttons. Her motor skills struggled.

Lucian's hand slid under the midnight blue lace of her panties and grabbed a handful of flesh.

One button was being a real prick.

"Rip it," he growled. Not needing to be told twice, her hands yanked at the silk shirt and buttons went pinging across the room.

He pushed her over and climbed on top of her. His shirt went flying and the moment his arms were free they pinned hers above her head. She arched over the soft, sensual sheets and his hot mouth latched onto her breast. Her raspy voice cried out as he sucked her nipple between his teeth.

Her panties were yanked over her hips. When she didn't lift to help him, the sound of lace tearing filled the air.

"I'm going to eat that pretty pussy of yours," he growled as his mouth kissed lower along her tummy and her thighs were roughly wedged apart.

The first lick of his flat tongue over her slit had her springing off the bed, "Lucian!"

"Don't move."

She struggled to stay still. His warm mouth kissed and tickled her creases. Cool air hit her folds as his thick fingers spread her open. She waited for him to do something, but nothing came.

"Lucian?"

"She's right," he whispered reverently. "You have a beautiful pussy, Evelyn."

Warmth spread from her cheeks to her breasts, and then he kissed an extremely sensitive spot and her fists knotted in the satin bedding as she cried out. It was a sensual assault. Wet strokes lashed at her folds as his fingers kept her spread wide. Her thighs opened as his shoulders drove harder between her knees. She slid up the bed and he gripped her hip, holding her in place as he continued to bring her the most intense pleasure she had ever imagined.

Pressure built and the width of his finger stretched her. He seemed to be reaching for something. He didn't thrust inside of her. Rather, he pressed deep and applied pressure as his mouth latched onto that most sensitive spot and he sucked relentlessly.

Scout screamed as rapid pulses took over her body and had her bearing down. He suckled hard and pressed into her belly with his palm as moisture flooded over her folds. The climax peaked and waned.

"Again," he growled and began driving his fingers into her. She couldn't take it. She began to struggle, needing to break away from the onslaught of pleasure.

"Be still," he commanded, holding her down.

Forcing herself to obey, another intense climax took hold of her. She was panting, mouth open like an animal in heat. Her body rocked and sweat glossed her skin. Her toes pointed as her knees drew up.

When he still didn't stop, she begged. "Lucian, please, I can't take any more."

"You can and you will."

His fingers swirled her arousal, gathering it and creating a slick path that ran down below her crease. His fingers pressed where his mouth had sucked her to climax and relentlessly rubbed over the extremely sensitized bundle of nerves.

His body rose above hers as both hands worked between her legs. "Look at me," he commanded and her eyes opened. Her lashes fluttered as she fought to watch him. "Feel me, Evelyn. Feel the pleasure I bring you."

Fingers pumped into her channel as his hand rapidly brushed over her flesh. He removed his fingers and brought them to his mouth. She watched as he licked at the evidence of her arousal and moaned. His eyes bored into her as he sucked one finger deep.

Her mind seemed to have sobered, the alcohol perhaps burned off by her orgasm. Although she was still a bit sluggish, she seemed trapped more in a sexual haze than a tipsy one.

He stared down at her, his dark, hooded eyes softening and a peculiar expression taking over his face.

"What?" she whispered.

His head shook slowly, fingers tracing whorls over her flat belly. "What am I going to do with you, sweet Evelyn? You have me in knots. Half the time I want to shake you and half the time I want . . ."

When he didn't finish, she asked, "Want to what?"

He continued to shake his head. The urgent way he handled her when they first arrived had transcended into something new and unfamiliar. Intimate. Oddly, she didn't shy from the quiet intimacy. The alcohol must have weakened her boundaries. They seemed cocooned in a whispered secret outsiders would never understand.

Her fingers touched his wrist and he stilled. Dragging the backs of her nails slowly over his arm, he watched her curiously. "You make me break my rules, Lucian," she quietly confessed.

His hand caught hers, lacing their fingers together. He gazed down at her in a way no man ever had. It was as if he actually saw her. She felt exposed, but for some reason it wasn't as frightening. *He* eased her fears of closeness and she had no idea how he managed it.

"You make me break my rules too, Evelyn. You tempt me more than any woman should."

Her body sank into the plush mattress as he leaned over her and kissed her softly. Lips pulled at hers as his tongue slowly seduced her mouth into a gentle serenade. As she reached for his shoulders, he carefully extricated himself from her hold and pressed her hands over her head into the feather pillows.

"Let me," was all he said as his mouth slid to her jaw and worked in tiny kisses to her pulse.

The moment was slow and sultry, languid molasses minutes dripping through time. Every caress had her twisting and moaning softly. When his mouth reached her breasts, his touch was nothing like it had been. His lips closed over her flesh tenderly, reverently, and all those tiny frayed edges of her being knit back together, tightening, blanketing her in a sense of security she only felt when with him.

Long fingers curved around her hips as he kissed her tummy. Dipping his head, his nose traced along her ribs, and soft hair tickled the underside of her breasts. She was trembling. He managed to unhinge some fundamental part of her control and introduce her to the exquisite liberation that came with surrender.

As his mouth journeyed from her breasts to her hips, down to her knees, and teased at her sex, she embraced the indescribable sensation of just letting go. He took her away from it all, the noise, the worry, the struggle. He presented an escape she never realized could exist in this manner of intimacy. This was definitely more than a business agreement.

He brought her to climax more times than she could count.

The tides had changed and there was something to be said for the gentle way he handled her. He was still intense and dominant, but reverent as well. Every touch solidified their bond, a bond she'd normally fear, but her mind was too lost to the pleasure to protest.

They fell asleep holding each other, waking here and there within the dark hours of the night when Lucian soothed her back to sleep with more tender caresses.

twenty-five
. . . . .

PRIDE

DARKNESS and heat surrounded her. Scout's head ached and she needed to pee. Lucian's arm weighed heavily over her waist. She lifted it and slid out of bed. Her body was incredibly weak. She was starving.

Stupefied, she sat in the bathroom longer than necessary. Her fuzzy head felt filled with cotton and her eyes were gritty. She was gross.

Her hands quietly shut the bathroom door and adjusted the dimmer. She winced when she accidentally made the lights too bright. Grabbing her toothbrush, she began brushing her teeth and stepped into the shower. The water washed over her and slowly memories of the night before returned.

Wow, she had been really drunk. Lots of memories of laughing, but she couldn't recall what had been so funny. Patrice was funny, but she wasn't sure why. Scout had the sense that Dugan was unhappy with her.

Lucian. Lucian had been . . . disappointed? No, that wasn't it. He wasn't mad. He hadn't yelled at her. Yet he didn't seem too pleased either. Visions of his fingers undressing her swam at the hazy edges of her mind. Somehow she had seduced him to join her, but how?

Images of Lucian touching her flashed through her head, his mouth on her breasts, her neck, between her thighs. The more she thought about the night before the more she remembered. He had made her scream in pleasure.

She stilled, pulling her toothbrush from her mouth, and she frowned. She'd enjoyed drinking, but the aftermath was annoying. She was sore and confused about events from the evening. Scout rinsed her toothbrush and finished showering quickly.

Did we have sex?

She hated how muzzy her memories were. Wrapping Lucian's robe around her, she then combed the knots from her hair. The bedroom clock proclaimed it was just after five in the morning. She didn't want to wake Lucian, so she went to the common area of the suite.

Scout picked up the phone and dialed nine. When someone at the front desk answered, she quietly whispered, "Hi, this is Evelyn Keats. I'm staying with Mr. Patras. Could you please have someone send up some pastries and a pot of coffee. Mr. Patras is still sleeping, so please have them just leave it outside the door."

Curling into the overstuffed chair, she stared out the window. With it still being dark she could see her reflection quite clear. Sometimes her reflection was like a stranger to her. There was certainly no recognition of the woman staring back at Scout now.

The soft clatter of the tray being placed outside the door and the sound of the elevator descending caused her to rise. She carried the heavy tray over to the table and poured herself some coffee.

As she watched the sun slowly rise behind the buildings dominating the view, she sipped from her mug and nibbled a cheese

Danish, contemplating the night before. Lucian and she had definitely not had sex.

This was a problem.

It was Saturday. Had she really only met him one week ago? As morning arrived the sound of movement began creeping through the building. Elevators dinged and vehicles played a quiet beat over the streets below. Growing tired again, Scout decided to just shut her eyes for a moment. Next thing she knew, Lucian was showered and dressed and pouring himself a cup of coffee in front of her.

"You're up," she rasped.

He nodded. "How do you feel? Hungover, I imagine."

The heel of her palm rubbed the side of her head.

"I was. I woke up at five and showered. I feel a little better now. Sorry about breakfast. I didn't want to order anything that would be cold by the time you woke up."

"It's fine."

"Are you going out?" It was Saturday. The sight of him in a suit made her fear he was leaving.

"I don't know."

"Lucian, can we talk about what's happening here? Honestly?"

He didn't answer.

"We didn't have sex last night."

"I'm aware."

She huffed. "Can you stop with the arrogant one-liners and talk to me? Why won't you fuck me?"

Her words had shocked him. Good. He sipped his coffee and put it down with a sharp click on the table.

"You are not meant to be *fucked*, Evelyn."

"Why?" Her eyes narrowed at him. He was going to explain what was happening between them once and for all. "Why not,

Lucian? You did it once already. My virginity isn't going to grow back, you know."

"I know it isn't," he sneered. "I took that from you and I can never undo that. I wasn't gentle as a man should be with a virgin and I was too fucking selfish to make sure you enjoyed it. I took from you like an animal and I wish you would stop pestering me to do it again."

His words hit her like a slap to the face. She reared back, not fully believing what she just heard. "I'm a pest to you?"

"Evelyn, that's not what I meant—"

"What else could you have possibly meant, Lucian? Please, tell me, because right now I'm torn between bursting into tears or walking out that door and never coming back."

"You're not a pest."

"Then what am I to you? Explain it to me. *Please!* Am I your lover? Am I your friend? Am I someone you see as a charity case? Do you feel indebted to me because you took my virginity? Explain it to me!" Her voice rose with each statement.

He turned on her, his arms boxing her in to the upholstered fabric. She leaned back into the chair. "You are not a fucking charity case. And yes, you are my friend. I want to be intimate with you, but I *can't.*"

"Why, Lucian? Why? You have all these reasons, but you won't share them with me—"

"Because I will hurt you!"

The lash of his words silenced them both. It was ridiculous. Lucian wouldn't hurt her. She was certain of it. It wouldn't make sense for him to be so overprotective with her and then go ahead and do her harm.

"Lucian—"

"Stop. Before you go on assuming you know what I need, just stop. Do you know why Slade's rude to you? Do you?"

She shook her head.

"Because he and I fucked the same woman for years. I don't do vanilla sex, Evelyn. When I met you, I immediately picked up on your submissive nature, but I was a blind fool. You had me so enchanted I missed all the signs of your innocence. My God, I think about how I touched you in front of Jamie and I want to find my best friend and rip out his eyes. But it's my fault because I let him!"

Her mind was still stuck on him and Slade fucking the same woman for years. Was it just one woman or several women and one just stuck around a little longer than the rest? Did they fuck each other? That would explain why Slade hated her, but she couldn't imagine Lucian with another man.

He forked his hand through his dark hair and groaned. "I brought you into this situation and I never should've. How could you have possibly understood what you were agreeing to when you didn't have the first clue about sex? I completely uprooted your life and now I feel responsible—"

"Shut up!" she shouted. Then in a calmer voice, "Just shut up. Don't stand there and act like you are in any way accountable for my life. You don't know the first thing about my life outside of this hotel. You couldn't even cope with me spending one night in a shelter. What about all the nights I slept under a bridge, or on a bench? I was born in an alley, addicted to heroin. Did you know that? Of course not, because you're too busy playing martyr to all my problems. Well they aren't your problems! They're mine! And I don't need you to feel responsible for them anymore." Pity was something she simply could not tolerate.

Scout stood on shaky legs. "I'm leaving. I don't want you to follow me or have Dugan follow me or anyone else for that matter. We clearly don't work together, because while I can overlook all your money and arrogance, *you* will never forget who I was or where I came from. I am *nobody's* charity case, Lucian Patras."

With a confidence she didn't feel, she marched into the bedroom and found her bag. Furious that her hands were shaking, Scout yanked the zipper hard enough that it broke. Her shoulders collapsed at such simple, yet complete, devastation. The bag was the only thing in that world that she owned and she just fucking broke it. Fighting back the fallout that was sure to come, she quickly dropped her robe and pulled her sweatshirt over her head. Once she had her jeans on she grabbed her bag and held the broken zipper together as best as she could and walked to the front door.

Lucian looked as though he'd seen a ghost. Her limbs trembled as she faced him, but he wouldn't meet her gaze.

"Thank you for everything. I hope you find someone who can make you happy." Scout turned and left.

lucian

twenty-six
·····

ALEKHINE'S GUN
A position in which the queen backs up two rooks

THE door slammed and a piece of Lucian's soul ripped away. Her words shredded him. It took everything he had not to bring her back, not to call the front desk and demand they hold her here. In one week's time he'd come to think of Evelyn as his, yet he was incapable of fucking her again.

That look, that haunted, broken look in her eyes, he put that there. It was right for her to leave, but she wasn't going back to her house or her life. She was going back to that goddamn shelter and the streets and she didn't even have a fucking coat!

He walked to the window and stared down at the streets thirty-two floors below. Cars wove in and out of spaces as pedestrians mingled and raced to where they needed to be. *Such monotonous bullshit.*

How had she ever made it this far and come out less damaged than him? Well, that wasn't true. She was notably more damaged since she became associated with him.

I was born in an alley, addicted to heroin.

Roaring in frustration, Lucian turned and swept everything off of the desk.

Stalking to the French doors, he pulled them wide. The blustery November air cut through his clothing as his feet stomped to the heavy railing. Leaning far over the edge until his muscles clenched in fear that he might plummet to his death, he gazed at the tiny people scurrying below. Looking for any sign of Evelyn's dark hair luffing like a sail or that ridiculous pillowcase she called a bag, something inside of him crumbled when he saw nothing but strangers.

There was something indefinable about Evelyn, something no other woman had. She was strong, yet fragile. He could help her in ways others didn't need, yet she didn't need him either. Convincing her to take from him was never an easy task, and now he might never be able to give her anything again.

Stubborn woman.

He tried to convince himself that she'd be back, but the unfamiliar presence of fear weighing in his gut told him otherwise.

Standing out there until his fingers felt bloodless, waiting, watching for any sign of her, Lucian's mind scrambled for a solution. She'd come back. She had to come back. Eventually able to admit to himself that she might never come back and that was for the best, he shut his eyes, swallowed back the lump of pain in his throat, and returned to the warmth of the condo.

A small black package sat on the side table. He hadn't noticed it there before. His brow creased as he slowly stepped closer. Ominous and finite, the little package was incredibly intimidating. A gift. His fingers ran over the sleek black paper and silver ribbon.

Lucian couldn't recall the last time he had opened a present. Visions of childhood holidays with Isadora and Antoinette took him to another place and time. Jamie handing him a pack of baseball cards on his thirteenth birthday he had subtly slipped a mint

Mickey Mantle into, Monique giving him a new set of dishes because she didn't care for the old ones. There was nothing in the past several years. How vacant and meaningless his life had become. His existence had turned into something utterly superficial.

Evelyn was so different from Monique. She lacked the sense of entitlement Monique had always displayed. He'd admired that greatly about Monique, saw it as confidence, but looking back it was more spoiled petulance than anything else. If she hadn't been so all determined to have everything how she wanted it, when she wanted it, she'd likely still be alive today. But he wasn't sure if they'd have stayed together.

Slade was always more indulgent when it came to Monique's tantrums and demands. He'd been the one that bought her that damn bike to begin with. She should have never gotten on that thing, but after getting her way for so long, she accepted the word *no* less and less.

Evelyn, although stubborn in her own way, had a more rational side than Monique could have ever possessed. Evelyn listened and observed and, many times, he could see her brain processing new things she otherwise wouldn't know about. He liked that about her. Years ago he would've referred to Evelyn's outward personality as meek, but now he knew better.

Of the two, Evelyn was definitely the stronger. He hoped she wasn't so strong she'd stay away for good. Maybe she was stronger than him, because while she decided she didn't need him, he very much felt like he still needed her. She saw him in a way no one else did and he didn't want to lose her.

Lucian's presence was sought after for functions in which the purpose had lost all meaning. He couldn't even recall what he was supposed to be supporting last Monday at the museum. Details of Evelyn's crystal eyes and her ice blue gown ate up his memories of that night. It had been so difficult not to maul her the moment he set eyes on her. The memory of her soft skin as he zipped her gown still took his breath away. In that moment he had never wanted anything more than to peel that zipper down instead of up and splay her naked body wide for his pleasure.

Gazing down at the gift box, his finger slid under the silver satin ribbon and tugged. It slackened and slid from the box in a loop closely resembling a noose. He carefully peeled back the heavy paper, recognizing the name on the box from the boutique downstairs.

Plucking the box open, Lucian found crisp black tissue folded, covering a tiny nest that held a treasure inside. Without seeing what the actual gift was, he decided to love it on principle. Evelyn had picked this out. She had seen it and thought of him and that made it special.

As he peeled back the tissue he spotted polished, sleek leather, coiled like a snake. It was a belt, the brushed nickel clasp faded metallic, like gunmetal. Gently, his hands pulled the gift from the box.

As if he'd been given a ribbon of honor, he smiled and wanted to put it on immediately. It was a badge, proof that she thought of him even when he wasn't there. Gingerly placing it back in its box, he shut his eyes, overwhelmed with gratitude for the thoughtful gesture.

This was not an inexpensive gift for someone of Evelyn's means. Scowling at the incredible gift, he wondered if she'd charged it to the room or foolishly used her own money.

"Oh, Evelyn . . ."

His thigh vibrated and he reached into his pocket for his phone. "Patras."

"Lucian, it's Shamus. How are you?"

"Hey, James. What's up?"

"I wanted to let you know that I met with the broker about the property on Macintosh. He says it's a go. You just need to have your attorney okay the paperwork and sign. Slade thinks it's a good deal. His attorney went over it yesterday."

"Where are you now?"

"I'm actually in your neck of the woods. Spent the night with a lovely woman by the name of Tammy."

"Sounds charming."

"Charming she certainly was not, but she could fuck like a sailor on leave so I'm not complaining. How's your little piece?"

It wasn't Jamie's fault the way he referred to Evelyn. He'd have no clue Lucian saw her differently than the rest, especially not after he provided him with a cheap show a few days ago.

"She's . . . she actually just left."

"Left, like ran to grab a paper or . . ." He let the question hang.

"She's gone."

"You okay, Luche? You don't sound too happy about that."

"I'm . . . I don't know. It's for the best I suppose. It wouldn't have worked out."

"That's a shame. She was a stunner. Those eyes . . . gave me something to think about for quite a few nights."

"She isn't like that, Jamie." His jaw locked. He didn't want Jamie thinking of her that way.

"All right. Settle down. Didn't know." He cleared his throat. "If she's so special, how come you let her go?"

"Slade hated her."

Jamie laughed. "Slade hates everyone at first. Lucian, please tell me you're not basing your choices on Slade's preferences. Monique's gone. You need to let her go. The both of you do. Besides, I think you're making a mistake if you find a keeper and decide to share her."

"You didn't think I was making a mistake when you were invited to watch."

"Watching and touching are two totally different things and you know it. Listen, I'm pulling up to Calgary's, then I'm coming over. You want me to grab anything before I get to the condo?"

"No, I'm good."

"All right, I'll see you in twenty."

twenty-seven

·····

BLOCKADE

A strategic placement of minor pieces intended to
provide shelter from an attack

SHADOWS crawled across the ceiling as the insidious ticking of
the clock filled the room. It would soon be dawn and Lucian
hadn't slept a wink. It had been the same for the past four nights.
All he could think about was Evelyn. Was she safe? Was she
warm? Was she thinking about him?

He tried to recall the shelter. He'd been in a rage the night he
found her, showing up with a sole purpose, to get her the hell out
of there. There were more men than women. Every time he imagined her sleeping on that floor alongside other homeless residents,
his gut twisted.

He must have slept for an hour or two. When he awoke at
seven, it was to the sound of his cell vibrating quietly on the night-
stand. Seeing it wasn't anyone he wanted to talk to, he silenced it
and went to shower.

By noon, Lucian was on his way out the door to a meeting at
Finks off the main line. Midweek check-ins clogged the lobby entrance. Jerome held the large glass-plated door and Dugan, in perfect timing, opened the passenger door of the limo.

"Good morning, Mr. Patras," the doorman greeted as he whisked by.

"Good morning, Jerome."

Nodding to Dugan as he outran the chill and slid into the back of the car, the door closed and he was again submerged in warmth. They were soon on their way.

Finks was an open little joint specializing in Italian cuisine leaning more toward lighter fare. Lucian spotted the woman he was looking for as soon as he arrived.

She was dressed in a style he considered understated money. Her clothing was finely made, but subtle, lacking any pompous flare or designer tags. She stood on her burgundy square-heeled shoes as he approached the table.

"Mr. Patras," she greeted and smiled. "It's a pleasure to finally meet you. I admire what you've been doing with the old Poplar building." Her handshake was completely asexual, not overcompensating; firm, but also lacking any feminine grace.

"Thank you for taking this meeting, Mrs. Morris."

"Please, call me Paula."

"Paula, then. And call me Lucian."

The waiter deposited menus and they each ordered their beverages. Business lunches were a strategy meant to distract and relax guests, and he always made sure not to fall too far into the comforts of the surroundings. He quickly ordered a light grilled chicken salad and handed back his menu, not wanting to waste too much time on the superfluous rituals of social etiquette.

"Slade tells me you're interested in St. Christopher's," Paula said before sipping from her sweet tea. "I must admit I'm a little surprised. I've watched your career at a distance and noticed you tend to stick to the more artistic charities. I'm flattered you're considering involving yourself with our shelter."

Leaning back, he eyed his lunch companion with friendly ease.

"I don't know anything about what it takes to run a shelter, I'll admit, but I'd like to make the conditions more . . . agreeable to the guests."

"Residents," she corrected. "That's wonderful. I'm not sure if Slade told you, but the fire inspector's been coming down on us pretty hard lately. The school is passable, but the church should've been condemned years ago. It's a constant struggle to run a charitable organization when repairs are needed. Most of our budget goes to utilities and supplementing the pantries when supplies are low.

"Being that tomorrow's Thanksgiving, we'll have a surge of donations from local food banks that will get the residents through the next two weeks, but after that, as the holiday season approaches, people tend to get caught up in securing their own luxuries, rather than considering what the less fortunate actually need."

It had completely slipped his mind that tomorrow was Thanksgiving. That meant he'd be traveling back to the estate tonight and heading to Isadora's in the morning. The tediousness of a day with family immediately registered itself, forming a knot between his shoulders.

Paula continued to list the various needs of the shelter. He decided that while food was not an immediate issue, clothing was. He'd order bulk shipments of coats, gloves, hats, socks, and shoes and have them sent over as soon as possible. Next week he'd look into the building's structural issues and see what could be done there. Slade was on the factions committee, and he'd know best where to start.

Paula admitted to not being too sure about the facility's structural needs. She said after last year's battle with the township, it was a wonder they remained open at all. Slade had spearheaded the campaign to keep the shelter alive. Lucian was grateful he had.

No matter how much Slade didn't support his interest in Evelyn, he was still a philanthropist on some level. The shelter had been a cause of his since he graduated, taking up right where his mother had left off with the charity. Lucian wondered if he was coming around on the Evelyn front or if he had called him the night he found her in hopes it would smother all interest Lucian had in the woman.

After taking care of the bill, he thanked Paula and promised to be in touch. Upon their return to the hotel, he told Dugan to hang tight and quickly packed his briefcase with things to keep him busy on the ride out of the city. Within the hour they were leaving Folsom and he was on his way to an intense, family-crammed holiday. His palms were already sweating.

twenty-eight

PAWNS

The weakest pieces in the game

ISADORA put out a beautiful spread. Distraction was easily found in asserting his skills of intimidation over Antoinette's date. Peter Cross was a slimy little crawler with a knockoff Rolex, who liked to touch his baby sister a little too much.

"You're rotten, Lucian," Isadora teased as he washed his hands at the kitchen sink.

"Quite, but what's brought about your scrutiny today?"

She laughed melodically as she transferred the remainder of turkey into a disposable silver tray.

"Poor Peter's going to need a new pair of underwear by the time he leaves here."

"I don't care for the way he handles Antoinette. He should have respect. He's in our family home."

"They're twenty-two and in love, Lucian. It isn't like he's grop-ing her ass at the dinner table."

"He better not be," he growled, tossing a dishtowel on the granite countertop.

"She's not a baby anymore, Lucian."

That was true. She was the same age as Evelyn, yet Antoinette still seemed like a little girl in pigtails.

Isadora sealed a lid over the leftovers and turned. "I talked to father today. He and Tibet send their regards and apologize for not making it back to the States."

"Like we ever expected them to."

Tibet was his father's mistress. She'd basically come with his father's marriage to their mother, like an unfortunate stowaway they all turned a blind eye to. When their mother passed away, when they were all under the age of twelve, Antoinette merely a toddler, Christos Patras had abandoned his children and legacy and taken off to Europe to fornicate with his mistress, where he wouldn't be under the judgmental eye of his and Lucian's mother's upper-crust circle.

Lucian's teenage years had been a navigation of misplaced anger and rebellion at being abandoned by the only parent he had left. Isadora took on the role of nurturer. Tutors saw to his education, ensuring he had the proper well-bred edification of any baron apprentice. He'd earned his master's just after he disenfranchised the company he saw as his father's last standing pride and joy, and earned his first million independent from his legacy shortly after.

The Patras name was plenty a foundation to stand on. By his midtwenties Lucian had held the impressive prestige of men twice his age, because none of them could compete with his family's worth. Their name had been a trusted brand since the turn of the century, when his great-great-grandfather had opened a charming little inn that catered to the upper class within the limits of a little metropolitan town called Folsom. They now had a fleet of luxury hotels spanning the globe and more money than any of them knew what to do with.

Lucian pulled his thoughts from the past with an effort. After the remainder of the meal was dealt with, they gathered in the great room to watch a little of the game. Although his eyes never left the television, minus the sidelong glances at Peter and his wandering hands, he wasn't even aware which teams were playing. His mind was focused on Evelyn.

Was she eating a turkey feast? Did the shelter acknowledge the holiday? What was she thankful for? He thought about the young man named Parker. It wouldn't surprise him if the two of them found comfort in each other's company. He cared for her very much, that was obvious in the longing way he watched her, whether Evelyn saw it or not.

Lucian's gut twisted at the thought of someone else holding her, touching her, kissing her. He didn't want to think of those silver blue eyes staring into someone else's face with the same awe she sometimes looked at him with. The boy would never be able to provide the right type of life for her, the kind that would extricate her from the gutters of Folsom and put her where she deserved to be.

Parker Hughes wasn't really a boy, though, was he? No, he was a man with a disadvantage. The prick that Lucian was, part of him wanted the other man to stay down so he'd never have her. He should be hoping Parker ran into some luck so Evelyn could maybe find some small measure of happiness, but he was selfish. She was his.

Evelyn was intended for something better. Everyone saw it, except for poor innocent Evelyn herself. He bet she hadn't even realized what a ruckus she had caused at the bar the other night. What would she have done if she knew not only that clinger hovering at her chair was hoping to get a piece of her, but her friend from the salon, Patrice, also would've been more than willing to follow her to bed that night?

When he arrived at Vogue after Dugan received a call from the manager that a woman was using his card, he wanted to stomp in there like a possessive animal and mark every inch of her. Eyes from all directions were crawling over her body.

While everyone else had painstakingly chosen designer duds and invested extra time in their appearances in order to patronize the ritzy bar, Evelyn had worn nothing but a cotton T-shirt and jeans with those sexy fuck-me pumps. She stuck out like a sore thumb. Not because she was underdressed, but because even without the effort made by the others, she was easily the most beautiful creature in the room.

His jaw popped and he unclenched his teeth. She was no longer his and he'd have to accept she would always gain the notice of other men and women. She was stunning and sweet and made it incredibly easy for him to go the extra mile and do something generous he normally wouldn't even consider. He'd do anything, just to see that look of admiration in her eyes. But what if that meant letting her go?

He realized the game had ended when Peter stood.

"Well, Annie, you ready to head home?"

This douche bag . . .

Antoinette lived in a cozy little condo at the top of a swank establishment he had finished just in time for her twentieth birthday. Lucian had no doubt Peter was making himself quite at home in her condo, using her cable, eating her food. He reminded himself, again, that Antoinette and Evelyn were essentially the same age and she had as much of a right to live her life the way she chose as Evelyn did. It didn't help.

Slapping Peter hard on the back, Lucian squeezed his shoulder until he winced. "Why don't you come down to the city sometime, Pete? I'd love to show you what it is I do, let you get your feet wet in the real world for a day or two, see if you got what it takes."

"Luche, Peter isn't interested in industrializing the world. He wants to be an instructor," Antoinette said with doe-eyed affection for her boyfriend.

"An instructor of what?" he asked.

"Martial arts," Peter chimed in, an unreliable worldliness to his voice.

Lucian's gaze narrowed as he skeptically took in his lanky build. "What belt are you?"

The younger man shifted his feet apprehensively. The motion was a complete contradiction to his upturned chin. "I'm not any belt yet, but I'm planning on starting classes this spring."

Good grief. Antoinette needed to drop this moron. Quick. "Well, good luck with that," he said, not bothering to disguise his unimpressed tone.

Once they all made their good-byes and his sisters promised they would get together in Folsom sometime before Christmas, he headed to his Rolls and planned to take the scenic way home in order to take in the open land. Hopefully the crisp air would erase the images of silver eyes and chestnut waves filling his head.

twenty-nine

COVER

To protect a piece, perhaps by placing the king in check

I T was bitterly cold on Monday when Lucian returned to the city. Climbing out of the limo, he hustled up the steps to Patras, the blustery wind chapping his cheeks in the mere seconds it took him to reach the warm interior of the lobby.

"Good morning, Mr. Patras," numerous attendants greeted as he passed quickly to the elevators. Sniffles and coughs filled the air, mixing with the low chatter of normal check-in traffic. Winter had arrived.

Entering the condo he found his mail and several messages awaiting him. He checked his phone and saw that Slade and Jamie would be arriving any minute. As he sorted through the mail, the soft chime of the elevator sounded and he moved to answer the door.

"Shit, it's miserable out," Jamie said as he undid his coat and tossed it over the back of a chair. Slade moved with quiet stealth, not needing to state the obvious like Jamie so often did.

"You guys eat?" Lucian stacked the mail on the heap of papers on his desk for later.

"I'm good. Coffee would be welcome though."

Coffee was ordered and they jumped right into business. Jamie took the signed contracts he'd been waiting for and Slade sighed with relief. This deal was one they'd all been anxious to conclude.

Papers were sealed in envelopes and a messenger arrived to deliver them directly to the Realtor finalizing the deal.

"Well, it's good to see that finally over," Jamie said, leaning back and exhaling a long-held breath.

Slade snickered. "It's just beginning now. This is going to be a nightmare once we get into zoning."

"It'll be fine," Lucian commented, wanting to move on to more important issues. "Slade, I'm having a shipment of winter clothing sent over to St. Christopher's tomorrow. I spoke to Paula and she said to check with you to make sure someone's there to receive the delivery."

Slade's expression became unreadable. An unsavory sense of dread ran through Lucian's veins.

"What?" he asked, knowing this wouldn't be good.

Slade, always so in command of himself, actually stuttered. "Uh, Luche, I'm not sure what Paula told you, but we've sort of been battling hard with the fire inspector lately."

"She mentioned that. I'm going to send a crew over there to see what needs to be done and have everything taken care of." There was no sign of relief in Slade's expression. "What?"

The other man squirmed uncomfortably, then stood, walking his coffee cup to the tray and reaching for his coat. "There's nothing that could've been done at this point. Our donors are tapped with the upcoming holiday and recent surplus of residents."

Irritated at his inability to get to the point, he gritted, "Spit it out, Slade. What are you getting at?"

"They barred the doors on Black Friday. The sprinkler system failed inspection and the fire inspector condemned the building."

Pressure built between Lucian's ears as a sudden red rage blurred his vision. He lunged at Slade, fisting his lapels and jerking him against the table. Jamie shouted and grabbed his shoulders. "You knew! You fucking knew this was going to happen and you didn't tell me!" he growled in his face.

Jamie ripped him off of Slade and he panted, ready to spring back at him again. Slade batted the wrinkles out of his jacket then glared at him. "What fucking difference does it make, Lucian? Another shelter will open eventually and they'll all move on. She's fucking homeless! Do you understand what that means? They're filthy and thieves and addicts—"

Lucian shoved Slade and he shoved back. Jamie jumped between them. *"Enough!"* Jamie shouted. "This is bullshit! Both of you back the fuck up."

They each took a step back and scowled at one another.

"Fuck you, Slade," Lucian spat. "She isn't like that."

He was a hypocrite, helping the homeless from afar, but never really believing they deserved to join the ranks of the working class. It was the same self-serving, pompous bullshit the rest of the upper class pretended at to make them feel less like rich snobs. Evelyn may not be upper class, but she didn't belong on the streets.

The sense of being betrayed cut through him. Evelyn was right. Slade didn't like her. But this was more than a matter of taste or his sensitive feelings regarding Monique's memory. This was an act of Judas.

"I don't get you, man," Slade said, shaking his head. "What did you expect to gain from associating with her? She doesn't have a clue about our world. You see this doll you've dressed up and fucked, but you're missing the big picture. I don't even want to think who's visited that well before you."

Lucian hadn't realized he moved. He only registered the sharp sting of Slade's face slamming into his knuckles.

"Get the fuck out of my home!"

Slade glared up at Lucian from where he was sprawled across the table. Dabbing the corner of his lip gingerly, he licked a bit of blood and spit on his carpet.

"You've changed, Lucian. She's a poor excuse for Monique, but you'll realize that eventually. Good luck finding her. I'm sure once you see the squalor that spawned her you'll understand what I was trying to tell you."

Lucian's jaw cracked as he breathed harder than a bull through his nose. Never again would he see Slade as anything more than a prick colleague. He was done.

thirty

SIMPLIFICATION

Strategy of exchanging pieces, which can amplify an opponent's
advantage and strengthen their endgame

THE scent of burning refuse permeated the frigid air. Tramps huddled over burning garbage cans stared as the limo slowly crawled by. Faces looked the same, vacant eyes peeking from dirty visages, hopelessly staring at the world moving around them. They'd been trolling the bowels of Folsom for days, with no sign of Evelyn.

It had begun to snow. December barreled in like a stampede, clearing the streets, leaving a hollow wake. Every night on the news there were posted advisories about the frigid temperatures. Lucian secured the permits for St. Christopher's yesterday and the crew was gutting the school and church at that very minute. He hired a night shift in order to get the job done as quickly as possible and get the shelter up and running again.

They took the corner slowly so that they could scan each body huddled in the cold.

"Stop." The limo halted abruptly and he climbed out. "Evelyn . . ." His words fell away as a young woman, similar in height and build, stared up at him with dark eyes and a toothless mouth, nothing like Evelyn's. "My apologies. I thought you were someone else."

Turning, he noticed several curious eyes on him. "I'm looking for a woman named Scout. Do you know her?"

"I may know her," an older man with a lazy eye and discolored beard jaggedly grown in over a ruddy, scarred face said. "What's it to you?"

His nose was made up of one pocked divot after another. His coat was worn and moth-eaten. Lucian could smell him from several feet away. Reaching in his pocket, he withdrew his phone and a few cards.

Dugan stood at the hood of the car, shivering. Flurries coated his shoulders. "Here, Dugan, take this."

Lucian handed Dugan his belongings and stripped off his Armani wool trench. Walking over to the man claiming to know Evelyn, he held out the lined coat. "Here."

The man eyed him skeptically.

"Take it. It's supposed to drop another ten degrees tonight. You need it more than I do."

He snatched the coat and quickly shrugged it on. It was too large for him. "What you want with Scout?"

"I don't wish to cause her harm if that's what you're wondering. I just need to know that she's safe."

The man's mouth worked, shrinking into a pucker over his toothless hole. "She comes to see Pearl now and then, but Pearl ain't been 'round much. Moved on some time ago."

"Pearl?" Lucian's fists dug into his pockets and his body jerked with shivers.

The man nodded. "Yessir. Pearl used to take care of us men here, so long as we get her a fix when she done her job."

Dread moved through him like eels in a swamp as his brain worked out what the man meant. *Fuck.* He needed to get to Evelyn.

"Do you know where I can find Pearl?"

He shrugged. "Lots of people know Pearl. She sick now. No one wants anything from her no more. Like I said. Moved on some time go."

Lucian nodded and mumbled a thank-you. Even the warmth of the limo did nothing to warm his blood. "It'll be getting dark soon, sir," Dugan announced as he pulled away.

"Keep driving."

They returned to the hotel sometime after two a.m. There was no telling where the needy went after dark. They had driven over every dilapidated road and looked in every dark alley, but found no one who could help them find Evelyn or this Pearl character.

The poignant reality he'd witnessed tonight was enough to haunt him for the rest of his life. The fact that these were people, human beings, living like rats among the gutters disturbed him to no end. Not because of their filth or pitiable circumstances, but because of their hardships, their hunger, and the bitter pain in their eyes. Such hopelessness.

Lucian awoke before dawn and stood on his balcony looking over the dark streets. A wash of light followed the swoosh of the random car cutting through the slush covering the pavement. Patras's walks had been maintained by the hour and were pristinely cleared for pedestrians while the rest of the world was two steps behind.

The low groan of plow trucks making their way down the city streets in a grid pattern brought about a familiar sound of winters past. The thick marble railing along the balcony was caked with at least six inches of white death. The reality that people died last night from the cold and precipitation made it impossible to focus on the ordinary mundane worries of his typical existence. It all seemed suddenly small.

Returning inside he picked up the phone and dialed nine.

"Front desk."

"This is Lucian Patras. I need a town car and driver brought around right away."

"Yes, Mr. Patras."

He hung up the phone and went to his closet to find another coat. Dugan had driven for over eight hours yesterday and would likely still be sleeping. He could take the second shift.

A young man by the name of Clint met him out front with a Lincoln Town Car. "Good morning, Mr. Patras," the man said, holding the door.

The interior was still cool. He climbed behind the wheel. "Where will you be going today, sir?"

"Head down to lower Folsom. Drive slow and be prepared to stop if I say so."

The driver's mouth opened, but he kept his questions to himself. He shifted and merged onto the street. The town car bumped and glided over the snowy streets as the vacant walkways passed by.

By eight, the streets were all plowed and he had still found no signs of Evelyn. "You know where the old St. Christopher's church is?"

Clint nodded and navigated in that direction.

The sky was a cocoon of gray, wrapped tight around the city. Snow was never a beautiful thing in Folsom. It was discarded as an inconvenience and stained black as soon as the plows forced it aside. Wet, salted walkways had pedestrians clumsily skipping puddles and drifts. The only good thing about the snow was where the plows wouldn't go, footsteps could be found. There were trails leading in and out of abandoned buildings and cutting across chained-off industrial parks. It gave away where someone without proper shelter might be hiding.

He'd visited over a dozen shelters. No one recalled seeing a woman that met Evelyn's description, not with her eyes or length of hair and petite frame. The town car pulled into the broken parking lot of St. Christopher's. The construction crew was in full swing. "Pull over by the steps."

Clint maneuvered the car as close to a snow-embanked curb as possible, and Lucian climbed out before he had a chance to get the door.

"Wait here. I shouldn't be long."

"Yes, sir."

Taking the steps two at a time, his tension eased slightly at the sound of hammers hammering, drills boring into fresh Sheetrock, and saws trimming. Progress was being made, and that was a good thing. Lucian stilled when he caught movement out of the corner of his eye.

Someone was lying in the brick embankment that was once a flowerbed alongside the building. Wool skullcap and a thickly wrapped scarf were all he could see at first. The bulk of the body was disguised by layers upon layers of clothing. When the person shifted to sit up, Lucian caught his scruffy profile and saw that it was male. Several days' growth of beard covered his chapped red cheeks. His light green eyes turned on him and he stilled.

"Parker?"

A rattling cough preceded his sardonic greeting. "Well, well, if it isn't Prince Charming. She's not here. No one is."

Dropping all underlying disinclination, Lucian looked at him with all the humility he possessed. "Do you know where she is?"

The other man glared at him for a moment, clearly taking his measure. Lucian poured all his worry and concern into the space between them, and Parker sighed. "No. I don't. I haven't seen her in three days."

Three days. That was *something*. Eleven days less than the time that lapsed since Lucian had seen her.

"Where was she?"

Parker's lips pressed tight into a thin, silent line between the scruff of his beard.

"I want to help her, Parker. I swear it. I . . . I care for her."

"Maybe she doesn't want to be found."

Lucian hesitated a moment, then leveled with him. "Look, I know how you feel about her. I could let her go and give you my blessing, but you and I both know I can offer her more. If you really love her, let me help her. Help me find her. Please. I swear I only want to do right by her."

When several minutes passed and Parker said nothing, Lucian figured he wouldn't help. Then he surprised Lucian by saying, "You hurt her."

"I did," Lucian admitted.

"I don't know what you did or said. Scout has a habit of fixing everyone else's problems and not letting anyone help her with her own. What I do know is that whatever you did, it hurt her bad. Scout doesn't cry and you changed that."

Guilt and shame cut through him. "I'll make it right," he vowed more to himself than to anyone else. "Please just help me. I'm begging you here, Hughes."

Parker smirked. "Not something a guy like you does often, I imagine."

"You've got me. I'm putting it all on the table. My hands are tied here. I've been driving around for days searching for her. I'm out of ideas. You have an idea of where she might be. What do I have to do to get you to help me?"

The other man's lips pursed and his green eyes jerked away, then back again. He exhaled noisily. "Fine. You want to help her? Well, I don't trust you. Guys like you don't do anything without an ulterior motive. Scout needs . . . stability. She'll do anything to get it. Problem is, she associates stability with money."

"She's right."

"Says you. Judge me all you want, but I want to see you fail. However, if you fail so does she, and that's not what I want. I want her to have the life she's after. I want to see her keep a good job, have her own home, and never have to worry when she'll eat next."

"I can do all that for her. That's the plan."

"Ah, but I won't see it." Parker stood and Lucian noticed him limp slightly. No matter how strong he pretended to be, it was obvious his circumstances left him quite weak. "You're an audacious fellow. I have a proposition for you. I'll take you to her, but I want to be there when she gets everything she wants. I want to *see* all those dreams of hers come true. I want a job. You give me a job and I get back on my feet. At that point, you give me a fair shot at her. I'm not saying right away. I'll need some time. But when I'm ready, I say the word and you back off and give me a fair shot. One month where you don't interfere."

Not a chance.

Lucian learned a long time ago how to act unaffected during the negotiations stages of a deal. "She may have a problem with that, you realize. Evelyn doesn't like being maneuvered without her feelings being considered."

"Then I suppose we both lose."

Lucian's eyes narrowed. Patient Parker had a very shrewd side to him. Something told Lucian the other man had no problem letting him walk away and never telling Evelyn he was here. Every hour of cold made a difference. This wasn't a situation where one could wait out the other.

It would backfire on Parker, of course. Lucian never broke his word once given, but Parker would somehow break the deal on his own. There was something about the kid that didn't stem from growing up on the streets. Something . . . informed, innate. Careful not to underestimate him, Lucian would do some research of his own and make sure he never got what he was after *without* cheapening the value of his word.

"Okay, Hughes. You've got yourself a deal, but let me give you some free advice. One, she'll eventually find out you only agreed to help her after securing your own chance at gaining something, and I give you my word I won't be the one to tell her this. Two, she won't like it when she does find out. Three, I haven't gotten where I am today by giving in easily. A challenge is just that to me. And four, I always get what I want."

"Keep your fucking advice, Patras. All I'm interested in is a job and your word."

"You have it." Lucian extended his leather-clad hand.

Parker eyed it and then grudgingly shook it with his own. "Let's go."

thirty-one

HANGING

Unprotected and exposed

ADRENALINE coursed through Lucian's veins at the twin snap of the doors on the town car slamming out the cold. "Clint, this is Parker Hughes. Hughes, this is Clint. Mr. Hughes is going to be your copilot. Talk."

The car kicked into drive, as did his heart.

Parker leaned forward. "Take Wisely two blocks and keep going. Don't turn left until you hit the tracks."

Clint drove for several minutes as Parker navigated through a winding labyrinth of neglected roads surrounded by dilapidated buildings, until they parked in front of a condemned old mill. Boards concealed the windows that weren't shot through, and graffiti was scribbled over everything that was reachable from the ground.

"She's here? You're sure of it?"

Parker pointed to a banged-up, rusted garage door at one of the raised bays. "See that door there? She slides under it. It's dark and there's worse things than glass to cut yourself on if you aren't careful. She'll be in the last room at the last corridor on the other end. Ready?"

Parker leaned forward and Lucian pushed him back with his palm. "Wait."

Parker sat back and scowled.

"Clint, call Dugan and tell him to meet me here. Take Mr. Hughes back to St. Christopher's. He's no longer necessary."

"We had a deal!"

"And I gave you my word. Be at Patras tomorrow at six a.m. Someone will meet you there to orient you with your new position. I'm giving it to you, Hughes, but mess up, show up late, do anything that's unacceptable and, like any other employee of mine, you lose it. Keeping the job's on you."

"And what about the other half of my deal?"

"You have until she agrees to marry me. Wait too long . . ." Lucian shrugged. "But Hughes, if she doesn't want to go to you, I won't make her."

Lucian noticed the front the other man had been putting up so far shifted. No matter what, the cards were always stacked in his favor when it came to something he wanted. He made sure of it.

He gripped the handle of the door and Parker quickly asked, "What if she isn't there?"

"Then both of us are fucked."

Lucian climbed out and slammed the door. Clint drove off. One fortifying breath and his legs were moving. He hoisted himself onto the cement bib outside the door. Like Hughes had said, it was propped open enough for a person to slide under. Sighing, his knees dropped to the cold ground, he gathered the tails of his coat to his body and slid under the opening.

The acrid stink of urine and waste practically choked him. His eyes adjusted to the dim light and he headed in the direction Parker had pointed. People lurked in shadows, and small fires burned here and there. No one seemed to pay him any mind, their focus purely on keeping warm.

There was a dense area that was set up like a compound of sorts. He pushed through the putrid odor of human waste, and the smell dispersed as the individuals thinned out. When he reached the last corridor, the silence seemed impenetrable. It was as if he'd left the last of the living and traveled somewhere altogether worse, some circle of Dante's, he was sure. Except it was so fucking cold.

The reverberation of his steps echoed down the quiet corridor, and the sound of a muffled cough trickled from the very end. His steps grew faster and soon he was running. He slowed as he approached the last door. Needing a steadying breath before he faced whatever he was walking into.

Turning the corner, Lucian found what looked like a dead body sprawled on a collapsed stack of cardboard boxes. Emaciated fingers protruded like sticks from fingerless gloves, and breath was sucked audibly from the rank cell, followed by a rattling cough. Not Evelyn.

As his eyes shut he heard a slight clatter and jerked around. There in the corner, back to the wall, curled in a little ball was his Evelyn. Taking two long steps to reach her, he fell to his knees and pulled her to him. She jerked, startled, and weakly struggled.

"Shh, shh, Evelyn, baby, it's me. I'm here."

Her body shook violently. Her skin was chilled right through her clothing. Her eyes were surrounded with purple shadows and her chin quivered as her teeth chattered.

"L-L-Lucian?"

"Yes. Come on. I'm getting you out of here."

Relief was a living thing, infusing him with energy and the strength to do whatever needed to remove her from this vile place.

The body in the corner began to hack violently. Evelyn scrambled out of his arms and crawled to the heap of flesh and bones hidden under layers of dirty fabric. She quickly uncapped a bottle of cloudy water and pressed it to the person's blue lips as she cradled the head in her lap. The person, a woman, gasped and choked, but eventually settled back into a restless sleep, mumbling and chanting nonsense.

"Evelyn, come on. Let's leave this place."

"How did you get here, Lucian?" He saw that his presence cost her a chunk of pride. She didn't want him to see her like this. He didn't care.

He went to her and took her hand, urging her to stand. "It doesn't matter. I'm here and we're leaving."

She snatched her hand back. "No. You shouldn't have come. I can't leave Pearl."

Pearl. He gazed down at the heap of rotting flesh. She was infected with some disease and clearly dying. He warred with choices, Darwinism versus compassion. He tried to understand the fierce loyalty Evelyn felt for this person.

"Who is she, Evelyn? She's sick and I'm not sure moving her is wise."

Her silver eyes, so incredibly weary, looked up at him. A sheen of tears built and trickled past her matted lashes. "She's my mother."

Her words cut through him with realization and sympathy. The woman was at death's door and Evelyn wouldn't leave her. The pain he felt for her, with her, in that moment was crippling. Lucian's mind went back to his mother's funeral, the agony of loss, the relentless force insisting he remain stoic and strong in the face of fear, the emptiness, the irrelevance of it all, the immeasurable consuming grief, the nothingness that had stolen all the color from his world for so long. He couldn't ask her to walk away.

Swallowing the lump in his throat, he stood and surveyed the room. Mold corroded the walls. Water trickled down the plaster, leaving a puddle in the corner. There was a flipped-over box with an oxidized candle, a spoon, a strap, and a syringe. Heroin.

His eyes landed on Evelyn's bag and he scooped it up and handed it to her. "Here."

"What're you doing?" Her breath formed a cloud of vapor between them in the frigid room.

Kneeling, he scooped up her mother, her body shockingly light, and stood. "We're getting out of here."

Her jaw shook and her eyes watered. "Lucian, w-why?"

He shifted the practically weightless body in his arms. "You ask me that entirely too often, Evelyn. Because I love you. Is that answer enough for you?"

Her face crumbled with emotion and she lowered her chin then raised it, breathing in a rough sob. "Yes."

thirty-two
· · · · ·

ODDS

An advantage given by the stronger player to a weaker player

EVELYN sat in the overstuffed chair facing the window, looking small and lost. Her pallid eyes were without expression. Her hair, still wet from the shower, was combed back, making those tired eyes seem huge, the soft skin appearing bruised around the silver pools. Lucian handed her a cup of coffee, and she stared at him for a moment as if she'd forgotten his presence and couldn't quite make sense of it. Her exhaustion was so evident. It showed in her motor skills as well as her reflexes, both verbal and physical. He fit her small hands around the warm, steaming mug, and she turned back to the window.

Several long, silent moments later, the guest room door quietly opened. Vivian stepped out and pulled the door shut, at the same time managing to leave it slightly open. Her face was somber. She discreetly sent him a bleak gaze before she approached Evelyn.

With perfect bedside manner, she gently touched Evelyn's shoulder, drawing her out of her contemplative trance. "Evelyn?"

She looked up at Vivian, desperate hope softening her features. "Is she going to die?"

Vivian's expression softened and for the first time ever, he saw his sharp vixen friend appear more of a nurturing woman than he ever imagined her capable of. "No, sweetheart, she's not going to die. Not today."

Evelyn's relief was evident. Her body crumpled as she sobbed a breath and folded her face into her hands. Vivian wrapped her in her arms and he wanted that honor, but wasn't sure his touch would be welcome.

Lucian watched from the shadows of the room as Evelyn cried, and felt absolute impotence with his inability to fix this for her, or perhaps it was his fear that she wouldn't want his help that had him paralyzed.

Her upset slowly faded and Evelyn wiped at her eyes, once again establishing the invisible walls that kept her apart from others and protected her from them all. "I'm sorry," she said to Vivian. "I was certain she wouldn't make it another day."

"Your mother's sick, Evelyn," Vivian stated empathetically. "Hepatitis is something that needs to be monitored and treated. Her immunities are very low right now, fighting off infection. Her bronchial passages aren't at their best and she's running a fever, but her biggest issue is the withdrawal symptoms she's suffering."

Evelyn's body tensed as if she wanted to stand, but she lowered her weight back into the chair. "She's addicted to heroin. I . . . I can get it for her."

"Absolutely not," Lucian said fiercely. Evelyn was never going into those dark corners of the city again. She seemed startled by his comment as if it reminded her of his presence in the room once again. She was all he thought about for weeks, yet she kept forgetting his presence with every passing minute.

She's tired. His self-assurance rang hollow and was cold comfort.

In a much calmer manner, Vivian said, "No, Evelyn. Drugs aren't what she needs. She needs to dry out."

"But she won't. If I don't get it for her she'll sell herself for her next high."

Vivian purposefully glanced around the penthouse. "No one's here for her to do that with now, and she's too weak to go back to where she came from. I know it won't be easy for you to hold her against her will, but you actually have all the power right now to get her through this. If you have the energy, that is?"

"We can't stay here."

Vivian glanced at him, then speculatively back at Evelyn. "I don't think moving her would be wise."

"You're staying," he said, putting the issue to rest. "Pearl can stay until she's well enough to move. At that point I'll pay to have her placed in a rehab facility with the best doctors who specialize in this sort of thing, and she'll get well."

"She won't go," Evelyn said in the most defeated voice he had ever heard her use. He didn't like seeing her so hopeless.

"Her other choice is to return to the streets and freeze to death. Surely once she finds her bearings she'll realize the danger of that. There's a blizzard coming in the next couple of days."

She bit her lip nervously. "You don't know what you're inviting into your home, Lucian. You've never seen someone go through withdrawal before, watching them tear at their skin because *everything* is agony. She'll soil your home and be so far out of her head she won't care about shitting on your sheets or vomiting on your carpet. What do you plan to do when she comes clawing at you like a feral animal because she resents all of your help and would rather die than live with it? She doesn't want a sober life. She'd choose death first. I know it."

"Do you think I'd blame you for her actions when she's sick? I don't care if it's a thankless, uphill, unending battle. I'm not letting you do this alone."

Several agonizing seconds ticked by like fortnights. The scratch of Vivian scribbling something down on a pad of paper was the only sound as he stared challengingly into Evelyn's tired eyes. He turned when Vivian touched his sleeve. She handed him a script.

"This is the name of a clinic outside of the city. Tell them I sent you and I'm sure you'll have no problem getting her in. It's pricey, but I doubt that will be an issue. She won't be ready to move for at least three days. Maybe seven. She's going to have to want to be clean or even the best facility, doctors, sponsors, and all the support in the world won't help her. There are teas she can take. I'll have a messenger send some over. She probably won't eat for a few days. When she does, start light, dry toast, soft eggs. Nothing too heavy. You have my number if you need anything."

There wasn't much time to talk after Vivian left. It seemed the moment the door closed, a tornado of misery unleashed within the walls of the condo. Evelyn went right into action, her weak body obviously struggling to endure far past the point of her own exhaustion in order to be there for her mother.

Pearl carried on for hours without allowing Evelyn a moment's respite. She screamed and feebly fought Evelyn back. It occurred to him the woman did not recognize her daughter. She often cried and called for Scout, rejecting Evelyn's touch, calling her vile names, and accusing her of killing her baby.

She was out of her head, and he worried that perhaps she suffered from more than destroyed brain cells and hard living. This couldn't be just from drugs. There had to be some level of dementia happening here.

Pearl's endurance outlasted even his own. He ordered several linens and soaps up and it seemed they'd fallen through a rabbit hole into a world of revolving ups and downs, Evelyn as poor desolate Alice, Pearl the Mad Hatter, and he the frightened rabbit. He consistently caught himself standing back, watching as Evelyn carried on, tapping into an empty well of energy and putting effort forth to ease her mother's mind and discomfort. There was no peace in the hours that followed.

Evelyn's affection for such a hateful, spiteful person amazed him. She simply accepted Pearl's behavior with stoic grace. Lucian knew he could never be as humble as she was in those horrid moments. He knew, even his mother whom he'd loved dearly, could not treat him as Pearl treated Evelyn and continue to be a part of his life. How Evelyn did not snap or retaliate left him speechless. He was completely inexperienced with such raw humanity.

Pearl shivered and glared as Evelyn bathed her with a damp cloth, cooling her sweltering, fevered skin as her temperature reached frightening heights. He feared many times they'd lose her, no matter what Vivian had said. Minutes felt like days, hours like years, and there was not an end in sight.

It wasn't until long after the sun had set and begun to rise that Pearl had finally exhausted herself. Evelyn was a shell of carbon and flesh, barely holding herself upright. In the corner sat a pile of wasted linens he knew would have to go directly to the incinerator.

Pearl fell back with a weak sigh that didn't fit her intrepid fight. He waited, skeptically, for her to rouse once more. Convinced her shattered mind substituted itself with an unstoppable will, when her breath leveled out, he remained. But she only slept. The forgotten clock told him twenty-six hours had passed since they arrived back at the condo. He had thought he'd rescued them from the depths of hell, yet now he was convinced he had brought the devil into his home.

Evelyn slipped into the chair like a wilted flower. Her vacant eyes still wouldn't leave Pearl's face. She seemed a delicate soul, barely held together by withered threads, yet the set of her shoulders told him she would rally again if her mother needed her. Her fortitude baffled him. He was exhausted, but she wouldn't give up her stoic vigil.

Quietly slipping from the room, he called the front desk to order food and several trash bags. He also ordered a maid's cart to be brought up, knowing Evelyn's pride would forbid another employee she saw as her peer to clean up after Pearl. He would tend to the mess, because there was no way he was allowing her to exert another ounce of energy.

The food came and he quietly placed it in the living room. Returning to the guest room, he found Evelyn slumped in her chair, holding her head up with one weak hand. She looked to be asleep, but he knew she wasn't. Her heavy eyes watched her sleeping mother's form through tiny slits.

"Evelyn," he softly whispered. Her motions were slow and delayed. She turned to face him with great effort. "You need to eat. Why don't you go clean yourself up and I'll stay here with Pearl."

She looked like she wanted to argue, but her verve had simply been too depleted to try. Weakly nodding, she stood on shaky legs. He helped her gain her equilibrium and waited as she staggered with the grace of a zombie into the bathroom.

As the door closed behind her, Lucian went to the hall and pulled the maid cart in. Careful not to disturb Pearl, he slipped on gloves and began bagging up the soiled linens, then sanitizing every surface. He heard the shower running and wondered how Evelyn was even still standing.

By the time the room was disinfected and put back to sorts, he called Dugan to come handle the disposal of items, knowing Evelyn wouldn't want people unnecessarily wondering at her private business. He held on to the maid cart, figuring they'd need it again, and simply tucked it out of the way.

She returned to the room, looking depleted and beaten. "You need to sleep, Evelyn. She's resting now and I promise to stay with her and wake you if she stirs. Take your rest while you can so that you have your strength when she wakes."

She nodded and turned to go to the master bedroom. He waited until she was asleep, then went to clean himself up.

Once he washed up and changed into fresh clothes, he returned to Pearl's side and settled into the chair beside the bed. Lucian drifted in and out of a restless sleep. Pearl moved very little, but often moaned quiet, agonized whispers of nonsense.

He had lost all sense of time. His phone had continued to ring until he finally shut it off. People would have to go on without him for the next few days. His priorities were here, with Evelyn.

thirty-three
. . . . .

SKEWER

A severe attack to a valuable piece that compels it to move

LUCIAN felt the weight of her gaze on him before he'd fully awakened.

"Am I in a hospital?" Pearl looked frightened and pitiful compared to the uncontainable force from the day before.

"You're at the Patras Hotel. I brought you and Scout here."

"Scout's here?" She asked the question with evident doubt.

"She is. I hope you know your daughter loves you very much."

Pearl moaned and gripped her stomach, curling into herself as sweat beaded on her brow. "Get Scout," she groaned. "I need Scout."

"Your daughter's sleeping."

"Get her!" she shouted. Knowing Pearl would only continue until she woke Evelyn up herself, he stood with resignation and much dislike for the woman resting in his home, and went to wake Evelyn.

Keeping an eye on the guest room door, he carefully sat on the bed of the master bedroom and touched Evelyn's cheek.

She started and came awake immediately. "Is Pearl—"

"Pearl's fine. She's awake and asking for you."

Evelyn rushed to stand and he eyed her wearily. She'd lost weight over the past two weeks. Her skin looked pale and her arms frail, but most disturbing was the change in her eyes. They had lost so much of the vibrancy he'd seen when they first met.

Pearl was sitting on the edge of the bed when Evelyn approached. He stayed at the door and observed them together.

"Scout," Pearl sighed with obvious relief. "Baby, where's my stuff? Someone's gonna steal it."

Evelyn smiled sadly. Gone was the glint of laughter in her crystal eyes. Her mouth held no happiness. He wanted to shake this rotten woman for what she'd put her daughter through.

"Momma, your stuff's fine. Don't worry about that now. You're sick and you need to get well."

Pearl only half listened as Evelyn went on about how worried she was and how delirious with fever Pearl had been. Her mother scratched at her arms, her eyes jerky and her demeanor skittish.

As Evelyn was professing how relieved she was that Pearl was awake and showing signs of life again, Pearl interrupted, "Scout, I need some money. I need a fix. Can you get me one? It hurts, baby. Make it go away."

His hate for this despicable woman doubled in that moment as her words visibly cut through Evelyn. Pearl was too entrenched in her own selfish need to notice what she was doing to her daughter. She was no mother.

He watched as Evelyn again stiffened her posture, refusing to be worn down. She was so incredibly strong. He'd never seen someone appear so beaten and so resilient at the same time. She was astonishing.

"Oh, Momma, no. You can't do that here."

"Then I got to go."

"Momma," Evelyn said, taking her mother's hand. "You're sick—"

Pearl snatched her hand back. "*Why you always bossing me? You're not the boss of me, Evelyn Scottlynn Keats! I am your mother—*"

"*Then act like it!*" Evelyn suddenly snapped. Her voice cracked and in a much softer voice she said, "For once in your life act like it. You almost died. I know you don't care, but what am I supposed to do without you?" She stood shakily. "Not this time, Momma. I'm not letting you go back to that. You're going to get through this because you owe it to me."

With pathetic sluggishness and pitiful strength, Pearl's hand came up to slap her daughter.

Evelyn caught her wrist with surprising preparedness. "Stop it!"

She released Pearl's arm as the other woman tugged. Pearl, now feeble, nearly fell back with her own ungainliness. She sneered at her daughter, "You little bitch! You're doing this on purpose, you hateful thing. Always jealous of how much they all like me. You're stupid! Do you hear me? Do you, stupid girl? Where's my daughter? I want my daughter! Scout!"

Lucian was speechless. The woman shouted cruel words in Evelyn's face and she barely flinched. She did cry, but silently and without visible emotion. As the tirade continued, he'd heard enough. He stepped in and took Evelyn gently by the shoulders and steered her out of the room, slamming the door hard behind them, stifling the insane diatribe.

Evelyn was nonresponsive as he laid her back in bed. He didn't know what to do, so he curled in behind her and held her as she wept, kissing her hair and offering any comfort he could provide. She silently sobbed for several minutes and eventually Pearl's screeches quieted.

Soft sniffles broke the silence every few minutes. "She didn't mean it," she finally muttered. "She doesn't know."

Her skin was cool to the touch as he ran his fingers over her arm. "I know, baby. I know." But he didn't. He couldn't understand because he'd never seen the like.

thirty-four

QUIET MOVE

A move, which does not attack or capture

VIVIAN'S final warning had been an understatement. The four days that followed Evelyn and Pearl's arrival at the condo had been one trial after another. Evelyn barely spoke. She tended to Pearl, bathed her, fed her, cleaned up after her, took unending abuse from her, and slept. While she slept, Lucian tended to her mother.

As they dropped Pearl off at the clinic Vivian had suggested, she was sedated and easily dealt with. Lucian understood that she could not be held there against her will, but the clinic was out in the middle of nowhere and Pearl would be stranded. His only hope was that, as Evelyn's mother's appetite returned, she would find the steady supply of food, heat, and shelter worth more than her need to inject herself full of dope.

Evelyn cried silently as she stared out the window the entire way home. He called and had chicken and dumpling soup sent up ahead of their arrival. He also asked for melon wrapped in prosciutto and a hot fudge sundae, but knew it would probably go to waste.

They dined in silence. Evelyn finished her soup but touched nothing else. He moved the tray to the hall and ran a bath for her.

Her tears had subsided through supper, which relieved him, but her continued silence increased his concern.

His fingers combed through her soft hair, pouring water over the thick strands and rinsing away the shampoo. She passively allowed him to bathe her. While cleaning her fingers and removing the dirt under her nails, she suddenly burst into tears again. Unsure what to do, Lucian reached for a towel, lifted her out of the tub, and held her as she cried.

Her warm tears burned through his shirt and the dampness from her hair soaked into his sleeve. He stilled when the light caress of her lips danced over the flesh on his throat. It was no accidental touch. Lucian turned and stared into her tired eyes.

She cupped his unshaven cheek and whispered, "Make love to me, Lucian. Take me away. Make me forget the last few weeks."

Tucking a strand of damp hair behind her ear, he met her gaze. "You're tired."

"Please."

His lips swept softly across hers and she leaned into the caress. His hands moved to her bottom and he stood, holding her slight body in his arms as he walked back to the master bedroom. Laying her back on the blankets, he stared at her as he slowly removed his clothing. The curtains hadn't been drawn and moonlight pooled onto the bed from the balcony doors, snowflakes dancing in the shadowy night's reflections.

His hands gently removed the towel from her body and she lay before him naked. Her small pink nipples puckered under his gaze and her hip cocked to one side, her legs twisting in absolute female perfection. He reached for the covers and pulled them over them as he crawled in beside her. Her skin was cool. His heated skin was in such contrast as he drew her close, pulling her under his protective embrace, wanting to shelter her from all the pain.

Softly, he sipped from her lips. His thumbs coasted over her delicate jawbone as he tipped up her face to meet his kiss. Her body cushioned his as her small hands drifted over his flesh. The satisfaction her touch brought him on so many levels was almost too much to bear. The pressure of the past few weeks unraveled inside of him. He was exposed, raw, and more helpless against his passion for her in that moment than he had ever been.

She owned him. He was completely possessed with his need to have her in his life. Such vulnerability would normally be unwelcome, but his mind couldn't fight the power she had over him. She was what gave him purpose. She altered his perspectives and made the unbearable bearable. She was his drug, his addiction. She was his heroine.

Closing his mouth over her breast, he drew her downy thighs apart. Her body was moist and warm, ready. His tongue licked at the sensitive flesh of her breasts, pulled on her nipples, and his fingers opened her tender folds. Kissing a trail over her soft belly, his mouth moved over the delta of her sex, now dusted with soft brown hair. His lips lowered and he tasted sweet ambrosia.

Lucian drank from her folds as if she were the fountain of youth. Her legs curled over his shoulders as her needy cries filled the room. When she came, it was intrepid and breathtaking, such an honest release lacking any modest insecurity.

Pulling her to his chest, he rolled to his back and brought her atop of him. Her thighs spread over his hips, anointing his stomach with her dewy arousal. She braced her hands on his chest as she seated herself over him.

Once their bodies were aligned he caressed her cheek and whispered, "I love you, Evelyn. Don't leave me again."

Her gaze drilled into his as a tear slid from the corner of his eye. She lowered herself onto him and he thrust slowly to meet her halfway. Her fingers scored his flesh as he moved under her, holding her tight. Her hips rocked and swelled with refined motions and he studied her, experienced the sensations of their bodies combining in every sense.

The sight of their bodies meeting, their pelvises kissing with each thrust, the sound of their moans and breathy sighs muffled by their closeness, the taste of salty skin as they stole kisses, the fragrance of their combined need; it was the most complete sexual experience of his life. Never before had he known the need to be so tender and savor every slide and shift, every sigh and breath.

Lucian rolled her to her back and moved on top of her, balancing his weight on his forearms, trapping her close. Restraint was no longer an option. It was beyond his will to deny himself her offering a moment longer. He longed for the intimate bonding that came with the physical act of possessing her wholly.

Their tongues licked and lips kissed. He pressed deep into her heat, needing to bury himself, irrevocably, in some secreted part of her soul no other man would ever know. She arched and called his name as he thrust back in hard and deep. Again and again, he took her with long deep strokes.

Her body gripped his. Her fingers bit into his shoulders. He sucked at the tender flesh of her throat, biting softly as she throbbed against him, milking his own climax with her contracting sex. His release burst from him with sureness and bathed her womb.

It wasn't until that moment it occurred to him that there was nothing between them. No emotional barriers, no lies, no obstacles, and no protection. He thrust again, wanting her womb to take his seed, wanting, needing to find her belly swollen in the coming months with his child.

As the aftermath of their climaxes faded, their hands refused to let go. His face pressed into the curve of her shoulder and he breathed her in, memorizing her feel, committing this moment to memory, knowing their lives would be forever changed from this moment on.

thirty-five
.....

AMATEUR
A rare term only relevant when an untried player faces a master

LUCIAN'S mind roused with the sense that he was being watched. He breathed and Evelyn's soft fragrance filled him with warmth. Opening his eyes, he found her at his side, chin perched on hand as she rested on her elbow. Her amazing eyes were fixed on him.

"Good morning," he whispered.

Sleep had restored some of the radiance to her eyes. The skin under them was no longer drawn or bruised. She smiled. "Good morning. Did you know you're entirely too beautiful for a man?"

"Should I pay someone to break my nose?"

"I'm sure you could find someone willing to do it for free," she teased and yipped when he rolled on top of her.

Her body was a soft sanctuary for his. He kissed her sweetly. Against her mouth he whispered, "Is that so?"

She giggled, her lips curving under his. "But anyone who'd want to hurt you wouldn't really know you. I know you, Lucian Patras, and you're nothing like the hard-ass you pretend to be."

He stilled, schooling his playful behavior. "Don't be so sure,

Evelyn," he said with total gravity. "I take care of the people I love, but those who betray me live to regret it. I didn't come this far by being easily maneuvered. Never doubt I'm in complete control of myself and those around me."

He regretted his words as a bit of the lightheartedness washed from her eyes. Her days had been wrought with hardship and he wanted to take away the pain. He softened his disposition and pinned her arms above her head with nowhere to move as his body boxed her in. He ran a thumb over the crest of her soft cheek.

"You don't intimidate me, Lucian," she whispered brazenly.

"Well, that's good. I don't want to intimidate you. I want to master you, love you so thoroughly, know you completely, in a way no one else ever has, and that doesn't happen when one feels threatened, coerced, or intimidated. I'd say we're making progress."

When her silver eyes moved as if calculating some in-depth equation, he knew she was overthinking things. He wished he could read her thoughts.

"What're you thinking?" he asked.

"I'm wondering, now that you have me here, what you are going to do with me."

His cheek pulled and his lips twitched as he fought a smile. He moved his knees between hers and nudged her body open. Heat from between her thighs scorched him. His erection fell heavily onto her soft tummy. He pressed his hips seductively and she arched into his suggestive hold.

"I believe I'm going to fuck you and you're going to let me."

Her lashes lowered and her gray eyes deepened with darker hues of blue. Her hands began to reach for him, but he pinned them to the pillows again. Uncertainty momentarily flashed in those stormy eyes.

"I want you, Evelyn, and I want you to let me take you. When I want, how I want, you are to be mine. Do you call checkmate?"

Her mouth formed the word *no*. Blood surged to his cock as her head shook slowly. She was his, and he was *never* letting her go.

Unbidden, thoughts of her friend Parker came to mind. Lucian had given him his word and his word was something he always kept. He shook off the thought. He'd move on, forget about the promise he made. If Parker kept the job, good for him, he'd meet new people and realize there were other fish in the sea. If he lost the job, which Lucian suspected he would—good work ethic was not something beggars usually possessed—then the opportunity would pass him by and he'd be nothing more than a memory. Evelyn was his, and he was a very possessive man.

Ducking low, Lucian took one soft nipple into his mouth and sucked it hard. Her belly pressed into his as her spine arched and she moaned softly. He treated the twin nipple with the same force, taking pride in the wet marks his mouth left over her tender flesh.

Her body curved and stretched in his tight hold. She needed to move and was growing frustrated with his restraint. She needed to learn self-discipline when it came to submitting. Even though her strong will sometimes amused him, and he adored her feisty little spirit, respected it, submission was a beautiful display of inner strength and he wanted to teach her.

"Don't move your arms, Evelyn."

He dragged his hips lower. Her arousal glazed his cock and he nudged between her soft folds, careful not to penetrate. He probed her clit as she jerked and sighed.

"I want to show you every form of pleasure two lovers can share when they trust each other. Do you trust me, Evelyn?"

He waited, not wanting to give away how much her answer would mean to him. He had confessed his love and knew, while she didn't reciprocate his sentiment, her presence in his life again was not meaningless. Love would come, but for the kind of relationship he wanted with Evelyn, trust was necessary.

Reaching down, he turned his wrist and pressed his palm into her clit, his fingers dipping into her honey, and waited. "I trust you, Lucian. More than I probably should."

Good enough. His hand pressed down and his finger plunged deep. She hissed and thrust her body into his touch. "That's it. Let me feel your wanting. I'll take care of you, baby."

His palm pressed and glided over her pussy as his fingers swirled and opened her slit. She was very small and he wanted to take her hard and fast, but would not fuck her until he saw to her pleasure first.

Her body writhed, but like a good girl, her arms remained above her head. Slick nectar coated his fingers. Her breath lightly tousled his hair with each panted sigh. Curling his middle finger, he plunged deep. Her body expanded in accommodation and she stilled.

"Feel that, Evelyn? That's me pressing on your G-spot. I'm going to teach you every part of your body, and you'll learn that no one will ever pleasure you the way I can."

He applied pressure onto the spongy inner tissue and rubbed his thumb over her clit. She shouted and came fast and hard over his hand. Her channel fluttered against him, throbbed and tightened around his deep grip. He smiled at the shock he saw in her stare.

Removing his fingers, he gazed into her lust-glazed eyes and sucked his digits deep into his mouth. Her sweet, tangy flavor tickled his taste buds. He pressed up, sitting back on his heels, and took himself in hand. His slick fingers tugged over his hard flesh, and he thumbed a drop of precome, massaging it into his heavy cock.

"Look at what you do to me, Evelyn."

Her lashes lifted as she gazed up at his length. His hand pumped hard over his straining erection.

"I'm going to teach you how to bring me pleasure the same way I bring it to you. Your body will know mine like I know yours. You'll crave my touch like a drug and I'll take you higher than you've ever been. I'm going to teach you every way possible to satisfy me and you're going to love it, need it, want it so badly you'd sell your soul for it."

Her breasts lifted as her breathing increased. Her eyes locked on his hand slowly stroking his hard flesh. "Do you want to be fucked, Evelyn?"

"Yes," she rasped.

"Yes what?"

"Yes, Lucian. Please."

Releasing his cock, his fingers sank into a plush down pillow and moved it to the center of the bed. He piled another on top. Once he formed a nice little mount, his mouth crashed over hers and he plunged his tongue into her, demanding, taking, and driving her to a point of need that was hopefully dizzying.

Her knees raised and gripped his hips. His hand lifted her head, sifting through her heavy waves of soft auburn hair. He kissed down her jaw, purposely scraping his rough stubble against her delicate skin, marking her. Lips nipped at her throat, licked and pulled at her earlobe. Her cries became frenzied, her muttered sighs a cross between a curse and a prayer. She begged and he made her wait awhile more, ensuring that when he did plunge into her she'd be so ready for his cock, she'd likely come immediately.

Lucian tickled and teased her pussy, his hand a constant presence at her sex, yet careful not to bring her to peak. She'd learn to accept his touch, depend on it. He was a demonstrative man, and

Evelyn would become conditioned to expect his touch in all things, be it carnal, corporeal, or spiritual.

He intended to possess her wholly, not just mind and body, but also her soul. She'd already taken possession of parts of him no one had ever laid claim to. It was unnerving, and he needed to balance the scales for his own peace of mind.

Once he had her trembling with need, he pulled her and flipped her over the pillows. His cock throbbed with delight at the vision of her succulent ass raised before him. One day soon he'd take her virginity there too. At first he had been appalled and uncomfortable with the fact that he had taken her virtue. Now, it made him want to howl with satisfaction.

She was his. Only his.

He adjusted her hips and kneed her thighs apart. The pink flesh of her pussy was drenched with cream. It practically dripped down her thighs. His finger traced from her nape, down the long column of her spine, between the crevice of her ass, and through the pool gathering at her awaiting pussy. She stretched like a cat and purred with need.

Crawling close to her backside, he lined his cock with her sex, bathed it in her slick fluid. "You're mine, Evelyn. I'll never willingly let you walk out of my life again. I intend to make it so that you never want to."

Lucian thrust into her in one smooth glide, gripping her hips hard, preventing her body from propelling forward with the force of his entry. Her tight little pussy strangled his cock in its moist heat. She cried out and he gritted his teeth, fighting back his own release.

He withdrew slowly, savoring every bit of friction along the way, and slammed back into her. Her channel constricted and pulsed around him. Extracting his length with painful gradualness, her body reflexively tried to suck him back in. He held the glossy tip of his cock at her rosy opening. His gut clenched, causing his come to stir deep inside, when he saw the muscles surrounding her pussy lips twitch and tighten, stretching around his girth. He plunged into her, burying himself to the hilt. Her head reared up, glorious chestnut hair arced in a wild mane, and she screamed as a violent orgasm took hold of her.

Lucian's hips cocked back. He angled himself over her and began drilling into her. He took her hard and he took her fast. Her pussy gripped his cock as if it never wanted to let him out. That was fine, because he never wanted to leave the shelter of her body.

He fucked her like an animal. Their bodies glistened with perspiration. Her narrow shoulders flexed as her arms extended into the plush pillows at the headboard and fisted the silky fabric. His balls tightened, drawing up tight, and his hips smacked into her ass. He dug his fingers into her sides, yanking her back on him each time he plunged forward.

Sharp cries of ecstasy echoed each thrust. He blinked as salty dampness burned his eyes. His tongue tasted the briny moisture along his lips as he panted through his teeth. He wanted her to remember his possession, still feel him inside of her when she lay down to sleep at the end of this day.

He needed to possess her ruthlessly in a way that the sense of him would never leave her, his presence entombing itself so deeply that once removed she would feel hollow without him, steadfastly aware that something was missing. Him.

Tingles of ecstasy shot up his spine, firing sparks of intense sensation into his nervous system and heating his blood. His release climbed up his dick, chugging thickly and forcefully until he shouted and it burst into her body. He fucked his seed deep into her, burying it. Deep satisfaction bloomed inside of him as, again, he considered they might be creating life. Lucian thrust his hips deep one final time for good measure and collapsed on top of her, catching his weight at the last moment.

They lay in a panting, sweaty heap. She continued to moan, and every few seconds her pussy fluttered with postorgasmic tremors that had his dick twitching in her flooded channel. He kissed her shoulder, and she chuckled quietly.

"Something funny?" he asked as he licked at her salty nape.

"You," she said, her voice muffled in the pillows.

"I wasn't aiming for that kind of amusement," he remarked drolly.

Her hand reached back and patted his sympathetically. "Oh, there was nothing funny about your performance. I was laughing because last time I was here I could barely get you to lay a hand on me and after the way you just fucked me . . . well, I guess you're over my virginity."

He bit her shoulder and she yelped. His mouth soothed the bite. "After this week there'll be nothing virginal about you, Evelyn. I intend to make sure of it. So yes, I suppose you can say I'm over it."

She sighed happily. "I'm glad."

thirty-six

DEVELOP

Moving a piece from its original square and putting it into action

EVELYN'S shoulders leaned against Lucian's chest, her bottom cradled between his legs, as he dragged the soapy sponge over her shoulders. Their fingers were pruned from sitting in the Jacuzzi tub for most of the morning, but neither of them were in any rush to get out. His clean hand reached for another strawberry and held it to her mouth. Her lips closed over the fruit and juice dribbled down her chin as her teeth bit into it.

Tossing the stem away, he turned her chin and licked away the red drops. "Delicious."

"You're going to spoil me, feeding me, washing my hair. Where's your palm leaf?" She laughed and he chuckled, his hand draping low over her chest and pinching her nipple. "Ouch!"

Lucian's fingers soothed the tender tip of her breast as he continued to pluck and pull as they talked. "I like taking care of you. I like when you let me."

"Keep doing what you're doing and you'll hear no objections from me." She slid down his front, allowing him to use his other hand as well.

His mouth closed over her wet shoulder and drank from the shallow pool that had settled in her collarbone. His cock grew and he shifted, fitting it just above the crease of her ass. Her breathing became labored and soft, little needy cries formed in the back of her throat.

"Turn around," he whispered, giving her a gentle nudge forward. Water sloshed as she turned onto her knees and faced him. "Kiss me."

She gazed at him, a touch of suspicion in her eyes, then slowly leaned forward and pressed her lips to his. He didn't wrap his arms around her, wanting to see how she'd handle herself. Her fingers threaded through his hair, droplets of water sprinkled his shoulders. The sultry air of the bathroom cocooned them in warmth.

Her soft, strawberry-flavored tongue tickled his lips and he opened. Her kiss was gentle, tender. Tentatively, her fingers moved down to his shoulders and she crawled closer. Lucian's mouth curved under her kiss and he slid his knees between hers, guiding her hips low. She straddled him and he fit his cock between her thighs.

"Put me inside of you."

She paused for a moment and shyly reached under the water for his length. Her small hands wrapped around his flesh like a gentle leaf catching the rain. She timidly directed him to her sex and he was tempted to tell her to wait so that he could show her how to touch him properly. But as her heat teased the tip of his cock he wanted nothing more than to be inside of her again.

"Now take me, Evelyn."

She lowered herself, rotating her hips in order to accommodate his size. Her hand returned beneath the water. Her fingers curled delicately around his length as she opened herself wider and slid down. They both sighed as their bodies fit together as one.

Lucian gripped her hips and held her to him, not allowing her any relief from his size. "Feel me inside of you, Evelyn. You take me so well."

Her bare breasts swayed before him temptingly. Leaning forward, he captured one turgid nipple in his mouth. Her head fell back as he sucked and nibbled on her tight little bud. He released her nipple with an audible pop.

"Now ride me. Make me come, Evelyn."

He allowed her to take the lead. Her palms pressed into his shoulders as she found her balance and she slowly lifted, her tight channel stroking him. His flesh pulsed within her heat. She rotated her hips and lowered her body. It took her a few tries to find a rhythm. She worked slowly and her expression changed with each discovered pleasure her movements elicited.

Water rippled and gently sloshed around them. She moaned when she discovered if she arched her pelvis forward she could drag her clit across his lower abdomen.

"Uh-uh," Lucian warned. "You're not to make yourself come." When she paused and looked at him in confusion, he explained, "Your pleasure's mine to give. You don't take it without my permission."

Her lips formed the sweetest little petulant pout. "Who says?"

"I say."

Her mouth opened to argue, but he swept up and kissed away her protests. As her motions became surer, she became lost in the experience. Her throat worked as her neck elongated. Her hair formed an auburn cloud behind her slender shoulders, the ends swirling over the surface of the water. She was as enchanting as a mermaid. With every gesticulation of her body she learned a bit more about her sexuality.

All that was needed was one hard thrust and he could come,

but he held off, wanting her to take this time to become comfortable with their coupling. It was important that she learn her own body's likes and dislikes as well as his own.

Her skin prickled with goose bumps. The water had cooled substantially from the time they first climbed into the tub. "Hop up. I want to turn you so I'm behind you."

"But . . ."

"Shh, do as I say."

She pouted, but obliged. *Good girl.*

With their combined maneuvering she settled back on his length, now facing away from him. Holding her breasts and pulling her damp back to his front, he guided her up and down. Lucian scooted lower, angling himself into her, and reached for the handheld showerhead. He turned on the faucet and adjusted the temperature of the water.

She had lost a bit of her rhythm in the new position. Once the lever turned, water flowed from the shower massager. Setting the dial to pulse he lowered it under the water. His hand went to her belly and anchored her back to his chest. Sliding lower, he splayed his fingers over her pussy lips, exposing the little bud of her clit.

The moment he directed the flow of water to her clit she jerked in his arms. "Stay put." His arm tightened over her as he fit the fast pulsing flow over her bud.

"Lucian! It's too much!"

Her knees trembled and her cunt locked down on his cock hard. Her cries echoed off the tiled walls as she came, her channel gripping him like a hot vise. Relentlessly, he continued to torture her hard, little clit. Every part of her came alive. The muscles in her ass tightened over his hips. Her legs trembled and her entire body quaked.

She screamed out one climax after another. The sharp edges of her nails bit into his arms. His hand rapidly shook the massager over her pussy, adding another degree of stimulation. When she came the fourth time her body practically shot out of the water.

Lucian released the impromptu chrome sex toy and moved over her, guiding her hands to the lip of the tub, and pressed his over hers, locking her in place. Cool air blanketed his back as he rose out of the water and drove into her. It didn't take long after how hard she had gripped him through her last orgasm. As he thrust into her his release bubbled up and suddenly shot into her. Amazingly, beautifully, she came again on the coattails of his own release.

He thrust into her once more, as was becoming his wont, and their bodies sagged into the water as one. Hers was lax, drained from her multiple climaxes. Lucian cradled her in his arms and dragged a sheaf of her now wet hair away from her face and kissed her deeply, pouring all of his emotion into it.

She panted. Whispering against his lips, she smiled. "You're going to kill me. We can't do that again for at least twenty-four hours."

Lucian chuckled. "We'll see. I'll just have to be gentle. I don't think I can go more than a few hours without being inside of you."

thirty-seven

. . . . .

SQUEEZE

Gradually increasing the pressure of a bind

NEEDING to get out of the condo for a bit, Lucian took Evelyn to a privately owned sushi restaurant off the main line.

"It's like cat food," she said, poking the sashimi with a chopstick. The waiter took pity on her and wrapped her chopsticks with a rubber band like he'd seen done before for children.

Lucian laughed. "It's a notch above cat food, I should hope."

Her lip curled. "If you can afford to have someone cook for you, why wouldn't you? I don't see how this is appetizing."

Reaching over the tray of ginger and spices, he plucked up the piece of fish she continued to poke and popped it in his mouth. Her throat flexed as if even watching someone eat uncooked fish was unsavory to her.

When he swallowed, he placed a piece of tempura on her plate. "Here, try this. It's cooked."

She eyed it cynically. "What is it?"

"Crab. If you like a little spice, try dipping it in this. There's wasabi in it though, so be careful. Even a dab can make your eyes water."

She clumsily lifted the piece to her lips and nibbled. Lucian chuckled when the roll fell apart. She cupped her palm under the sprinkling of white sticky rice and cucumber. With a huff, she dropped the mess onto her plate and put her chopsticks down with a click. "This is too much work."

They laughed throughout dinner. Evelyn enjoyed the vegetarian roll the most because it didn't include fish, only a wrap of raw vegetables. He offered her some Japanese beer, but limited her consumption, keeping in mind she was not yet accustomed to drinking much.

"Do you really not know when your birthday is?"

She sipped the glass of beer and shook her head. "Nope. I've never had a birthday either, made up or otherwise. I think it would be nice to blow out candles and make a wish."

Lucian's heart ached for her. Such a simple statement, but so telling of the kind of existence she'd led. "I intend to make that happen. Pick a date and we'll declare it your birthday from here on."

A tight little smile formed at her lips. The outside edges of her eyes creased with contained joy. "Really?"

"Really. We'll have a great celebration with cake and candles and presents galore."

Her eyes took on a dreamy wonderment, and she tapped the space between her upper lip and her nose with her petite finger. "When's your birthday?"

"October eighth."

"Can I pick January eighth, then?"

"You can pick whatever you want."

A smile bloomed on her face. "That's what I pick, January eighth. Can we get balloons?"

Lucian considered her request. "I suppose we can arrange for balloons."

Her mouth opened as she gazed at him, smile still fresh on her face. He thought she would say something, but then the waiter came to drop off the check, interrupting the moment.

On the drive back to Patras, she lounged into his side. Lucian found himself always touching her. His fingers played with a strand of her hair, and he watched it turn shades of dark copper under the passing lights and the glow of the moon seeping through the skylight.

"How do you feel about coming to my home with me for the next two weeks until Christmas? I'd like you to meet my sisters, and we'd be closer to your mother. If she's doing better and ready for visitors, maybe we could visit with her."

She shifted and looked at him. "You're leaving?" Vulnerability showed in her eyes. He squeezed her shoulder reassuringly.

"Not if you'd rather stay. Just because I'm not always in the city, Evelyn, doesn't mean you'll be out on the street. I promise you'll never be without a place to stay again."

"Lucian," she said reluctantly. "What we have right now, it won't always be this easy. I mean, don't get me wrong, I like the way things are, but people grow apart. You can't expect us to last forever and it isn't safe for me to expect you to always be responsible for me."

"I want to be responsible for you."

"But you can't. I need to be accountable for myself."

"Evelyn, there'll be ups and there'll be downs. It's part of every relationship. You have to roll with the punches and cross those bridges when they come. Worrying about problems that don't yet exist is useless. As long as we're always honest with each other and communicate when something's bothering us, I have no doubt we can work through anything. Now, tell me you'll come home with me for Christmas."

Lucian sensed her doubt in his words. He was coming to learn that Evelyn doubted a lot in her life and didn't place her trust in anyone but herself. It was difficult for her to depend on others. She smiled, but it wasn't her true smile. Time would convince her.

"All right. I'll come home with you."

When they returned to the condo, Lucian carried her to the bedroom. He slowly stripped her of her dress, leaving her in nothing but her stockings and shoes. She shook as he dropped to his knees in front of her and licked from the tops of her lace-covered thighs over her exposed flesh and teasingly close to her sex.

"Lucian," she whimpered, balancing her hands on his shoulders.

"Has it been twenty-four hours yet?" he teased, biting the sweet swell of her hip.

She groaned impatiently. "You're doing this on purpose!" Her petite heel stomped into the carpet.

"If you want something, Evelyn, all you have to do is ask for it." He sat back on his heels and fondled the strap of her garter. Her lips stubbornly pressed together, and he sighed. "Since when are you shy?"

"I'm not. I just don't know how to ask for . . . that."

Holding back a laugh, he said, "That's simple. Just repeat after me. Lucian . . ."

She smirked and repeated, "Lucian . . ."

"Only you can bring me satisfaction. Your talented tongue is comparable to the mouths of gods. Please lick my sweet pussy and make me come."

She laughed long and hard. It was a beautiful sound, so free, almost childlike. "I am *not* saying that. You aren't quite ranking with the gods. 'King' is where I draw the line."

"Is that so?"

He grabbed her around the waist, and she folded over his shoulder in a fit of giggles. He smacked her ass and dragged her to the floor. His mouth took possession of hers, each of them laughing over the other's lips. "I'll take that as a challenge."

He kissed down her body quickly, nipping at her tempting breasts, swirling his tongue in the shallow indentation of her belly button. Wrenching her thighs apart, he found her pussy glossed with honey and waiting for his touch. He lifted her to his mouth and licked from the tight pucker of her anus, through her slit, and to her clit. Her taste was spectacular. She moaned and pressed her body to his mouth, all signs of humor gone and now replaced with desire.

Bracing her thighs in the gap between his thumbs and fingers, Lucian thumbed her opening wide. His tongue stabbed in and out of her. He couldn't get enough of her sweet taste. He loved the way her clean folds tasted under his lips, and he made a mental note to schedule another salon visit for her soon. He was sure Patrice would appreciate it.

As he toyed with her clit and licked at her tight little cunt, his mind wandered. He considered how Evelyn would feel about a woman like Patrice kissing her here. The thought made him incredibly hot, but then surprisingly displeased him. While he had no interest in fucking anyone other than Evelyn, the exhibitionist in him rallied at the idea of fucking her in front of her lusty friend, yet something about sharing Evelyn with anyone no longer sat well with him.

His mouth traveled down to the tight rosette of her anus, and he tongued the little knot. She practically leapt out of his grip.

"Stay," he growled and continued to seduce the tiny hole because he knew it unnerved her. She settled obediently, although he could tell her conscience warred with her desire. Under his gentle ministrations there was no doubt that Evelyn enjoyed some light anal play. He intended to school her in all the wonderful pleasures that could come of such things.

Lucian fed his index finger into her wet pussy and she moaned, her body rocking into his hand. He was in no rush. It was important she learn to savor the journey and control her body's reactions. He'd teach her tolerance of the most excruciating pleasures in the weeks to come. Excitement jittered through his bones.

Withdrawing his dewy finger, he glided it to her back entrance. She tensed as he pressed into the tight opening. "Relax." He teased her rosette and reminded, "You have a safe word. Do you want to use it?"

Slowly, she shook her head, hooded crystal eyes meeting his challengingly. She grunted quietly at the subtle intrusion.

"Push, Evelyn. Press into my touch and your body will accept me." She squeezed her eyes closed. "You can do this, baby, push."

Her eyes opened as the endearment was whispered from his lips. She was breathtaking in that moment, watching him with brave, lust-filled silver eyes. Her need was evident in the tang of her scent, the arch of her spine, and the seductive curve of her plush mouth. Biting down on her plump lower lip, determination setting her features, she pressed down on his finger.

The tip of his finger slipped past the delicate tissue and penetrated her hole, sinking deep, and she whimpered. His finger and thumb clamped down over the wall separating the digits, and glided in and out in tandem. His arousal became a fire burning in the wild, unable to be contained.

Lucian blanketed her with his strength and held her there as he took her body places her mind likely couldn't follow. He pinched down on the swollen bud of her sex, and her jaw locked as her neck curved. Eyes forced shut, she breathed through the intense orgasm as he fucked his fingers inside of her. Flutters of untried muscles pulsed against his digit as he held it inside of her.

"Feel it, Evelyn. Adjust to it. You need to get used to it so you're ready for my cock in the weeks to come. I plan on taking every bit of you and filling every virgin hole you have with my come. I'll show you how to accommodate me here, how to suck my cock, and how to enjoy every minute of it while pleasing me."

Her rapid breathing was loud. He was pushing her. Lucian rewarded her submission with a few quick licks over her clit. She moaned and writhed. His finger withdrew from her tight hole and plunged back in. This time her resistance was less. He continued to torment her clit, whispering words of love over her tenderized flesh as he kissed, nibbled, and sucked, all the while driving his finger in and out of her ass.

When he plunged two fingers from his other hand into her sex and pulled her clit tight between his lips, flicking the bud with his tongue, it became evident that her pain transcended to pleasure. Like strings cut from a cluster of balloons, he watched as all her thoughts seemed to float away. She writhed, moaning, appearing disconnected from her body, floating, floating, floating, until she eventually settled back to earth like an exhausted feather falling to the ground. Lighter, looser, replete.

His fingers grew slippery with her release. He drew out her orgasm, then flipped her to her hands and knees.

Her shoulders trembled as his fingers undid his pants. The sweet curve of her ass was too tempting. His cock pressed at her hot center, bathing in her arousal. His palm slapped one rounded globe and he drove into her pussy, burying himself and nearly driving her to the floor in the process. His palm, still hot from the slap, gripped her hip as he plowed into her. He should've laid a blanket down, but the two of them were too far gone to consider such things. He'd have to make it fast so her knees didn't get burned from the carpet.

Lucian focused on his release and two pumps later he was filling her. Cries of pleasure, hers and his, filled the room. They collapsed to the floor in a puddle of flesh and limbs. He pulled her to him and kissed her damp temple. Declarations of love built in his throat, but he held them back, knowing they wouldn't be reciprocated.

As his strength slowly returned, he stood and lifted her to the bed. She wasn't yet asleep, but her eyes were closed. She smiled and sighed softly. Lucian went to the bathroom and quickly cleaned himself, wet a cloth, and returned to her. Bathing her pussy, he gently kissed her knees and folded her legs together, easing her into a more comfortable position. When he returned from the bathroom the second time, she was asleep.

thirty-eight
. . . . .

DYNAMISM

A style of play in which the activity of the pieces
is favored over the position

THE next few days passed much the same. Lucian worked while Evelyn watched television. She visited the salon on days he had other obligations. He purchased her a laptop, but she didn't show much interest in the Internet. He assumed she didn't really have computer experience, so he showed her how to play games like Scrabble, but again, she didn't seem interested. For some reason he suspected it made her uncomfortable, so he didn't push.

There was a change since he'd discovered what Evelyn's life outside of his world was truly like. Perhaps he'd become more attuned to her or perhaps she'd given up on keeping so many secrets. He understood the weariness he sometimes saw in her. There was a tiredness about her that came, not with the excursion of a day, but with the unending battle that had been her life.

It seemed an unspoken agreement that she'd take some time to simply be. He'd notified Tamara Jones of Evelyn's leave of absence and assured the manager that—when Evelyn was ready to return to work—she would. He preferred her home, so he hadn't pressed the subject. It was clear she needed this time and he was happy to provide it.

They often had breakfast in the condo and dined in the restaurant for lunch. In the evenings, they either ordered in and played chess or he took her somewhere in the city. After offering to take Evelyn to a local club, she admitted that she didn't know how to dance. He arranged to have a teacher come in twice a week for private lessons in one of the Patras ballrooms.

There were quiet moments here and there when a sadness stole over her eyes, so hopeless, it disarmed him. She'd admitted to missing Pearl, something he couldn't quite comprehend, but empathized with all the same. He never denied her the chance to call or visit her mother, but she seemed reluctant to take that step. He assumed she just needed a little more time.

He'd gotten reports from the facility regularly about Pearl's slow progress and that seemed to satisfy Evelyn to some degree. He knew she missed her mom, but visiting her, she explained, wouldn't take that longing away. He finally was beginning to understand that, while Pearl lived, Evelyn's mother was gone. She was mourning and afraid to hope for more.

After the past few weeks, Evelyn was emotionally tender. He enjoyed the moments her feistiness showed, liking that challenging, playful side of her, but he also valued her softer side, which shared whispered confessions about her past and fears for the future.

They made love regularly. Evelyn was developing her own addiction to sex, which pleased him greatly. Lucian took great joy in those moments when he caught her gazing at him with bashful need. It amused him to press her buttons in those moments and tease her into confessing what it was she wanted. Just thinking about it made him hard with lust.

She sashayed by his desk, eating an apple and wearing a pair of loose-fitting cotton pants and one of his dress shirts. He turned and grabbed her hips, halting her progress and pulling her onto his lap. His hands wandered over her curves. Guiding her hand to his mouth, he bit into the juicy fruit.

She sighed and snuggled into his hold. He cupped her breast through her shirt and slid his other hand between her legs. She squirmed and pulled away from his touch.

He frowned and pulled her back. "What's wrong? Are you sore?" She lowered her face and looked away. "Evelyn, answer me. Did I hurt you?"

"No."

He turned her chin until she met his gaze. "Then what is it?"

She sighed. "I'm getting my period."

Lucian's mouth opened and shut. A million thoughts occurred to him at once. Most prominent, however, was the realization that she wasn't pregnant. Disappointment bloomed within him and he tried to hide it.

"Oh, well, that's okay." Something else seemed to be on her mind. "What else is bothering you?"

His hands gently massaged her thighs and she relaxed again. "It occurred to me that we haven't been very responsible as far as . . ."

"Birth control?" he offered grudgingly.

She nodded.

"Well, we should talk about that."

"I like not having anything between us," she admitted. "But I don't really know much about our other options."

"Are you opposed to using nothing?" He had to ask.

She pursed her lips and frowned at him. "Lucian. Be serious."

Okay, definitely not ready for that.

"Okay, well, how about if I make you an appointment with Vivian? The last time I talked to her she mentioned wanting to see you again."

"Do you think I should?"

His heart clenched at her question. Every time Evelyn placed trust in his guidance, they were one step closer to where he needed them to be. "I'll make the appointment and we'll go together."

Later that night as they went to bed, Evelyn was in rare form. She huffed and batted at the covers and tossed and turned. Finally, he pulled her close and held her. "What's the matter, Evelyn?"

"You turned me into a sex addict!" she accused and he laughed. He cupped her breast and massaged her gently. "Don't."

Reflexively, his fingers pinched on her nipple, a fast reprimand. "Excuse me?"

"Lucian," she huffed, turning to face him. "Nothing can come of that, so don't torture us."

Drawing in a deep breath, his gaze smoldering into hers with challenge, he whispered, "Evelyn, if I want to fuck you, I will." Before she could argue, he added, "I'm respecting your need for space right now. Tell me no again, and I'll do as I please."

Her lip trembled and he could read the challenge in her eyes. She whispered, "No, you won't."

She gasped and Lucian had her pinned beneath him the second she mistook his promise for a bluff. His finger pressed through her cotton pants and zeroed in on the tight ring of her ass. "Try me, Evelyn. There are plenty of ways for me to fuck you. I could put my cock in this tight little ass of yours or I could fuck your mouth."

She panted. She was excited and sexually frustrated, but he also noted a bit of reluctance and fear in her eyes. Not of him, but of the unknown.

"Is that what you want?" he asked smoothly, applying a bit of pressure to her bottom.

Her excitement was building. She was getting aroused.

"I don't think you're ready to take me here, but perhaps you're ready to take me orally. How does the thought of my cock in your mouth make you feel, because it makes me damn hard imagining those pretty lips of yours stretching wide to accommodate me."

Her breath hitched and he removed his hand from her ass and pinched her nipples pressing through the thin fabric of her cotton tank top.

"I could also fuck these pretty tits." He ground his erection into her. "As a matter of fact, all this challenging talk has made me decide I *will* fuck you. I'll be gracious and let you choose where."

Her pupils dilated and a needy moan left her lips as he ground himself into her again. "I want you in my mouth," she whispered, and he smiled slowly at her acquiescence to his authority over her body.

"Very good, Evelyn. Remove your shirt so I can look at you."

She nodded and pulled her shirt off.

"I want you to enjoy giving me pleasure as much as I enjoy giving it to you." Lucian gently held her chin and ran his finger under her full lip. "You okay with this, Evelyn?" He gave her an opportunity to voice any concerns. "I want you to know you can always tell me when something makes you uncomfortable. I expect you to confess *all* of your concerns to me."

"I'm okay. I want to do this to you. I'm excited."

Pride welled up inside of him, plumping his cock another inch. "Good girl. You make me very happy."

He eased her into a sitting position and then helped her off the bed.

"I want you on your knees. It'll be easier than having me over you."

Lucian dropped a plush pillow onto the floor, and she lowered gracefully to the ground. He looked into her upturned face and said, "I never want you to tolerate or do anything you aren't comfortable with. When we do things and you're in a position that doesn't allow you to speak, you still need to communicate with me.

"If I ask you if everything's okay, I expect you to answer me, vocally or otherwise. When you can't vocalize, this will be our sign for okay." He formed a V with his index and middle finger, mimicking a peace sign.

"If you need a time out, you'll cross your fingers like this, which is sign language for the letter *T*. *T* for time. If you want whatever's happening to stop altogether, you'll use the universal signal for stop by splaying all five fingers wide. Do you understand?"

"Why can't I just pull away?"

"That won't always be an option."

She drew a deep breath and shivered.

"Are you still okay with my conditions?"

"Yes."

"Do they frighten you? Be honest."

A deep pink flush climbed from her breasts to her ears. "No. It excites me. Does that make me a deviant?"

"No, it makes your lover one." He laughed and in a more serious voice said, "Evelyn, so long as it's safe, sane, and consensual, we aren't doing anything wrong. There's no shame here. Okay?"

She nodded.

"Good. And when I do this"—he gently tapped her throat twice with two fingers—"that's your signal that I'm going to come so that you can prepare." They ran through each signal a few times until he was sure she understood.

"Are you wet, Evelyn?"

"Yes," she rasped.

"Good." He took her hand. "Feel how I take your finger into my mouth."

He sucked her finger deep, curving his tongue along the bottom, and applying firm pressure. After thrusting her digit into his mouth a few times, he released her from his mouth. "That's how you'll take me, firm but gentle, deep and long. Are you ready?"

"Lucian, if you don't let me touch you soon I'm going to explode."

His shoulders shook with laughter. Feeling his eyes crease with mirth, he whispered, "Undo my pants."

She sat up eagerly. Her nimble fingers made fast work of the silk drawstrings at his waist. His pants loosened and fell to the ground in a puddle. He lifted his feet free, took his cock in hand, and stepped up to Evelyn. Her eyes were focused on his hand as he stroked over his flesh.

Brushing a hand over her hair and cupping the back of her head, he said, "Lick your lips." She did. He painted her wet lips with a tear of come that seeped from the head of his cock. "Now lick them again. Good girl." He watched her eyes widen at the taste of him, then tapped the weight of his dick on her lower lip. "Now open."

Her lips parted, and he slowly fed his cock into the warm cavern of her mouth. Taking gentle hold of her hair, he urged her forward. She pulled back the moment she felt uncomfortable with his depth, but eagerly drove forward again, building her tolerance. Her mouth felt fucking fantastic.

"That's it, baby, adjust to it. Get used to me being there, because I'll be back again real soon."

She became bolder with each thrust. Her tongue experimented with swirls and her lips dabbled with different variations of suction. His toes curled into the carpet and he moaned when she did something he found especially pleasant. She was too careful to do anything unpleasant.

He kept a gentle grip on her hair. "Put your palms on my thighs for balance."

After several minutes he said, "Now take me deep, as deep as you can."

She drew a deep breath and sucked him almost to the back of her throat. It was exquisite.

"Now you'll do it again and this time I'm going to hold myself there for a few seconds. Trust me to know how long is too long and remember our signals."

She nodded and he plunged deep. His grip tightened in her hair. Her eyes widened and then glazed with lust. He held himself at the back of her throat for only a second, then tugged her head back.

"Beautiful. Again."

She became putty in his hands. She moaned as if she were vicariously experiencing his pleasure. Her fingers dug into his thighs as he slowly pumped in and out of her mouth. Lucian shut his eyes for a moment, fighting back his climax. As he withdrew his cock, she leaned forward, reluctant to let it go, until his grip in her hair drew her up short.

"Who's in control, Evelyn?"

"You, Lucian."

"Do you want to make me come?"

"Yes."

"Then lower your hands and suck me deep as I fuck that pretty mouth. Give me control. Surrender. When I'm ready to come you'll lean back and I'll show you what you do to me."

Her hands lowered, and her mouth opened a second before it was stuffed with his cock. Showing her what pleased him, he did not keep his touch gentle. Rather, he fisted her hair and pumped her hot mouth over his thrusting cock.

"God, you're fucking amazing," he said through gritted teeth. "Tighten your mouth. That's it. Now drag your tongue from side to side . . ." He moaned deep as his release powered from deep within him.

He tapped her throat twice. "Now, baby, now!"

She released him with a pop and threw her body back, bracing herself on her elbows.

"Watch me, Evelyn."

Lucian gripped his cock hard and jerked as hot come jetted out in long ribbons and coated her tits. She gasped and watched his release mark her and dribble down her front.

She was crazed with lust, and he couldn't leave her in that condition. Dropping to his knees, he took her mouth hard. His fingers trailed over her sticky breasts, collecting his come, and reached into her pants.

She broke the kiss. "Lucian!"

"Hush. It's fine."

His come-covered fingers found her clit and rubbed hard. He pressed into her bud, giving her the friction she needed. It only took a few firm strokes and she was coming. Her body quivered in his arms and he cradled her to his chest, kissing her shoulders, throat, and panting lips.

"You were beautiful, Evelyn. You please me very much."

She nestled against his chest, a sort of affection he was slowly coming to expect from her. It warmed him, and he drew her closer. Essentially, they hugged for several moments, neither of them willing to let the other go just yet.

She quieted. Slowly, he stood and went to the bathroom. Running warm water over a cloth, he returned to where she lay on the floor and gently lifted her. Lucian cradled her pliant body to his chest and settled her into the bed. The cloth cleared away the remnants of their passion, and she shivered. Carefully tucking her under the heavy satin covers, he discarded the cloth and climbed in beside her, drawing her body close to his, needing to hold her.

His hands coasted over the gentle curve of her shoulder as his gaze watched her drift slowly to sleep. He couldn't tear his touch or his gaze from her. For some reason he needed to see her, feel her, know she was real and right there beside him.

As her breathing settled and her body drifted off to sleep, his mind seemed to waken, a thousand thoughts running through his head, each one triggering the next. His fingers twirled her soft hair, admiring its silken sheen, loving the subtle weight of it in his palm.

This was more than finding her to make sure she was safe. This was more than fucking her because he had to have her. This was more than anything a casual proposition for company should become, but he was glad it had evolved to something else entirely.

Evelyn provoked a possessive side in him that had been dormant too long. He was not an easy man, no point in pretending to be. He knew it, his business partners knew it, Evelyn knew it. But this territorial side of him that came out around Evelyn was different than anything he ever felt. It was . . . softer. Beyond the intense need to claim her as his came some sort of tender desire.

It wasn't enough that she be with him. She needed to be happy, fulfilled. Emotionally, physically, and any other way a person could be made to feel content.

A soft little sound escaped her lips as she nestled closer to his chest. Her warm flesh was soft and smooth, so different than his own. Lucian cuddled her close, wrapping his arms around her delicate form protectively, not wanting to let her go, never *intending* to let her go.

PART THREE

evelyn

thirty-nine

THE HOURS TO COME . . .

ALL of Scout's life she'd essentially been the same person, but that person she had always been suddenly seemed unrecognizable. She was losing Scout and becoming Evelyn. She was changing.

Evelyn had visited the spa early that morning and had her appointment with the girls, getting everything trimmed, waxed, painted, and plucked. She was acutely sore, but glad to have it done with. She was coming to take pride in such regimens and loved the way Lucian noticed such things and appreciated her efforts.

On her way back from the salon, she almost mistook a Patras attendant for Parker. The resemblance was uncanny. The man she saw had the same soft eyes and careless posture she had come to recognize as Parker's, yet this man had a bit more meat on his bones and his skin had a healthy rosy glow. His hair wasn't as long as Parker's. She wanted to get the man's name after he'd looked directly at her in the lobby, but, as a group of guests cut through the foyer to the elevators, she'd lost track of him.

Probably best she didn't approach him anyway. What would she even say? *You look just like my friend.* Like he would care.

Since the incident in the lobby, however, her mind had stuck on Parker, and she wondered how he was. The snow was now gone and the bitter cold relented to uncomfortably arctic. Not perfect conditions, but certainly less bite.

Evelyn asked Lucian about the progress being made at St. Christopher's and was pleased to discover the shelter had reopened its doors that past weekend in time for Christmas. Lucian also informed her that he'd replenished the facility with a month's worth of food and other goods like cots that would lift the residents off the ground, blankets, a free laundry facility, showers, and a huge shipment of coats, gloves, hats, and boots. He was a master of hospitality and basically turned the shelter into a free hotel for the needy. This information was extremely dangerous for her heart, which was already hazardously close to falling in love.

She couldn't love Lucian. She just couldn't. Love was a trap. It led people to depend on others who might not always be there and gave them the ability to hurt you more than anyone else ever could. She'd only ever loved one person, and she'd done nothing but show Scout all the reasons she should have protected her heart.

As they made the ride out of the city one afternoon, the highway opened up and Evelyn recognized the familiar route. Much like the last time they made this trip, she was anxious. Although she'd visited Lucian's home once, it felt like years had passed since then. And that time didn't include his family.

She had a chilling thought. "Will Slade be there?"

Lucian's otherwise serene expression shuttered. "No."

He didn't offer any explanation, so she let the topic of his friend go. Lucian must've detected her unease, because he pulled her close and rubbed her shoulders. She'd become dependent on his constant touch. Another dangerous thing.

"Are you anxious about leaving the city? We'll be back."

"No, this time I'm anxious about going to your home."

"Why?"

"Well . . . what if your sisters don't like me?"

He rolled his eyes. "That's nonsense. They'll love you."

She hoped he was right.

"You know," he said, interrupting more of her anxious musings. "If you need a distraction I'm sure I could provide one."

Evelyn elbowed him. He was so full of himself. But he was right. Lucian could drive her to distraction like no one else could. "I can't."

"Why?"

"Patrice told me no fooling around for at least twelve hours."

He gave her a sidelong glance. She knew that look in his eye. He looked at her like that whenever he was having dirty thoughts. "Did she now?"

"Yes. I'm puffy and I hurt."

He pouted dramatically. "Oh, I'll have to kiss it all better. What else did Patrice say?"

Frowning, she asked, "What do you mean? She asked me how I was and how you and I were doing, where we were spending our holiday, stuff like that."

"She didn't have anything to say about your pretty pussy?"

She smacked his arm. "Girls don't talk like that!"

He laughed. "Wanna bet?"

"Well, Patrice doesn't."

He hugged her close. "Oh, Evelyn, how innocent and trusting you are."

Trusting was the last word she'd use to describe herself, and she didn't appreciate the patronizing tone in his voice. She turned and scowled at him. "What're you suggesting? That I don't know Patrice?"

"Not at all. I'm merely acknowledging that your memory suffers when you drink."

A frown crinkled her brow as she thought back to the night she'd hung out with Patrice. Nothing specifically came to mind out of the ordinary. Pursing her lips, she said, "Explain."

He chuckled. "Patrice is very fond of you. She made it quite clear when I came to collect your little drunken ass the night of your bar escapades."

"I did *not* have escapades," Evelyn said, crossing her arms.

"The four-hundred-dollar bar bill I paid says otherwise. It was very thoughtful of you to buy so many rounds for the house, by the way."

Her eyes widened and her gut twisted like she was going to be sick. "Oh my God, Lucian, I'm so sorry. I'll pay you back. I swear."

He waved off her concern. "It's nothing. I'm glad you enjoyed yourself. Now, let's get back to Patrice. She's quite pretty, don't you think?"

"I guess, but I don't see why you should notice."

He smiled and pinched her chin. "Don't be jealous. My observations were purely for your benefit."

He was ruffling her feathers on purpose. "How's Patrice being attractive going to benefit me?"

"Because I enjoy exploring your sexual appetites. She seemed quite fond of your beautiful pussy."

Evelyn stopped breathing. He had to be teasing. Lucian surprised her on a daily basis, but that was just taking things too far. Her throat was dry as sand, and she swallowed. It didn't help. Her mouth gaped like a fish, but again, it couldn't be helped.

He laughed and patted her knee. "Don't worry. It'll only be me who touches you. I won't ask you to do anything you're uncomfortable with—much. I'm not sure my possessive nature could tolerate you touching someone else, no matter how titillating the thought is."

She finally snapped out of her dumbness. "Lucian, Patrice isn't like that—"

"Yes, Evelyn, she is. Not only is she like that, she informed Dugan and me that you had a beautiful vagina. There was no mistaking her intent. Especially after seeing the way she touched you."

"We're friends!"

He shrugged. "Sometimes friends fuck."

She scowled at him. She wasn't stupid. She knew about gays and lesbians. She just wasn't one. "Well, I don't fuck my friends."

All jovialness disappeared. "Oh, I know. I'm glad you do too, so we won't have to have that talk in the future."

"Besides, girls can't fuck other girls."

She saw him tilt his head curiously in the reflection of the window. "Why, because they don't have a penis? That's ridiculous. I could stay completely clothed and fuck your brains out. In fact, your ignorant certainty on the matter makes me wonder if that's exactly what I should do tonight."

She didn't like his choice of words. "I'm not stupid, Lucian." She glared at him from over her shoulder.

"I'd never say you were, and I'd beat the shit out of anyone who ever even hinted at such a falsehood. I'm merely saying that you underestimate all the ways a woman can be fucked when a flesh-and-blood cock is not available."

She turned back to the window. "I don't want to talk about this anymore."

A few minutes went by and he leaned close to her. He whispered, "There are toys, Evelyn. A myriad of playthings meant to bring a woman to climax faster than any hand, mouth, or living cock ever could."

Evelyn shivered as his warm breath tickled her ear. Her pussy clenched of its own volition, and she told herself it had everything to do with Lucian's closeness and tone of voice and nothing to do with the mention of other women.

"Imagine," he continued softly, his fingers tickling under the delicate wisps of hair that had slipped from her bun. "What would it feel like to have a dildo up your cunt that turned and vibrated, and pumped over your G-spot without the need for a break? I bet it would feel sensational, probably better than the water massager—which by the way, if I hear you bringing yourself to orgasm one more time while you're taking a bath I'm going to spank that little ass of yours. Those are my orgasms to give, and you don't take them without asking."

Blood rushed to the surface of her cheeks. How the fuck had he known that? She always made sure she wasn't loud. He gave the warning teasingly, but there was real disappointment behind his words. Knowing that she'd somehow disappointed Lucian did odd things to her. She hated the shame that came with the knowledge that she somehow let him down. His praise felt a hundred times better.

"I'm sorry."

"Let's not dwell on it. You've been warned. Now, where was I? Oh, yes, there was a big vibrating dildo up your pussy about to make you come. Now, Evelyn, imagine that dildo also had an attachment that stimulated your clit a mile a minute." Her body shivered.

Lucian's hand reached under her arm and undid the snap of her jeans. She watched as his finger slowly undid her zipper. He placed an arm over her shoulders and drew her back until she was reclining on him. Lucian took her hand and guided it under the denim V of her open pants and placed it over her warm panties. She was drenched.

"Be very gentle," he whispered. "Let's not forget about all of Patrice's warnings."

Evelyn could scent her own arousal. Her fingers massaged over the wet patch at the front of her panties. The smooth surface beneath the silk was hot and sensitive from being waxed only hours ago.

Lucian's fingers opened the buttons of her coat and the buttons of her blouse. His fingers slipped between the panels of fabric and found her nipple. He plucked leisurely.

"Now let's say your hands are restrained and you're at my mercy while I'm fucking your wet little cunt with that big nasty toy. Oh, I bet you're begging for release, practically crying for it. In fact, perhaps you're making such a ruckus that I climb on top of you and force my cock in your mouth."

She moaned at the thought.

"Keep rubbing, Evelyn, but don't come."

Her finger slowed, but continued to play over the saturated silk. Her body throbbed. She was so close, so close that she feared accidentally pushing herself too far and not being able to draw herself back in time to stop the wave of release once it crested.

Lucian nudged her wrist. "I said keep rubbing."

Her breathing quickened and she shook with the tension of holding back her orgasm.

Lucian's deep, gravelly voice only made things worse. "So you have my cock deep in your mouth and you're loving it. Meanwhile, I turn the vibrator between your thighs and the part that was just vibrating your clit is now tapping on your tight little asshole. I imagine you scream out the exquisite pleasure and my cock moves a bit deeper."

Her heart was going to beat out of her chest.

"Then," he said silkily, "perhaps I turn you, so while you're swallowing my cock my mouth's sucking on your clit and you're suddenly coming hard."

Her gasp turned to a guttural moan as her hand was suddenly ripped from her pants. She needed to come. "Damn it, Lucian!"

He clucked his tongue. "I'm afraid not, Evelyn. Not when you already stole one orgasm from me this morning. No, I think you'll have to wait until your twelve hours are up. Patrice's orders."

She hated him. Her teeth gritted and she stifled all the nasty names she wanted to call him. And then it occurred to her that she was her own person and if she wanted to come, all she had to do was reach between her legs and make herself come. Lucian be damned!

Her teeth slowly unclenched. It wouldn't be as good. In fact, it would be the opposite of good. Lucian's disappointment would weigh on her until she felt as though she were drowning. Imagining him frowning at her and the shame she'd feel at not doing what he asked made her want to turn and apologize. And she hadn't even done anything! She was seriously fucked up.

For several minutes her brow lowered in confusion as Evelyn thought of this obsession she had with pleasing Lucian. She didn't do it out of fear. On the contrary, she did it because his praise made it that much better. He never yelled at her or punished her. Even though he was always in control, she never felt forced into anything. She had practically forgotten her safe word. She would have, if Lucian didn't remind her of it on a regular basis.

What was wrong with her? *Was* there anything wrong with her? She had no prior experiences to go by. All she knew was Lucian. She knew what he liked and she knew that she liked it too. She couldn't imagine it being any other way between a man and woman. She needed him to be in charge. Otherwise nothing would ever happen, because she certainly wasn't asking.

She pressed her fingers to her forehead. Dear God, she was like a brainwashed puppet. Yes, Lucian. Please, Lucian. Thank you,

Lucian. Yet every word out of her mouth was genuine. She wanted to be polite to him because she respected him. She wanted to thank him because he thought about her more than he did himself. She wanted to please him. Everything she did somehow always brought her back to him. She was addicted to Lucian.

forty

CHRISTMAS CARDS

ONCE they arrived at the house, their things were brought in and Jamie joined them for a late lunch. Evelyn found it difficult to look at Jamie after the last time they were in the dining room together, but his easygoing disposition helped. It was almost impossible to associate the carefree man with the one who watched her come with nothing but pure lust and intensity in his eyes. It was easier to forget about what he'd seen when they were at the penthouse, but when they were at Lucian's home the past came hurtling back to her.

"Are you enjoying your holiday, Scout?" Jamie asked as they sat in the library after lunch. Lucian was called away for a few moments with an important business call.

The library wasn't overly formal, which didn't really match the name. Rather, it was like a cozy living room, but a television was absent and the walls were covered with books. She sat cross-legged on the overstuffed sofa facing Jamie. "Lucian has a way of making every day feel like a holiday."

Jamie's cheeks were dusted with freckles that made his pigment appear darker than it was. He was actually quite pale. When he smiled, like he did now, twin dimples formed in his freckled cheeks. His smile was quite charming. "Lucian does have that ability when he chooses to use it. I think you've been good for him. I haven't seen my friend this lighthearted since we were children."

Lucian definitely had an intense side. He brought that side out when they were intimate, but it wasn't the same as the severe side she'd caught glimpses of when he needed to accomplish something important. She had no doubt that Lucian could have anything he wanted, because his determination and tenacity was almost frightening at times.

"I'm enjoying myself," Evelyn said.

"I'm glad," Jamie admitted. "I hope that you stick around for a long time, Scout. I like you. I like what you do for my friend and I like the kind of girl you are. Luche's never had a girl like you before."

"What do you mean, 'a girl like me'?"

"Tough. You're not a pushover. Lucian's extremely domineering with women. Not everyone can handle a demanding male and draw a line between being submissive and being completely subjugated. You won't lose yourself to him. You've a strong little will under all that beauty."

"Thank you?" What did you say to that? *Domineering with women* . . . Lucian didn't have women. He had her. There had better not be any other women.

The sound of Jamie's laughter eased the tension weighing on her face. "Relax, Scout, I meant it as a compliment. Oh, yes," he said, holding his trim belly. "I think you'll be quite wonderful for Lucian. As a matter of fact, with the fierce look you just had on your face, I wonder if maybe I should fear for the day that Lucian truly pisses you off, because trust me, love, he will."

She believed him. When Lucian returned, he seemed flustered. "Evelyn, will you get me a drink, please?"

Caught off guard, because Lucian rarely requested her to wait on him, she did a double take. He wasn't looking at her, so she simply stood and went to the bar. Crystal was incredibly heavy for glass. Evelyn's hand trembled as she tipped the decanter over the tumbler. Lucian and Jamie were speaking in hushed tones over at the sofa. Distracted by trying to hear what they were saying, she almost overpoured and spilled all over the bar.

Amber liquid topped the glass, almost forming a bubble. If she moved the glass, the placid surface of liquor would ripple and make a mess. Her eyes shot to Jamie and Lucian, then back to the glass. Leaning over, she put her lips to the rim of the glass and sipped. Fire burned through her esophagus like tunneling lava. She gasped and choked.

Her eyes watered and she turned, fighting to suck in a deep breath. A bottle of cool water was shoved in her face. Her hands gripped the bottle and drank from it greedily as someone patted her back. Swiping a finger under her runny eyes, she turned, totally embarrassed. She was such an idiot. Never a dull moment.

"You okay?" Lucian's expression was wholly concerned. Knowing he wasn't laughing at her, she felt a little better.

"Yeah. Thanks. What the hell's that crap you're drinking?"

"Brandy."

Evelyn made a gagging face. "It's like trying to swallow melted glass."

Jamie chuckled, reminding her of his presence. Lucian's eyes softened and he leaned forward and kissed her temple. The gesture wasn't unfamiliar, but there was something intimate about it. It surprised her that he'd show such simple affection in front of his friend. When she turned, Jamie looked equally surprised, but also pleased. The smile hovering around his lips also touched his eyes.

"Well, kids, I believe I'll be taking off. Perhaps I'll visit Christmas Eve," Jamie announced, and Lucy, who seemed to always show up at just the right moment, disappeared, then reappeared with his coat. Jamie shifted his long arms into his dapper coat and buttoned the double-breasted panel in the front. The style reminded her of something Parker would look great in.

"Do, Jamie," Lucian said, patting his friend on the back. "I know the girls would love to see you."

The side of Jamie's smirk kicked up. "Antoinette's in her twenties now."

Lucian scowled. "No."

Jamie laughed merrily and slapped his shoulder with what appeared as sympathy. "It's inevitable, Luche. You know it and I know it."

Jamie kissed Evelyn's cheek and walked out of the library in high spirits. "She's got a boyfriend, Shamus. He's a martial arts instructor. He'll kick your ass!" Lucian shouted and Jamie's laughter echoed from the foyer.

Once she was sure Jamie had left, she asked, "Does Jamie like your sister?"

He pinched the bridge of his nose and sighed. "Not as much as Antoinette likes him. She used to follow him around like a puppy. Jamie's always kept his distance, but once he lost a bet and Toni made him give her his word that after she turned twenty he'd stop seeing her as only his friend's baby sister."

"You don't want her to be with Jamie?"

"Jamie's a great guy. Couldn't ask for a more loyal friend, but Toni's my sister, and Jamie's my friend for a reason. We have very similar tastes."

A small bit of hurt formed in her belly. Why were Lucian's "tastes" good enough for her, but not good enough for his sister?

"Hey. What's that face for?"

She shook her head. "You don't want a man to treat your sister the way you treat me?"

He opened his mouth, but the tension in his brow faded and he seemed to understand the conclusions she was drawing. "Evelyn, there's nothing wrong with what we do. My concern with Jamie getting involved with Toni is . . . let's just say that I'm very private about my appetites around my family. Toni's a blabbermouth. She likes Jamie because the little girl inside of her said one day she'd marry him. She doesn't have a clue about what she'd actually be walking into with him. My sister doesn't have a submissive bone in her body and I'm not sure Shamus has the fortitude to help her be what he needs. The entire thing could end badly and I don't need Toni running to all her little friends, painting Jamie's name in a bad light when he does nothing I wouldn't do."

His words reassured her. She understood the desire for privacy. "Well, you said she has a boyfriend. I don't think Jamie's the kind of guy to poach."

Lucian's head jerked with a short bubble of silent laughter. "Baby, Jamie and I are very similar. If there's something we want, we go after it. It doesn't matter who's guarding it from us. Once we set our sights on it, it's already considered ours. And we always get what we consider ours."

"Well, what about Antoinette's boyfriend? Surely Jamie wouldn't fight—"

"Antoinette's boyfriend couldn't kill a spider. He's a tissue. Jamie would destroy him if it came to that."

CHRISTMAS Eve morning Lucian woke Evelyn up by gently making love to her under the covers. They held each other close, tucked away from the chill in the air, and he rocked into her with such intense tenderness she was off balance for a good part of the morning.

Lucian laid out clothes for her to wear, a thick cable-knit turtleneck sweater, long johns, thick wool socks, and new fur-lined boots. When she met him downstairs, he was dressed much the same in boots, a heavy sweater, and rugged jeans. He looked like a lumberjack. He looked delicious.

His broad arms spread, holding out a puffy down coat for her. Evelyn slipped her arms in and he zipped it tight. As he placed a wool cap over her head and wrapped a cashmere scarf at her neck, she asked, "Where are we going?"

"It's a surprise."

They went out front. Expecting to see Dugan, she was surprised when Lucian unlocked the passenger door of a luxury SUV for her and got behind the wheel. "You drive?"

His eyes crinkled. "Of course I drive. Buckle up."

She snapped the buckle and watched as Lucian navigated his way through the back roads. He drove like he did everything else, in complete control. They listened to carols on the radio and Lucian quietly sang along with the chorus.

"You know all of them," she said and he glanced at her without fully taking his eyes off the road.

"All of what?"

"The carols."

"Doesn't everyone?"

"I don't."

Sometimes she felt like her background was a piece of Swiss cheese with great big holes in it, while Lucian's was some expensive aged kind that had been around long enough to see everything. Rather than comment on her lack of holiday experiences, he simply placed his hand on her knee and rubbed and tapped with the beat of the carols.

They pulled up to a small shed with a large sign and an enormous wreath on the peak. Lucian parked and smiled. He pointedly glanced at the sign and then back at her. She looked at the letters, wishing she could read, and then shook her head.

"It's a tree farm," he said.

"A tree farm?"

"Yeah. They grow trees. We're going to pick out our Christmas tree."

Her cheeks rose as her grin bloomed. "Really?"

"Yup. Come on."

They went into the shed, which was actually a store. A man in a heavy flannel jacket handed Lucian a receipt, Lucian took her hand and led her to the back of the store. They stepped out a set of double doors and Evelyn gasped.

An elegant open sleigh with a single horse hooked to it awaited them. The horse drew her near, his glossy black coat tempting and stunning. Clouds of moisture formed in the air in front of the animal's large snout. Its eyes seemed so alive behind the dark side blinds. His nostrils were huge. Heavy harnesses connected to his shoulders, and his mane was a glorious shade of black. She stepped close, needing to touch him to know he was real.

His pointed ears twitched and he whickered, his harnesses pulling, the creak of the leather pronouncing their weight. He was incredibly strong and likely the most impressive living thing she'd ever seen. He reminded her of Lucian.

"Shh," she soothed as she reached up a steady hand.

His wild eyes watched her, but he stilled as she petted the side of his mane.

"You're quite handsome," she whispered to the impressive beast.

Turning to Lucian, who was watching her with a soft smile on his face, she asked, "What's his name?"

"Pegasus."

"Hello, Pegasus."

Snow crunched as Lucian quietly approached. "He appears as charmed by you as every other male that crosses your path." His hand smoothed over the powerful neck of the horse.

She stepped back. Pegasus's feet were covered in white fur that resembled snow boots. The sleigh was as sleek and black as the horse drawing it. A driver sat perched in the front seat, wearing a top hat with a sprig of holly tacked in the brim.

Lucian directed her to the rear. There was a black leather upholstered bench seat and a red fleece blanket draped over the back. As she stepped up her gaze fell on a single red rose sitting on the bench. Her cheeks pulled tight as she reached for it. There was a note attached. She unfolded it and tried to read it, but couldn't. It didn't matter. It was still the most romantic thing anyone had ever done for her. She knew it was from Lucian because at the bottom of the note she recognized the signed *L*.

Evelyn clutched the rose in her hands and faced him. "Thank you."

He kissed her temple and they settled into the seat, tucking the blanket over their knees. Her heart raced.

"Ready, sir?" the driver called over his shoulder.

"Ready," Lucian answered as he wrapped his arm around her shoulders and drew her close. Sleigh bells jangled as the sleigh lurched forward. They moved swiftly over the icy ground. Wind pressed into her cheeks and she shut her eyes, breathing deeply in the fresh air.

As they rode, they passed many displays of lighted Christmas scenes. Although it was daytime, they were still beautiful. When they crossed through a field, the tall pines became denser. They followed a narrow trail, and then the land opened up and they faced a nursery of young evergreens. The driver pointed out trees that he thought were notable, and Lucian did the same. She never had a Christmas before, let alone a Christmas tree, so Evelyn simply sat back and let the men decide.

Lucian had the driver pull over by a tall Douglas fir. "What do you think, Evelyn?"

"It's perfect." It was. She remembered seeing an enormous tree when she was a child outside of Mackles's department store. It was tall and full and as soft as this one.

Lucian reached in the back of the carriage where a chest was stored and removed a saw. She was completely impressed as he sawed through the trunk. The driver tossed a rope over the top of the tree to direct it away from the sleigh as it went down with a soft thump. They wrapped the branches tightly with rope and secured the tree on a board. The tree was towed behind the sled back to the store, and the men attached it to the top of Lucian's SUV. It was perhaps the most magical afternoon she'd ever had in her life.

That evening after the servants moved the tree to the foyer, boxes were placed all around and she and Lucian decorated it. Each ornament was made of glass or crystal or some other fragile material. They reminded Evelyn of jewels. They were beautiful.

Carols played, but other than that the house was quiet. "Where is everybody?" she asked, realizing she hadn't even seen Lucy in some time.

"They went home to be with their own families. They won't be back until the first. What? Why are you laughing?"

She pressed her lips tight, but her amusement was impossible to disguise. "Lucian, you'll starve. How are you going to make it a week without people waiting on you hand and foot?"

He smiled and grabbed her by the waist. His fingers dug into the tender, ticklish skin at her side and she squealed. "It just so happens, Ms. Keats," he said, pressing his lips against her neck, "I'm a wonderful cook."

His mouth sealed to her throat and his hold gentled. Her body went slack in his hold as he kissed her. Breathlessly, she whispered, "I doubt there's anything you don't do wonderfully."

He gazed at her. Twinkle lights reflected in the black of his eyes. Evelyn's lashes lowered as he pressed his lips to hers, and her body sang as he deepened the kiss. He lifted her off the floor and she held on to his shoulders, legs wrapped tight around his hips, as he carried her up the stairs, never once breaking the kiss.

Fingers tugged at buttons and zippers until they were both naked. Lucian kissed her with such passion, she slowly melted into a puddle of wax. His palms turned her hips until she faced the tall post of the four-poster bed. He guided her hands above her shoulders and pressed his fingers over hers until she was holding on to the post.

His mouth traced the gentle curve of her neck. The heat of his tongue trailed down her spine. She yipped when his teeth pinched her ass, but he soothed away the bite with languid kisses.

Shivers scattered up her back and over her breasts as he continued to kiss her everywhere with those soft lips of his. She was wet and needy. Her breathy moans whispered through the room. He licked at the backs of her knees and ran the tips of his fingers over the swell of her hips. His eyes caressed her right alongside his fingers and mouth.

When he had her truly trembling with need, he turned her toward the high bed and planted her palms on the edge of the mattress. Her feet were nudged apart and his finger trailed down her spine. She arched with his touch, completely under his seductive command.

He filled her in one hard thrust that had her up on her toes. It was intense, but not what she would consider rough. His body blanketed hers as he took her from behind, possessed her. His cock sank deep into her sex and his arms wrapped around her waist, holding her tight. Fingers grazed her swaying breasts, and her nipples sent shock waves to her center every time he pinched the tender tips.

She was grateful Lucian had taken her to visit with Dr. Sheffield. The birth control she was now on was a forgotten matter she wouldn't have to readdress for another year. The doctor had inserted something inside of her that pinched for only a minute, and now they were safe to touch each other freely and as often as they pleased.

Lucian drew her hips back forcefully, possessively. He owned her body in that moment, and she never enjoyed surrendering more. Slow, deep thrusts filled her and soon she was crying out her release. He withdrew and her sex was suddenly lonesome and cold.

The mattress pressed into her back as she was lifted and turned. Lucian raised her ankles and kissed the soft spot just below where his thumbs held. He pulled her legs into a wide V, and she was full once more. His gaze never left her, and she felt as if he were looking into her soul.

His dark throat worked and his jaw ticked as he filled her with his hot release. Her body was no longer her own. Her body felt free and cherished, as did her mind. A tremor of fear slipped past her contentment. This feeling she kept hiding from, the one that kept chasing her thoughts into corners, was becoming too big to ignore. It made her want to place distance between Lucian and herself, yet at the same time, the thought of even a brief moment without him terrified her. Giving up Lucian, she feared, would be worse than living without air.

EVELYN awoke to something tugging at her hand. Turning, she blindly felt for Lucian, but his side of the bed was cold. Something tugged at her finger. As she rubbed her eyes, she heard the quiet hum of Christmas carols. She could smell the piney fragrance of the tree from downstairs and the trace of fresh-brewed coffee.

There was a thin, red satin bow tied to her ring finger. The ribbon hanging from it pulled taut and her finger pinched. She stood. Inching one hand over the other, she followed the red ribbon trail out of the bedroom. Once she reached the hall, she unraveled the ribbon from where it looped over the clawed foot of a chair and discovered a note. Evelyn collected the slip of paper and followed the ribbon farther down the hall.

The carols grew louder, but still remained only a soft part of the background. She discovered one note after another, wishing more and more that she could read just one of them. When she approached the top of the stairs, she found Lucian sitting in a chair that had been moved to the foyer. He wore a satin robe and held the other end of the long ribbon. Smiling, he gave the ribbon a tug.

He was like no one else in this world. Common sense told her nothing lasted forever, and sublime happiness only meant the sadness that followed would hurt all the more. But Evelyn recognized how happy she was and pushed away her ever-present trepidation.

As she stepped off the bottom stair, she gathered the bundle of ribbon and walked to Lucian. He tugged until she leaned down and kissed him. "Merry Christmas," he whispered.

"Merry Christmas."

He took her hand and traced a finger over the bow. "Just what I wanted, already wrapped for me in a pretty bow." He undid the bow and pulled her to his lap. He kissed her soundly and left her dizzy. "Now that I've opened my present, which I cannot wait to play with all day, how about you open yours?"

She tilted her head and he tipped his chin, gesturing toward the tree. She swiveled in his lap and gasped. Boxes and boxes of beautifully wrapped gifts covered the skirt of the tree, spilling onto the floor.

"They're not all for me . . ." Evelyn said, a bit overwhelmed by such grandeur.

"Of course they are. I had twenty-two Christmases to make up for. Come on." He pulled her to the floor and she sat paralyzed. There was just so much.

"Here," he said, placing a small box in her lap. "Open this one first."

She hesitated. "Wait. I have something for you too."

Slipping off his lap, she returned to the bedroom. She quickly used the bathroom and went to her bags stowed in the closet. There, inside her small, rumpled sack sat his gift. It was not enough to fill beneath a tree or even weigh down a single branch, but it was what she could afford and she put a lot of thought into it.

Her lips thinned nervously as she made her way back down the grand staircase. Lucian looked up, his expression curious and adorably childlike. He smiled. "You got me another gift?"

He'd worn the belt she'd purchased often. This was nothing as extravagant, but she hoped he'd like it all the same. She handed him the small box. "It's nothing special."

He took the package and glanced down at it then back to her. "Of course it's special. People don't give me things often. Your thoughtfulness is a gift in itself, Evelyn."

She lowered her gaze, his praise warming her heart. "Open it."

The sound of paper tearing played over the soft hum of carols. He lifted the lid and stilled. "Oh, Evelyn."

"I saw it at a pawnshop months ago and asked Dugan to pick it up for me. It isn't new, but I liked it and thought you would too."

She held her breath as he lifted the vintage pocket watch out of the box. It was scratched and slightly tarnished, but it still told time. She wanted him to always remember their time together, even if a time came when they were no longer a part of each other's lives.

"It's beautiful. I love it." His expression was sincere. As a matter of fact, he seemed beyond moved by the gift.

"It really isn't much."

His gaze shot to hers and his brow lowered. "I think it's one of the nicest things anyone's ever given me. I'll keep it with me always." He pulled her to his lap and kissed her. Tucking the watch into the silk pocket of his robe, he leaned over and handed her the gift she'd left on her chair. "Here. Open it."

Her fingers trembled as she carefully undid the tapings. She had never unwrapped a present before. It made her sad to destroy such lovely coverings. Some odd hoarder part of her personality that she didn't know she had wanted to save every bit of paper and tuck it away to look at on rainy days, memories of brighter times.

Once she had the box opened she peeled back the tissue and pulled out a canvas bag. "It's a bag."

"A *new* bag," Lucian stated the obvious. "You can finally get rid of that ratty old thing you take everywhere."

She appreciated the practicality of the gift. When the time came, a new bag would come in handy. She tried not to overanalyze the fact that Lucian had just given her a gift that would only be used if they separated.

"Thank you."

"Here, do this one next." He seemed to enjoy giving the gifts as much as a little kid opening them.

The next was a gorgeous sweater, after that, a pair of sapphire earrings. She didn't mention that her ears weren't pierced. They were as lovely in their velvet box as they would be on her lobes.

The morning continued in the same pattern. She'd open a gift, thank Lucian, and then she'd find another in her lap. She simply couldn't comprehend such generosity and indulgence. The pile never seemed to end. She'd been given clothes, gowns, shoes, jewelry, an iPad, perfume, expensive soaps and lotions, a robe, and more. It became so overwhelming, she lost track.

She peeled back the paper of a heavy box and lifted the lid. Books. Her smile trembled nervously and Lucian said, "It's Henry David Thoreau. *Walden* is by far one of the most eloquently written pieces of literature I've ever read. I think you'll like it."

It was simply too much. Her eyes stung and she blinked. "Oh, Lucian . . ."

"What's the matter? Have you read it?"

Emotion choked her. She worked to make her voice audible. "No," she whispered. "I've never read it."

He pulled it from her lap and placed a thinly wrapped package in her lap. "Open this one."

Her fingers trembled. She didn't want to open any more presents. As the corner tore and the pretty paper was spoiled, she stopped. She just couldn't do any more.

"Evelyn?"

Lifting her brow, she looked at Lucian apologetically. "Can we stop for a while?"

She saw his confusion, but he nodded. "Okay, baby. How about I make us some breakfast?" She nodded, needing to get away from all the gifts for a while.

Lucian made French toast for breakfast. It was delicious. She loved watching him cook. He seemed so relaxed, so ordinary. She found herself wishing he were.

"What time will your sisters get here?"

He glanced at the clock. "Probably sometime in the next two hours."

A nervous tickle danced across her chest. "Should we be cooking something?"

"The turkey's been in the oven since five. Isadora will bring the sides, and Antoinette will bring the desserts. I provide the booze, and Lucy dressed the formal dining room before she left."

"What should I wear?"

"Wear whatever you're comfortable in. It's just family."

Yes, but not her family. Evelyn thought about Pearl and wondered how she was enjoying her holiday. So much time had gone by since she spoke to her. She'd never been away from her mother for more than a few days. "Lucian, can I call my mom?"

He stilled as if he hadn't considered Pearl. "Of course. I'm sorry, Evelyn. I should've let you do that first thing. If you want, we can go see her before my sisters arrive."

She shook her head. "No. I don't think I'm up for that. I just want to call and wish her a merry Christmas."

He handed her a phone and a business card with a number handwritten on the back. He busied himself with the dishes as she made the call. Pearl sounded . . . anxious.

She was very curious about how long she'd stay at rehab and when Evelyn was coming to visit. Evelyn promised they'd come in the next couple of days, and in a paranoid whisper Pearl asked if she could come alone. She figured that would be okay, so she said yes. Her mother admitted she was very tired and they ended the call.

That was the first time she had ever talked to her mother on a phone. It was impersonal and distant. Evelyn didn't like not being able to see her face. She thought hearing her voice would help her awkward mood, but it didn't. She felt . . . lost.

Everything was unfamiliar. Even Lucian wasn't being his usual self. He was doing dishes for Christ's sake! She excused herself to go take a shower, thinking that might help.

After her shower she selected a burgundy sweater dress paired with black tights and spiked black leather boots that went to the knee. She wore her hair down, not because Lucian preferred it that way, but because it acted as a shield. With every minute that ticked by she grew more and more nervous.

Lucian entered the room and eyed her curiously. She had been sitting on the edge of the bed staring at nothing for the past twenty minutes.

"Evelyn?"

"Hey."

"Baby, what's wrong?"

She shrugged. "I don't know. The best way I can explain it is . . . I feel . . . homesick. I know that doesn't make sense because I don't have a home, but that's the best way I can put it."

He sat next to her and pulled her close. "You have a home, Evelyn, with me. I'm sorry if I went a little overboard on your gifts. I just wanted to spoil you."

"It's so much, Lucian. I don't even know how to use half that stuff. And the books . . ."

"I'm sorry about the books. I should've gotten you something more girlie. I just figured since I liked them . . ."

Without warning, a sob hiccupped from her chest.

"Hey, hey, what's wrong? Evelyn, please don't cry. I'll take them all back."

Shutting her eyes, she pressed her lips together and shook her head. Forcing a deep breath, she stood and went to the top drawer of the dresser. She removed the notes from the morning and the one that had been attached to the rose. Evelyn handed them to him and he frowned.

"Read them," she asked.

"What?"

"Read them. Please."

For the first time ever, Lucian looked unsure. He glanced at the first note. His voice was a thin thread of what it normally sounded like. *"I love the sound of my name when it crosses your lips. It is the sweetest whisper my ears have ever been sung."*

He looked at her and she pointed to the next one.

He read, *"On the days that I cannot hear your heart beating beside mine, you're too far away and I want nothing more than to go to you and hold you close, and never let go."* He began breathing heavily. He frowned at the notes and his fingers tightened over the delicate parchment.

"And this one," she whispered.

He read this one a little faster. *"I feel as though you sip from my soul every time our lips touch and when you look at me as I'm deep inside of you, you breathe life back into me, and I know, before you, everything was only an imitation of what living truly is."*

Her heart pinched and her stomach rolled with too much emotion to keep inside.

Lucian suddenly stood. "What is this, Evelyn?" he barked. "I'm not a writer. If you don't like them, throw them away." His fists closed over the papers, crumpling them into a ball.

"No!" She jumped to her feet and grabbed his fist. As she tried to unknot his fingers he scoffed and let them all flutter to the floor. She chased them down to the carpet and quickly uncurled them.

Lucian threw his fingers into his hair and turned. "I don't get you, Evelyn. I thought today would be perfect, but every time I look at you you're more upset than you were the moment before. I can't win for losing!"

He stormed toward the door and she panicked. "Lucian, wait!"

He stopped but didn't turn around. His shoulders heaved slowly with irritation. She hadn't meant to embarrass him.

Her voice was watery and breathless. "I'm sorry. I don't know why I'm so emotional today. I'm just overwhelmed. You have to understand, before today, Christmas just meant ham instead of stew at the shelter and hot chocolate for dessert instead of going without. I've never been given gifts before I met you and your overindulgence is at times more than I can comprehend."

"I'll send them all back." He was hurt and that was her fault.

"No, Lucian, you don't have to do that. I just want you to know, all of those gifts down there don't mean a fraction of what this means to me," she said, holding up his love notes.

His eyes narrowed. "Then why did you make me read them like that? You made me feel like—"

"Because I can't read them."

"What?"

She stared up at him, so tall and powerful. His image shimmered behind the wall of tears covering her eyes. "I don't know how to read."

It took a minute for her words to sink in. His expression softened and he blinked at her.

"Evelyn . . ." he rasped. "I . . . I'm sorry. I didn't know."

"I didn't want you to know. I didn't want you to think I was stupid."

He lowered himself to the floor. "I could never think that." His hands gently turned her face and kissed her tear-streaked cheeks.

A watery laugh bubbled from her. "Bet you believe me now when I tell you I wasn't snooping at your desk the day we met."

He didn't laugh. His strong arms wrapped around her and he rocked her. His warm lips pressed into her temple as he whispered over her skin, "I'll teach you to read, Evelyn. I'll teach you anything you're interested in learning. I never want you to feel like you're less because you can't do something. Anything you want to learn, I'll teach you. Even without those skills, you're so much more than anyone else in this world."

He held her for a long while, there on the floor. She asked him to read the rest of the notes and he did. By the time they were heading back downstairs, hand in hand, to welcome his sisters, she was sure of four things. One, she'd finally learn to read. Two, Lucian loved her very much. Three, she loved him more. And four, this would end very badly and her heart would likely never beat right again.

forty-one
.....

ON THE THIRD DAY OF CHRISTMAS
MY TRUE LOVE GAVE TO ME . . .

L UCIAN'S sisters hung around for two days. Isadora stayed at the house, but Antoinette returned home each night after Lucian declared that there was no way she and her boyfriend Peter were sharing a bed under his roof. On the last day they were there, Jamie showed up. Jamie wasn't his jovial self around Lucian's younger sister. He studied her with an intensity much like the way Lucian watched her. Evelyn observed them with interest. So did Peter, yet he seemed a little insecure about what everyone saw between Toni and Jamie.

Isadora was even more beautiful in person than she was in the picture Evelyn had seen. While Antoinette was a fiery ball of energy in a package of curves and dimples, Isadora was a willowy, elfin creature with skin as silky as rose petals and eyes as dark as sin. She definitely seemed the matriarch of the siblings, and it was interesting watching her tease Lucian the way no one else could.

Although they were probably one of the wealthiest families in the world, an outsider would never be able to tell by their easy manner. Evelyn's nervousness disappeared the moment Isadora grasped her in a tight hug and welcomed her to the family. She failed to inform her that her greeting was a bit presumptuous and found herself falling into a cozy little world of make-believe.

The day after Christmas, she visited Pearl. Her mother still looked quite ill. She was lethargic and quiet and barely sat up when Evelyn knocked on her door. Evelyn gave her one of the sweaters Lucian had given her for Christmas, but Pearl didn't acknowledge the gift. Her blinking eyes stared into nothingness as Evelyn made small talk.

The hollow welcome left her cold and heartsick. When they returned to the estate, greeted again by Lucian's sister, it was a welcome distraction. Perhaps with time, her mother would forgive her.

Evelyn was sad to see Lucian's family go, but also anxious to have Lucian back all to herself. As he closed the door behind them, he smiled at her. They had made love tenderly and quietly over the past few days. It was nice, but she missed the intensity they usually shared.

He faced her after locking the door behind his sisters. "I want you to go upstairs, remove your clothing, and wait for me on the bed." She shivered and quickly moved to do as he instructed.

Lucian entered the room a short time later, carrying three small gifts in his hand. She inwardly groaned at the thought of more presents.

"Open this," he instructed as he placed a gift on the bed.

She did. "It's a blindfold."

"Correct. Now open the other two."

The second package jangled when she shook it. After unwrapping the paper, she lifted the lid and found two leather cuffs attached by a long chain. She swallowed.

"And the last," he instructed.

She peeled back the paper carefully and found a bottle of liquid. She looked at the label. "What is it?"

"Oil."

Evelyn knew what the oil was for immediately and her heart quickened as blood rushed to her cheeks.

"You have several more gifts like this downstairs," he said. "Each night I'll give you three to open and you'll choose which one we'll use. Choose now, Evelyn."

Her fingers traced over the soft leather of the cuffs and the soft satin of the eye mask. She picked up the oil and looked at him.

"Are you sure?"

She nodded.

"Tell me your safe word."

"Checkmate."

"Lie back."

Her legs uncurled from beneath her and the soft bedding pressed into her back. She heard the whisper of Lucian removing his clothes.

"Spread your legs for me," he said.

He still remained off the bed. She looked up at the chandelier hanging above her and drew her knees apart.

"Open yourself so I can see you."

Her fingers reached for her sex and she opened her slit. She was already wet.

"Whose pussy is that, Evelyn?"

"Yours."

"Very good, Evelyn. And whose tits?"

"Yours, Lucian."

"And after tonight, who will own your ass?"

"You will, Lucian."

He grumbled his approval. "Make yourself come. You have two minutes."

Her fingers closed over her clit and she rubbed in fast, tight circles. Her body tightened. She replayed Lucian's words in her head, his commanding tone echoing in her mind, and her sex clenched. The orgasm was quick and slight, nothing like the releases she experienced at Lucian's hand. She understood its purpose, however. The sharp release eased some of her tension and helped her relax.

"Very good."

The bed dipped, and Lucian's mouth latched onto her nipple. He sucked hard and released the tip with a pop. He repeated the action on her other breast, then climbed over her torso, straddling her. He was naked. His weight sunk into her and she felt deliciously restrained.

"Open."

Her lips parted and he leaned forward. His cock pressed into her mouth hard and fast. He took her wrists and held them above her head. Her back arched slightly, lifting her breasts. He thrust several times in quick succession, and then withdrew and scooted back.

His warm palms plumped her breasts and he fit himself in the tight crease he created. He fucked her there with his wet cock as his thumbs circled over her nipples. Other than the skid of his fingers and her building anticipation, there was little else that stimulated her out of what he was doing. This was purely for him and she understood that.

Lucian could be achingly tender, but every once in a while he needed to assert his authority and show her that he could take his pleasure as he saw fit. Her pleasure was his to give and there was no promise as to how often she should receive it. Although what he was doing was intentionally selfish, it excited her.

It made her wet to watch him take from her with such confidence as though it were his due. She probably wouldn't feel that way if he wasn't such a generous lover for the majority of the time, but he was, and she found great pleasure in getting him off.

The selfless surrender he demanded of her made her feel powerful and strong in her own way.

Heat seeped from the dark head of his cock onto her chest. His fingers stopped teasing her nipples and simply held her as he fucked faster. He grunted, and hot come shot between her breasts and trickled over her shoulder.

He slid down her body and wedged her knees apart, surprising her by driving himself deep into her pussy. "Rub my come into your breasts."

Her fingers slid through the warm fluid and massaged it into her skin.

"You're very wet, Evelyn. It turns you on when I take my pleasure from you, doesn't it."

"Yes, Lucian."

He ground himself into her. "Pinch your nipples and don't let go until I give you permission."

She did as he asked and he drove into her hard. His fingers worked over her clit and he pumped in and out of her sex.

Her breasts stung and grew surprisingly numb. She didn't let go as he slammed into her. Her orgasm built, but she fought back her release, not wanting to take it without his permission. Suddenly he pinched her clit.

Evelyn screamed and he said, "Now, Evelyn. Release them now and come."

Blood rushed to the tips of her breasts, a delicious mixture of sharp, biting pain that was quickly replaced with fiery pleasure. The same sensation filled her clit as he relinquished his hold and she came hard, arching off the bed and calling out his name.

She wasn't given much time to recover. Lucian climbed back up her body and tapped her mouth. She opened her eyes and realized it was his cock that had bumped her.

"Taste yourself on me and suck me until I'm fully hard again."

She took him into her mouth and licked over his solid flesh. He wasn't flaccid, but he also wasn't as erect as he usually was. It didn't take long to get him there. She tasted her arousal mixed with his and found herself growing wet for him again.

His hand sifted in her hair and he quickly directed her mouth over his cock. The feeling of his flesh twitching and growing over her tongue as he filled her mouth was an empowering and heady thing. He released her hair and she dropped back to the pillows. He climbed off of her.

"It's time."

Lucian set pillows in the center of the bed and guided her on top of them. The soft downy fabric cushioned her abdomen, and her ass remained high in the air. Lucian kneeled between her legs and crawled close to her backside. Heat from his body warmed her thighs.

His hand slid up her spine, and she lowered her shoulders when he applied pressure there. "Rest your cheek on your arms, Evelyn," he said softly.

The snap of a cap sounded like the crack of a gun at the start of a race, drawing her shoulders tight, flooding her veins with adrenaline, and then he was separating her cheeks and massaging the cool oil around and into her hole. It heated under his touch.

Her clit swelled as he nudged the tight knot of her ass with his finger. She relaxed, having grown used to his fingers penetrating her there. When he sunk his digit deep, she sighed at the expected slow burn as it bloomed into something dark and pleasant.

There was a difference with the oil from when he used her own moisture like he usually did. This was easier, smoother. It didn't absorb as quickly as her own lubrication. He worked another finger in and she breathed out through her teeth against the intrusion, all those nerve endings jangling and protesting. Her flesh grew hot and she worked hard to remain still as he fingered her ass.

Pressure expanded from within as his fingers opened and closed, and she realized he was stretching her. As he continued she crept very close to coming, but was missing that one tiny shove that would send her over the edge.

His fingers withdrew and with the sensation of new hollowness came a sense of dark anticipation. Heat from the head of his broad cock pressed on her hole. He was too big, several times larger than his fingers. He slicked his flesh and hers with more oil and her outer skin burned as he pressed in.

She couldn't help it, her spine stiffened and she tensed. His thumb replaced his cock and he easily slid it in and out of her back entrance. "Relax, baby. You're doing great. Once I'm in you'll love it. Relax so I can get there."

Evelyn breathed out and forced her shoulders to lower. Her hot cheek burned her arm and the scalding pressure at her ass returned. He leaned over her, blanketing her with his weight. She couldn't escape. He pressed into her and she shrieked at the pressure. Then he was in. She panted, feeling incredibly full and hot.

She was sweating, perspiring in places that were normally dry. His mere presence in her exerted her in ways she had never felt. He didn't move. He remained buried deep inside of her and her inner muscles fluttered. There was no relief, only Lucian, so deep inside of her she feared she would never get him out.

His breath beat over her back. She tasted the salt of her own lips as his pressed into her shoulder. "Beautiful, Evelyn. Absolutely beautiful."

He slowly drew his weight off of her and pulled. *Pulled* was the only word to describe it. It wasn't the same as vaginal sex. He didn't withdraw. Her body clung to him and he pulled her with him as he retracted his cock from her ass. It felt tight and fulfilling. When he slammed back in, she gasped.

Yes! So forceful, the cushion of her behind and her legs, fitted more together than when he usually fucked her, allowed him to take her hard. Possession.

He pulled out and drilled into her again. Her fists twisted in the bedding. Each time he pulled, she wanted him back harder and deeper. As his pace increased so did her breathing. There was an ever-present emotional intensity when they made love. That was still there, but being taken like this brought about a physical intensity she hadn't known she was craving.

Evelyn wanted him to take her as hard as he could. When he gripped the back of her shoulder, pinning his thumb at her nape, her sex fluttered and throbbed, building into an intense wave that would soon crash over her, cooling her scorching hot skin. Lucian grunted, as did she.

She called out a myriad of filthy words, begging him to relentlessly fuck her. Encouraged, he rode her harder. She needed to come. Oh, God, did she need to come.

Fire blistered over her ass as Lucian's hand came down hard on her hind flesh. "Come!"

Her soul soared out of the cage of her bones, and white noise washed out all sound as a tsunami of an orgasm broke from within. She shouted through the quivering and Lucian fucked her so fast, both of them were practically flat on their bellies. His shouts echoed hers, and then hot come was drenching her ass. Holy shit, there was nothing that compared to anal sex. It didn't outdo regular sex, but it was an entirely different sort of animal. All she knew was that she wanted to do it again.

They fell to their sides and panted. She tipped her head back and stared into Lucian's dark eyes and they watched each other for several moments, too exhausted to do anything more than breathe. They slept for a while. When Evelyn awoke, it was to Lucian pressing a warm cloth between her legs and cleaning her. Knowing this was something he needed to do more for himself than for her, she shut her eyes and went back to sleep.

forty-two

THE MENU

LUCIAN had shown Evelyn how to use the iPad he bought her and set it up with several reading games. She felt ridiculous, being in her twenties and playing such juvenile games, but she was actually learning quite a bit. He also left notes around for her to discover throughout the day. They were never written in cursive anymore and were only ever made up of small words.

She now knew that *L-O-V-E* spelled love. She was getting pretty good at sight words too. It helped that Lucian usually had meetings during the day, because that gave her time to practice without someone listening.

On New Year's Eve she visited Pearl. Lucian drove her, but waited in the lobby of the clinic, understanding that Pearl wanted to see Evelyn without him there.

Separating from Lucian, even for only a brief time, told her a lot about herself. She felt his absence and didn't care for the empty feeling. She'd not only come to depend on his being with her, she had come to depend on the shelter he provided. He blurred the lines of reality and took her away to a safe place where nothing bad could touch her.

Pearl was happy to see her the second time she visited, which meant more to Evelyn than any words could describe. She looked healthier than she had in years. She said the doctors had put her on steroids and an antibiotic and she'd gained a few pounds. Evelyn was both shocked and thrilled at her progress. Her mind seemed markedly sharper, but all of her optimism faded when the old Pearl showed up.

Her eyes had skittered to the door and then back at her. She gripped her hand and whispered, "Scout, baby, you gotta get me somethin'. I can't take it anymore. I can't sleep. I can barely eat. My muscles shake like my bones're gonna rattle right out of my skin. I got such pain in my belly, you'd scream if you felt it." Pearl looked around nervously and tapped her emaciated arm. "I just need one hit and then I'll be all right. Just one, baby."

Anger and disappointment welled up inside of Evelyn like a storm. Her eyes prickled with tears and she instinctively searched for Lucian, but he wasn't there. Her breath beat from her lungs fast and she couldn't seem to pull any back in. She felt sick. "No, Momma."

"What'ch you mean no? I don't wanna be here, Scout! I hate it! It's like a prison and where're my things?"

Pearl rubbed her lips hard over her teeth and gums and quickly reached into her drawer for a piece of hard candy. You would've thought it was heroin itself the way she moaned over the sugar rush. She'd told Evelyn before that sugar somehow soothed the toothaches.

Evelyn took her hand and tried to soothe her panicky motions. "Listen to me, Momma. It's just temporary. Just a little while longer. You're getting better and soon—"

"Aren't you listening to me, Scout? I don't want to be here a while longer. I wanna go home! This place's killing me slowly. I don't fucking care anymore! *Do you hear me? I don't care!* I'd rather die than feel the way I do, but I'm too fucking weak to kill myself."

Evelyn's tears spilled past her lashes. "Momma, it'll get better. I promise—"

Pearl flicked Evelyn's hand off hers with surprising force. "What do you know?" Her mother sneered, her face distorting with hate. "I don't wanna get better. I want to go home! You don't know nothin' and it's you who's keepin' me here. *Get out!* Get out and don't come back. I ain't got no daughter no more! You hear me?"

Evelyn ran out of there like the hounds of hell were chasing her. Lucian comforted her the best he could, but his protective instincts rode him hard to do something in retaliation. She could feel it thrumming in him. There was nothing he could do. Pearl was her mother and she had the power to hurt her more than anyone else ever could.

They returned to the penthouse on the first, and as soon as they did, that sense of homesickness she'd been suffering disappeared. She tried to put distance between Lucian and herself, but he wouldn't tolerate it.

That night he had taken Evelyn's chin firmly in his hand while he was inside of her and fiercely said, "Look at me, Evelyn. I love you and you can't put up walls between us because love scares you. Keep all your words locked in, but silence does not make your feelings any less real. I will not let you put distance between us, so stop. Enough. I'm not Pearl and I will never abuse your love the way she has."

He was right. She couldn't run from what Lucian and she shared, because her love for him would reach across any distance. Silencing her emotions did nothing to weaken what she felt for him. He ran through her blood. He was her drug of choice, and she'd likely rip off her flesh before she'd be able to give him up willingly.

She nodded and cried as they made love slowly. Although they had started out anything but gentle, they each needed the tenderness after his emotional allocution. As she had fallen asleep, she vowed to do her best and no longer categorize Lucian's love with the kind of self-serving love Pearl treated her to.

As Evelyn plugged along at her game, waiting for Lucian to return from his meeting, she thought about how much had happened in the past two months. Sometimes she missed Parker, but she tried not to think about him. She cared deeply for Parker, but he'd always laughed at her dreams of making it off of the streets and never showed much ambition to save himself. He was a dangerous person for her to care for, because he could so easily pull her back to the world she never wanted to visit again.

With all the improvements Lucian had made to St. Christopher's, things were better for her old friends than they had ever been. Lucian informed her every time he made some sort of shipment to the shelter, like on Christmas Eve when he had a truckload of toys delivered for all the children and forced Dugan to dress as Santa and hand them out. *Poor Dugan.*

There was a knock at the door and she stood, shutting off her iPad. Still thinking of Dugan Claus as she opened the door, she grinned, but her smile was quickly replaced with surprise.

"Patrice, what are you doing here?"

"Hi. Mr. Patras told me to drop off the salon ledger. Every once in a while he does an audit of our books. He's known to be quite thorough. How's everything going with you?"

"Uh . . ." Evelyn stepped back and she entered the suite. Her soft floral scent was pleasant and familiar. "I'm doing okay."

She hadn't seen Patrice since her last visit to the salon, the same day Lucian teased her about Patrice saying she had a sexy pussy. Her mind went to a place it really shouldn't. Realizing she was just standing in the door, she pasted on a nervous smile and said, "Would you like a glass of wine?"

"Sure."

Was this really about bookkeeping or was Lucian testing her? Memories of their last conversation regarding Patrice resurfaced. Evelyn found it difficult to look the other woman in the eye. If Lucian expected anything more than conversation to happen in her presence, he had another thing coming.

She poured two glasses of red and awkwardly backed out of the space and took a seat in a chair in the common area. Patrice filled the seat closest to the chair. "Cheers," she said, holding out her glass.

Evelyn clanked hers to Patrice's. "Cheers."

"To new experiences in the New Year."

Evelyn emptied her glass in deep gulps. Where was Lucian? As Patrice prattled on about her day and a customer who dicked her on a tip, she refilled her wine and planned Lucian's execution. The more she drank, the more she convinced herself Patrice's presence was intentionally meant to throw her for a loop. She could hide a body. She knew lots of hiding places.

The door opened and she turned. Already feeling the effects of the two glasses of wine she had chugged in about two minutes, she stood.

"Darling!" she purred, narrowing her eyes. "You're back. Good thing. I was worried about you. We have a visitor." Evelyn pressed up on her toes and leaned in for a kiss. When he pressed his lips to hers she bit him.

He pulled back and glared at her. "Behave yourself, Evelyn," he muttered in a warning tone.

She blew out a puff of air and rolled her eyes. "Good luck with that." She turned to flounce away and he grabbed her arm. The smack against her ass stung and her front was again pressed against his chest.

He took her mouth hard. His tongue forced between her lips and she bit at him. His hand squeezed the still-burning cheek of her ass and his fingers reached between her thighs and clenched over her crotch until she settled. He ripped his mouth away and gave her a warning look. He was obviously not impressed with her greeting.

"Don't be a brat." He handed her a boutique bag. "I was going to save this for later, but I think I'd like you to wear it now. Go change. Dinner will be arriving shortly."

Evelyn took the small bag from him and recognized the hotel's logo on it. She peeked in between the layers of black tissue and spotted pale pink lace. Lingerie.

"Lucian—"

"Evelyn," he growled. "I do not like being accosted the moment I arrive home. Nor do I appreciate cattiness. You were disrespectful and you will not disobey me again or I'll toss you over my knee and show you what a real punishment feels like—in front of your friend. I suggest you choose option A."

His threat scared and excited her. The image of Lucian bending her over his knee and spanking her was oddly titillating, but she was also wise enough to see that she'd pissed him off. If he were to spank her in the mood he was in, it might actually hurt. She huffed and turned to go change.

The sight of Patrice sitting on the chair watching them made her stumble. Being that she was upset with him for inviting her, Evelyn had no idea how she forgot Patrice was there. She hoisted her chin in the air, collected her glass, filled it again, and marched into the bedroom.

Taking a great big gulp of wine, she placed the glass on the dresser and eyed the offensive little lingerie bag. She remembered

when she'd first met Lucian he'd told her that clothing was courage. Well, she sure hoped that counted for underwear, because
she needed some. STAT.

Evelyn groaned as she pulled the wisps of lace from the bag.
She turned the bag over and shook it, but nothing else came out
except for tissue. She held up the dental floss doing a weak impression of panties and frowned. There were four loopy openings
instead of three. *What the . . . ?* She turned it and realized they
were crotchless underwear. The demi bra wasn't much better.

She stripped out of her clothes and slid on the lingerie. Looking in the mirror she nibbled her lips and evaluated the outfit, if
one could even call it that. Her breasts were lifted and little half-
moons of brown showed where her nipples peeked past the lace
edging. The panties were delicate, pale pink with black lace scal-
loped edging below her belly. A thin black bow tied over the delta
of her pussy and a white pearl nested in the satin knot. Nothing
covered her sex, only two thin strings holding the garment together that rode along her lips.

She turned. A tiny little swatch of pink lace made a triangle
above the crease of her ass. The rest disappeared between. Fuck.
There was no courage here. There was barely coverage.

Spontaneously, she turned and went to her jewelry box. She
found the string of pearls Lucian had given her for Christmas and
wrapped them twice around her neck. She snapped the matching
bracelet around her wrist and twisted her hair high on her head.
In the closet she found a pair of black satin stilettos. She applied
some gloss to her lips and walked as proudly as one could manage
in such an asinine ensemble into the common area of the suite.
Thinking back to the special she and Lucian had watched on the
Kennedys, she imagined she looked like JFK's greatest fantasy,
somewhere between Jackie and Marilyn.

Gratitude swamped her when she saw dinner had been

delivered. It was bad enough Patrice had to see her like this. Lucian stood and there was a noticeable moment when he stopped breathing.

Huh, maybe there is some courage in lingerie. Magic undies!

He held out her chair and she gracefully sat. She placed her napkin over her lap with all the hauteur she could manage then frowned. "Where's Patrice?"

Lucian's eyes darkened as he sipped from a glass. "I sent her home. You look stunning, Evelyn."

"But . . . I thought . . ."

He shook his head. "I know what you thought. I'm disappointed in the way you welcomed me home. You'll make up for that after dinner. Eat." Her eyes never left him the entire time they ate.

She'd love to say the tilapia was delicious, but for all she knew it might've been pasta. He kept the wine and conversation flowing and eventually she forgot she was in her underwear.

When he wiped his mouth and tossed the linen napkin on the plate, she swallowed. Maybe she'd overreacted. Her breath filled her lungs as she considered what he might have in mind for her penance. Evelyn lowered her gaze as she realized her reaction to Patrice in their home might have been less about being sexually pushed and more about not wanting to share Lucian. Her brow creased as she examined this territorial side she hadn't realized she possessed.

"Can I interest you in dessert?"

She looked up at him, quite concerned about what he'd planned next. "No, thank you."

He smiled under hooded eyes. "Why don't we have a seat on the couch?"

She stood and walked to the settee. The cool air of the condo played over her exposed curves. Lucian sat, pose relaxed as his elbow dangled over the armrest. He patted the space next to his thigh and Evelyn settled beside him. She was excruciatingly aware of her lack of clothing and was sure she wore a deep blush down to her barely there bra.

Evelyn stiffened as Lucian's lips pressed to her shoulder. "Do you remember our discussion when we last left Folsom?" he whispered, breath hot and teasing the escaped wisps of hair along her neck.

She'd thought of little else over the past hour. Her lashes lowered. "Yes."

His long fingers traced over her hip and up her belly. Apprehension, paired with the sensual way he was fondling her, had her trembling. He cupped her breast and pulled away the lace, exposing her even more.

She feared he was still angry with her, but his touch was gentle. He slipped a hand beneath Evelyn's knees and lifted her legs onto the sofa. The pointy toes of her black high heels tilted toward the arm of the settee. He plucked at her nipples, both now exposed. "Part your legs for me, Evelyn."

She hesitated and Lucian whispered, seeming to sense her nervousness. "You have a safe word if you need it. Trust me to know how much is too much."

It was silly to be nervous. They were alone and he wouldn't hurt her. However, she'd obviously upset him, perhaps even embarrassed him earlier, and that scared her. Taking a steadying breath, her knees slowly parted and cool air tickled the bare flesh.

Lucian drew her hands to her side, pressing them into the seat, a quiet command not to move. His fingertips trailed over her stomach and down to her pussy. "Are you wet?"

Evelyn shut her eyes. "Yes, sir."

"Mmm, I like when you call me that." Lucian's fingers traced down her folds and he chuckled, feeling she was indeed wet. "You belong to me, Evelyn. Just because an unexpected guest stops by, does not give you the right to make assumptions about my motives. I know where your mind went tonight and I can't say I'm happy with your behavior. I am quite protective of what I consider mine and I don't take kindly to others trespassing on my property. You should know this by now."

There was so much Evelyn could've taken offense to in that statement, but her relief outweighed her outrage. Her shoulders sagged at his unmistakable proclamation that no one would touch her aside from him.

He must have sensed her relief, because he kissed her temple and whispered, "Trust."

Lucian continued to fondle her folds. He spoke as if this were just another business meeting. "I want to be very clear. You're quite important to me and what might have been okay in the beginning, no longer is. Tell me, Evelyn, whose pussy is this?"

"Yours, Lucian." Her voice was a mere rasp. Her shoulders subtly lifted with each breath.

He rewarded her with a gentle tug on her clit. His hands slid up to her chest. "And whose breasts?"

She sighed as he cupped her in his warm palms. "Yours."

"And who owns that delectable little ass of yours?"

Her body tightened. "You do, Lucian. Only you."

She sensed his satisfaction.

"Did you think I would let her touch you?"

Evelyn slowly glanced over her shoulder at him. "I didn't know."

His lips twisted in a disapproving smile. "I meant what I said, Evelyn. I won't share you. Ever. I believe you've found a place in my heart no woman has ever visited before. I fear for anyone who tries to lay a hand on you."

A bit of her confidence slipped back into place. She turned

onto her hands and knees and pressed a kiss to his soft lips. Smiling, she said, "I should slap you for calling me a possession."

He smiled unapologetically. "Is that so?" She nodded and jumped when his palm slapped down on the exposed cheek of her ass. "Bring it, Ms. Keats. I like it rough."

Before she could answer, she was flipped onto her back and he was on top of her, pinning her arms above her head and ravishing her mouth. He somehow managed to strip his clothes away while never depriving her of his touch.

When he filled her, it was fast and potent. She arched into him as his mouth marked every curve of flesh he could get his lips on. Their lovemaking had never been so furious, so possessive. She clawed at his shoulders, wanting to mark him as well. He bit and nipped at her tender parts, and when they came it was an act of nature, so potent, so all-consuming, the earth could have fallen from its axis and neither of them would've known.

He carried her to their bed some time later, and she sighed as he pulled her close. Her mind was off in some place only Lucian could take her, and she luxuriated in those calm moments, surrendered to them, knowing he'd hold her as long as she needed.

forty-three

WISHES

AFTER her dance lessons, Evelyn was always in a good mood, but today not so much. Lucian had to cancel because something "extremely important" came up. She still enjoyed herself. Their instructor, Ferdinand, was a very sweet man.

Lucian hired him for her lessons because he was the best around and also because he loved men. Evelyn laughed when she remembered him ranting about how he would never tolerate another man's hands on her, yet once Ferdinand admitted he was gay, Lucian reconsidered.

She wasn't sure if it was her instructor's taste for men, or more specifically, Lucian's taste for her, but the dancing today lacked the intensity that usually came when she danced with Lucian.

Evelyn hoped whatever had pulled him away didn't keep him long. She stepped into the elevator, missing him, and slid her key in the slot and pressed for the penthouse. Odd; there was a pink balloon floating by its lonesome at the ceiling, its long pink string curling all the way to the floor.

She shrugged and stepped off the elevator. Walking to the private bank of elevators, she spotted another pink balloon floating in the hall. There must be a party in one of the ballrooms. She took the elevator up.

At the master suite she keyed open the door and glumly walked in, wondering if she should order dinner or wait for Lucian. Her shoes kicked off by the door and she stilled as something caught her eye.

Raising her head slowly, her jaw dropped as she took in the sight. Hundreds, no, thousands of beribboned pink balloons danced along the ceiling. Evelyn turned as a light clicked on to her right.

She frowned. "Hello?"

She saw a note and navigated through the long curling strings to get to it. It was a big word. She took a deep breath and quietly sounded it out. "Ha-p . . . hap-pyah . . . happee-yah . . . hap-pee . . . *happy*!"

Evelyn turned and another light flickered on over at Lucian's desk. She ran over and found another note. "B-ih-r-tuh . . . bihr-tuh . . ." She frowned and took a deep breath. She looked at the word. *Th* said *thhhh* . . . "Bih-rrr-th . . . bihrth . . . birth . . . *Birth*!"

She smiled, expecting another, and turned. A small lamp flicked on in the hall. She ran over. She picked up the small paper and recognized the word. "Day!" she shouted and jumped. "Happy birthday!" The bedroom light flipped on, and Evelyn ran in and slid to a stop.

Lucian stood in his tuxedo, holding a cupcake with a candle. He was surrounded by at least twenty-two other cakes. Big cakes, wedding-style cakes, chocolate cakes, ice cream cakes, each one with a tall candle burning on the top. One for every birthday she never had.

She shook her head, speechless.

"Happy birthday, Evelyn. Make a wish."

Three staggered steps and she was in front of him. She looked in his beautiful dark eyes, candlelight shining back from their soft depths. How had she ever mistaken his eyes as being hard? Gazing down at the candle burning between them, she thought of the one thing she wanted most. She had twenty-two other candles to get to and plenty of wishes to fill each extinguishing breath, but this one was the important one. This one would count.

She took a deep breath and blew.

Don't let anything take him away from me.

parker

forty-four
·····

FAST

FUCK.

Parker picked up the wallet and fought back the temptation of pocketing it. If someone saw him, he'd lose his job. With a sigh he looked for the three-piece suit who had dropped it and saw him climbing into the back of a sleek black limo.

The limo pulled into traffic and started stealthily down the busy street.

"Son of a bitch," he muttered and began chasing after the car.

"Parker? Your shift's not over," Philippe shouted. No time to stop. He lost sight of the limo as it turned off of Gerard and onto Washington.

The sidewalks were clogged with pain-in-the-ass, pokey pedestrians. His Patras hat flew off his head, but Parker didn't slow down to retrieve it. He bumped a woman in the shoulder, and taking a second he couldn't really spare, he stopped to steady her and offer a quick apology. When he looked up, the limo was blocks ahead and moving in the turning lane, heading down the main line.

His soft-soled dress shoes skidded over the pavement as he took off again. Once Parker caught up to where the limo turned, he stopped. In a sea of yellow cabs there were three limos. He did a quick assessment of each black car and decided the one two blocks up on the left looked to be his guy.

Parker's knees pumped hard as he sprinted after the car, hurdling small obstacles along the way. He almost lost it again, but some traffic snagged the limo's progress. His breath sawed in and out of his lungs. He practically collapsed on the back window as he banged his palm on the glass.

The chauffer poked his head out the window and frowned. "Hey! Get out of here!"

Too out of breath to offer an explanation, Parker banged on the window again. The black glass slowly lowered. He sighed when he recognized the man with bright blue eyes and caramel-colored skin.

"Can I help you?" the man asked.

He panted and held up the billfold. "You dropped—" Parker breathed. "Your wallet."

The man's expression relaxed. He looked out the back window as if checking where they were at the moment. He then read the Patras emblem on his blazer. "You ran all the way here from Patras?"

"I didn't . . . want you . . . to lose your stuff."

The man popped the door open and scooted back. "Get in."

Parker hesitated a moment and then nodded, sliding onto the soft leather seat. It had been a while since he had been on the inside of a limo but the memory suffused him before he shook it off. "Thank you." He was finally catching his breath.

The man eyed him as he flipped through his wallet once Parker handed it to him. His brow rose. "Everything's here. Thank you. I'll give you a ride back if you don't mind a little detour."

"I appreciate it, but I can't." Parker pointed to his blazer. "I'm on the clock."

"Does it really matter?" the man asked, and Parker frowned.

What kind of question was that? "Uh, yeah, to me it does. And I'm sure to my boss. I can't accept my paycheck if I didn't earn it honestly, and I need the money."

It was tempting to bail on the day, but he pushed his ethics forward. *Don't be a cheat like your father.*

The man grinned as if his answer impressed him. Parker wondered if his comment had been some sort of a test. "Slade Bishop." He held out his hand.

He shook the proffered hand and introduced himself. "Parker Hughes."

"Hughes, that's a big name around these parts."

"Used to be," he remarked dryly. He hated his name. It was the last link he had to his father.

"Any relation to Crispin Hughes?"

Parker grimaced. He could lie, but the man's vibrant blue eyes seemed to be reading him keenly for any falsehoods. "He was my father."

"No kidding," the man said, leaning back in his seat and crossing his arms over his chest. "Quite an impressive man your father was. I'm sorry about what happened. He led a decent life up until the end."

Until he shot himself and left his family bankrupt, Parker silently finished. "My father was a crook."

"He wasn't the first to dabble in insider trading and he won't be the last."

This was not a conversation Parker expected to be having. The car moved. "Uh, look, I just wanted to make sure you got your wallet, but I really gotta go." He sat up and the man gestured for him to stay put.

"Stay. I'm sure your boss will understand."

He snorted. "Doubtful. It was Lucian Patras who gave me the job, and he and I aren't on the best of terms."

The other man cocked his head curiously. "Why offer a job to someone you aren't on good terms with? Well, regardless, I'm just as much your boss as he is. I'm his silent partner."

Parker hadn't realized Patras was owned by partners. Before he could remark on his statement, Mr. Bishop asked, "What did you do to piss Lucian off? Usually he doesn't keep employees he doesn't like."

"He didn't have a choice." His answer came out a little too arrogant and he regretted the show of emotion.

Mr. Bishop laughed. "Really? I'd be very interested to hear how a doorman maneuvered Lucian Patras into an uncomfortable predicament. Lucian has a reputation of always coming out on top."

"I made him a deal. He owes me. Half of our bargain was for a job. The other half's a little more valuable, but I'm not ready to collect on it."

"And you trust Lucian to keep his word with this other valuable half of your deal?"

Parker nodded. "I do. A man like Lucian Patras doesn't get as far as he has unless his word's worth something."

Mr. Bishop tapped his chin and eyed him peculiarly. "You seem rather sharp for a doorman."

"Probably because I never intended to be one. I was already taking college-level courses when my father killed himself and we discovered the courts and banks owned everything we had and then some."

"Impressive. That would've made you what? Seventeen at that time?"

"Fourteen."

His brow shot to his hairline. "Fourteen and college-level courses? What the hell are you doing holding doors?"

"I wasn't in a position that made people eager to hire me." He'd also been content until Patras had stolen Scout away. After that, the asshole owed him. "Mr. Patras did me a favor by giving me a job."

"Some favor." Mr. Bishop laughed. "The way you tell it, he didn't have a choice."

The car continued to move, now out of traffic. Parker figured he was safe since this guy was also his boss. He relaxed a little. "He had a choice. He chose what was in his power to give me." The man smirked and Parker continued, "And now he owes me." He shrugged.

"And what does Lucian owe you?"

He pressed his lips tight.

Realizing Parker wasn't going to answer, he then asked, "Okay, how about what did you have that he wanted?"

He shrugged again. "It wasn't so much what I had as much as it was my knowledge of where something Mr. Patras wanted was hiding."

"Scout," the other man whispered and Parker stilled.

How the fuck did he know about Scout?

"Holy shit, that's it isn't it?" Mr. Bishop's eyes narrowed. "That's why you look familiar. You're from St. Christopher's."

Knowing he'd blown his hand, Parker asked, "How do you know Scout?"

"Anyone associated with Lucian knows the woman who managed to wedge his head up his ass."

"Excuse me?" He wasn't following.

"He thinks he's in love with her and hasn't been himself since she showed up."

Parker's jaw popped. He hated thinking of Lucian Patras

loving Scout. Nothing about Patras was right for her. Scout had an unhealthy obsession with money. She thought of it as security. Little did she know that the kind of money a man like Patras had wasn't the kind of security she was after. Money at that level was power, entitlement, ownership, and it always led to corruption.

Parker needed a little more time, and he'd secure a place to live and be able to provide food on the table and other necessities, and she'd see that kind of life was better than one of such extravagance, simpler. There was too much expectation when one dealt with real wealth, too much society and judgment. The public eye, once you were in it, never blinked.

He must have a terrible poker face, because the other man then said, "Ah, I'm beginning to understand why Lucian doesn't like you. You're a threat."

Parker scoffed. "I'm hardly a threat to a man like Lucian Patras."

"Don't underestimate yourself, Parker. You're someone from her past, a past a man like Lucian will never be able to relate to or wrap his brain around. You also happen to be a decent-looking man and I assume Scout's friend. You've been in my car now for what? Five? Ten minutes? Like me, Lucian's good at picking up on talent. I recognized you were more than a doorman two minutes after we met. Don't be naïve. Lucian knows exactly who your father was. Before Lucian Patras, there were two men who held equal or more power than him in Folsom. His father was one of them. The other one was yours."

Parker scowled inwardly, hating any comparisons between himself and his father.

Mr. Bishop laughed and said almost to himself, "It was probably a relief to give you a job. It allows him to keep an eye on you." He looked Parker in the face. "You say he owes you something else. What is it?"

Parker looked away, knowing this man could read him like a book.

"How about this," Mr. Bishop offered. "Tell me what it is and if it's what I think it is, I'll give you a job that will get you to the top a lot faster than doorman or bellhop. I have a business that Lucian has no share in. I could offer you a position where you wear something a little more dignified than a blazer with your enemy's name on it. If you're as smart as you say, and have half of your father's aptitude for business, you could find yourself in a corner office before you know it. You said you need money. I'll start you out at triple what you're making at Patras, *if* your answer is what I think. What do you say? Sounds like a good deal to me. If it's not, I'll keep your secret quiet and you go on holding doors for us. What do you say, Mr. Hughes?"

"Why would you do that if Patras is your partner?"

Mr. Bishop hesitated, clearly debating what he should share. "There's been a falling out. We're approaching my next stop and I'm afraid my offer leaves with me. Better decide fast."

Shit. He'd be crazy to turn down an offer like that, but there had to be a catch. The limo pulled over and Mr. Bishop stared at him impatiently.

"Fine," Parker snapped. "It's Scout. He had to promise me a job and then, when I decide I'm ready, I call in his other IOU, a month with Scout in which the rich prick cannot interfere."

The man's smile was almost reptilian, and Parker worried that he'd made a grave mistake in confiding in him. "Excellent," he purred. "Meet me here, tomorrow morning at seven." Mr. Bishop eyed him from head to toe. "I believe I have some older suits to start you off. I'll bring them with me in the morning and you can change then. My driver's yours for the next twenty minutes. He can take you back to Patras, or now that you have a better job, wherever you want."

He opened the door and Parker gripped his arm. "Wait."

Bishop narrowed his eyes at his hold on him, but Parker didn't let go.

"You seemed pleased when you found out Scout was the bargain. Why?"

"I have my reasons," the man said.

He quickly considered the offer. Lucian had promised him a job, but specified that keeping it would be up to Parker. The other part of the deal, the part involving Scout, was contingent on two things: Parker being ready to call in his debt and doing so before Patras got a ring on her finger. He could take Bishop's offer and Patras would still owe him. There was only one concern. "I won't work for someone who wishes her harm," Parker said, meaning every word.

"I wish the lovely Evelyn no harm. I only wish her out of my partner's life."

acknowledgements
.....

There are so many wonderful people who helped The Surrender Trilogy come to be. I must first thank my husband, Mike, who made my dreams a possibility and gave me the wings to fly. You are my rock. My parents, who raised me to believe I could be and accomplish anything I put my mind to. Trudy Kozak, you have been my courage and advisor throughout this journey. You are truly a great friend. My book club girls, you are the foundation on which my hopes stand and the catapult that propels me into action. And my daughter, who has the patience of an angel and the sweetest soul I've ever known. These are the people behind the scenes who have made my life extraordinary, but there are those I've met along the journey that kept me moving and inspired me to never stop.

To the students and teachers of Pennwood Middle School, you listen to my stories of yesterday and inspire so many tomorrows—hold your dreams tight and never let go, no matter how high they take you!

And then there are those who played a special part in this magical moment. Lori Foster, you are an opportunity giver, a dream maker, and proof of everything any writer hopes to be. Duffy Brown, you saw something in me and told me the best way to go. Leis Pederson, there are no better words than thank you. Roberta Brown, thank you for believing in me. Gayle Donnelly and Robyn Mackenzie, you rock—enough said. And to all the wonderful people at Penguin, my gratitude is immeasurable.

Finally, my greatest acknowledgement of all goes to you, my readers. I love you. Without all of you, the days would be dull and the journey would only be half as sweet. I am humbled by your love and support. Thank you for everything.

Keep reading for an excerpt from the next book in
The Surrender Trilogy

BREAKING OUT

*Available now from InterMix and in print from Berkley
November 2014*

·····

THE JOB

EVELYN smoothed her clammy palms down the front of her pencil skirt. The narrow belt at her waist winked under the artificial, amber lighting of Patras's lobby. Reflections danced across the toes of her patent leather Mary Janes as her feet clicked over the polished marble floor, suddenly muffled when she crossed the threshold and the four-inch heels landed silently on the red runner. Dugan waited just past the gold tassels.

Her hands tightened the lapels of the nipped jacket she wore over her pearl-button blouse as the brisk March air cut through her clothing. Dugan nodded at her and opened the door to the limo.

Silk slid over leather as she slipped inside the warmth of the car. The door shut with a gentle snick and she adjusted the nude lace at the top of her stockings. Nerves twisted her stomach into a spring that coiled and released adrenaline, heating her blood.

Dugan glided into the driver's seat. "Where to, Ms. Keats?"

Pulling in a slow breath, she carefully exhaled, forcing away any trepidation. Her lips were done in a deep crimson shade one of the girls at the salon had suggested after she had them style her hair in a sophisticated French twist that morning. She was very aware that she looked nothing like her normal self.

"Patras Industries," she said with as much confidence as she could muster.

Dugan's untamed brows lifted to the brim of his hat. She had never been inside Lucian's office. It was a part of his world she didn't like to trespass on, but after their conversation this week, she knew it was time to cross into that part of his domain. After all, he had brought so many of her fantasies to life it was time she returned the favor.

Dugan maneuvered the limo carefully away from the curb and eased into traffic with practiced skill. The pearls at her neck hung low in her cleavage. Her fingers twirled over the opalescent, heavy beads. Her mind toyed with images, predictions of Lucian's expression as she unveiled her surprise.

Her legs crossed and uncrossed as the limo navigated through the busy streets of Folsom. A jolt of nerves had her questioning her motives. What if Lucian was busy and became upset when she interrupted his day?

She pushed the thought away. This was one of *his* fantasies. He'd taught her to be adventurous. As much as she worried he would be upset with her brazenness, she couldn't truly imagine her handsome exhibitionist being too put out.

The corner of her mouth pulled into a secret smile. Breath filled her lungs as excitement spun wildly in her belly.

The limo pulled up in front of Patras Industries. The glass façade reflected a distorted version of the car back at her. "Would you like me to phone Mr. Patras and inform him you're here?"

She tensed. "No. No, thank you, Dugan. I'd like to surprise him."

"Would you like me to wait?"

Her palms again smoothed her skirt. "That won't be necessary. Lucian will see that I get home safely."

"Very good, Ms. Keats."

Dugan exited the car and came to her door. Sweet anticipation had her knees softening. Sliding out of the car, she stood and found her footing in her high heels. She was doing better with the walking in heels thing. Her clothing adjusted with gravity and her eyes momentarily widened as she became suddenly aware of a minor wardrobe shift down below. Heat rushed to her cheeks as the gusset of her panties sagged under the weight of her arousal. She was already starving for him. Luckily, no one could see her panties. Yet. Lucian would know soon enough how excited she was.

She cleared her throat. "Thank you, Dugan."

He nodded. "Do you know where you're heading?"

"Fifteenth floor, right?"

"Yes."

Taking a deep breath, she pivoted and stepped through the revolving door. The lobby was quiet. A man sat on a chair beside the elevator, typing something into a Blackberry. Evelyn's manicured finger pressed the elevator button and it instantly took on a golden glow.

The man looked up from his phone, his gaze traveling from her heels, up her stocking-clad legs, around her curves barely concealed by the tight skirt, and settled at her breasts. Her lips tightened as she watched the antique metal arrow clock the floors. When the cart arrived, she breathed a sigh of relief and stepped inside the elevator, away from Sir Staresalot.

Knuckling the button for the fifteenth floor, she stepped back and ran a quick hand over her clothing and hair, making sure everything was in place. The car alighted with a luxurious purr and slowed just as the arrow reached fifteen. Shutting her eyes, she took a calming breath.

Showtime.

The metal doors parted and Evelyn carefully stepped out onto burgundy carpet. Phones rang and quiet voices carried. A woman in a brown skirt and ivory blouse leaned flirtatiously over the reception desk, a ballpoint pen twirling in her dainty fingers as she whispered to the young man who manned the area.

He cleared his throat and his visitor straightened. She stood straight, stepping aside so that Evelyn could be seen. "May I help you?"

Evelyn smiled. "Yes, I'm here to see Mr. Patras."

The man stilled, glanced at his computer, and frowned. "Did you have an appointment?"

"No."

His mouth opened and snapped shut. "Mr. Patras only sees people with appointments. If you'd like to leave a name—"

"Could you please just let him know Ms. Evelyn Keats is here?"

The man's eyes bulged. "Ms. Keats?"

She smiled, seeing recognition in his eyes. "You must be Seth. It's a pleasure to put a face to the name."

He seemed suddenly self-conscious. "The pleasure's mine. Let me inform Mr. Patras you're here." He pressed a button on the receiver at his desk. "Mr. Patras?"

"Yes, Seth?" Lucian sounded harried.

No backing out now.

"There is a lovely Ms. Evelyn Keats here to see you."

There was a momentary pause and then his voice sounded, tinged with curiosity. "Is there? Please, send her in."

Seth smiled and pressed a button. "You may go in."

"Thank you."

She carefully stepped to the door labeled *President* and turned the brushed nickel knob. Lucian was coming around his desk to greet her. "Evelyn, is everything all right?"

She smiled and quietly shut the door. "Everything's fine, Mr. Patras." He raised a brow at the use of his formal title. "I came for my interview."

Pausing, then extending his arm, he gracefully invited her into the lion's den. His face split with a slow grin and he nodded. "Ah, the interview. I'd forgotten. Please, have a seat."

He returned to the executive chair behind his desk, this one just as messy as his desk at the condo. The lavishness of the office compensated for its sloppy surface. She slid into the butter soft leather chair facing him and crossed her legs. His gaze followed the action and she hid a smirk.

Folding her hands over her lap, she waited for direction. He waited as well, the pregnant silence tightening her muscles as each second ticked by.

He cleared his throat. "Why don't you tell me a bit about yourself," he suggested. Easing back into his chair, his steepled fingers seemed to hide his mouth. Her own lips twitched with a sense of playfulness, but she shut her eyes and drew in a slow breath. Fantasy was about fulfilling a psychological need with physical illusions. In other words, she needed to be convincing in order to do this right.

She licked her lips, again drawing his attention to the subtle movement. "Well, I'm told that I have an aptitude for taking direction. I'm a fast learner, I like to please, and I do well with praise."

"And if there is need for correction?"

His eyes darkened and she drew in a slow, heated breath. "I do well with that as well."

It was nearing four o'clock and his throat showed shadows of a day's growth as his Adam's apple bobbed slowly. "I'm quite particular with my expectations, Ms. Keats. I do not tolerate anything less than perfect."

Her mouth went dry. "I understand."

He leaned forward and gathered some papers on his desk, stacking them haphazardly and tossing them into a tray to the right. "Let's take a look at your briefs."

"Pardon?"

"Come here, please."

Her lips parted as she rose to her feet. Slowly, she stepped around the edge of his desk. Heavy brass wheels rolled slowly as his gaze traveled over her outfit. "You are looking very professional today, Ms. Keats. I like it."

"Thank you, sir."

"Show me your briefs."

Her fingers glided to the hem of her skirt. She slowly lifted the fabric, exposing the lace of her stockings, the snaps of her garters, and the pale pink lace triangle of her panties. Lucian's eyes darkened and his nostrils flared. Her gaze slipped to the bulge beneath his Armani belt buckle.

"Very nice." He made no move to touch her. "Remove the garters."

Carefully, she bent and undid the beribboned snaps holding her stockings in place. They hung like the seductive branches of a weeping willow. Once the last was undone, she stood.

"Did you bring duplicates?"

Her brow pinched and he nodded toward the apex of her thighs. He was referring to her panties. "No, sir."

He tsked. "I'm afraid you will have to leave the originals then, Ms. Keats."

Her chest rose and fell with shallow breaths. "Yes, sir. I apologize for being unprepared."

"I believe in correcting employees immediately after an infraction. Please hand me your briefs."

Her fingers fit under the string of her damp panties and slowly lowered them. Rising once again, she held the garment from her pinky and offered them to him. He caught the shred of silk and brought it to his nose, inhaling deeply.

"These are wet." He crumpled the fabric and slowly stuffed it in his pocket.

"I'm sorry, sir. I was excited for the interview."

"Come here, please."

There wasn't much room between him and his desk. She took a small step forward. The weight of his palms circling her hips caused her to sigh with pent-up relief. Since morning, she'd been starved for his touch. He turned her. "Palms on the edge of the desk, Ms. Keats. I'm going to look over your proposal."

Her hands pressed into the fine wood of his desk as his palm caressed the rounded cheek of her ass. Chills raced up her spine, curling her toes in her Mary Janes, and causing her heart to gallop in her chest. She arched and his palm lifted, coming down quick and sharp on her rear. A delicious heat bloomed at the surface and seeped deep beneath her skin.

A sharp gasp of excitement slipped past her lips as she jumped and his fingers gently scraped over the sensitized skin. "This is an office, Ms. Keats. Discretion is important. I'm going to have to ask that you keep your voice down."

Sucking her lips between her teeth, she bit down. His palm slapped upon her flesh again. She hummed quietly, drawing her shoulders back. Her neck rolled, her head tipping back.

"You take direction very well, Ms. Keats."

"I aim to please, sir."

His palm came down a third time. Her flesh was alive and needy. The blunt tip of his finger followed the line of lace around her thigh and traced the seam down the back of her leg to the heel of her shoe. He wrapped his fingers around the heel and lifted her foot off the ground.

Her weight shifted as he bent her leg back. "These are new. I like them."

"Thank you, sir."

"Spread your legs." He released her and she widened her stance. His palm pressed like a brand into her lower back, easing her slightly forward. Her spine stiffened as his fingers bit into the rosy cheeks of her ass, spreading her wide. His tongue licked up her crease, over her waxed folds. "Fuck, you're sexy."

She moaned. He released his hold on her ass and bit her sensitized flesh. Her heart raced and arousal flooded her sex. Her lungs sucked in a breath as his finger breached her folds and entered her. He quickly withdrew the digit and replaced it with two.

She was embarrassingly wet. The sound of his fingers fucking her could be heard all around the room. His other hand reached around her hip, bunching up the front of her skirt gathered there. The first touch of his fingers to her clit had her jerking her body forward.

He was suddenly on his feet, his mouth biting through her blouse, into her shoulder. "Don't move, Ms. Keats."

She loved the way his body managed to hold her in place as he tortured her so sweetly. The press of his arousal against her could be felt through his suit pants and the sensation of heat added to the thrill of his thrusting fingers.

"You see," he said in a gravelly voice as he blanketed her from behind. "I seem to have made a mistake with my schedule. I have a meeting in about two minutes with a man from accounting. I'd hate to cut your interview short. I've yet to test your oral skills."

She was breathless as he plucked at her clit. Her knees trembled. "I'm told my oral skills are quite notable, sir."

"I'll be the judge of that." His hands suddenly disappeared. The echo of his zipper was followed by the clank of his silver belt buckle coming undone. She was pressed forward until her breasts grazed the surface of his desk through her silk top. "But first I'm going to fuck you. Don't make a sound."

His cock nudged her opening and then he filled her in one swift movement. She bit down on her lip, stifling a moan as she went up on her toes. Spine arching, her upper body lifted from the desk.

He grunted and grabbed her breast roughly over the silk of her shirt. His mouth sucked at the tender flesh of her neck. His tongue slid over the pearls as he pulled them between his teeth.

He thrust hard and she couldn't help the moan that escaped. The weight of his palm settled over her lips, fingers curling gently into her cheek. His breath beat at her ear. "Shhh, Seth will hear you."

His other hand slid down her front and found her clit. He pinched the sensitized bud and she squeaked, eyes going wide. He thrust faster and tightened his hand over her mouth.

His warm breath tickled the shell of her ear. "Is it good, Evelyn? You want to scream, don't you? But you can't. If you make a noise I'll spank you again, this time until you come."

Her body tightened. Breath rushed out of her nose, over his fingers.

"You want to come, don't you, baby?"

She quietly moaned her agreement. "All right. Because you performed so beautifully during the first part of your interview, I'll let you come. I need to come too. Then you're going to suck me hard again while I meet with my accounting rep. When I come the second time you're going to swallow every drop, never letting anyone know you're here."

Her body gushed around him, pulsing and tightening. He

rubbed her clit rapidly and her muscles locked. As she came in a rush, he moved his grip to her hips and fucked her relentlessly, groaning softly as he filled her with his release.

When he withdrew from her sex, she was trembling. He cradled her on his lap and kissed her temple. The intercom buzzed.

"Mr. Patras?"

"Yes, Seth."

"Mr. McElroy is here from accounting."

He glanced at her, tipping her chin back so he could see her face. "How are you, love?"

She smiled dazedly. She was wonderful. "Mm, I'm good, Mr. Patras."

"Would you like to proceed with your interview?"

"Oh, I don't plan on leaving until the job is done."

He grinned. "You know what I expect."

She gently kissed his lips then slithered off his lap, lowering her body to the floor. He stood and zipped his pants and fastened his belt as she fit herself beneath his desk.

Lucian leaned forward and pressed a button on the phone. "Send him in, Seth."

The door clicked open and Lucian greeted the man from accounting. Evelyn quietly backed farther into the niche beneath Lucian's desk. The other man said a quick hello and settled into the seat she had originally occupied at the start of her "interview". The fine leather on the chair squeaked beneath his weight. She wanted to peek under the small space to see the other man's shoes, but was too afraid of inadvertently bumping her elbow or accidentally making a noise that would give her away.

"Let's see what you have," Lucian said, his tapered legs coming back into view as he lowered himself into his chair. His shiny shoes eased forward, his chair gliding him closer.

Evelyn fit herself between his knees and was comforted when

his hand lovingly petted over her hair and down her cheek. Like a cat, she pressed into the caress affectionately.

His hand disappeared as the sound of papers shuffled above her. Their voices were muffled. Her cheek grazed the tailored thigh of his pants. She'd never done anything like this before. Swirls of delicious, erotic tension knotted in her belly. Perhaps she was turning into an exhibitionist too.

Lucian had taught her early on just how much he enjoyed an audience. When he'd explained his fantasy of having her in his office for the day, servicing him like this, she knew it was the idea of being watched that made the fantasy so erotic for him. It didn't matter that the other person had no idea what they were witnessing—at least she hoped they didn't.

Shaky fingers steadied as they coasted up the inside of his thighs. Her body still bore the results of their last coupling, making her thighs sticky. She rubbed them together with pleasure, reveling in the sensation, Lucian's mark of possession. She found his belt and bit down on her lip as she quietly fed the leather through the small metal buckle. His torso elongated purposefully, giving her easier access.

The space under the desk grew warm and her range of movement became limited as he hardened. Once the buckle was undone she pushed it to the side, wincing as the clip accidently clanked against the metal catch on the other end. Lucian cleared his throat and continued talking. She had no idea what he was saying.

Her fingers found the tab of his zipper and slowly lowered it. The sophisticated snap of his pants was inside his waistband. She frowned as she worked to unlatch it. Once she had his pants undone, she spread the material into a wide V.

With nimble fingers, she unbuttoned the lowest three buttons of his shirt and spread the material wide. Lucian's muscled abdomen twitched beneath her gentle touch. Her lips pursed play-fully as she teased him by blowing softly over his tight stomach.

Knowing she wouldn't be able to get him out of his briefs—she smothered a laugh. He had *her* briefs—she ran her fingertip along the front seam of his underwear until she found the opening.

His knee jerked as she fed her fingers inside and withdrew him. It was no easy task. He was already fully aroused. Once she had his length in her hand, she gripped him, marveling at the softness of his skin over steel, the firm weight filling her palm.

Easing up on her knees, she took him in her mouth and had the satisfaction of hearing his voice shift in timbre. Her lips stretched over him as she pressed forward, taking him to the back of her throat. His knees clamped into the sides of her body, squeezing her tight, restricting her breathing.

The other man's muffled voice filled the office as she wrapped her fingers at the base of Lucian's cock and quietly pumped him in and out of her mouth. He eased back in his chair and there was suddenly a tapping sound rattling over her.

Her brow knit with confusion. Releasing him, she turned her face and looked up. He was rapidly twiddling a pen between his fingers, tapping the edge of his desk. She smirked. It must be kill-ing him, having to keep his hands to himself. Lucian was very hands-on when it came to oral sex, or any sex for that matter.

Knowing she was making him insane only made her go at her task with more zest.

Ms. Keats shows great enthusiasm for tackling objectives on the job. She giggled.

"Did you hear something?" the muffled accountant's voice asked.

There was a sudden pinch at her scalp as Lucian's hand tight-ened over her snugly wrapped hair. "My apologies, McElroy. I skipped lunch," Lucian quickly explained. His warning touch was gone before the other man could notice his hand disappearing beneath the desk.

She returned to her task a bit chastised, but also a bit cocky. The meeting continued and she wondered if Lucian would really allow her to finish him in front of the accountant. She had no idea how he would manage to keep a straight face.

She sensed him getting close when his thighs lifted. Voices continued to travel overhead as he toed off one shoe. She frowned and released him as he shifted his legs. She eased back, unsure what he was doing.

His right leg adjusted in the cramped space, the tip of his socked toe fitting between her knees and extending until he found her core. She jumped at the contact. Breath stuttered out of her as his socked foot grazed her clit and her labia. She bit her lip to keep quiet.

There was a sudden clatter. "Pardon, I dropped my pen," Lucian apologized. Her eyes dropped to the carpet and spotted the pen. Dark eyes suddenly had her pinned. They creased with mirth. He smiled and reached for her.

She was huddled against the kickboard of his desk. Her eyes widened, unsure what he was doing. Since his foot had joined the play she'd grown incredibly distracted.

His fingers wrapped around the back of her neck and drew her back to his lap. *Oh, okay, keep going then . . .*

He rose just as his fingers swept up the pen. "My apologies. Got it."

The other man continued talking. Her lips slid to the base of his cock as his palm pressed her head low. He held her there a few seconds. When his grip on her disappeared, she bobbed up and down quickly. He was being a bit brazen. She could be brazen too.

She relentlessly went at him. His foot continued to tease her. "Well, this all looks great. I'm going to call over to Shamus now and fill him in." Lucian's voice was strained, but barely. He had remarkable self-control.

The other man made a muffled good-bye. The sound of footsteps faded and there was a click as the door closed. His cock popped from her lips and his chair propelled back. She was suddenly dragged out from under the desk and he was on her.

The rough carpet burned her sensitive rear as his lips crashed over hers, his body pinning her to the floor. "So fucking hot, Evelyn," he growled as his tongue knifed into her mouth. His fingers hooked beneath her knees and wrenched them up. He filled her almost violently.

The moan was unavoidable. He pounded into her, chafing her backside as he fucked her, propelling her from behind his desk. There was a sudden knock on the door.

Evelyn's eyes bulged, her head jerking toward the door, and, as if in slow motion, the knob on the door turned. She smacked at Lucian's shoulders, but he was like a man possessed.

"Mr. Patras, is everything okay? I thought I heard . . ."

Evelyn screwed her eyes shut and turned her face away from the door and into his shoulder. Lucian suddenly stilled. "Not now, Seth," he growled.

"My apologies!" Seth made a fast exit. The door practically slammed shut.

Neither of them moved for several heartbeats. Lucian's shoulders shook. He was laughing. She was mortified and he was fucking *laughing*!

She shoved at him. "It's not funny."

His shoulders trembled as he sucked in a deep, audible breath and loud laughter spilled from his lips. She rolled her eyes. Her face was likely the color of the burgundy carpet. When she attempted to squirm out from under him, he stilled and frowned at her, his body locking down on hers.

"Where do you think you're going?" he asked, all humor gone.

"I'm embarrassed and you're laughing. We were just caught."

His mouth spread into a tight, satisfied smile. He was too beautiful. At the moment his attractiveness irritated her.

With complete seriousness, he said, "Ms. Keats, the interview is far from over."

She narrowed her eyes and his crinkled with humor. He rotated his hips and she groaned. No matter how mortified her brain was her libido was still raring to go.

Her head dropped to the carpet. "You damn exhibitionist pervert," she grumbled.

He chuckled. "You know you love it."

She did, but she'd never freely admit it. Her chin pressed into her chest as he awaited her reply. "I'll never be able to come here again."

"Nonsense," he teased. "I plan on making you come here at least twice before I take you home."

She mashed her hand into his face and shoved him. He laughed and kissed her. It wasn't long before she gave in and they were at it again, this time, however, there was no rushing. He made love to her, slow and thoroughly.

The arrogant bastard was right as usual. She came twice more before he took her home.